The Bridal Season

The Bridal Season

CONNIE BROCKWAY

ISLAND BOOKS

ISLAND BOOKS
Published by
Dell Publishing
a division of
Random House, Inc.
1540 Broadway
New York, New York 10036

Dell ® and its colophon are registered trademarks of
Random House, Inc.

ISBN: 0-7394-2149-2

Printed in the United States of America

For Marcia Howard,
the jock,
who taught me to throw a ball
and swing a racket;
the "undercover" author,
who taught me to love books;
the champion of the neighborhood kids,
who taught me to stand up to bullies;
the best pie maker in the world,
who (unfortunately) taught me
the pleasure of good cooking;
and best of all, my mother.
I love you, Mom.

In writing this book I owe a debt of gratitude to Damaris Rowland, my über-supportive agent, and also to Maggie Crawford and Wendy McCurdy. And finally to Grace Pedalino, whose contribution to my literary craft is ever shrouded in mystery. Thank you.

The Bridal Season

Chapter 1

*When someone drops a pearl
in your palm, make a fist.*

London, the last decade of Victoria's reign

"BUT HOW CAN I?" LADY AGATHA WHYTE asked Henri Arnoux in a hushed undertone, painfully aware of the other passengers waiting in the lobby to board trains. "The Bigglesworths are depending on me. They fear that unless they make some sort of statement with the wedding ceremony and postnuptial celebration, the Marquis of Cotton's family will never accept young Miss Bigglesworth as their equal, and she will be forever marked as socially inferior to her new in-laws."

"But, how is this your problem, my dear, my darling, Lady Agatha?" M. Arnoux begged in his wonderful French accent.

Lady Agatha stared at him helplessly, trying to think of some way in which to phrase her unique position, and subsequent power, in Society. It would be immodest to call attention to her undoubted influence, but she had to make him understand just how important her services could be . . . couldn't they?

Perhaps she was deluding herself, she thought in alarm, and what influence she had was not as extensive as she herself had been led to believe.

"The Bigglesworths are convinced only the cachet of my involvement will gain Miss Angela entrée into Society. Indeed," she said apologetically, "they say the only reason Society will venture to so remote and provincial a place as Little Bidewell is because I will have planned the postmatrimonial celebration. As I did for your daughter, sir." She felt a blush rise in her cheeks. How many years had it been since she'd blushed?

"And a lovely celebration it was, too," Henri Arnoux assured her. "Yet, delightful as it was, it was not the basis for my daughter's future happiness. Unlike the decision I am asking you to make, which most definitely forms the basis for *my* future happiness and, dare I be so bold, perhaps in some measure your own? That is, if you can feel for me something of the regard I have for you, *dear* Lady Agatha." He secured her gloved hand and raised it to his lips.

Lady Agatha's reservations began to melt. He spoke so chivalrously and his face was so earnest—and hadn't it been romantic, the way he'd followed her all the way here, to the train station? Yet, how could she even consider eloping to France with M. Arnoux instead of going to Little Bidewell, the ticket for which she held in her hand?

If only she hadn't agreed in the first place. But the bride's aunt, Miss Eglantyne Bigglesworth, was an old classmate of Lady Agatha's favorite cousin. And when dear Helene had asked, it had seemed a fairy-tale sort of endeavor: a simple country girl wedding a man who, as well as being one of the ton's most eligible bachelors, was the scion of one of Society's haughtiest families.

"I fear Miss Bigglesworth might feel my loss acutely, and how would I forgive myself if—"

"Ach! I never 'eard such flummery," a disgusted female voice muttered from somewhere behind M. Arnoux. "I don't mean no offense, mum, but believe me, if this 'ere chippy has managed to land 'erself a marquis, she ain't needing no 'elp from you."

Nonplussed, Lady Agatha leaned sideways to look around M. Arnoux. She stared. The person who'd delivered this blunt advice was not the Cockney girl Lady Agatha expected to see, but a genteel and well-to-do-looking young lady perched decorously on a bench.

She looked to be in her mid-twenties and was remarkably handsome in an unconventional sort of way, with high, chiseled cheekbones and a sharply angular jaw. Her warm, brown eyes were deep-set and heavily lidded, the thin brows above them straight and dark. Only her mouth failed to be exactly ladylike, being too wide and full-lipped to be precisely . . . nice.

Lady Agatha's gaze rose to the enormous and ornate picture hat perched atop a mass of upswept auburn tresses. Sprays of silk lilacs nestled amidst striped ribbons, while a long purple dyed plume flirted rakishly with her temple. An amazing confection.

And while her dress was unsuited for travel, it was

the absolute height of fashion and obviously expensive. From her slender throat to her narrow wrists, delicate ivory-colored lace overlay a snug sheath of rich periwinkle-hued silk. The frock hugged the narrow span of her waist and curved out to accommodate the swell of her hips before falling free and sweeping the tops of kidskin half-boots. One could purchase a gown like that for no less than twenty-five guineas. Certainly no Cockney girl could afford it.

Lady Agatha looked around quickly for another possible source of the unsolicited advice. No one else was near.

The young lady smiled brightly. "Crikey, ducks. If a well-'eeled-lookin' bloke like this one 'ere asked me to peel off with 'im, you wouldn't see me for the dust!" She grinned cheekily and winked. "Best look lively, dearie."

"Excuse me?"

"Listen to her, Agatha," Arnoux urged. "Come with me."

"But—" Agatha's attention, momentarily diverted, returned fully to M. Arnoux. "I have made a commitment. I can't simply leave this poor motherless girl and her father..." She struggled to find the appropriate words.

"In the lurch?" the auburn-haired young woman supplied helpfully and then shook her head in disgust. "Coo! That's a dodge if ever I 'eard one. I've got your number. Taken to overstating your own importance, you 'ave. Made your bit of talent out to be all the thing, and why? Because you're afraid if you don't 'ave something, you'll *be* nothing."

Agatha remained mum. The young woman's words too closely echoed thoughts she'd more than once entertained.

"Well, that's fine and good if you ain't got nothing, but you do. You've got 'im." The young lady jerked her thumb at Henri Arnoux. M. Arnoux nodded eagerly. "Take my advice. Don't be a chump. Life grants you only a few choice bits of plum, far too few to be spitting out those what's already in your mouth. If this 'ere muck-a-muck wants to set you up on easy street, you let 'im. It's now or never, ducks."

The amazing creature leaned forward, her dark eyes sparkling, transformed from a fashionable young aristocratic Miss into an irresistible vixen. "Besides which, it don't take a genius to see you're in love with 'im and 'e's a fair goner where you're concerned!"

Finally, something Agatha understood. She blushed fiercely.

Her unsolicited advisor was about to say something more, but a shaggy little dog that had been rooting about the refuse bin suddenly darted past her, the oily wrappings from a sandwich in his maw. With a cry, the young woman nabbed him by the scruff of the neck and set about wresting his prize from him. "Fool mutt! Could be rat poison on this!"

The mangy creature began to growl, the young woman shook him in response, and—

—and M. Henri Arnoux kissed Lady Agatha Whyte. Right there, in full view of everyone in the station!

Oh, my! It had been years, nay, over a decade since Agatha had been kissed. Her knees began to buckle.

Her eyelids fluttered shut. Her reasons for refusing him suddenly seemed pitifully inadequate and the advice of the young woman like the wisdom of Solomon.

"Who would have thought when you took over the arrangements for my daughter's wedding that you would also take over my heart?" Arnoux said, stepping back. "I love you, Agatha. Marry me. Now. Today. Come with me to France."

Dimly, Agatha heard her counselor sigh with pleasure.

"It's as the young lady says, Agatha. You must decide now. Now!" He spoke so manfully and his little black mustache quivered so passionately and yet... and yet...

"But M. Arnoux, what of Nell?" Agatha motioned vaguely toward the area where her lady's maid had discreetly taken herself. "What about all my trunks and my things? Except for some few personal things, they are already in Little—"

Gently, he placed a finger over her lips. "Nell will come with us, of course. As for your trunks, if there are sentimental items amongst them, we will send for them later. But for now, let *me* buy you things, Agatha. Let me dress you, bedeck you with jewels, cosset you—"

"Gorblimey, let 'im!"

The young woman had the little canine in a stranglehold, half the greasy wrapper in her hand, the other half clamped in the dog's maw. Both sets of brown eyes, canine and human, gazed unblinkingly at Agatha.

"Really?" Agatha whispered, amazed she should seek advice from a stranger and such a remarkable stranger at that.

"Without a doubt."

The last of Agatha's hesitation evaporated. Happiness washed over her. Henri Arnoux cupped her face in his hands.

"Will you marry me, *ma chère, mon coeur*?"

"Without a doubt," she answered.

He kissed her soundly and, wrapping an arm around her waist, hastened her from the railroad station. So dazed and happy was Lady Agatha that she didn't even notice her train ticket fall from her fingers and drift to the ground, like confetti at a wedding.

But the young woman sitting on the bench did.

"Well, I'd say we've done our good deed for the day, eh, Fagin?" Letty Potts said to the dog. All traces of the Cockney accent had vanished. She watched the couple exit the London train station, a plump woman scurrying in their wake—doubtless the soon-to-be-expatriated Nell.

"Ain't love grand?" she asked, reverting to the cheeky Cockney accent. "Gor, sweet as treacle puddin', it be. Fair makes me teeth ache."

But the twinkle in her eyes belied the sarcastic comment and she dropped a fond kiss on Fagin's nose before bending to retrieve the fallen ticket. She peered at the name inscribed on the destination line.

"*Little Bidewell, Northumberland*," she read. "Coo, now that is remote. Where in the world is it, do you suppose? Not that it matters, eh, Fagin me lad?" Fagin's tail thumped against her side. "If a ticket to Little Bidewell is what we have, Little Bidewell is where we're going."

Her smile slowly faded. With the amusing diversion provided by the tall, thin redhead and her potbellied French swain at an end, Letty's thoughts turned to her own problems. Nick would be looking for her soon. But he wouldn't have started yet. He'd still be sitting at his "office" awaiting her arrival.

After all, in burning down the lodging house where she lived, he'd destroyed not only her home, but everything in the world she owned, except the gown she wore. It, too, would have burned if Letty hadn't donned her one truly elegant dress in a futile attempt to impress the manager of Goodwin's Music Hall.

After two weeks of searching for employment she should have realized it was useless. One way or the other, Nick had found the means of "persuading" every theater manager in London to blacklist her, in spite of the fact that she was one of the musical theater's rising stars. Or could have been if she could only cut herself a break.

The critics would come round in time. They already loved her voice; sooner or later she'd land a role that allowed them to see that she could sing with this "emotional depth" they all seemed to think she lacked, as well as comedic lightheartedness. But that break would have to be delayed some, it seemed.

She smiled bitterly. Nick must be congratulating himself on finding a way, short of murder, that left her no options but to come crawling back to him and be part of the nasty confidence game he was plotting.

But she hadn't crawled back. Instead, she'd come straight from viewing the fire at her boardinghouse to St. Pancras Station, where she'd counted out her few coins and asked the ticket master how far the small bit would take her. The answer had been disheartening: not even as far as Chelsea. Not nearly far enough.

Only then had desperation begun to unravel the tight hold she'd maintained over herself during the past weeks. She'd sat down to think, fighting the unfamiliar wash of helplessness. She was Letty Potts, by gad! Known for her spit-in-your-eye spirit, quick wit, and ready smile. Saucy, bold Letty Potts.

She wasn't going back to Nick. She wouldn't be part of his latest confidence game. This wasn't the usual bait-and-switch where they hoodwinked some peer's overbred, overornamented slumming son. Nick's newest enterprise was a cruel bit of work involving filching middle-class widows' much-needed inheritances. She'd have no part of it.

Then, as Letty sat deep in thought, the Society folks had appeared and literally dropped the answer to her woes at her feet. She could go to this Little Bidewell and lie low for a good while. Maybe she could even get a job doing a spot of millinery work—supposing this town was big enough to have a milliner. At the very least, she'd be out of Nick Sparkle's way.

Now, Letty was nobody's pigeon. Benevolent guardian angels were about as likely as snow in July. But she'd seen enough to know that every now and again Fate cracks open a door that only a fool refuses to slide through. She tucked Fagin under her arm and rose to her feet, looking about for the platform number printed on the ticket.

Letty Potts was no fool.

Chapter 2

*If a minor character is introduced in
the first act, you can be sure
he'll be carrying a knife by the last.*

"I WON'T BE BULLIED INTO GRANTING MY water rights to some vile Whig!" Squire Arthur Himplerump thumped his cane against the train platform's floor.

Sir Elliot March placed his hand on the older man's shoulder, turning him. As soon as he had the elderly curmudgeon away from the ladies, he intended to put an end to this nonsense once and for all. The old reprobate had seen him drive the Bigglesworth ladies up to the train station and had immediately cut across the main street to speak with Elliot. Or rather *at* Elliot.

That was the charm as well as the problem with living in so small a market town as Little Bidewell. If one were "in town," eventually one was bound to come across everyone else "in town"—whether at the greengrocer's,

Murrow's Tearoom, the dry goods store, the bank, or the church.

"It is, of course, your decision," Elliot said, fixing Himplerump's florid face with a steady gaze. "But, Arthur, even though you have a legal right to deny Burkett's easement request, the law was intended to protect your rights, not punish a man for his political leanings."

Himplerump's jowls quivered with indignation.

"I know you are not a vindictive man, Arthur." In actuality, Elliot knew exactly the opposite, but was willing to sacrifice the truth in the name of harmony. A short distance off, the incoming train whistle blew.

"Drat," he said, looking around at the approaching train and then back at his companion. "At least wait a while before doing anything you may regret. Now, if you'll pardon me, I must greet this society lady Miss Bigglesworth has hired to produce Angela's marriage celebration."

But Himplerump wasn't willing to let the matter go yet. "Kip says I ought to stand by my guns."

Kip was Arthur's only child and heir; a handsome youth who'd, unfortunately, discovered the mirror at an early age.

Elliot's mild voice grew steely. "I assure you, you will be best served by making your views known in a manner that offends neither your conscience nor Burkett's pocketbook."

"All right," Squire Himplerump blustered. "But mind, only because you say so, Elliot, and I know that you, unlike another I could name, are—like me—a gentleman."

Elliot's lips twitched but he managed to say gravely enough, "I certainly aspire to be so, Arthur."

With a sniff, Himplerump turned and stomped back to the platform where the London train was shuddering to a stop. Eglantyne and Angela Bigglesworth pushed forward, anxiously anticipating the appearance of the miracle worker. And a miracle worker is precisely what this Lady Agatha Whyte would have to be in order to convince the Marquis of Cotton's family, the Sheffields, to unbend backs stiffened by one hundred years of self-conceit and welcome little Angela Bigglesworth into their fold.

Elliot had met the Sheffields long ago when, for one brief season, he'd cut a minor swathe through Society. The Sheffields had not been impressed with him. Or rather his lack of title *had* impressed them with the knowledge that they needed to extend him no more than the barest civilities. No, the Sheffields would not take kindly to a little nobody's daughter marrying into their illustrious ranks. No matter that the Bigglesworths, like the Marches, had been working this land while the Sheffields were but up-and-coming villeins on some Viking's farm.

Elliot glanced at Eglantyne Bigglesworth. Her homely, narrow face was fraught with worry. Beside her stood her niece, Angela, blond, pretty, the picture of budding English womanhood, except for the uncharacteristically pinched set of her rosebud mouth and the slight shadows beneath her eyes.

Eglantyne noticed Elliot's attention and offered a wan smile. As the Bigglesworths' groom was laid up with the gout and Angela's father Anton had stayed behind at home to prepare for their guest, Eglantyne had enlisted Elliot and his carriage to bring the wedding planner to The Hollies.

He could not refuse. Sir Elliot March was, first and foremost, a gentleman. Besides, he was vastly fond of the Bigglesworths. It was Eglantyne who'd offered him solace when his mother had died. He only hoped Lady Agatha could do a tenth of what Eglantyne expected of her.

The train conductor threw open the door and leapt down to the platform, turning to pull out a stair block from inside. "Little Bidewell! All off for Little Bidewell!"

The few occupants began to emerge. The vicar's housekeeper preceded her two giggling girl cousins, come to spend a summer in the country. Following them came a middle-aged gentleman in a checkered coat clutching to his chest the raggedy portmanteau that marked him as a salesman. And then . . . no one.

The conductor checked his pocket watch and hurried toward the station, muttering about getting his "cuppa tea." Eglantyne and Angela traded alarmed glances.

"Well," Angela swallowed, "I am sure there is a very good explan—"

"There she is!" Eglantyne cried. "Lady Agatha! Here! Yoo-hoo!"

Elliot turned his attention to the first-class compartment. A woman was moving along the inside aisle past the windows. There was some sort of enormous contraption on her head. A hat, he supposed dubiously. The door at the end of the car opened and the woman paused, silhouetted against the bright setting sun.

Elliot's gaze sharpened. She had the figure and style that the American chap—Gibson, was it?—had recently made so popular, a figure revealed by a form-fitting lace dress that flowed like a second skin over a frankly voluptuous form.

Apparently she'd not heard Eglantyne, for she did not acknowledge the older woman's greeting. Instead, she looked behind her, pivoted, and bent sharply at the waist, displaying her lushly curved bottom in a most provocative manner. Beside Elliot, Squire Himplerump caught his breath.

"I say, Lady Agatha! Lady Agatha!"

Lady Agatha, still bent over, looked around. The broad brim of her ridiculously huge hat shadowed most of her face, but Elliot could make out a decisive chin, angular jaw, and unexpectedly large mouth. She was younger than Eglantyne had led them to expect. Much younger.

His gaze narrowed. He'd made some discreet in-quiries about Lady Agatha Whyte as soon as Eglantyne had told him of her plan to employ the sup-posed duke's daughter to produce Angela's wedding festivities. He'd discovered that Lady Agatha Whyte of Whyte's Nuptial Celebrations really was a "lady," the eldest child of the impecunious Duke of Lally. But he'd somehow formed the idea that she was in her thirties.

Lady Agatha straightened, scooping up a small, disreputable-looking black dog that had been hidden by her skirts, and turned. The sunlight hit her full in the face, revealing her best features, her eyes, which were a deep, rich brown. Not a spectacular beauty, by any means, but her looks were interesting, catching one's attention.

"I'm sorry," she said in a husky voice. "I'm afraid I didn't realize you were addressing me. I am—"

"No need to apologize, my dear lady," Eglantyne interrupted in her enthusiasm. "Drat hard to hear over the train engine, isn't it?"

"Indeed. But you see I am not—"

Whatever Lady Agatha "was not" was lost in the sudden bawl of the train whistle.

"We are so glad you are here. I admit, we were a bit worried, what with the train being late and all. But no worries now, eh? Everything is just fine now that you are here!" Eglantyne bellowed, blushing when the whistle abruptly quit and she was still shouting. She cleared her throat. "Your things arrived a few days ago."

Lady Agatha, in the act of redistributing the weight of her dog, stilled. "My things?"

"Yes," Angela said, finding her voice. "All sorts of fascinating trunks and boxes and bags."

"Really?" Lady Agatha said.

"Not that we pried!" Eglantyne quickly assured her. "We just saw them passing up the stairs, don't you know."

They waited, Eglantyne with a sheepish smile, and poor Angela looking as though she wished the earth would open up and swallow her whole.

"Elliot!"

Elliot turned to see Paul and Catherine Bunting coming toward him down the platform.

"Saw you from across the street, Elliot," Paul greeted him on making his side. "Thought we'd come over and say hallo. Catherine claims she had a positive pash for Murrow's treacle pudding, but I 'spect she really wanted to get a glimpse of this Lady Agatha," Paul said loudly. He leaned forward, saying only slightly less loudly, "Suppose you're here to fetch her back to The Hollies, what?"

"Yes," Elliot agreed, his gaze returning to the auburn-haired woman.

Paul's loud voice had caught her attention. She looked directly at Elliot. It seemed to him she realized his slight embarrassment and it amused her. He inclined his head.

And then she smiled.

Elliot forgot his manners. Certainly he forgot Paul and Catherine Bunting. He simply stood staring at *her*, because when she smiled everything changed.

The maturity her face lacked in repose appeared in the knowing crook of her brow, in the irrepressible shiver of her lower lip. There was wry humor there, and mischievousness, but an intangible sweetness, too.

It looked as if she didn't want to smile but couldn't help herself. One had the impression that she owned the most delicious secret and *so* wanted to share it. Her dark eyes danced and unexpected dimples appeared in each cheek.

She returned her attention to the Bigglesworths. "Why, how very kind you are to have personally come to collect me!" she trilled. She scrunched the dog up against her face. It stared up at her in canine incredulity. "Look, er, Lambikins," she cooed, "see the nice people?"

She set the dog down and swept one arm out in an embracing gesture. A handkerchief appeared in her hand and she brought it slowly up to dab at her eyes, the picture of a sentimental woman overcome with appreciation—an image utterly belied by her wicked eyes. "Thank you. Oh, thank you so very much."

Elliot's natural skepticism resurfaced. Lady Agatha Whyte was reportedly extremely shy of publicity. She avoided self-promotion as vulgar; she'd never even allowed her image to appear in the newspapers. Yet here she stood, accepting Eglantyne's accolades with every appearance of delight.

She dimpled coquettishly and flowed down the steps.

Flowed. There was no other word for it. One minute she stood poised atop the stairs, the next she was on the platform. He had never seen a lady walk like that, move like that.

He gave himself a mental shake. He was being absurd and—dear God. Paul and Catherine must think him an utter fool! He turned to speak but Paul, too, seemed to have succumbed to whatever spell Lady Agatha had woven.

"You are Lady Agatha, then?" Eglantyne was saying, and when the redheaded woman nodded, wide-eyed, she went on. "Of course you are! But when you didn't answer at once, well . . . Never mind.

"*Dear* Lady Agatha! I do hope your trip was uneventful and not too uncomfortable? Such a long way to come and such close quarters.

"And what must you think of us? Allow me to introduce myself; I am Eglantyne Bigglesworth, who has had the pleasure of corresponding with you. It's so nice to meet you at long last!"

"Entirely *my* pleasure, ma'am, I assure you," Lady Agatha said with the utmost sincerity, even though amusement still played about her wide, ripe mouth.

"And this," Eglantyne's eyes shone with pride, "this is our bride-to-be, our little Angela."

"I am captivated, Miss Bigglesworth, utterly captivated," Lady Agatha enthused, taking Angela's hands in hers. "Such a pretty thing! How lucky your young man is!"

Eglantyne caught sight of the Buntings and Elliot and waved them over. "Oh! How delightful! Here are our neighbors. May I present Lord Paul Bunting and his wife, Catherine?"

Catherine inclined her head, a little stiffly Elliot thought. He hoped she wasn't coming down with something. Even though it had been years since they'd once been engaged, he still cared deeply for her. Paul bowed, beaming with pleasure.

"And here's a happy chance! The Vances. Hallo! Miss Elizabeth! Come and meet Lady Agatha!"

Eglantyne hailed the Vances, who were making slow progress down the sidewalk. Beth's studied nonchalance was a bit too exaggerated for their sudden appearance in front of the train station to be purely coincidental.

Old Colonel Vance leaned toward his long-suffering, middle-aged daughter and shouted, "What? What did she say?"

"*Lady Agatha*, Father!" Beth answered in a loud, calm voice. "Come to make Miss Angela's wedding pretty!"

"Miss Angie's already pretty enough without some ass—"

Turning bright red, Beth wrapped an arm around the old man's shoulders and hustled him along before he could finish his sentence. "Pray excuse us! I fear Papa's not feeling well!" she called over her shoulder.

"Later, then!" Eglantyne turned in relief and spied Elliot. "Oh! And how could I be so remiss? Please, allow me to introduce our dear friend, Sir Elliot March."

He approached slowly, hoping his gait adequately masked his limp. His leg often stiffened in colder weather and the day had been unseasonably cool, if bright. Eglantyne leaned toward Lady Agatha and he heard her whisper, "War wound."

He removed his hat and bowed, feeling doubly awkward. If only he could cure Eglantyne of her heavy-handed romanticization of his military career.

He raised his head and met the red-haired woman's gaze. Her eyes widened, as though in startled recognition. They were the oddest shade of brown. Rich, intoxicating, like tawny port.

"My pleasure," he heard himself say as if from far off.

"Sir." She sounded breathless.

"Sir Elliot and his father share bachelor quarters about a half mile from The Hollies," Eglantyne rattled on. "We take terrible advantage of them, I'm afraid."

"Not at all," Elliot murmured, captivated by the soft stain of color climbing Lady Agatha's cheeks.

"Indeed, yes," Eglantyne said. "Sir Elliot's been kind enough to offer to drive us to the house since our own driver is indisposed."

"Gout," Angela announced. "Suffers terribly for it."

The lovely young woman reluctantly looked away from him toward Angela. "In my experience, people with the gout are given to drink. My maid drank." She nodded sagely. "Like a fish."

At this, Angela muffled a startled laugh. Elliot welcomed the sound. It had been quite a while since he'd heard Angela laugh.

Lady Agatha's eyes twinkled. "Terrible for the drink, she was. I only realized the extent of her problem when she showed up at the station yesterday too sozzled to board the train." Her eyes narrowed. "Needless to say, I left her behind."

Eglantyne had said Lady Agatha had a reputation for eccentricity. Apparently it was well warranted. No lady of his acquaintance would speak so complacently about such matters. He couldn't imagine Catherine saying the words "like a fish"—not even in reference to a fish. Indeed, Catherine had been unusually quiet.

Eglantyne didn't seem to notice anything odd. But then, Eglantyne was amazingly unworldly.

"I'm afraid our Ham is similarly afflicted," she confided. "But he won't stop. So what can we do?"

"Dismiss him?" Lady Agatha suggested.

"Aye," sighed Eglantyne. "But what would he do then? It's not likely anyone else would employ him."

Elliot nearly smiled at Lady Agatha's flummoxed expression. Little Bidewell residents had quite strong, if unique, views on social responsibility.

"Don't worry, Lady Agatha," Eglantyne said, misreading her expression. "Ham will be right as rain come the wedding. He'll not let the family down on a really important occasion. . . ." She trailed off in embarrassment. "Not that *you're* not an important occasion, Lady Agatha!"

Lady Agatha squeezed her dog to her face. "How charming! Do you hear that, Lambikins? We're an 'occasion.' "

"Indeed, yes!" Eglantyne said, hooking her arm through Lady Agatha's. "Now, Paul and Catherine, I know you'll excuse us. Lady Agatha must be quite weary after her long journey."

Elliot silently applauded Eglantyne. At this rate the entire town would show up. "Of course," murmured Paul, his gaze admiring. "It has been an honor, Lady Agatha."

"You are too kind, Lord Paul," she replied. "But you'd best all beware lest I take your professions seriously and decide to stay on forever."

"Ma'am?" Paul said, confused.

She laughed. "Well, within minutes of my arrival in your quaint little village I'm declared an honor as well as an occasion. How shall I ever hope to surpass that?" Her glance slewed toward Elliot and glinted merrily, wickedly, and yes, provocatively.

She wasn't at all what one might have expected. And that was interesting—and interesting things, in Elliot's experience, were not always welcome ones.

She was waiting for him to answer. But before he could frame a reply, Catherine said, in a silky smooth voice, "I wouldn't lose any sleep over it, Lady Agatha. I am somehow confident you will."

Chapter 3

There are moments on stage when
everything comes together.
Then the kid in the front row coughs.

LETTY SIMPLY COULD NOT BELIEVE HER good fortune. What with the train ticket first and then these poor, dear saps mistaking her for this Lady Agatha, she was having a hard time keeping herself from grinning like an idiot. Well, if life insisted on handing her flowers, she would simply make herself a bouquet.

A day or so spying out the lay of the land, so to speak, then pack up Lady Agatha's more portable precious pieces and bid a fond adieu to Little Bidewell. She nearly rubbed her palms together. And in the meantime, the scenery was decidedly better than one would expect in a backwater little burg like this.

Sir Elliot March was, in the modern vernacular, *yum*. Even breathtaking in a reserved, elegant, and utterly toothsome sort of way. Letty, seated opposite the

Bigglesworth ladies, kept having to forcibly drag her gaze from his broad shoulders to the landmarks her hostesses kept pointing out.

Letty made appropriate noises of interest, but as she'd spent her first eight years on a country estate, trees didn't exactly give her palpitations. The way Sir Elliot's dark curls, ruthlessly combed into gleaming order, grazed his snowy white collar—now that caused some fluttering. She'd always been partial to the dark, courtly ones, but he ... well, he raised the bar on masculine beauty. Blue-green eyes, black hair, a sensualist's mouth, and an emperor's nose.

Not that she was the sort of girl to indulge in a spot of slap-and-tickle just because a man was good-looking. And a rude surprise that had been to any number of stage-door Johnnies, she thought cheerfully. Besides, Sir Elliot may not want to play slap-and-tickle with *her*.

She frowned.

Not that *that* was likely, and there was nothing of vanity in thinking it, either. To paraphrase the Bard, "A man was a man was a man." When all was said and done, Sir Elliot March would prove no different from any other. They all wanted what they wanted, some just asked more graciously. And looked better doing it.

She sighed just as the carriage hit a deep rut in the lane.

Eglantyne squelched a squeal and Angela gasped. Immediately, Sir Elliot drew the horses to a halt and swung around, his concern evident. "I'm sorry. Is everyone all right?"

"Yes, Elliot. Thank you."

"Lady Agatha?"

"I'm fine."

He turned back and flicked the reins, starting the team up again. Good manners were so ... *attractive.* And Sir Elliot had really, really good manners.

Of course, Letty thought, forcing down her enthusiasm, there wasn't likely a whole lot more to do in a place like this other than practice elegant reticence. Sir Elliot would probably stutter into silence if he ever had to put more than a few polite phrases together.

The jump the carriage had made had jounced her into the corner of the bench seat. From this angle she could see Sir Elliot's profile. The final rays of the sun refracted off irises banked between thick, silky-looking black lashes. The firm contours of his lips were outlined against the sunset, as was the clean angle of his jaw. But it was his nose that bespoke his breeding.

It was a fine, bold nose. A straight, aggressive nose, flaring at the nostrils. It was a nose that a man could proudly look down ... and that's just what his ancestors had done. Most likely on *her* ancestors.

The thought sobered Letty. Her lips twitched in equal parts chagrin and amusement. If she had any sense at all—besides a disastrous sense of humor— she'd have as little to do with Sir Elliot as she could. From what she'd seen, he was the only one not so enamored with the idea of Lady Agatha Whyte's sprucing up the Bigglesworth wedding that he wouldn't take note of some little social misstep she might make.

Another rut sent Fagin, newly christened "Lambikins," tumbling to the floor. Eglantyne clucked her tongue sympathetically. Fagin, opportunistic little bugger that he was, immediately jumped into her lap and gazed mournfully into her eyes.

Eglantyne responded with a spellbound widening of her eyes. With a deep sigh, Fagin laid his head gently on her flat maidenly chest. The poor old girl didn't stand a chance. Fagin had perfected his melting gaze on the theater's hardest hearts. Hesitantly, Eglantyne began stroking Fagin's silky head.

Another mortal felled by a canine cupid's arrow! Letty thought before dismissing her dog's newest conquest, and considering the plan that had sprung full-blown to mind as soon as she'd heard Eglantyne say the words, "your things."

The only possible clunker in her plan would be if the real Lady Agatha wrote a note and explained that she was on her honeymoon. Which eventually she would.

It didn't take a genius to see that Lady Agatha was a woman of high principles—a characteristic that made her the perfect dupe for people like Letty: One could count on how she would act. That being so, it would still be three or four days before a letter arrived, and Letty would be long gone by then.

Still, Letty was glad she wouldn't be here to witness Eglantyne's disappointment. The sweet-faced woman obviously put a lot of stock in all this wedding rigmarole.

Vehemently, Letty squashed the tiny pricks of guilt in her ruthlessly anesthetized conscience. These folks certainly didn't need Lady Agatha's things. Letty did. In the end, the Bigglesworths would be no worse off than before they'd mistaken her for Lady Agatha, and she'd be a good deal better.

If she could pull it off. Which she might do if she was careful. And stayed away from handsome "sirs" with broad shoulders, elegant hands, and pretty eyes that held the memory of laughter in their depths.

But why just the memory? Letty wondered.

Eglantyne tapped her arm, distracting her from silly musings. "Almost here, Lady Agatha, watch for it now," she said. "The Hollies."

They rode up a slight poplar-lined elevation and rounded a heavy flowering bank of rhododendrons, and there stood The Hollies, sprawled atop a grassy knoll. It was a broad, complacent, somehow happy-looking accident.

Ells, projections, and porches gave evidence of years of haphazard, if fond, enlargement schemes. Part of it was covered in ivy; the rest bare and mellowed with age. Copper gleamed atop a set of cupolas and the myriad windows sparkled with the deep orchid hues of the setting sun.

"I hope it is large enough for your plans," Eglantyne said. "We've opened all the rooms. Even those that have been closed since last century. I'm sorry it's such a hodgepodge. But it's only a farmhouse. I do hope the marquis's family think it up to snuff," she said worriedly.

"The marquis," Letty repeated. Now this was getting interesting.

Eglantyne looked at her with dawning inspiration. "Why, I never thought to ask before. But how absurd of me! You probably know the Sheffields," Eglantyne said eagerly.

Sheffields? Not bloody likely. She knew *of* them though, everyone did. Only thing the family had more of than money was starch. Starchier than wallpaper paste, they were. Too good for the likes of music halls.

"No, I'm afraid I've never had that honor," Letty murmured, her thoughts racing as she glanced at Angela. The girl's face had pinked over becomingly and no wonder. The pretty little puss had won herself the Marquis of Cotton. And she looked such a naïve, unprepossessing little thing.

Well, well. Who'd have thought? Letty eyed the pretty puss with a new respect.

"I'm sure it will do," she said to Eglantyne.

Only a farmhouse? Letty thought. Though she'd been raised in one of England's grandest manor houses, she'd been a servant's bastard, tolerated only because of her mother's unparalleled skill with a needle. She'd never been allowed to venture into those parts of the house where the Fallontrues lived. Certainly she'd never spent a night as a guest in anything as grand as The Hollies. It was so large it could have contained the entire row of attached houses where Letty had rented rooms.

Until Nick had burnt it down.

He'd be looking for her now. Searching. A few questions at the right railroad station might lead him to her. And this time he might step over the line and hurt someone in order to bring her to heel. Maybe even her.

For a while she'd been so lost in the unexpected

boon of being mistaken for Lady Agatha, and then the gorgeous Sir Elliot, that she'd forgotten what had brought her here. Not a well-contrived confidence game, but chance and necessity. By the time they'd circled the old-fashioned lime-lined drive and drawn to a halt, her mood was sober.

"We generally use the east door," Eglantyne explained. "It leads into the oldest part of the house and, well, to be honest, we rather like the Great Hall. That must seem rather feudal and silly to you."

"No," Letty said, automatically answering the anxiety in Eglantyne's voice. "Not at all. In fact, feudal things are the latest craze in London."

"Craze?" Eglantyne echoed.

"Yes, craze. You know. Rage. Fad. Too-too and all that," Letty explained.

"Really?" Angela piped in, wide-eyed.

Letty hesitated on the brink of recanting her claim. But the women were regarding her so hopefully and it only took a simple fib to make their day all the brighter, and besides, maybe feudal things *were* all the rage in High Society. Stranger things had happened. "Oh, most definitely."

"Hard on the heels of last year's vogue for gladiatorial themes, no doubt," Sir Elliot said.

Letty's gaze shot up to meet Sir Elliot's. One of his dark brows was arched inscrutably. Apparently he was capable of more than rote phrases.

And in such a voice. Gads, it wasn't fair that a man with such looks should be given such a beautiful voice. If sound could caress, she'd be purring right now. It was that silky and low, but masculine. Decidedly masculine.

With an unfathomable quirk of his lips, Sir Elliot descended from the carriage and came round to the side. He even moved elegantly, Letty thought. Not like a slumming lordling, all slouching indolence and loose-limbed hauteur, but with precise military grace.

He must have been devastating in uniform.

He opened the carriage door and lifted out the steps.

"Is it true, Lady Agatha?" Eglantyne—whom Letty was quickly marking down as being nearly flawless in her credulity—breathed. "I mean about the gladiator thing?"

Letty pondered. She didn't think so. Probably not. Besides, how would Sir Elliot know anything about anything, stuck way up here, twenty miles from nowhere? Or could he? Blast. "Ah, mmm."

Elliot handed Eglantyne down before extending his hand to Letty. He looked directly into her eyes. He had lashes that would make a girl weep with jealousy, and his gaze clearly revealed he hadn't believed a word of what she'd said.

I must remember, Letty thought, still staring, *that just because a gentleman lives in a backwater burg does not mean he is gullible.*

Fagin, tired of waiting for her, squirmed under her skirts and, spying a rabbit, jumped to the ground and hied off after it.

"Lady Agatha!" Eglantyne exclaimed. "Your little doggie!"

But Letty could not pull free of Sir Elliot's gaze, nor did she see any compelling reason to do so. Fagin was a London native. A bunny posed no threat to him. "Little doggie," she muttered, "will be fine."

His big, warm hand wrapped around hers. She stared. "Lady Agatha?"

Her heart tripped in her chest and her cheeks grew warm. . . . Gads! She was blushing, she realized in horror. She hadn't blushed in years!

She erupted from her seat, snatched her hand from his, and clattered unaided down the steps.

Next, Sir Elliot helped Angela Bigglesworth from the carriage.

Letty's gaze sharpened on Angela and thoughts of Sir Elliot momentarily receded. Angela Bigglesworth didn't look to Letty like a woman who was about to achieve the matrimonial coup of the decade. Instead of gloating—which to Letty's mind a woman who'd achieved more than God, economics, or Society had intended of her, had not only the right but quite possibly the obligation to do—she looked more like a girl who'd found something unpleasant in her treacle pudding.

Now that was interesting.

"You'll stay for dinner, won't you, Elliot?" Eglantyne asked and Sir Elliot once more claimed the center of Letty's attention.

"Thank you, but I am afraid I must decline, Miss Bigglesworth. I've some work I must attend to."

"Well, at least we'll see you at the picnic tomorrow," Eglantyne said. "And remind the Professor that Grace has made some of those saffron buns he's so partial to." She leaned toward Letty. "The Professor is Sir Elliot's father."

"We are spoiled by your attentions, ma'am," Elliot said, and Letty had a glimpse of the affection he felt for his father. Why that sent a thrill through her, she didn't know. Men with dueling scars, men with wicked smiles and brooding good looks, untamed men with wild ways—now those were the kind of men who had always thrilled her.

Men like Nick? an inner voice sneered.

She was potty, that was it. Fire, unemployment, and Nick Sparkle had all conspired to drive her daft. It was just that Sir Elliot was—no, she abjured herself—*seemed* so different from the other men she'd known. In her present state she was just as likely to develop a passion for the vegetable gardener.

"I hope the business is not of a serious nature?" Eglantyne asked.

"Oh, no. Just a small matter that needs some looking into, and I'd best get to it," Elliot said. "If you ladies will excuse me?"

"Of course."

Once more his gaze touched Letty's face and she was visited by an unwarranted impulse to fuss with her hair and powder her nose. He tipped his hat and climbed up into the driver's seat. "Miss Bigglesworth. Lady Agatha. Miss Angela."

"I am sorry Sir Elliot had to leave," Letty said, watching him drive off. "You will miss his company."

"Oh, yes," Eglantyne nodded. "But that's what happens when a conscientious man holds an office of such responsibility."

"And what office might that be?"

"Oh? Didn't I say? Why, Sir Elliot is our local magistrate. He is responsible for all the criminal cases—" She stopped. "Lady Agatha! My dear, are you feeling all right?"

Chapter 4

If you forget your lines,
you had better mumble with conviction.

"*THE LOCAL MAGISTRATE?*" LETTY ECHOED faintly. *The bloody local judge and jury for the whole bloody county?*

Her head swam with new interpretations for Sir Elliot's sidelong glances and frowns of puzzlement, one that had nothing to do with her irresistibility as a woman. And then, just as she was castigating herself for her conceit, her sense of humor saved her and she stifled a laugh.

"Yes. He was a barrister until a few years ago when he accepted the position, Little Bidewell being the county seat and all," Eglantyne said.

And who had his clients been, Letty wondered, linking her arm through Eglantyne's, the local livestock? She was amazed a barrister could even make a living in a burg like this, but then maybe Sir Elliot didn't need to make a living. He certainly dressed beautifully. And expensively.

They mounted the front steps and the door swung open, held by a small, rosy-cheeked, redheaded maid who took one look at Letty, scuttled backward, and slammed the door shut.

"Merry." Eglantyne sighed and rapped sharply on the door.

"Our Merry is in awe of titles," Angela explained. "It was a full three months after he was knighted before she could bring herself to open the door to Sir Elliot."

The door abruptly swung inward with nary a sign of Merry to be seen. Lambikins, née Fagin, appeared out of nowhere and trotted past them into the hall as though to the manor born. Letty followed, looking around in delight.

Feudal? This was positively *arcane*. The oak-coffered ceiling soared two stories overhead, while beneath her feet an enormous Oriental carpet glowed in the last of the sunlight pouring in through a bank of west-facing windows. Tapestries, suspended from the minstrel gallery railing above, fluttered in the evening breeze. The headpiece from a suit of armor peeked sheepishly from behind a lush arrangement of potted palms.

"Stop popping your head in and out of the door, Anton," Eglantyne said, interrupting Letty's looking about.

"Confound it, Eglantyne, I wasn't popping." A slight gentleman with thin, snow-white hair appeared in a doorway at the side of the hall. The sharp upward tilt of his bristling white eyebrows stamped his face with an expression of perpetual surprise, while beneath them sparkled small, raisin-dark eyes. On his shoulders, fluffy white muttonchops bobbed like frothed egg white.

"Ahem." He cleared his throat.

"May I introduce my brother, Lady Agatha?" Eglantyne said. "Anton Bigglesworth. Anton, Lady Agatha Whyte."

Anton crossed the room with a scurrying gait and, before she realized what he was about, grabbed her hand and shook it eagerly. "Pleased to meet you, Lady Agatha. Kind of you to . . . That is, it's deuced nice . . . Er . . ."

He flushed profusely.

Poor old duffer. He didn't have any better notion about how to go on than she. Though socially her inferior—or rather Lady Agatha's—he was still her—or rather Lady Agatha's—employer, and the social niceties of the situation were obviously right posers for him.

"That is to say, I am honored . . . You do us a great fav—"

She couldn't let the poor little grub quibble himself into a stew like this. "Not at all, Mr. Bigglesworth. I am only too pleased to be able to offer my services."

He broke into a relieved smile. "Thank you. I suppose we ought to go into my office and see about paying you your fee?"

"Father!" Angela broke in, scandalized. "Not now! Lady Agatha has traveled all the way from London. She must be exhausted. She'll want to see her rooms and rest before dinner."

"Indeed, Anton," Eglantyne said, equally shocked. "Tomorrow will be soon enough to discuss, er, business."

The color that had slowly been ebbing from Anton's puckish face returned with renewed vibrancy. "Of course! Inexcusable of me. Merry!" he shouted before remembering Merry's problem with titled persons. "Drat! Grace!"

Within seconds a tall, buxom, middle-aged woman with suspiciously black hair appeared in the doorway wiping big, square hands on an apron tied about her narrow waist. "Aye?"

"This is our housekeeper and cook, Grace Poole."

Grace bobbed a quick curtsy. "Pleased I am to meet you, Lady Agatha."

"Where's Cabot?" Anton asked.

Grace's expression soured. "Labeling the bottles in the wine cellar, sir." She turned to Letty. "I suspect you wants to know what's been done in preparation. Well, your man from London's been up last week, mum, and between us and the instructions you give, we managed to make a neat bit of work."

Letty's face froze. Lady Agatha had a man who worked for her here? Damn. She barely kept herself from looking around. She had to get out of here before this bloke appeared.

"Grace, please," Anton said severely. "Lady Agatha is exhausted from her trip. Kindly show her to her rooms."

"Of course. If you'll follow me, Lady Agatha?"

"Yes, thank you," murmured Letty. "I *am* fatigued."

"Of course," Eglantyne said, smiling. "We won't expect you this evening. We'll have a tray sent up and see you in the morning."

Not if she was hotfooting it to the coast they wouldn't. "First thing," she promised brightly and turned to the housekeeper. "If we might?"

Grace led the way out of the room, Letty falling into step behind the housekeeper. Her glance kept snapping to and fro, fully expecting Lady Agatha's man to appear at any moment and denounce her.

The saints deliver her, she could get caught.

The frisson of fear that had been born with the revelation of Sir Elliot's position as magistrate grew. If she was lucky, her rooms would be on the first floor and she could duck out of a window as soon as it was dark. But then, hard on the heels of fear, came an imp of devilment. If she had to, how long could she avoid Lady Agatha's man? She bet she could . . .

That, m'girl, she told herself curtly, *will be your downfall, this notion that life is all a grand game pitting you against your "betters."*

One of the reasons she'd become involved in Nick's swindles had been because, besides feathering her rather underdressed little nest, it gave her a chance to thumb her nose at Polite Society. She'd never wasted her sympathy on Nick's gulls. She'd seen where they spent their money. They didn't have enough ways to waste it. Horses, fighting cocks, the dog pits, opium, women . . . the list didn't have an end as far as Letty could see.

Nah, a few bob donated to the Letty Potts fund didn't hurt them any. But then Nick had grown greedy and cruel and the word "gull" had been replaced in

Letty's mind with the word "victim." There was some that might say that Letty Potts was hard-hearted, and some who'd say she was an opportunist, and maybe both would be right, but she had standards. And while she was a right good confidence trickster, and a more than fair music hall performer, she wasn't a common criminal. There was no sport in taking from those that couldn't afford it.

Like these Bigglesworths. Oh, they may well be able to *financially* afford a run-in with Letty Potts, but they'd still be hurt. They didn't know any better; they'd stumbled into her life just as she'd stumbled into theirs. It wasn't their fault. And that's what made the difference.

Or seemed to, Letty cautioned herself. But then, Lady Fallontrue could seem every bit as kindly and ingenuous, *if* you didn't happen to be living in her house and your mother didn't happen to be blackmailing her into letting you sit in on the lessons the governess gave the Fallontrue daughters. With that grim reminder, Letty pulled her thoughts away from the moral implications of what she did to more practical matters.

As bad luck would have it, Grace led Letty up a curved flight of stairs and down a long hallway. So much for her window escape . . . unless there was a tree. She'd worked a tightrope act one season, been good at it, too, until the upper part of her anatomy had gotten more interesting than her act and her stepdad, Alf, had retired her from the routine.

Midway down the corridor, Grace Poole opened a door. Fagin casually pushed by them and sauntered into the room. He took one look at the four-poster bed piled with pristine white linen and launched himself into the center of it, where he promptly flopped down and began snoring. Apparently Fagin, son of the bards that he was, was intent on immersing himself in the role of "Lambikins," pampered lapdog par excellence.

Letty looked about. The room was huge and airy, the walls painted white, the upholstered furniture butter-yellow. A huge wardrobe stood against one wall, while on the opposite wall a pair of primrose yellow-and-blue-striped chairs flanked a marble fireplace. Tall windows overlooked the back vista, an elegant dressing table between them. And even with all this furniture there was still room for a divan, a piecrust table, and all that luggage.

There were at least three trunks and half a dozen sizeable pieces of leather luggage standing in a regimental line along the wall. With an effort, Letty kept her eyes carefully averted. She might start drooling.

"The bathroom's through that door. There's towels hanging inside." Grace pushed a little button on the wall. The chandelier overhead burst into light. Letty blinked in the sudden brilliance.

"Mr. Bigglesworth is most progressive. We got electrical from our own generator and have had for ten years now," Grace said proudly. "And, of course, there's hot and cold running water. Though why I should say 'of course' is a mystery. Not every fine house in Little Bidewell can boast that."

Grace liked to talk. God bless her. Now for a bit of fact-gathering.

Letty turned, her smile in place. As much as she wanted to tear into that luggage, she couldn't let such an opportunity pass. Information was always valuable, especially in her present circumstances. "And are there so many fine houses in Little Bidewell?"

Grace nodded. "Oh, a few. There's Professor March's house what is all modernized, and Lord Paul's, too. The Grange is lovely from the outside but a bit shabby inside, to my mind. And Squire Himplerump's next door is rather grand. Though no electrical. I'll warrant the marquis' house ain't any better lit."

"I'm sure you're right," Letty said, unbuttoning her lavender-dyed kid gloves. "You must be very excited about the wedding."

"Oh, yes," breathed Grace. "It's like something in fairy tales now, isn't it?"

"Is it? How so?" Letty asked invitingly.

"Well," the housekeeper said, settling her arms comfortably across her middle, "last year Miss Angela is invited by one of her former school chums—she went to a very fine finishing school, you know—to go on vacation with her and her family to one of those lakeside hotels in Cumbria. The second morning there she goes down to the pier to fish, and while she's there a very nice-looking young bloke joins her.

"However, it soon becomes clear that he don't know one end of the hook from another, and Miss Angela, who is the soul of kindness, offers to bait his hook for him. He accepts and introduces himself as plain old Hugh Sheffield—never mentioning as how he is a marquis.

"As will happen, one thing leads to another and the young people get to know each other and gets fond of each other," Grace's dark eyes glanced up quickly, "in a purely innocent sort of way."

Where a healthy boy and girl are concerned, innocence seldom enters the picture, let alone *pure* innocence, Letty thought, but only said, "How romantic!"

"It gets even better," Grace replied. "At the end of the month the marquis—who Miss Angela still don't know is a marquis—leaves, and Miss Angela comes home and mopes around until another friend of hers from school—a friend what's family is well up in Society—invites her to London for the Season.

"And Miss Eglantyne, thinking that a spot of gaiety might be just the thing to lift Miss Angela out of the doldrums, packs her off. And guess what?"

"She meets Prince Charming again? Or rather Marquis Marvelous," Letty said.

Grace nodded vigorously. "Yes, and *he* tells *her* that he's been looking for her all about town and had begun to think that she was just like Cinderella, and that some wicked stepmother was keeping her in the scullery, washing vegetable marrows, and that he was going to search for her door to door only he hadn't even the clue of a glass slipper to guide him by. Ain't that just lovely?" Grace sighed.

"Couldn't he have contacted the hotel and asked for her address?" Letty asked. "Hotels always ask for forwarding addresses in case something gets left behind. A marquis certainly would know that."

Grace scowled, opened her mouth, shut it, scowled harder. "I suspect he wasn't thinking very clearly, bein' so madly in love and all," she said in a hard, brook-no-argument voice.

Oops, Letty thought. Now she'd done it. Romantics hated being hit square between the eyes with logic.

"Undoubtedly you are right," she said soothingly. The deep furrows between Grace's brows relaxed. "And that *is* a pretty story. I suppose it was only a matter of weeks after their meeting in London that the marquis revealed himself as the heir to a wondrous fortune and begged Miss Angela to be his bride."

"That's right!" Grace said, delighted.

"And I imagine Miss Angela at first said, 'No!' thinking herself by far his social inferior?"

"Why, yes!" Grace intoned, clearly impressed.

"But he squelched her fears, finally convincing her that he would never be complete without her!" she finished dramatically.

"Exactly!" Grace said wonderingly. "How'd you know?"

Because three quarters of London's Gaiety Theatre operettas were fashioned on those exact same lines, and she'd seen every one. Even been in the chorus of a couple.

She smiled wisely for Grace's benefit, but inside she couldn't help but feel a bit gratified that real life actually sometimes worked out like that. It gave her a bit of hope.

Of course, if any bloke with a title and pockets full of gold asked for her hand, he wouldn't need to be asking twice. She wasn't a fool.

"I've seen much in my career," she said enigmatically and let it go at that as she began unpinning her hat.

"I heard how you haven't got a maid," Grace said. "So, I'll just send a girl up to help you—"

"No!" Letty swept her hat from her head and tossed it next to Fagin. Which one of these pieces of luggage contained Lady Agatha's clothing? "I'm not exactly sure what's where. That's one of the reasons I gave my maid the sack—I mean, terminated her employment. She didn't keep things straight."

"Oh."

"I daresay I'll deal well enough on my own this once. You mentioned the man I sent?" Letty hurriedly tried to channel the conversation to safer ground.

"The caterer? Nice enough fer a foreigner. Seemed to know his business and all. Left a lot of notes for you."

"Left? You mean he's not here?"

"Mr. Beauford went back to London three days ago," Grace said in puzzlement. "You didn't know, mum? Well, that's help for you."

Gratitude nearly brought Letty to her knees. Mr. Beauford was a caterer! Then, her relief fading, she said, "I suppose he'll be back soon?"

"Three days before the wedding to prepare the food and his staff. Just like usual, he said." Grace responded.

"And so it is," Letty said happily, patting the older woman's arm. She was safe for the time being. No need to hurry off. She could have a tray of food, sleep on a feather mattress, and tomorrow she could search through Lady Agatha's trunks.

A clean escape depended on the Bigglesworths' thinking that Lady Agatha had run out on them, taking some of her things with her. She had to be careful that even after she left they still thought she was Lady Agatha. She disliked the idea of Sir Elliot on her trail even more than Nick Sparkle.

"Grace," she said, "as you are the most senior member of the staff here at The Hollies—"

"Not me, mum. That'd be Cabot."

"Cabot?"

"The butler. Miss Eglantyne imported him from London as soon as Miss Angela got herself engaged last year. Give the family panache, she said."

"Oh. How nice."

"Some say," the housekeeper returned primly. "But I thinks a true gentleman don't need panache. Like Sir Elliot. You won't see him bringing in some hoity-toity butler to tell him how to dress or what wine to drink."

Letty, in the act of wandering about the room tallying the net worth of various bits of expensive bric-a-brac, stopped like a hound on point. "Sir Elliot."

Grace nodded. "A true gentleman."

"Indeed." She affected nonchalance, sauntering over to the bed and picking up her hat. She fussed with a spray of lilacs. It only made sense to learn what she could about the local magistrate. "Sir Elliot does, indeed, seem most agreeable."

"Oh, he is that," Grace answered enthusiastically. "Lest you stand before him in court. I hear he can flay a man to honesty using just his words and his wit."

And where had he sharpened those wits? Letty

thought sardonically. By trading barbs with the local poacher? "He's most agreeable to look at, too."

"Oh, my, yes! And even more so now than when he was young." Grace leaned forward and whispered, "He's grown into it."

"Into it?"

"The nose."

"Ah! I see. Yes, I suspect so grand a feature would overwhelm a young, callow face, though Sir Elliot hardly seems the sort to have ever been callow." She let her words trail off into a question.

"Never," Grace said. "Always been the first to answer duty's call. Never seen him shirk a responsibility, nor shun an issue what needs addressing."

"Damn."

"Mum?"

"Damp." Letty said, lifting up one of Fagin's limp forelegs. "His paws are damp. I'm afraid he's marked up the coverlet. Now what were we talking about? Ah, yes. Sir Elliot March. I confess," her eyes grew innocently round, "I find it amazing that such a paragon has escaped the matrimonial nets that must be cast his way."

"That's a fact. The ladies do go on somethin' about Sir Elliot. Not that any stands a chance of, er, nettin' him."

"No?"

Grace pulled a long face and shook her head.

"And why is that?"

"It's his heart, mum," the housekeeper sighed. "It's been broken lo these many years and ain't no one been able to mend it."

"Who broke it?" Letty asked.

"Catherine Bunting."

"That charming blond bloke's pasty-skinned wife?"

Grace choked and Letty clapped her on the back. After a minute she regained her breath and continued. "That's the one, mum. Before Sir Elliot went off to foreign parts to fight fer Her Majesty, he and Mrs. Bunting, what was then Miss Catherine Meadows, had a sort of understanding."

"They were engaged?"

Grace shifted uneasily on her feet. "Well, practically. At least everyone expected them to get married, but then Sir Elliot come back from those heathen climes as thin as a reed and white as chalk. That's where his limp comes from, you know. War wound."

What limp?

"But then, afore we know it, Catherine Meadows is engaged to Sir Elliot's best friend, Lord Paul, and Sir Elliot is standing up for him at the wedding. But he'd changed, you see. He went off a lighthearted rascal and come back a harder man." She sniffed, glanced sidelong at Letty, and said, "Not to say a word against Catherine Bunting."

Letty could have found plenty to say, but managed to hold her tongue. Poor Sir Elliot. How must he have felt, a war hero returned to find his sweetheart had left him for his best friend? Though how any woman could prefer Paul Bunting to Sir Elliot March was a mystery.

"A regular saint, she is," Grace's voice cut across Letty's thoughts. "Tends to the poor, visits the sick, organizes the annual church bazaar, and provides the

altar flowers. If only she'd see straight on women's suffrage . . ." Grace shrugged.

"Hm," Letty said noncommittally.

A few minutes later Grace left and Letty, feeling
vaguely dissatisfied and unable to pinpoint the reason why, decided to have a look-see around the outside of the house. It always paid to know the quickest
way out of a place and, as the Bigglesworths would be
dining, now was as good a time as any.

She opened the door and peered outside. Seeing
no one about, she slipped into the hall and retraced
her earlier steps. Someone, she thought, should teach
Sir Elliot a fundamental rule of the heart; there was
no sense in crying over spilt milk. Especially since
once spilt it spoiled.

She stopped. *Why* was she thinking about him? She
should be applauding herself on her impersonation of
Lady Agatha, or thinking about the best way to go
once she left Little Bidewell, not imagining ways to
rekindle passion in the man most dangerous to her. A
man who would have her in jail if he even suspected
what she was about to do.

She started walking again.

But, try as she might, her imagination would not
shut up.

Chapter 5

An enigmatic smile is worth
ten pages of dialogue.

"GUESS WHERE I BEEN?" GRACE COLLAPSED against the door in the servant's hall, her hands clasped over her heart.

"Where?" asked Merry, pausing with her tea half raised to her lips. The other servants seated about the table waited.

"*I* been bein' chatted up by none other than Lady Agatha Whyte herself, that's where I been."

"Never!"

"True." Grace pointed to the steaming pot of tea. Immediately Merry poured her out a cup and set it at the housekeeper's place at the head of the table. At the other end of the table Cabot, the butler, attempted to look uninterested. Grace wasn't having any of it.

She took her seat, arranging her skirts as eight faces watched her expectantly.

"Well?" Merry demanded in exasperation. "What's she like?"

"She ain't a bit hoity-toity," Gracie said, daintily sipping her tea. Cabot wasn't the only one with good manners. "I can see why she's managed so well. She has a chatty way with her and is ever so common."

Cabot snorted with disapproval.

"In the nicest sense of the word," Grace went on, ignoring him. "She asked all sorts of questions."

"What sorts of questions?" The boot boy asked.

"About Miss Angela and the marquis, of course, but mostly she was interested in—" Grace set down her teacup, placed her palms flat against the table, and leaned forward "—Sir Elliot."

"Go on," breathed the tweenie.

Grace settled back. "Tha's right. And I'm thinkin' that what with Sir Elliot bein' recommended fer a barony and Lady Agatha bein' a duke's daughter, she would make him a right proper bride."

"You must be jesting," Cabot said. "You can't seriously be playing matchmaker for Sir Elliot and Lady Agatha?"

Grace sniffed. "Wot if I am? Where's the harm? If things don't work out, well, Lady Agatha is going to be gone in a few weeks. And if things *do* work out, well, don't you think Sir Elliot deserves a duke's daughter?" She impaled Cabot with a glare. The others, quick to take umbrage over an imagined social slight to the local hero, followed suit.

"It has nothing to do with what Sir Elliot does or does not deserve," Cabot replied. "It has to do with interfering in people's lives."

"Ach!" Grace flapped her hand, dismissing his conceits. "Who of us would have ended up where we are if someone hadn't had the good sense to interfere with us?"

And with that impeccable piece of logic effectively stifling Cabot's protests, the conversation turned to the particulars of "interference."

"Elliot?" Professor Atticus March called out upon hearing the front door close. A breeze stirred the curtains covering the library's French doors and Atticus shivered. He was an old man and the night was cold.

Fighting the impulse to simply wait for Elliot and then request that he shut the doors, Atticus rose with difficulty and closed them himself. Elliot had come home when he'd had heart failure eighteen months ago. That was long enough.

He'd returned to his seat and was lowering himself into it when he found his arm being supported. With his usual unobtrusive manner, Elliot eased him into the chair.

"I was just thinking of having a whiskey and soda, Father," Elliot said. "Can I tempt you into joining me?"

"I'd like that," Atticus replied.

Elliot moved to a small credenza and busied himself with decanter and soda bottle. The problem, thought Atticus, watching his son, is that Elliot made *having* problems so easy. He simply shouldered any difficulties, whether or not they were his own. The result was that little was required of a person in Elliot's care, except to graciously cede his troubles.

Had Elliot always been so bound by duty? Atticus wondered, watching his last surviving child. He thought not. Oh, Elliot had always been attentive and conscientious, but it was only after Terry's death that he'd acquired that genteel polish, a polish so smooth that one could not easily see past its brilliant surface to the man beneath. It was an insidious sort of thing, Elliot's gentility.

After Terry had died, Elliot, filled with misplaced guilt, had abandoned his budding legal practice and joined the army. He'd returned wounded and covered in honors—not the least being a knighthood.

Since then, he'd not once deviated from the course on which circumstance and fate had set him. He'd funneled all his considerable energies into judicial reformation. Then, a few weeks ago, word had arrived that the Prime Minister had recommended that Elliot be made a baron. Which meant that Elliot would be able to take a seat in the House of Lords and eventually win his way into the appeals court.

Anxiety over the new pressures his son would face had given Atticus sleepless nights. Not that Elliot resented the burden; he considered it an honor and his duty to accept that honor. Atticus was vastly proud of his son. It made no sense, this feeling of dissatisfaction that arose when he thought of Elliot's future.

There was no reason for it. Elliot was well liked and respected, and though some would say he was too private and self-possessed, Elliot himself seemed content. Nothing wrong with contentment. Atticus considered it a fair compensation for a long life. And perhaps that was the problem. He was seventy and Elliot was thirty-three, far too young to have abdicated passion for contentment.

Elliot's appearance at his side postponed Atticus's troubled musing. He handed Atticus a whiskey and took the seat opposite, stretching his long legs out before him. He scowled slightly, his expression distracted, his thoughts filled no doubt with the demands of the day.

Atticus remembered that Elliot had fetched Eglantyne's wedding planner from the train station. He hoped Angela understood the difficulties she'd be shouldering upon wedding a marquis, with a termagant like his mother for an in-law. She was so young, barely eighteen. At church last Sunday she'd looked pale and fatigued.

"How is she, do you think?" Atticus broke the silence.

Elliot looked up, his expression baffled. "Who can say?" he said slowly.

"One could ask her, I imagine," Atticus answered in surprise.

"I barely know her," Elliot muttered. His gaze fixed inward on some image he alone could see, one that amused as well as troubled him, for his mouth softened into a grudging smile.

Atticus watched him, puzzled until he realized he was speaking of the wedding planner.

"She's not at all what one would expect," Elliot said.

"No?" Atticus asked, feeling his way.

"She's too young and too—" Elliot lifted his hand in a gesture of frustration, looked for a word, failed to find it, and repeated, "She's not what one would expect."

"She's young?" Atticus prompted, intrigued by the emotion this young woman who was "not what one would expect" had inspired in his son. "And ... beautiful?"

Elliot shot him a frustrated glance. "No," he said. "Yes. No. I don't know. Not beautiful like Catherine."

"But attractive."

"Lord, yes."

Atticus's brows shot upward.

"There's something in her face that makes it unusual, riveting. A sort of rueful joy. And the way she moves ... like a dancer. But not a ballerina. Like a Gypsy dancer."

"Doesn't sound like any lady of my acquaintance," Atticus admitted regretfully. He despised the stiff posture imposed by whatever contraption women currently wore under their garments.

"No," Elliot agreed slowly. "But she speaks well. Her voice is perfectly modulated and her accent is aristocratic."

"But ... ?" Atticus prompted.

"But she uses some extremely modern cant."

"Vulgar?"

"No, not exactly. But there are other things as well," Elliot said slowly. "She doesn't have a maid. She had no one with her except a little dog."

"What is this amazing woman's name?"

"Agatha. And I've never seen a less likely Agatha," Elliot muttered discontentedly.

"Anything else ... *interesting* about her?"

"Only her singular animation ..." He trailed off and shut his eyes for a moment.

His son was a handsome man, Atticus thought, and yet seemed completely unaware of it. True, Elliot paid attention to his appearance, but Atticus knew this to be a demonstration of his respect for others rather than any desire to impress.

Suddenly Elliot shoved himself to his feet.

"What is it, Elliot?"

"I have completely forgotten Lady Agatha's personal luggage."

"I thought a dozen trunks of hers had arrived a few days ago," Atticus said in surprise.

Elliot smiled. "Apparently those were but the tools of her trade. Her personal effects came with her."

"I see."

"They'll have unloaded it by now. I promised Eglantyne I should retrieve it as soon as I deposited the ladies at The Hollies. I ought to fetch it and bring it there at once."

"At once, I'd imagine," Atticus agreed.

With a nod, Elliot rose and strode across the room, pausing before the small gilt-framed mirror on the wall. He smoothed his hair back with his palms, frowned at the shape of his tie and quickly retied it, adjusted his cuffs, and turned. He grinned—yes, a decided grin—at Atticus. "I'll be back shortly."

"Take your time. It's a very nice evening," Atticus said. He smiled into his glass of whiskey when he heard the front door shut a moment later.

The excitement surrounding Angela's marriage had never particularly interested him, but in the last few minutes, he'd become positively fascinated.

Chapter 6

*No director directs as well
as a rapt audience.*

LETTY STUDIED THE LIGHTED WINDOW ABOVE. She knew it was her bedroom because she'd put her hat on the sill. She wrapped her hand around a good, thick vine snaking up the stone façade and gave it a hard yank. It held. Of course, there was only one way to be truly certain.

She wedged the toe of her boot amongst the leaves, gripped tighter, and pulled herself up onto the stout branch. She bounced up and down experimentally.

"Lady Agatha?" It was *his* voice—deep, incredulous, and wary. *Of all the vile luck!*

She swung about, holding onto the vine with one hand and pivoting on her foot, a smile already plastered on her face. He was standing a short ways off, the night swallowing up his dark clothes and midnight-hued hair. No wonder she hadn't seen him.

He'd changed into evening attire. Only his shirt was easily visible, bleached blue-white in the moonlight.

She, by contrast, had not changed. She still wore the lavender frock.

"Why, Sir Elliot!" she called breezily. "Lovely evening, what?"

"Quite." Hard to read anything into his tone, and she had only a vague impression of his features. "May I assist you in . . . in whatever it is you're doing?"

The question was implicit; what the devil *was* she doing? Only the fact that he was a gentleman and therefore must eschew anything that even remotely resembled an accusation kept him from asking her flat out what she was up to.

"As a matter of fact, you can," she answered brightly. "What is the name of this extraordinary plant?"

"Ivy?" His incredulity was only slightly evident. Of course, he couldn't very well say "bullroar," as he must have longed to.

"How interesting," she mused. "Do you know, it cleaves so tightly to this brick that it actually bears my weight? I can scarce credit it, it looks so fragile."

"Hmm. Deceptive."

"Ivy, did you say? I simply couldn't resist climbing up to test its strength. In the spirit of adding to my store of knowledge on natural history, you understand."

"Bullroar," he said under his breath. She was quite sure of it.

"Excuse me?"

He didn't answer. Instead, he came to stand below

her and looked up. The light from inside gilded the planes and angles of his face. His thick lashes laid crescent-shaped shadows on his cheeks. His dark hair gleamed. He inclined his head and she had the oddest notion he was trying not to smile.

"Perhaps you'd like to come down now that you've tested the vine?"

She nodded. It was hard to act the grande dame while clinging like a bat to the side of a house. She lowered one foot, seeking the ground, and—

His hands wrapped about her waist and he lifted her, lowering her slowly to the ground. He released her but did not step back. She did, however, warned by the little shiver of alarm that began when she looked into his eyes. Dusky and mysterious and compelling.

She took another step back and bumped into the ivy-covered wall. Her breath came rushing out on a little whoosh of nervous laughter. His brows tipped in silent inquiry. Desperately, she sought a way to regain mastery of the situation, running through her trove of maxims until she found one that answered: A befuddled man is a malleable man.

"Now, then," she said in a chill tone, "what exactly brings you lurking about The Hollies after sunset, Sir Elliot?"

His beautiful eyes narrowed. "As you may have already divined, I was 'lurking about' in hopes of encountering you, Lady Agatha."

Drat. It would take more than a few words to muddle Sir Elliot's brain.

"Really?"

"Well, I may not have come with the express idea of strolling about the grounds. I had, in fact, driven in all blessed innocence to the front door." His smile was vulpine and gentlemanly all at once. "I collected your personal effects from the train station and had just unloaded them with instructions that they were to be taken up to your room when I saw you disappear around the corner of the house.

"In short, Lady Agatha, I came to tell you your things had arrived, not to *spy* on you."

His forthright attack left her slightly breathless. He wasn't playing by the rules! He was cheating. A gentleman wouldn't accuse a lady of accusing him of spying on her! Even if she was! Damnation!

She laughed, not quite as lightly as she'd intended. "La! What a fanciful notion. You're teasing me, of course. I'm sure you realize that I lead an entirely boring and blameless life. If you *were* to spy on me, you'd be bored to tears."

"Oh," he said, his mouth still smiling but his eyes hard, "I sincerely doubt that."

"You are too kind." And this was too dangerous to continue.

She moved past him, intending to lead him back into the house where others could dilute the tension between them. He fell into step beside her.

"And you, Lady Agatha?" he said, his tone conversational and therefore doubly suspect. "You were simply taking the night air when you were overcome with this horticultural curiosity?"

"Exactly." If she moved any faster she'd be trotting. The realization brought her up sharply.

Maxim number two: A person who runs away always looks like they have a reason to—Her foot caught in her hem and she tripped. Immediately, his hand was beneath her arm, setting her back on her feet. She forced her eyes forward and kept walking.

He did not release her arm. His clasp was light and she liked it. And she disliked that she liked it.

"I couldn't think of dining after such a long trip and, too, the thought of being inside on such a lovely night was unconscionable," she said, pleased with her explanation.

"It is a most lovely night," he agreed. Then, after a long moment's hesitation, "Would you care to continue your walk . . . with me?"

"Yes." It popped out before she'd stopped to think. He smiled, his gaze averted. He looked disconcerted and a little flattered. Amazing. What was wrong with the women of Little Bidewell that this man was still walking about unclaimed?

Oh, yes. It wasn't what was wrong with Little Bidewell women, it was what was wrong with Sir Elliot: Catherine Bunting. The thought soured Letty's mood.

"I trust you're finding everything to your satisfaction at The Hollies?"

"Oh, perfectly delightful."

"And you have met Anton?"

"A charming fellow."

They walked a ways farther, Letty fearful that any topic of conversation she brought up would lead to her unveiling and Sir Elliot, for whatever reasons, just as mute. The air had cooled since she'd come out and dew had developed on the lawn, soaking through the thin soles of her boots.

"Your absence from London for such an extended period presented no difficulty?" His voice broke the silence.

"No. I was actually quite eager to be off."

"Ah, you enjoy the country."

She could think of no reason to answer dishonestly. "I lived in the country as a child, and all in all I must say I prefer the city. I am, you see, a woman of the world."

"Obviously."

She glanced sharply at him, thinking she'd heard laughter in his voice, but he appeared quite sober.

"Thank you. And as a woman of the world, I find that those things that most appeal to me are most often found amidst the bright lights of civilization."

"Yes?"

"Oh, I grant you, rustication is very peaceful and quaint and I suppose if one were convalescing from an illness or suffering from a nervous disorder, living in the country would be . . . all right . . . but I am quite robust and not given to nerves."

"And here I thought all ladies, even women of the world, liked to be thought appealingly fragile."

Lady Fallontrue had always pleaded some malaise or another when she'd wanted something from her husband. Letty had despised her for it. It was one thing to manipulate gentlemen on a level playing field, but it was quite another to victimize a man by making use of one of the few decent qualities he might own.

"What," she asked, stopping, "is 'appealing' about weakness?"

He studied her before answering. "You have a forthright way with words, Lady Agatha. It is most refreshing."

"Comes from owning my own business, I imagine," she said. "This wedding thingie, you know."

She hesitated and then, encouraged by some misplaced desire to draw Sir Elliot out, she said, "My experiences have led me to believe that honesty in conversation, while not always strictly diplomatic, is the most rewarding." As soon as she said the words, she realized how hypocritical they were. She blushed and was glad the night hid her heated cheeks.

"I shall endeavor to remember your good advice," he said. He'd withdrawn his hand from her arm when they'd stopped; she rather missed it.

"I must own, I *am* thought somewhat sage," she said modestly.

"Are you? By whom?" She shot a sharp sideways glance at him, but his bland expression put to rest the dawning suspicion that he was teasing her.

"Oh, all sorts of people," she said airily. "Tradesmen, servants, actresses, actors, singers, artists . . . They come to me, tell me their troubles, and ask my advice."

An idea had begun to form in her imagination. She had no right entertaining it, let alone acting on it, but that had never stopped her before and it didn't stop her now. He was simply too handsome to spend his life mourning the loss of "Saint Catherine."

"Yes. Why just the other day, Mrs. Dodgson—You do know Mrs. Elmore Dodgson, do you not? No? Oh. You must endeavor to be introduced. Charming woman.

"At any rate, the other day Mrs. Dodgson was lamenting the fate of her son Charles." She leaned closer to him. He smelled nice. Soapy and male. "I tell you this in the strictest confidence, of course."

"Of course."

"Well, Charles had developed a tendresse for a young lady, feelings he had every reason to believe were reciprocated and that he'd hoped would end in ..." She searched about the imaginary Charles's ultimate goal.

"A wedding thingie?" Sir Elliot suggested helpfully.

"Exactly! But then, just as their relationship was popping along smoothly, her father required that she go abroad for a long while. When she returned, he discovered her feelings had changed." She fixed him with a telling stare. "Charles has been moping about ever since."

"Poor fellow."

Once more she stopped walking. Once more he followed suit. She met his gaze squarely.

"Poor fellow, nothing," she said. "Self-pitying fellow. Foolish, self-indulgent fellow. Uselessly-pining-after-a-floozy-who'd-proven-herself-both-shallow-and-immature fellow."

He strangled a sound in his throat. Ah. So, he'd not missed her veiled reference, then.

"You don't believe that po—pitiful Charles's lengthy mourning for his lost love indicates the, er, depth of his feelings?" he asked.

"Pining after what can never be for months—or years—doesn't testify to the depth of a man's love, it testifies to his predisposition toward melodrama. The stage already has enough cheap histrionics without amateurs adding their voices. Believe me. And that is precisely what I told Mrs. Dodgson."

She'd been perhaps a trifle obvious in her little fiction and prepared herself to meet stony silence in return for her charitable hints. Instead, he burst out laughing. It was a deep, rich laugh, warm and full.

"My dear Lady Agatha," he said, "I daresay no one ever accuses you of rank sentimentality. Wherever did you learn to take such a hard view of life?"

Hard? He thought her *hard*? The idea hurt. She considered herself practical, tough, a bit of an opportunist, but an optimistic one. She'd never thought of herself as "hard." Nick was hard.

She disliked the word applied to her. Immensely. And since she disliked it, she answered without stopping to think.

"I've had to be," she said, and then too late realized that Lady Agatha had probably never "had" to do anything in her life. "I mean, in my years of planning nuptial ceremonies I've seen many couples wed. They are seldom fairy-tale unions. No matter how very much one wants them to be. Perhaps if one sees disillusionment often enough, after a while one becomes inured to it."

He moved close to her, his brow furrowed. He gazed out into the darkness and after a moment said, "You'll do your best for Miss Angela's particular fairy tale though, won't you?"

"Of course." She began walking forward. His hand stayed her. She turned. His hand dropped to his side. "Excuse me."

But she'd seen the question in his eyes. "I promise I will do everything in my power to make this wedding go as smoothly and uneventfully as possible."

And in her case, her best efforts meant vacating The Hollies as soon as possible. But since she'd promised, she decided that when she slipped off she'd leave the Bigglesworths a note advising them to find another wedding planner. That should satisfy him. Certainly she'd be doing more than the real Lady Agatha to assure the "smooth uneventfulness" of the Bigglesworth nuptials. *She* hadn't even written. Yet.

Sir Elliot offered her his arm and she took it, feeling somehow that he'd won concessions from her she'd not intended to give. "You must be in some way related to the Bigglesworths to be so concerned."

"Not by blood, but certainly by association," he said. "I grew up on the estate between here and the Himplerumps. My mother died when I was very young. The Bigglesworths more or less adopted my brother and me while my father went through a rather rough period of adjustment.

"Anton was an excellent surrogate uncle and Eglantyne was always motherly without ever presuming to take the place of my mother. Their efforts were much appreciated," he finished softly.

"And is your brother also appreciative?" Letty asked curiously.

"While he lived," Elliot said. "Terry died in Africa, during a military campaign."

"I'm sorry."

"Thank you," he replied, robbing her of the uneasiness of having stumbled unwittingly into private matters. "And you, Lady Agatha, your family is quite large."

His comment ambushed her. Was he speaking from certain knowledge that Lady Agatha's family was large or from an assumption?

"A large extended family," she said carefully.

"I recall."

Drat! Why did he have to know *anything* about Lady Agatha's family? Because every muck-a-muck in Society knew every other muck-a-muck, that's why. They probably spent free evenings poring over Burke's Peerage. She should have realized it.

She smiled without replying.

"And I also recall that personal experience must give you sympathy for uneven matrimonial matches," he said earnestly.

What sort of personal experience? He must be speaking of some particular incident. Had Lady Agatha nearly made a disastrous match? Is that why she was still a spinster? Was there something unsavory in her past that she'd had to overcome?

"Your grandmother's own story was most illustrative."

Lady Agatha's grandmother! Letty thought in relief, but it was short-lived. She didn't know anything more about the old lady's peccadillo than she did Lady Agatha's. He waited. Drat it all. She'd have to say something.

"I didn't know anyone still talked about ... that."

She imbued her voice with frost. "It was a long time ago."

He was immediately contrite. "Forgive me. I didn't mean to discomfort you. I do not like to think of myself as a snob, nor would I like you to think me one."

Snob? Than Granny Whyte had done something scandalous. Something that had caused her to lose her social standing. What had it been? Child out of wedlock? Cheating at cards? Caught with a lover?

"Oh, not discomfort. I am just surprised that something so," she took a leap of faith based on his wording, "lurid should interest you."

He shot her a quick glance. "I am afraid I have overstepped myself and caused you unease. I am sorry."

"Think nothing of it." She breathed an inner sigh of relief. However, just to circumvent any future problem, she should pry what Granny Whyte's sin had been out of the Bigglesworths.

What was she thinking of? She wouldn't be around long enough for it to matter. A day. Perhaps two.

But having successfully wriggled out of one difficulty filled Letty with a feeling of omnipotence. She reminded herself of the warning she'd given herself this very evening and promptly dismissed her earlier caution as a case of the jitters.

The night was lovely, she was free of Nick Sparkle, Sir Elliot was completely taken in by her, and she had a whole day in which to pretend to be the witty, sophisticated, admired Lady Agatha. Perhaps, she thought, glancing at Sir Elliot's clean profile, two days.

He led her silently to the entrance by which she'd left the house. At the door she turned to face him. She smiled. "Thank you for the walk, Sir Elliot. I enjoyed it."

"No more than I."

"Will we see you tomorrow, then?"

"Most definitely," he said, his low, intense voice sending a delicious ripple up her spine.

He lifted her hand to his mouth and dipped down, brushing a kiss against her hand. His lips were warm and soft, so warm and soft that she failed to note the chill in his smile when he took his leave.

Chapter 7

Give me a strong back
over a soft heart.

WHO WAS SHE, IF SHE WASN'T LADY AGATHA Whyte? Why would anyone want to impersonate her? He must be wrong. . . .

Elliot raked his fingers through his hair.

It had been such a long, long time since he'd been so intensely aware of a woman. He flexed his hand, seeing the tanned outline of his fingers imprinted on her lace gown. He could feel her waist beneath his palms as he'd lifted her down from the wall. He could hear her laughter, see the merry tilt of her lips, smell the fragrant warmth of her rising from her skin . . .

He shook his hand, as if in doing so he could shake off his awareness of her. She couldn't be an imposter, a filthy confidence trickster.

He scoured his mind for some other explanation for her extraordinary behavior. Perhaps she'd come here on a wager. He remembered enough of his days amongst the ton to know it wasn't impossible that in their boredom or mischievousness or both, one of her set had dared her to impersonate Lady Agatha. Perhaps Lady Agatha herself.

Or maybe she was Lady Agatha and simply a confirmed eccentric. Certainly the reports he'd heard of her suggested such. And that might account for her occasional startling lapses into street argot. Though it couldn't account for her dress. Even the oddest lady he knew would rather die than remain a moment longer than necessary in the gown in which she'd traveled.

And how to explain her youth? For not all the creams and salves in the world could imbue the buoyancy in her step, the porcelain whiteness to her eye, or the rich sheen to her hair.

And finally, tellingly, how did one account for the fact that Lady Agatha Whyte did not know that her grandmother, the eighth daughter of an inconsequential Irish landowner, had, through judicious console and blameless reputation, become one of Queen Victoria's ladies-in-waiting?

Clearly *this* Lady Agatha thought he'd been speaking of some disgrace attached to her grandmother.

There was none.

He'd referred to the fact that even though she'd begun so humbly—like Angela—Lady Agatha's grandmother had risen to be not only accepted but also feted by Society. No breath of scandal had ever touched her. Indeed, she'd been famous for her virtue. Nothing in her history had ever been referred to as 'something so lurid.'

The woman had to be an impostor.

Didn't she? Unless she'd been referring to her other grandmother . . . About whom he knew nothing.

He moved away from the stables, heading for the house, his face set. Tomorrow he'd telegraph London and begin making some discreet inquiries. The answer, he knew, could be some time coming. In the meantime, he'd stay very, very close to this lady.

Whoever she was.

Letty spread her arms wide and fell straight back, sinking deep into the feather mattress. Fagin, bounced rudely awake, grumbled and settled down again.

Letty glanced at the mantel clock. Two o'clock in the morning and she'd just finished unpacking Lady Agatha's things. She'd been too wide-awake after her evening stroll with Sir Elliot to even think of sleeping. She looked around with satisfaction.

Strewn over every surface in the room were dresses and materials, some still in bolts of yardage and others in tissue-wrapped parcels: Sheerest batiste, thick polished brocades, glimmering faille and shimmering silk, dense lustrous satin, rippling crepe de chine, and gauzy muslin, tissues and sarcenets, moirés and tulles. The variety was amazing. And the colors endless!

Letty had never imagined so many whites existed. She'd unwrapped hard, gleaming nacre white and white as soft as a dove's wing; brilliant snow-white and white as mellow as ancient ivory. Dense chalk-white and thin, milky-white. Silvery-white and cool alabaster-white.

And after the material, she'd started on the trunks.

She'd unpacked every decorative accoutrement a woman could want. There were kidskin gloves with four buttons or six in half a dozen colors, silk stockings so sheer they seemed transparent, silk tassels for hats and bird's wings for headdresses, tippets and scarves to drape around the neck, sashes and ribbons to tie about the waist.

Lady Agatha hadn't scrimped on the underpinnings, either. Cartons of frilly unmentionables stood open about the room; pads and tounures to shape the hips, and chemises and corsets to enhance the bust. And there were petticoats, beautiful, soft, draping petticoats, designed to tantalize the imagination of anyone who might catch a glimpse of their frilly hems.

Letty's mother would have fainted dead away in ecstasy. Veda had always claimed that she'd stayed with Lady Fallontrue because in return for her talents, her ladyship had allowed Letty to be educated with her own children. But Letty suspected that as good a reason for Veda's putting up with the woman's cruel tongue and pitiful wages was that Lady Fallontrue gave Veda free rein to create all the wondrous gowns that crowded her imagination.

For all her flaws—and there were a great many— Lady Fallontrue had two distinct gifts: she knew genius when she saw it and was wise enough not to interfere with it. Who else would let a nobody like Veda create as she saw fit? Certainly not the music hall owners with their cheap velveteen and cheaper chintz.

But that's where Veda had ended up—as costume designer to second-rate music hall performers. Not that they'd always been second-rate, Letty thought loyally. When Lady Fallontrue had hired The Amazing Algernon as a divertissement for one of her "at-homes," he'd been at the top of his career, a handsome, acrobatic, and charming magician.

Lady Fallontrue was not the only one who thought so. Veda had taken one look at The Amazing Algernon—born Alfie Potts—and for the second time in her life, fallen in love. This time with happier results.

Not that Letty wasn't the sunshine of her life, Veda had always said, but frankly put—and Veda Potts was nothing if not frank—Letty was likely the only good thing that had ever come from Letty's father, Viscount Napier.

Twenty-four hours after Alf's performance—and just which performance Letty had never had the nerve to ask—Veda had given Lady Fallontrue her notice. The rest, as the storytellers liked to say, was history. Alfie and Veda had married and Alf had happily stepped into the role of stepfather. The three of them had moved to London where Letty had lived ever since, raised behind a hundred stages' crimson curtains, sung to sleep at night by racy ditties, and apprenticed in the myriad crafts of the theater, both legit and un.

Then, six years ago, Veda had caught a cold that had turned into pneumonia. She'd died. Alfie, brokenhearted, had left the stage. Veda would have hated that. She hated a quitter and she hated a soft-heart. "Give me a strong back over a soft heart any old day," she'd said. And even on her deathbed had managed to croak out, "Don't cry, Letty. Tears are for the weak and the weak don't survive."

Letty refused to leave London with Alf. She was a good singer and, regardless of what the know-nothing critics said, a good actress, too. And she was beginning to be noticed by those who could get a girl a leg up.

Like Nick Sparkle ...

Letty flopped over on her stomach, refusing to entertain thoughts of Nick and her mistakes related to him. She studied the cascades of material thoughtfully. Oh, the things her mother would have done with this windfall!

Letty smiled.

Veda had been no saint and, Lord knows, neither was Letty. But mostly they'd been pals. Especially after Alf had come into their life. Alf had knit them together, made them a family.

It had been too many months since she'd visited him. Maybe once things with Nick had blown over she could look him up in his little rural cottage. He'd said the door would always be open to her. On the other hand, she wasn't about to bring her troubles to her stepfather's door. She'd go somewhere else. Maybe France.

And in order to do that, she needed money. Which a few of these dresses and some of these costly baubles would bring. *If* she could find a buyer for them. She sat up.

The first order of business was to continue to string these folks along in their belief that she was Lady Agatha. Particularly Sir Elliot. And that meant making a grand show of herself. She looked down at her once-lovely lavender gown. The lace was pulled out of shape and the underdress was stained. She couldn't wear it again. She sighed. No rest for the wicked.

She glanced down at Fagin, sleeping blissfully. The fool mutt hadn't left the bed since he'd landed on it. Well, he'd best not get too used to a life of luxury, she thought. Though no one deserved it better than he did.

She wasn't rightly sure just how she and old Fagin had teamed up. Fate, she supposed. She'd come out of the back alley of a third-rate music hall one night after finishing her act and found a pack of boys torturing a little dog. They'd had it cornered. She hated above all things to see a creature cornered like that.

So she'd waded into their midst with fists flying and legs kicking and, most importantly, screaming at the top of a pair of incredibly gifted lungs. Afraid a copper would show, the mob had dispersed. The ragged little dog had scooted in with her when she'd returned to the music hall. Fagin had been with her ever since. Not a pet she owned, not something she was really responsible for. He was just *with* her, was all.

"All right, then," she murmured. "Until we're back in London, you can consider yourself officially on holiday. But don't you get too used to finer things, m'lad, because they're temporary."

She pushed herself to her feet and fetched the sewing basket she'd found in one of the trunks. She rummaged through it until she found scissors, needles, and thread. Then, with the eye of a connoisseur, she began sorting through the dresses she'd unpacked, looking for the one that would take the least amount of alteration to make it fit her smaller, riper figure.

A gauzy white muslin, the skirt figured with black swiss dots and the bodice piped with black velveteen caught her eye. She held it up, pulling it to her at the waist and studying her reflection in the full-length mirror. It was lovely. In the very first stare of fashion. Or would be once she tweaked the bodice and hips. Sir Elliot wouldn't spare a glance for his former fiancée once he got an eyeful of her in this dress.

Well, she admitted after a moment, of course he would spare a *glance* for Catherine Bunting. And words. And a dance or two. Because he was a gentleman, and gentlemen always paid equal attention to all the ladies of their acquaintance. Added to that, even if he wanted to, a gentleman would *never* monopolize one particular lady.

But, Letty grinned, spinning around and setting the skirts swirling out, wouldn't it be thrilling if he did?

Chapter 8

Find out what people want to do,
then tell them to do it. They'll think
you're a genius.

"GOOD MORNING, MISS BIGGLESWORTH."

Eglantyne, who'd been waiting in the breakfast room since nine o'clock for their celebrated guest, or rather their employee, rose from her seat. "Good morning, Lady Agatha . . ." Her voice trailed off.

Lady Agatha, posed dramatically in the doorframe, smiled. "Is something amiss?"

"No, not at all," Eglantyne hastened to say. "It's just that your dress . . . It's . . . it's so . . . so exceptional."

The black piping decorating the bodice drew attention to Lady Agatha's happy abundance in that area. Almost as much attention as the glove-close fit of the gown across the hips and nether regions. From there, the black dotted skirts fell in a long cascade of material that brushed the floor.

Lady Agatha's vastly expressive face lit with

pleasure. She twirled, setting the light skirt swirling about her ankle in a froth of ruffles. "It's all the thing in town."

With a sickly smile, Eglantyne sank down in her chair. Dear Lord, she hoped Lady Agatha wouldn't suggest Angela's wedding gown look like that.

Lady Agatha paused beside the buffet, inspecting the scant leavings from the breakfast that had been put out hours before. She picked up a piece of dry toast. "I recall your saying something to that charming Sir Elliot about a picnic today?"

"Yes," Eglantyne said, hoping Lady Agatha liked the outdoors. She certainly looked like a, er, *healthy* young woman. "Our other guests will be arriving at about four o'clock."

"Delightful!" Lady Agatha smiled happily. She returned to the breakfast table, her hips undulating in a graceful and impressive manner. Not that Lady Agatha needed to move in order to be impressive. Not in that dress, Eglantyne thought, feeling the warmth creep into her cheeks.

Lady Agatha began to hum, a catchy little ditty that stuck in the mind and sounded somehow . . . well, a bit *fast*. Eglantyne, as bemused by the ditty as the dress, picked up the breakfast bell and rang it frantically.

She wished Cabot would hurry. Cabot would know what to do and how to react. He was the perfect butler. She didn't know how to respond to Society ladies or what to say. This whole affair of hiring an aristocratic employee, the marquis's exalted family coming so soon, Angela's impending marriage, and then the fact that she'd be going away and never coming back again—

Eglantyne's eyes clouded over with tears. She had the most awful foreboding that everything was going to go horribly awry. And then Lady Agatha was beside her, sliding into the chair next to hers and laying a hand gently on Eglantyne's forearm. "What's wrong, du—darling?"

"Nothing," Eglantyne said bravely, but the unexpected sympathy in Lady Agatha's voice threatened her composure. She *couldn't* confide in a stranger, especially such an illustrious one.

"Are you sure?" Lady Agatha prodded gently. Her warm brown eyes were steady and just a little bit amused, not in a mocking way, but in an oddly reassuring way, as if there was no trouble in the world that one couldn't laugh away.

"I am so glad you are here," Eglantyne burst out. "I feel so inadequate for the whole ugly—Oh!" As soon as the horrible word was out she regretted it. Heat flamed in her cheeks. "How awful you must think me!"

"Why? Whatever for?" Lady Agatha said.

Eglantyne gazed at her thankfully for kindly ignoring the all too obvious fact that she'd just about called her dear, darling Angela's upcoming nuptials "the whole ugly task." As if it were some onerous chore, like scouring a floor or blacking shoes and not a cause for . . . for cele . . . celebra . . .

Eglantyne burst into tears.

Letty stared at her, stricken. She couldn't imagine what had set Eglantyne off. Not that she was concerned, mind you; why should she be? Eglantyne

Bigglesworth had everything a body could want. And it was only that she was curious about what could cause a rich woman to sob so pitifully that she put her arm around the older woman's shoulder and gave a little squeeze.

Eglantyne lifted her head. Her eyes were puffy and red and her nose was dripping. As Letty didn't suppose Eglantyne was the type who'd take advantage of her sleeve, she picked up the tidily folded napkin beside her plate, snapped it open, and held it under Eglantyne's nose. "Here, dear, blow your nose. There's a girl. . . . Now then, why don't you tell me what these tears are about?"

"I really shouldn't trouble you . . ."

"Nonsense. It is my job to be troubled. I mean, to facilitate weddings. If something is amiss, then I can't do my job properly, can I?"

"I suppose not. But there's nothing amiss, really. It's just that . . . I don't know. I suppose I'm a foolish, selfish old woman. I want Angela's happiness more than anything in the world, but oh! I shall miss her so—oo—oo."

She burst into tears again.

"Of course you will," Letty crooned, wrapping her arm around Eglantyne's shoulders and rocking her gently. When Eglantyne's shaking subsided, Letty shoved the wrinkled napkin into her hand again. "That doesn't mean you are selfish. It simply means you love Angela."

"Oh, I do! I do!" Eglantyne blew her nose.

"And you've been mum to her for how long?" Letty asked.

"Ever since her mother died giving birth to her.

Over eighteen years." She smiled tremulously. "She was so sweet and tiny and the dearest little creature you can imagine. I simply couldn't leave her in the care of someone we *paid* to—" She blushed. "Oh! I am sure I didn't mean that simply because one was paid for one's efforts they were somehow less valuable!"

"Never mind, dearie," Letty said comfortably. "I'm not offended. And I quite understand. You can rent a chap's talents, but you can't buy someone's affection, and clearly you'd fallen in love with the little squib."

"Squib?"

"Baby."

"You understand. I just want her to be happy and I am worried that my misgivings about her becoming a marchioness spring from an entirely selfish desire to keep her here with me."

Letty patted her shoulder. "You mustn't fret. I'm sure your Angela will be ecstatic in her grand castle." *I would be.* "As a marchioness, she'll have no more to do than order about a horde of servants and count the family portraits. She'll dine on caviar and champagne every night and have two dresses for every hour in the week."

Eglantyne sniffled around a little laugh. "Oh, Lady Agatha, you are too kind, playing the jester for me."

Jester? She'd been dead earnest.

Eglantyne's expression sobered. "I wouldn't mind so much, not really, if I were only certain Angela was looking forward to it. But lately Angela doesn't seem the same happy girl I have always known and loved. She looks pensive, and sometimes actually morose."

"Wedding jitters."

Eglantyne shook her head. "Angela's never been a flighty sort of girl. When she told us about Hugh Sheffield's proposal, she was ecstatic, otherwise Anton would never have agreed to the match."

"Maybe she's having second thoughts? That's natural."

"I thought so, too, but when I asked her if she'd prefer not to marry the marquis, she burst into tears and swore that she desired to be his wife above all things."

Well, thought Letty, at least the chit hadn't gone daft.

"I think," Eglantyne said, leaning toward Letty, "I think it's the Sheffields."

"How so?"

"They've already made it clear how low Hugh is stooping to marry Angela. I hesitate to make any accusations, but it seems to me that his mama has found every excuse by which to keep Hugh away from The Hollies and at her side.

"Don't misunderstand me, I don't pretend to know anything about High Society, Lady Agatha, but surely it is a bit unusual for the groom not to spend any time visiting his future in-laws at their home?"

Was it? "Ah, well . . . not necessarily," Letty said cautiously.

"Really?" Eglantyne fell on her words. "You give me hope. And," she went on as though to herself, "it is true that Hugh is coming at the end of the month, and his family has answered my latest invitation by promising to arrive shortly thereafter."

Letty smiled brightly. "Seems right as rain to me."

Eglantyne looked at her hopefully. "Hugh *is* most attentive to Angela. He writes to her daily. Though lately she doesn't seem so eager to read his letters." Her face fell. "I think it might worry Angela that they'll find us provincial and that we'll feel badly for it. Or they'll think the wedding reception is shabby. Or we are shabby. We simply can't appear second-rate! You must help us, Lady Agatha."

She held out her hand appealingly. She spoke so earnestly, her expression filled with such an odd mixture of affection, tenderness, and frustration, that it quite touched Letty's heart.

She gave herself a mental shake. She was getting soppy; she must be nearing her monthlies.

"Of course, I will," Letty said, disconcerted by these surprising treacly feelings. "Rather than worry about whether your Angela is good enough for the Sheffields, you might better concern yourself with whether the Sheffields are good enough for her."

At this mild suggestion, Eglantyne's eye widened and she clasped her broad hands across her chest. "I never thought of it that way, Lady Agatha! I can see why you are so successful. You are a paragon as well as a confidante and adviser. If only . . ." Eglantyne trailed off wistfully.

"If only what?" Letty prompted, in full charity with this unexpectedly canny woman.

"I couldn't possibly impose."

"I am not a falsely proud woman, Miss Bigglesworth," Letty said. "I should not hesitate to remind you that I am here in the capacity of your employee."

Instead of encouraging Eglantyne, Letty's words

seemed to have the opposite effect; her pink and powdered countenance crumpled in misery. "You're right. I could never take advantage of a situation in which my position is in any manner superior to your own."

Letty sighed. Gads, but the rich made things needlessly difficult! "Then perhaps as a new *friend*, I can encourage you to ask what you will."

"Oh, thank you!" Eglantyne clasped Letty's hands fervently. "It's just that, as one so close in age to Angela, and being a woman of the world, I was hoping that you might counsel Angela. Such advice would be invaluable to her. For *you* to give her the benefit of your experience and wisdom would be a gift that I, poor little country spinster mouse that I am, could never offer."

Her? What would she say to the girl? She'd never been married. In fact, she'd never even—Well, no one ever said that women of the world had to be *fast*.

She looked at Eglantyne. The older woman was regarding her anxiously. Ah, hell. What could it hurt to say she'd advise the girl? She wouldn't be here long enough to do the kid any lasting harm. Might even do her some good to hear a few frank facts. Letty capitulated with a deep inner sigh.

"Why, Miss Bigglesworth," she said, "of course. I will be only too happy to advise her in any small way that I might."

"How ever can I thank you? You are an inspiration!" Eglantyne's gaze traveled over Letty's person. "Why, one has only to look at you to realize that you are your own woman, Lady Agatha, and piffle to anyone who tries to tell you how to behave or how to live."

"True," Letty allowed, flattered.

"*You* don't let convention and small-mindedness govern your life," Eglantyne went on, warming to her subject.

"Righto," Letty said.

"You don't give a fig what people say about how you dress or act!"

"You bet I—" Letty stopped. *She didn't? She should. Lady Agatha would.* "What do you mean?"

"Well, most ladies wouldn't *dream* of wearing something so interesting. Nor would they be so devil-may-care, if you'll excuse the term. I imagine you'll cause quite a stir in our little community when you appear in that gown."

"Really? The ladies will talk?"

"Yes. Enviously," Eglantyne said.

"And do you think the gentlemen will approve?"

"I dare say so!"

"Even . . . Sir Elliot?"

"Oh." Eglantyne considered. "Well, Sir Elliot is a different kettle of fish, isn't he?"

"Is he?" Letty asked.

"He is," Eglantyne confided, "a very private man. Not that he isn't amiable. Indeed, Sir Elliot is everything one could ask in a gentleman. He'd never let a lady's appearance affect his opinion of her."

Letty stared at Eglantyne to see if she was joking. She wasn't. The old dear really believed it. "Sir Elliot is a man, is he not?"

"Oh, yes," Eglantyne said wistfully. If she were just twenty years younger ...

"Then, believe me, Miss Bigglesworth, his interest in a lady is most definitely affected by how she looks. No man, gentleman or not—"

"Miss Bigglesworth?" The butler's voice interrupted them.

"Ah, Cabot." Eglantyne turned toward the door with a little whoosh of relief. She wasn't entirely sure she wanted to hear what Lady Agatha had been about to disclose about men. "Would you please see that Grace makes some fresh coffee for Lady Agatha?"

She turned to ask Lady Agatha's preferences. As she did, Lady Agatha's little doggie Lambikins sauntered in from the hallway and, as though these exertions were quite enough for one morning, sat down squarely on Cabot's foot.

"Just give him a nudge," Lady Agatha said, lowering her gaze at Lambikins. "He'll—" She looked at Cabot and abruptly stopped speaking. Her eyes grew round.

Cabot, imperturbable stone-faced Cabot, swallowed audibly.

"Cabot?" Eglantyne asked. Whatever was going on? Cabot looked as though he'd seen a ghost. "I say, Cabot, are you quite all right?"

"Quite all right, madam," Cabot said. "Do you require anything else?"

Eglantyne looked askance at Lady Agatha. She had recovered from whatever had momentarily nonplussed her. "If there are any strawberries?" she asked demurely.

"Very good, madam." Cabot said. "Will there be anything else, Miss Bigglesworth?"

"Yes," Eglantyne said, seized by a sudden inspiration. There was no time like the present to get things rolling along between Lady Agatha and Angela. "Cabot, would you fetch Miss Angela at—"

"Ahem."

Eglantyne turned toward Lady Agatha. "Yes?"

"Might I suggest that you bring her here yourself, Miss Bigglesworth? It will give you an opportunity to lay the groundwork, so to speak, for our little chat." She glanced at the stoically waiting Cabot.

"A fine idea, Lady Agatha," Eglantyne agreed, rising. "I'll get her directly."

As she passed Cabot, he turned to follow her out of the room. But then she heard Lady Agatha say, "Oh, don't run off yet, *Cabot*."

Chapter 9

The past keeps showing up
wearing new makeup.

"IS IT REALLY YOU, SAMMY?" LETTY PEERED AT the portly, stern-looking butler in amazement.

"Yes, Letty. It's me," he said, his voice hushed with astonishment.

And then she was across the room, flinging her arms around him and hugging him tightly. He returned her embrace awkwardly, a man unaccustomed to demonstrations of affection. She chuckled. The same old Sammy.

The last time she'd seen him had been a half dozen years ago when Veda and Alf had been working the Saturday variety acts at the Palace Theatre. They'd known all the other performers from years past—including Sammy, who'd knocked about the "human oddities" shows for years as Sam-Sam, The Spaniel-Faced

Boy, Nature's Fantastic Amalgamation of Characteristics Both Canine and Human.

She smiled into his shoulder. One would never tell by looking at him now, but at one time his face had been covered with dense fur. But now... she lifted her head and regarded the furiously blushing butler delightedly. By gum! The Spaniel-Faced Boy had a receding hairline!

"Letty Potts," Sammy exhaled taking a step back and clasping her shoulders. For a moment his expression was as soft and pleased as her own and then the pleasure dimmed and his smile faded. "Whatever are you doing here? And why are you posing as Lady Agatha? Where *is* Lady Agatha?"

"Hush!" She darted behind him and hurriedly pulled the door shut. "Come across the room and I'll tell you."

The butler followed her slowly. "Last thing I heard about you, Letty, you'd taken up with that no-account Nick Sparkle." Worry supplanted his earlier pleasure. "I warn you, Letty, if this is one of his schemes to bilk people—"

"No one's going to bilk anyone!" Letty said, waving her hand to quiet him.

He didn't look convinced. Which hurt. Sammy and she had once been friends.

Indeed, she'd sharpened her impersonation of a lady on his suggestions, since Sammy, when not snarling and feinting at the enthralled women in the first row, had always comported himself as a first-class gentleman. Or rather, first-class butler, she now realized.

She'd never inquired about how he'd come by his impeccable deportment—those who made their living on the stage didn't ask too closely after another's past.

"What happened, Sammy, er, Cabot? Where's all your . . . your—"

"Fur?"

"Yes. I didn't recognize you. And what's with the butler act?"

"It's not an act," Cabot said. "My father served the Earl of Prescott as a butler, Letty. From the time I could toddle, my dad raised me to be a butler like him."

At Letty's querying expression, he chuckled. "I wasn't born covered with hair, you know. But the closer I got to adolescence, the hairier I grew. It soon became apparent that my physical appearance would keep me from following in my father's footsteps. So I came to London where I found work in the music halls. And that's where I met your mother and stepfather. It was a good enough life," he said, a nostalgic gleam in his eyes. "But as the years went by, my hair started to fall out. Got to the point where I had to glue fur on to make myself look like my posters. Finally, about four years ago, I had to quit the stage altogether."

"I'm sorry," Letty said softly.

Cabot looked at her in surprise. "I'm not. I could finally look for work as a butler. I applied at several of the employment agencies but few people wanted a fifty-year-old butler with no work experience. Then, one day I was interviewed by this dear, unsophisticated woman wanting to hire 'a real London butler' for her brother up north. I gave her Lord Prescott's name as a recommendation, and ... well, here I am."

"And you enjoy it?" Letty asked curiously. "Don't you miss the city, the lights, your old mates?"

"Not too much," he said. "Though I still trade letters with Benny," he said, referring to Ben Black, The Human Dynamo. "I have everything I want, Letty. I have the respect of my peers—at least, most of them—the care of a fine home, and most importantly, I am able to do what I was brought up to do."

She nodded thoughtfully. "I envy you, Cabot."

He cocked his head quizzically. "How so?"

"You know what you are. It seems you've always known."

"Well, Letty, you know who you are, too," he offered kindly.

She shook her head. "Who I am. But not *what*."

"Why, Letty," Cabot said, casting about for an answer to her unvoiced question. "You're ... you're ... the best time the English stage has ever known, that's what you are! No one could make folks tap their toes or smile like you did, Letty."

"A good time," she whispered. "Is that what I am?" She met his eye. "Well, I'm afraid I'm not even that, anymore. Leastways there's certain people in London who wouldn't think so."

"Nick Sparkle being to blame?" Cabot asked flatly.

She wasn't about to accuse Nick of those things she'd done, or been party to, of her own free will. If she had it all to do over again, she'd do the same. Or would she? The prickly question posed by her conscience caused her to lift her chin defiantly. She'd done what she'd done and she wasn't going to start apologizing now.

"I won't talk about Nick. You only need know that he's not here and he's not coming here. Other than that, the subject's closed." She forced a smile to her lips. "I still can't believe you like rusticating up here in the midst of nowhere."

He regarded her closely a moment before relaxing. "But I do. The only thing that has kept me from being perfectly content is the fear that someday someone will find out that the very proper butler Cabot was once Sam-Sam, The Spaniel-Faced Boy."

"Snobs, are they?" Letty said knowingly.

"Something terrible," Cabot confirmed.

Of course they were, Letty thought. The Bigglesworths were blue bloods, even if they didn't have a title. Just because Eglantyne had seemed so down-to-earth didn't mean that she couldn't toss her nose as high as the next aristocrat.

Letty knew the type well. She remembered one stage-door Johnnie particularly well. He'd had lovely manners and respectful ways, until a lady of his acquaintance showed up at the restaurant where he'd taken Letty for lunch. Then he'd not only forgotten Letty's name, it seemed he didn't even know how they happened to be dining together. After that, Letty had declined any more gracious offers to dine and stuck with her own kind. Still, it was a bit of a disappointment. She'd thought just maybe the Bigglesworths were different. Ah, well.

"To blazes with them," she told Cabot. "And good riddance."

"Easy to say," Cabot answered with a sigh. "You don't have to work with them."

"Work *with* them? My, that's a nice democratic way of putting it."

"I try," Cabot said, "to encourage by example. If I treat them as equals, I hope eventually they will learn to deal with others in the same way. Especially that harridan of a cook, Grace Poole—"

"Grace Poole? What are you talking about?" Letty asked in bewilderment.

"The staff," Cabot said. "Who else?"

"The *staff* are snobs?" Letty asked in amazement. "Not the Bigglesworths?"

"The Bigglesworths are the most fair-minded and generous people I have ever known," Cabot said. "Their staff, however, is another matter. They are magnificent in their snobbery." He smiled. "And speaking of snobbery, you've the way of a grande dame down pat, Letty. You've quite taken everyone in, I don't mind telling you."

"Really?" Letty asked, flattered.

"Oh, yes. But you always did have a knack for an impersonation. It's a shame you squandered your talents in Nick Sparkle's scams."

Letty's smile faded. "I thought we'd agreed that subject—"

"I suppose I haven't any right to judge," Cabot broke in. "But you were a nice kid, Letty. Tough as nails, but good-hearted."

"I'm still good-hearted," Letty declared.

"Then don't mention to the staff anything about my former career. I'd never live it down."

"Not I," Letty vowed, and then, "if you don't tell anyone about *my* little secret."

"That," Cabot answered slowly, "I cannot promise. I owe the Bigglesworths gratitude as well as loyalty, Letty. They assume people are decent. So, you see, *I* have to look after their best interests, Letty, since they refuse to do it for themselves."

"Well," Letty said, "they won't be harmed by me."

Cabot didn't look overly reassured. "I trust your word, Letty, but what about Nick Sparkle?"

"I *swear* to you, Nick has no part in this. No part at all," she vowed, hesitating a moment before going on. She would have gone into the details about her split with Nick Sparkle, but time was flying. Soon Eglantyne and Angela would be back. But she had to tell him something to reassure him.

"I was in a bit of a spot in London, Sammy, er, Cabot. So I went to St. Pancras even though I didn't have much money and I didn't have anywhere to go. I was just hoping something would turn up. And it did! While I was sitting there I saw the real Lady Agatha throw away her train ticket. So I picked it up."

"And came here," Cabot said.

Letty nodded. "I didn't even *mean* to impersonate Lady Agatha, I was just taking advantage of a spot of good luck. I'm only here for a day or so, then I'm off. When I go I'll take some of Lady Agatha's things, I won't lie to you about that, but I promise I won't take anything that belongs to the Bigglesworths."

Cabot eyed her closely a minute. "Where *is* Lady Agatha?"

"On her honeymoon." Letty leaned back in her

chair and smiled ruefully at Cabot's amazed expression. "That's why she dropped her ticket. Her husband-to-be chased her to ground at St. Pancras Station. Quite romantic. 'Leave everything behind and come with me now or never, Agatha!'"

Cabot shook his head. "The poor Bigglesworths."

Letty frowned in exasperation. "I told you, I won't—"

"I'm not speaking of you, Letty. I'm talking about Lady Agatha. She couldn't pick a worse time to elope. The Bigglesworths were counting on her to see that Miss Angela's wedding comes off properly."

"Well, that's not my problem, is it?" Letty said defensively. "In the final tally, whether I'm here or not won't make a bit of difference to the Bigglesworths."

"Maybe they'd have time to find someone else if they knew Lady Agatha had failed them."

"Two days isn't going to make that much of a difference." She stared at him imploringly.

"All right, Letty," Cabot finally said heavily, "as long as you don't nip off with any of the Bigglesworths' belongings, I won't say anything. Probably serves Lady Agatha right for being so cavalier with Miss Angela's fate. But if you're here three days from now, I'm going to Sir Elliot."

"You do what you have to."

He did not reply.

"What does Cabot have to do?" Eglantyne asked.

Letty swung around to find Eglantyne and Angela standing in the doorway. She smoothed her face to a bland expression. "Find me some fresh strawberries. Apparently your cook's hoarding them."

"Oh." Eglantyne nudged Angela into the room. "Cabot, please find Lady Agatha some strawberries."

"At once, madam." Cabot inclined his head and withdrew.

Eglantyne twisted the watch pinned to her bodice. "Oh. My. Look at the time," she said. "Our guests shall be arriving soon and there's still so much to do. Angela, won't you keep Lady Agatha company while I see that the croquet field is properly set up?"

Letty held back a smile. As a means of throwing the two of them together, Eglantyne could have been more subtle. Poor Angela blushed as Eglantyne fled the room.

"I'm so sorry if this is an imposition," Angela said.

"Not at all, Miss Bigglesworth," Letty said. "Won't you join me?"

Angela took a seat, looking as happy as if she'd just been asked to answer a few questions for the Inquisition. Fine lines framed her mouth, and sleeplessness had bruised the area beneath her eyes. Eglantyne was right: Something was definitely amiss with the bride-to-be.

"I hope your rooms are in order," Angela finally broke the silence.

"Everything is lovely. Thank you." They smiled at each other uncertainly.

"Here you go, ma'am." Grace Poole came bustling into the room wheeling a cart piled with a bowl of strawberries, clotted cream, scones, and a pot of coffee.

Letty's mouth watered. She hadn't eaten since early yesterday morning and that a greasy bit of fish from a street vendor.

"I'm eager to see the materials to which you referred in your letters," Angela said.

"Um," she said, nodding enthusiastically when Gracie pointed at the berries and cocked a brow inquiringly.

"I only wish I didn't have to wear a white gown. I have never felt very attractive in white."

Letty held up three fingers in response to Grace's silent inquiry as to how many sugar lumps she wanted in her coffee, then gave her attention to Angela's words. Anyone in the theatre understood the importance of color in stage design. And what was a wedding anyway but a production, only with the audience seated in pews? "Not every white looks the same on every complexion, Miss Angela."

"Really?" Angela asked hopefully

"Really." She studied the girl. Angela's self-assessment was right. A bleached blue-white would make her look pasty, and dull her soft blond hair. "A pinky-white for you, Miss Angela," she mused, an image of the shatoosh silk she'd unpacked last night springing to mind. It had a breath of delicate abalone-shell pink beneath its glowing surface. Body without stiffness. Virginal yet stylish.

Warning bells went off in her head. She didn't stop to heed them, she simply plowed ahead. "I have just the thing up in my room."

"You do?" Angela's face was a study in hopefulness.

"Hm." She reached for a scone and took a bite. Delicious! Her eyes rolled back in her head and she directed some sort of yummy sound in Grace's general vicinity. Grace accepted the accolade with equanimity and retreated from the room.

It took Letty a few minutes to realize that while she was methodically tucking away every bit of food on her plate, Angela was watching her in surprise.

"A healthy appetite is indicative of a generous nature," Letty said, dredging up a maxim.

"I am sure that your appetite must be quite large, then." Angela frowned as if her words hadn't quite come out right, colored, and continued. "I mean, you are most generous in giving up all your High-Society endeavors to come to us in Little Bidewell."

"My dear Miss Angela," Letty said, "what Society could possibly be higher than a marquis's?"

Angela's face crumpled.

"Why, m'dear, what's wrong? You don't look very happy."

"Oh, I am," Angela said quickly. "I wish to wed Hughie above all things! I love him so! It's just that, well, things would be so much simpler if he *weren't* a marquis.

"You can't imagine what it's like, Lady Agatha. Whenever I'm with his family I go in terror that I might make some unforgivable faux pas and be revealed as the insignificant creature I am."

"Oh, believe me," Letty murmured, "I understand."

"I'm just not comfortable pretending to be something that I'm not," Angela said.

Finally, a subject Letty knew something about. She waved her fork instructively. "First and most important, you must *believe* yourself into the role. When push comes to shove, simple self-confidence can mask any little missteps."

"I can't believe *you* have ever misstepped, Lady Agatha."

"Well," Letty lowered her eyes modestly, "I'm sure I must have made *some* mistake at some time or other."

"I'm just not going to be any good at being a great lady. There's all these rules and codes and dictums . . ." Angela said.

"Just be guided by your own good sense and, of course, a discreet observation of those whom you would emulate, and you will succeed."

"I've been studying this." Angela said, reaching into her skirt pocket and withdrawing a well-thumbed, softbound book. She handed it to Letty. *Our Decorum: Etiquette and Manners for Ladies of Breeding.* "But I see now that your advice is the best. I shall simply watch how you do things and comport myself accordingly."

Only supreme self-control enabled Letty to keep from choking. "Now, Miss Angela, that isn't what I meant," she croaked. Dear God! If she ended up being responsible for breaking this girl's engagement, she'd never forgive herself. "I am quite sure you could find more suitable people to pattern your manners after. After all, I am sure my deportment has . . ." she cast about, "has suffered through the necessity of my having to work for a living."

"Never," Angela said staunchly.

Letty smiled weakly. "Besides, you are already as admirable and well-bred a girl as any man could wish to wed. Sheffield is lucky to make you his wife."

Angela stared at her in stricken silence, as if a friend had suddenly turned on her.

"Angela? What is it?" she asked in alarm. The girl's face was pale and her lips trembled.

"Nothing," Angela said hastily, turning her head. "It's just that I'm not as good as you ... or ... or Hughie think I am." Her breath caught on her betrothed's name and she blinked rapidly.

There was more here than Letty had first thought. But Angela wasn't ready to confide in Letty. Not yet, but—Letty gave herself a sharp, mental slap. What was she thinking, 'not yet'?! If she was lucky, not *ever*.

But then, it wouldn't hurt to give the poppet a spot of joy, would it? It certainly wasn't because of maudlin sentimentality or some misplaced desire to be a do-gooder that she decided to show Angela the shatoosh upstairs; it was only out of artistic curiosity. To see if she still had as good an eye as her mother had once claimed.

"I know," she said. "Before the guests arrive for your aunt's picnic, why don't we nip upstairs and take a look-see at that material I was talking about?"

The suggestion worked like a charm. What woman could resist the pleasure of sorting through fabrics and poring over patterns? Ten minutes later they were in Letty's room, Angela's eyes dry as the desert and bright as the stars as she sorted through all the wonderful things Letty showed her.

Chapter 10

Kindness costs nothing.

THE AFTERNOON WAS FINE. ONLY A FEW clouds disturbed the porcelain-blue tranquility overhead. A freshening breeze had earlier flirted with the ladies' picture hats, but even this subsided as the afternoon drew on.

The croquet field had been set up on the back lawn and along one side of it the servants had raised several open-sided marquees. Beneath the striped awnings, tables and chairs waited invitingly, while rugs had been spread beneath the open sky. At each place waited a wicker picnic basket overflowing with cold meat pies and fruit, jellies and flaky scones, fresh cheese and the promised pièce de résistance, a mouthwatering strawberry trifle. Sweating tin canisters stood beside these, filled with lemonade for those who chose not to imbibe and ale for those who did.

Lady Agatha Whyte, standing in the reception line beside Anton and Eglantyne Bigglesworth, did. And had before, as evinced by the easy way she quaffed the ale from a ceramic mug and licked the froth from her upper lip.

Sir Elliot arrived with his father and greeted the Bigglesworths, and tried with only moderate success to keep his eyes from straying toward Letty. But her eyes were alight with private laughter and her dark auburn hair blazed in the bright afternoon sun. She'd dressed in a swirling, close-fitting gown, her every movement exaggerating the ripe—

He gave himself a mental shake and bowed over Eglantyne's hand. Then Eglantyne turned toward Lady Agatha, saying something about having introduced him yesterday, and he was before her, carrying her hand to his lips. He lifted his eyes as he kissed the back of her hand. Her eyes darkened, her lips parted. He heard her inhale softly.

He straightened, smiling calmly though his pulse had begun racing. She returned his smile with equal aplomb and equal duplicity; the thin material covering her breasts shivered and his body reacted instinctively. It had been years since a woman had had such a physical effect on him.

Then he and Atticus were moving down the line and from there out onto the lawn toward where Paul and Catherine Bunting stood. Atticus was silent, and for this Elliot was glad. Was Lady Agatha the lady she claimed to be or an imposter? He did not trust his own judgment.

"Lady Agatha is a most handsome young woman,"

Atticus said as they approached the Buntings. "Quite lively. It's the red hair, you know." His father nodded sagely. "It invariably decries an ardent nature."

"I suppose."

"I suspect it's why she's unmarried. Too volatile."

"Hm."

Atticus glanced at him in surprise. "You take a different view?"

"I suspect it has more to do with a lack of ready than a superfluity of passion."

"Superfluity? Passion?" Atticus's brow furrowed.

"Vivacity, then. And I was being ironic, Father. One could hardly be too alive, could one?"

His father smiled. "You'd be surprised at the odd notions some men entertain regarding the fairer sex. I have little doubt that there are men who would consider Lady Agatha's, ah, joie de vivre disreputable."

"Then they'd be fools," Elliot said shortly.

He made his obeisance to Catherine, kissing her hand before shaking Paul's. Catherine, warmhearted and affectionate by nature, linked her arm through his.

"Who's a fool, Elliot?"

His father answered. "Men who do not understand Lady Agatha's charm."

Catherine looked surprised. "You think her charming, Elliot?"

He had never been the sort of man to easily disclose his feelings, and he wasn't even sure what they were in regard to Lady Agatha. "The Bigglesworths obviously find her entirely delightful."

"Ah!" Catherine said, smiling kindly. "The Bigglesworths are such dear, undiscriminating people."

Before Elliot could answer, she'd tapped him playfully on the cheek. "And you are entirely unworldly where women are concerned. Come, Elliot. Let us find a glass of punch and I shall explain to you about the wiles of the *average* woman."

She'd secured his arm and he had no choice but to escort her to where a servant was dispensing punch.

Paul watched them go without any appreciable interest, as Lady Agatha approached him in company with Dr. Beacon and his wife. She greeted Paul and Atticus, looking about with unfeigned interest.

"Ah, drat," Beacon said. "I missed Elliot."

"I suspect he'll be back shortly," Paul said. "Went off on some errand of Catherine's making."

Atticus glanced at Lady Agatha. Should he, or shouldn't he? He should.

"Does that a lot, doesn't he?" Atticus said mildly.

"All the time," Paul answered. "Still feels something of the old tenderness I should imagine," he added proudly, "and Catherine always goes out of her way to make sure she shows him a little extra attention. She's so tender-hearted." He glanced at Atticus. "Not that I'm suggesting that Elliot's feelings aren't entirely honorable."

"Of course not," Atticus agreed at once, and noted with satisfaction the chill expression on Lady Agatha's face. "It's fortunate for Elliot that Catherine doesn't feel uncomfortable being at the center of an old swain's as well as a loving husband's attention."

"She always says it's important that Elliot feel welcome," Paul said.

"Perhaps she enjoys the attention?" Lady Agatha suggested.

Paul shrugged. "Maybe."

His answer, as well as his obvious unconcern, had the effect of making Lady Agatha's eyes flash with annoyance or disapproval. She smiled brittlely. "Dr. Beacon, isn't that your lovely sister over there? I would so like the opportunity to know her better."

Somehow Atticus kept from grinning until after Lady Agatha and Jim Beacon were gone. But it was an effort.

Having gotten Catherine her punch and returned her to her husband, Elliot was about to join Lady Agatha's party when he noted Elizabeth Vance and her father sitting by themselves at a table under an awning. He went to them at once.

"Miss Vance, would you and the Colonel mind terribly if I joined you for lunch? There are some matters about the current Boer situation that I would like the Colonel's opinion on."

"Of course. Of course, m'boy!" Colonel Vance thumped the empty chair next to him with his cane. "You'd best go off to some of your women friends, Elizabeth. Sir Elliot wants my advice. Nothing of interest for you here, I'm sure."

"I'm afraid not," Elliot agreed apologetically. Elizabeth all but leapt to her feet and, after making a breathless promise to return soon, fled.

Elliot settled in to listen. Though he was usually

content to hear the old man's tales, today his gaze kept straying to the lawn outside, where the sun danced between newly minted leaves and women and men strolled beneath the branches, laughing, chatting, and flirting.

He was thirty-three years old. At one time he'd been as easy and careless as those around him, but then obligation had required him to don a mantle of authority and purpose.

Bad luck, a horrific miscarriage of military justice, and a dervish's blade had aided that transformation. In a zariba seven miles from the Nile, he'd caught a sword in the leg but, made oblivious to pain by the sheer fury he'd felt at a dishonorable and spurious piece of injustice he'd stumbled into the night before, he'd managed to keep his company together. They'd rewarded him by shipping him home and giving him a knighthood. He'd vowed never again to presume justice was available to all men, and to henceforth do all in his power to see that it was.

Since then, he'd subordinated everything in his life to fighting to make the legal system a viable and honorable one. Now it looked as though the care with which he'd led his life and the scrupulousness with which he performed his legal duties would be rewarded in the premium he had sought. The Prime Minister himself verified it; come New Year's Honors, Elliot would be made a peer.

He should be elated. He should be taking this opportunity to prioritize a laundry list of reforms and concerns. But his attention kept wandering. Lady Agatha sat on a large rug, finishing her luncheon along with a group of picnickers that included John and Rose Jepson, Jim Beacon and his sister Florence, and Squire Himplerump's scion, Kip.

"Don't you agree, sir?" Colonel Vance's voice grew steadily in volume.

"Most definitely, sir," he avowed, not having a clue as to what he was swearing.

John Jepson hadn't said a word since Lady Agatha sat down. He kept grinning at Rose, both of them pink-faced with pleasure over finding themselves in such august company. Jim sat beside Lady Agatha, chivalrously plucking daisies for the necklace she was weaving for her dog's necklace, while Kip lolled on his stomach, his broody good looks marred by an insolent smile.

As Elliot watched, Lady Agatha called out for Angela to join them. Angela started over, but abruptly changed her mind, begging off and turning away. Kip pushed himself to his feet and hurried to catch up to the girl.

Elliot wished the boy luck. Perhaps he could find out what was troubling Angela. The two had been friends since the cradle. Indeed, Angela was one of the few people—besides Kip's doting parents—who insisted the boy was good at heart.

Like a magnet, Elliot's gaze had returned unerringly to Lady Agatha, when a sudden lull fell on the conversation. Into that brief stillness Colonel Vance's voice boomed like a foghorn, "I'd be staring, too, if I could see half as well as I used to! Quite an eyeful, by God! Makes one's mouth water."

Elliot closed his eyes and wished himself a

thousand miles away. Someone tittered nervously. He opened his eyes. Archibald was leaning across the table, regarding him with insistent inquisitiveness, his eyes as bright and black as a malevolent crow's and just as oblivious to the commotion he'd caused.

"Well, Elliot?" Archibald demanded. "Ain't that toothsome? Or have you no appetite for a fancy piece of work like that?"

Dear God, could it get any worse?

"Father!" Elizabeth, arriving just in time to hear her sire's comments, covered her mouth. Her face bled of all color. "Oh, Sir Elliot!" she whispered from behind her hand. "Please, I pray, forgive him, us. *Me.* I should know better than to leave—"

She was near to sobbing. And her father was regarding her in hurt befuddlement. And if Elliot didn't do something immediately, Elizabeth, whose social life was already as severely curtailed as genteel poverty and dutiful daughterhood could conspire to make it, would never be able to bring herself to accept another invitation. *If* she ever received another one.

He looked directly at Colonel Vance. He must take the onus for the Colonel's words but, if he was to pull this off, everyone must think he was unaware that they'd become the center of attention. He smiled—though he doubted the stretching of his lips bore much resemblance to anything remotely pleasant—and in a loud, distinct voice said, "Ah. Then you did hear me, sir. As I remarked earlier, she is, indeed, most delectable." A female gasped. He steeled himself and plowed on. "Not the usual find at a country picnic. You retain an excellent eye."

Well, Elliot thought, so much for becoming better acquainted with the mysterious Lady Agatha now. She'd shun him like the swine he'd acted. For him to speak of her as if she was some consuma—

"Well, really, Colonel Vance," a throaty voice cut across his thoughts. "It *is* Colonel Vance, is it not? And Sir Elliot."

He froze upon hearing her voice, but his training stood him in good stead and he rose to his feet and turned. She'd every right to personally deliver the set-down he so richly deserved.

"Lady Agatha." He inclined his head, his voice betraying none of the self-disgust he felt.

Her clever, angular face was tilted to the side, one brow cocked, her wide mouth ripe, richly amused, her eyes dancing in perfect comprehension. In her hands she held a glass bowl filled with cake and strawberries.

"I could not help but overhear your conversation," she said, glancing at Archibald. At least the old roué had grace enough to avert his eyes. Her gaze released him and swung back to Elliot.

"Your *entire* conversation," she said in a voice that, though carrying clearly, somehow gave an impression of intimacy so that anyone listening—which nearly everyone within shouting distance was—would think she spoke to him alone. Nice trick, that, and for a second he wondered where she'd learned it, but then she moved closer.

"Forgive me for eavesdropping, but that is how I learned how delectable both you gentlemen find *strawberry trifle*. I also noted that your table doesn't seem to have been set with one, and so confided to my fellow diners."

She gestured graciously to the doubtful-looking group behind her. "Generous souls that they are, they simply could not enjoy this one knowing you were without, Colonel Vance. Oh," she batted her eyelashes innocently, "and you, too, of course, Sir Elliot."

He stared.

She knew full well they hadn't been speaking of any cake. It was there in her eyes, in the teasing tilt to her smile. She also knew that since she'd claimed to have heard their conversation, no one could say they hadn't been speaking of cake without calling Lady Agatha a liar.

He smiled, grateful for her generosity, but on seeing the amused arch of her brow, realized, as she already had, that he was also now in her debt.

Chapter 11

Charm is getting people to say "yes"
without ever having to ask them a question.

"HERE," SAID LADY AGATHA, OFFERING HIM
the bowl.

"You are too generous, Lady Agatha," he mumbled.

"Aren't I just?" she replied smoothly.

"I thought you disliked strawberries, Elliot,"
Catherine said from beside him. He hadn't even seen
her approach.

"Perhaps at one time; not anymore," he said, looking across Catherine at Lady Agatha. "Quite recently
I've developed a veritable passion for them. Amazing
the things one can discover about oneself. And under
the most unusual circumstances."

Lady Agatha stifled a laugh.

"Piffle," Catherine said severely. She took the trifle
and placed it in front of Archibald Vance who, in a
rare instance of prudence, had decided to stay mute.

She linked her arm through Elliot's and gave it a little hug.

"Remember when we were young and Cook used to give us bowls of strawberries as a treat? You always gave me yours. Come to think of it, I wouldn't be surprised to learn that you *have* always liked them. You have always been chivalrous to me."

"Chivalrous? Not I," he said, directing his comments to Lady Agatha. "Though I am most recently reminded that chivalry is not dead."

Lady Agatha colored the faintest bit.

"But you were always kind to me, weren't you, Elliot?" Catherine said with a touch of insistence. He looked down at her pretty, expectant face.

"You were an easy girl to spoil, Catherine," he said.

She laughed, hugging his arm tighter as she leaned toward Lady Agatha. "I'm afraid I still am. Paul and Elliot and . . . well, I'm shamefully overindulged."

"Don't worry, m'dear," Lady Agatha said. "I can assure you, you do a splendid job of masking any character flaws such pampering oft engenders." She paused. "Besides, I'm sure you've exaggerated your situation."

Elliot glanced at her sharply, not quite trusting her innocent expression. Though the words themselves were reassuring, the tone was mildly sardonic. And, as disloyal as he felt it to be, he couldn't help but feel Catherine deserved it.

For whatever reasons, since the moment she'd met Lady Agatha, it had seemed like Catherine had been set on making her ladyship feel like an outsider. Already today he'd heard her make several casual remarks about Lady Agatha's "interesting fashion sense" and "peculiar—albeit charming—conversation."

Of course, he was probably misinterpreting what was going on. Catherine had no reason to feel any animosity for Lady Agatha. Nor Lady Agatha for her.

Still, Catherine's voice was decidedly frosty when she murmured, "You are too kind."

Lady Agatha didn't demur. She simply smiled sunnily and said, "So I've been told."

Elliot damn near burst out laughing. She'd make a formidable opponent, would Lady Agatha. She'd turned the tables on Catherine right enough, and though he should be supporting his one-time fiancée, he found himself too busy trying to keep from grinning.

Into this mire of tension sailed Eglantyne, Grace Poole at her side and young Hobbs from the stable bringing up the rear. He was pushing a wheeled cart filled with croquet equipment.

"See, Grace? More than enough food," Eglantyne said. Her gaze fell on the abandoned trifle. "But what is this doing here? Don't tell me you haven't had your dessert yet, Colonel Vance! Miss Vance? Elliot? Well, I'm afraid I'll have to ask you to delay enjoying it until later or you'll miss the croquet, and I do so need you, Elliot, to make an equal number of ladies and gentlemen."

"Of course."

"Thank you. Now, then—" She clapped her hands, drawing the attention of the rest of the picnickers. "If you please! We're going to have a croquet tournament this afternoon with prizes for the winners," she announced. "So please divide yourselves into teams of one lady and one gentleman. The only requirement is that," she wagged her forefinger playfully at Catherine, "you must not pair up with your spouse."

"Oh, Elliot!" Catherine exclaimed. "Remember how we won the lawn tennis tournament at Tumley?"

"I do," Elliot answered. He knew where this was going, yet he was reluctant to ask. Beside him, Grace Poole whispered urgently in Eglantyne's ear. He glanced at Lady Agatha. She'd turned in another direction, her expression a little bored.

Catherine regarded him with confident expectation. He cleared his throat. "Catherine, it would be—"

"I'll tell you what it would be," Eglantyne cut in abruptly. Grace Poole folded her hands at her waist, her expression supremely complacent. "It would be a great favor to me, Catherine, if you would partner Anton. You know how shy he is about his lack of athletic abilities, and what with your talent, you might just keep the pair of you in the game beyond the first round. If you would be so kind, my dear?"

Catherine's smile wavered. "Well, of course, Eglantyne dear. If you think he really *wants* to play . . ."

"Oh, I am certain he does." She raised her voice. "Yoo-hoo, Anton!"

Anton, who'd been in conversation with Atticus and the vicar, looked around.

"Grand news," Eglantyne called with strenuous cheer. "Catherine has just been telling me how much she would like being your partner!"

"She has?" Anton asked.

"Yes! Come on, then. Don't keep her waiting."

Anton, his florid face bemused, hurried over. Eglantyne turned to Elliot. "Oh! I have *just* had a grand idea, Elliot! Perhaps *you* might partner *Lady Agatha*."

"I would be delighted," he said promptly.

"Oh, no!" Lady Agatha exclaimed. "I mean, I am certain Sir Elliot is an ace player. Indeed, that's the problem. I'm not. In fact, I've . . . I've never played croquet before."

"Never?" Eglantyne echoed disbelievingly.

"I'm . . . very busy, and when I was a child we didn't play many games. Not that sort of game."

"Well," Eglantyne said, "it's high time you learned. You'll enjoy it. Capital game. Elliot will have you flying through wickets in no time."

She drew a pair of mallets and two balls from the cart and plopped them unceremoniously into Elliot's hands.

Lady Agatha darted a glance at him from beneath her lashes. She looked a little uncertain and suddenly quite young and quite shy; an attitude that contrasted strongly with her oft-repeated insistence that she was "a woman of the world." In fact, several times now he'd seen Lady Agatha surprised into ingenuousness, making it seem ever less likely that she could be some hardened confidence artist.

"I wouldn't want to be a bother," she said.

"It would be my pleasure, I assure you," he said.

"Dear Eglantyne, Elliot," Catherine said sympathetically, "if Lady Agatha doesn't want to play, I don't think we should badger her into complying."

"Oh. Of course not," Eglantyne agreed, at once red-faced and contrite. "I am sorry. I did not mean to insist."

Once more, Lady Agatha saved the situation. She laughed, taking Eglantyne's hand between hers and giving it a little shake. "Don't be silly, dear. I was simply being coy," she admitted with charming artlessness. She dimpled adorably. "I am secretly all atwitter to learn the game. Because," she straightened, "it's always so much more fun to be *in* the game," her gaze flitted over Catherine, "rather than sitting on the sidelines. Don't you agree, Miss—oh! Excuse me! What a goose I am! It's *Mrs.*, isn't it?—Don't you agree, Mrs. Bunting?"

"Yes," Catherine clipped out, her body stiff and her face stiffer. "Come along, Anton, we'd best collect our gear while Elliot instructs Lady Agatha. Though I wouldn't doubt she could teach him a thing or two— She looks very much the *sporting* sort, doesn't she?"

She turned to Letty. "I look forward to meeting you on the playing field, Lady Agatha."

"No more than I, Mrs. Bunting," Letty replied.

"Whatever is going on?" Eglantyne asked, watching Anton being led off by Catherine.

"Nothing," Lady Agatha said.

"Well, then, I'll leave you in Elliot's good hands. You have a quarter hour to turn her into a prime player, Elliot. Ah!" She raised her head like a hound sighting a hare. "Dr. Beacon! I need another gentleman," she called, taking off after him, "I say, Dr. Beacon!"

Elliot turned to Lady Agatha; she was smiling after

Eglantyne as though any minute she might shout an encouraging "tally-ho!"

"That was most kind, what you did with the trifle."

"It was nothing." She accepted the mallet that he held out to her. "How do you hold this thing? Like a golf club?"

She was not being falsely modest. She really was discounting her generosity as a matter of no importance.

"I beg to differ."

She looked up from swishing the mallet experimentally at some weed heads. Clearly she'd considered the subject closed and he'd surprised her by pursuing it. A roguish glint appeared in her eyes. Her wonderfully mobile mouth pursed contemplatively. "Sir Elliot, *I* am a woman of the world."

Somehow he kept from smiling, but then his humor was supplanted by another sensation altogether as she placed one hand on her hip and in the other swung the mallet as a dandy would his walking stick. She sashayed toward him, her playful mood infectious.

"Really, now, Sir Elliot," she said, her eyes flashing, her hips . . . God, what those hips were doing! "What else should I have done? I looked over, immediately understood the situation, and—well, I saw at a glance that this proud, straitlaced darling would suffer from his comments far more than I was ever likely to do."

She stopped and leaned on the mallet, a comic caricature of a London dandy. "It seemed a little enough thing to save him from the torture he was bound to put himself through. Especially since his supposed 'crime' in no way warranted so grievous a punishment."

"You are kindness itself, Lady Agatha," Elliot said. "And you were correct in your estimation of Colonel Vance's character. He would, indeed, have put himself through—"

"Oh," she cut in, "I wasn't speaking of Colonel Vance."

It took a full ten seconds for her meaning to sink in, and when it did, he took one look at her naughty, lovely, teasing face, and burst into laughter.

Sir Elliot's many friends and neighbors looked around in surprise. They'd not heard such full-blown laughter from him in years, and seeing the smile on his face they found themselves smiling, too, for he was a great favorite in their community.

A few dozen yards away, Eglantyne and Grace Poole exchanged glances as congratulatory as they were conspiratorial. Atticus, deep in conversation with the vicar, paused at the sound of Elliot's rich amusement and smiled. And even Cabot, offering an uncharacteristically petulant Catherine Bunting a different glass of iced tea, hesitated before a grin flickered and vanished on his austere face.

Only Lady Agatha failed to understand the rarity she'd produced. She grinned back cheekily in response to his laughter, as though they'd traded bon mots all their lives, and as she did, a breeze caught a tendril of her hair and whipped it across her face.

Elliot, still smiling and before he could think better of it, reached out and brushed it away. As soon as his fingers touched her sun-warmed cheek, he under-stood his folly. Instantly, the casual touch evolved into something too like a caress for comfort.

He stared into her eyes, suddenly wide and ques-tioning and young and...frightened. His hand dropped. He stepped back and gestured for her to precede him. "Perhaps we ought to go to the playing field," he said, despising the stilted tone in his voice.

But she was having none of it. Her expression had smoothed out; her eyes glittered. "I could have sworn we were already *on* the playing field," she murmured, invoking another laugh from him. Something inside of him struggled for expression.

He was in trouble. He liked her, liked her enor-mously—which was far, far more worrisome than sim-ply wanting her.

Chapter 12

If you trip, make sure the leading man
is there to catch you.

"BECAUSE THE BIGGLESWORTHS HAVE SUCH a large lawn they play a six-wicket game of croquet, though we do have to be careful on the edge of the field." He gestured to a ridge of land across from where they stood. "It's an embankment. There used to be marsh on the other side, but it filled in with sedge years ago."

Lady Agatha studied the layout of the playing field. "And the wicket is that wire arch there?" she asked.

"Yes. The object of the game is to shoot our balls—these black-and-blue ones—through the wickets in a particular order and hit that peg at the end of the field there." He pointed to where Hobbs was driving a stake into the ground. "Then return to the other end of the field in reverse order, our ultimate goal being this peg."

"It doesn't sound very challenging," she said doubtfully.

He smiled at her with a touch of condescension. "The addition of other players provides the challenge. One tries to go through the pattern in as few shots as possible, each team getting one stroke per turn. However, upon driving your ball through a wicket, you get another turn."

She frowned and he decided not to complicate matters by explaining "taking croquet" and "roquet" until the need arose, or rather, *if* the need arose, which it very well might not. Little Bidewell society played a notoriously, if excruciatingly, civil game.

"Very well," she said. "What next?"

"You hit the ball with the flat end of the mallet. May I suggest you take a few practice shots? Wrap your hands around the handle and swing it to get the feel of it."

She grasped the handle at the very end, like a walking stick. "Like this?"

"Not exactly. Use both hands." He gripped his own mallet in demonstration.

She choked the middle of her mallet as though wringing some poor chicken's neck. "Stand back while I hit the ball."

He obliged and she drew the mallet back and swung. The mallet flew from her hands, hit the ground, and cartwheeled across the lawn. Her nose wrinkled. "I can safely assume *not* like that?"

"Not quite."

She sighed heavily. "I'm afraid I'm hopelessly inept."

He regarded her closely. She'd been climbing up an ivy vine last night, and now she claimed to be unathletic? He dismissed his suspicions. He'd not had an answer to the telegraph he'd sent to London this morning. Until he did, the wisest course was to take her at face value.

And isn't that a nice rationalization? his conscience taunted him as he kept his eyes from lingering on her feminine figure. Her brows rose to a saucy angle. She knew full well her impact on him—on him and all the rest of Little Bidewell's male population. She was a woman accustomed to being ogled.

"If you'll allow me to take your hand?" He held out his own. Wordlessly she placed hers in his, her eyes guileless. "Here. You wrap this hand like so." He positioned her fingers near the top, curling them around the handle. "And this hand like this."

His one hand nearly enveloped both hers. Her fingers were fine-boned; her skin was warm and smooth. "There." He removed his hand and stepped back.

"Thank you! This is much better," she said, swatting ineffectually at a blade of grass.

He frowned. Her grip looked more or less correct, but the manner in which she was swinging the mallet was wrong.

"You're frowning!" she accused him. "Pray, don't spare my feelings, Sir Elliot. Above all things I loathe incompetence. What is the problem?"

"It's your swing."

"My swing."

"Yes. It's not even. You need to lean over more, using your shoulders as the fulcrum from which your arms depend—no, no," he said as she suited her actions to his words and hunkered inelegantly above the ball, like a hen preparing to roost. "Try standing farther back from the ball. . . . On second thought, don't. Please."

She'd taken a giant step back away from the ball and was bent at a right angle from her waist. The position thrust her posterior out and set it straining against the glove-tight fit of her skirt. His mouth had gone dry.

She straightened. There was a hint of frustration in her pose, a frustration echoed by the line of her brows. But there was something else as well: amusement. She found the whole situation vastly entertaining, he'd wager his father's library on it.

"Well," she said gruffly, "can't you show me somehow?"

Oh, yes. He could. It wouldn't be proper, but he had the distinct impression she knew that and was daring him. In his youth he'd been quite fond of the games played between men and women. And he'd been rather good at them.

"Well?"

"I will need to adjust your person," he warned her.

"I see."

"And stand closer."

Her smile was confident. "I am a woman of the world, Sir Elliot. I can assure you I won't read anything improper into your proximity."

"Of course not. Excuse me for being so gauche. But then, *I* am a simple country gentleman," he added humbly, winning a sharp, assessing glance from her. "Would you please turn around?"

She complied. He stepped behind her, moving his arms to encircle her. Immediately he realized his mistake. His body tensed the minute his arms wrapped around her, and when she shifted slightly, her derrière inadvertently flirted with his loins. Tension became an ache. He ignored it, his jaw tightening. Grimly, he readjusted her grip. But in doing so he needed to press closer. His breadth encompassed her; his shoulders covered her.

He covered her . . .

He had been born and raised in farming country and the three simple words flooded his imagination with a hundred images of male and female, of primal want overriding every other drive. He tried desperately to douse them in the cold waters of restraint.

But she . . . she brought passion to vibrant, fulsome life with her knowing eyes and her wide, gay lips. He could only hope the layers of her skirts kept her from discovering a great deal more than she would care to know about her effect on him.

Still, shamefully, he could not keep himself from deriving pleasure from the situation. After a moment of fruitlessly trying to do just that, he gave up, tallying sensations: the warm, floral scent that veiled her skin, the jut of her shoulder blades against his chest, the silken feel of the tendrils of her titian hair that flirted with his lips . . .

"Watch out!" someone shouted.

Instinctively, he jerked her up into his arms, pulling her back and around just as a croquet ball whizzed beneath her feet. His first thought was that he didn't want to release her. He wanted the feel of her crushed against him like this, her body tense.

For one brief moment she was still and then she was struggling fiercely, her brows dipping angrily as she tried to free herself. He came to his senses at once, cursing himself for an utter cad. He set her on her feet.

"I must beg—"

"She tried to hit me!" Lady Agatha said in a stunned, furious voice. She whirled around, her skirts snapping angrily. She pointed. "You saw, Sir Elliot. *She* tried to hit me with that ball!"

Catherine stood twenty yards down the field, her face a picture of contrition. Beside her stood Anton, wide-eyed with amazement.

"I am *so* sorry, Lady Agatha!" Catherine said, hurrying over. "I was just practicing my swing and, well, I'm afraid I'm a bit rusty. I'm sure you understand."

Lady Agatha turned back around to face him. "Does she honestly expect us to believe—"

Whatever she'd been about to say died on her lips. She regarded him with an expression of increasing incredulity. He couldn't begin to imagine why. Catherine had apologized for the accident.

"Lady Agatha?" Catherine called tentatively. "You do forgive me?"

Lady Agatha glared at Elliot before turning around. "Of course, I do, m'dear." Amazingly, her voice sounded perfectly pleasant. Yet, Elliot could have sworn that she'd been about to call down curses on Catherine's head not half a minute ago. Either he was mistaken, or Lady Agatha Whyte was more of an accomplished actress than he'd imagined.

"I daresay one does find oneself growing rusty with age," she went on, and then gave a little gasp. "Oh, my! That came out all wrong. Of course, I meant that one's *talents* become rusty. And now *I* must beg *your* forgiveness."

Catherine's lips curled into something that vaguely resembled a smile. "Of course."

Elliot watched the exchange in profound befuddlement. It had been a croquet ball, for God's sake, not an artillery shell.

"Once more, *my* pardon," Catherine said. "And good luck to you in the tournament, Lady Agatha."

"Think nothing more of it. And good luck to you, too, Mrs. Bunting," Lady Agatha replied and turned away as Catherine took Anton's arm and went after her yellow ball.

"I am certain it was unintentional," Elliot said.

In a flash, Lady Agatha's expression went from calm to exasperation.

"Catherine sews nappies for the parish orphans," he explained. "She routinely brings beef tea and blankets to the poor. Why, she single-handedly set up a reading room for returning soldiers. Now, really, would such a woman purposely shoot a croquet ball at another woman?" he asked in the spirit of reconciliation.

At least his words drained the ire from her. Her face reflected amazement. She stared at him a long minute before finally shaking her head and bending down to retrieve her mallet. And as she did so he heard her mutter one word: "Men!"

The Bigglesworth croquet tournament would go down in memory as the longest and most fascinating match in Little Bidewell history. From the beginning it looked as though Sir Elliot March and Lady Agatha Whyte would win. Sir Elliot was a sportsman of some repute and, despite her earlier claims, from the outset Lady Agatha gave a good account of herself: She was as natural an athlete as the game had ever known. She had a marksman's eye and an acrobat's balance. Time and again she swacked her black-and-blue ball decisively, sailing it through one wicket after another. It soon became apparent that no one could touch the team of Whyte and March.

But then halfway through the game, after Lady Agatha had finished a lovely run of two wickets, Catherine Bunting hit Lady Agatha's ball, knocking it ten feet. Lady Agatha, who'd been regaling a small group of gentlemen with a spicy tale of her exploits in Paris while she awaited her turn, turned toward the sound. She took stock of the situation and graciously called out to Mrs. Bunting not to fret over the incident.

A decidedly unrepentant Mrs. Bunting snorted—a first, as far as Elliot could remember—and told Lady Agatha she didn't intend to fret. With that, she repositioned her ball next to Lady Agatha's and proceeded to take one of the longest stop shots Little Bidewell had ever seen. Lady Agatha's ball flew and bounced and rolled to the very farthest corner of the field.

Lady Agatha, who'd been watching Mrs. Bunting's activity with increasing perplexity, stared in open shock. Only after her ball finally came to rest between the gnarled roots of an oak tree, did she turn to Elliot.

"Can she do that?" she asked gravely.

"Yes, she can," Elliot said with a tinge of guilt. "It's called a 'roquet.' When she put her ball next to yours in preparation for the shot, she did what is called 'taking croquet.' "

She nodded. "I see. Hence the name of the game."

"Yes."

"And," she tried to smile but had to settle for a stiffening of the lips, "why, might one ask, did I fail to be told of this rule?"

He couldn't very well tell her it was because Little Bidewell's croquet players considered the roquet bad manners. It was one thing if one *happened* to hit an opponent's ball, but to purposely set out to hit another's ball was ... Well, in Little Bidewell, despite what the rest of world did, it simply wasn't done.

At least, it *hadn't* been done.

"I should have told you," he said. "I am remiss. I beg your pardon."

She gazed at him with an odd combination of composure and resolution. The look was familiar—rather like the expression on the faces of men about to ride into battle. "Quite all right. Just tell me when it is my turn."

The rest, as they say, was history. By the end of that

famous game, croquet as played in Little Bidewell had been forever transformed.

At first, the two women made at least a cursory effort to go through a wicket on their way to hunting down each other's balls. Soon, however, both had abandoned all pretenses, and long after even the worst teams had hit the final peg and retired, they charged from one end of the field to the next, smacking into each other's balls. And they did so with smiles like rictus and voices dripping equal parts honey and venom, every civility attended.

"Ah, Mrs. Bunting," one gentleman heard Lady Agatha say, "*however* do I conspire to keep hitting your most unfortunate ball?"

Mrs. Bunting replied with a shrill little laugh. "I dare not venture a guess, Lady Agatha, but whatever imp of perversity guides your ball must certainly be incensed by my own amazing inability to shoot past your ball without striking it!"

And so it went.

Despite initial heroic efforts by both Anton Bigglesworth and Sir Elliot March to bring the game to an end, eventually the two male factions surrendered to the inevitable and withdrew from the field altogether, leaving it to their partners.

By six o' clock the other members of the party were milling about the back entrance to The Hollies. Eglantyne, with Lady Agatha's disreputable little dog Lambikins curled in the crook of her arm, flitted nervously about, casting worried glances toward the kitchen where Gracie Poole could be heard to make increasingly loud comments about overcooked food.

By this time, only Sir Elliot seemed to have any real interest in the outcome. He'd appropriated a folding chair and set it on the edge of the playing field. There he sat, boot on his knee, his expression mildly quizzical and totally masculine.

If not for Squire Himplerump, the contest may well have gone on until dark, what with polite Little Bidewell society not willing to offend either Lord Paul's saintly wife or the vivacious, highborn Lady Agatha.

The squire's appetite would not be gainsaid. He'd gone foraging for leftovers under the empty marquee when he'd spied Lady Agatha's abandoned trifle. Unfortunately, it was on the far side of the trestle table. Unwilling to exert himself, he'd stretched across the table for it, lost his balance, and pitched forward.

The poor table was no match for his two hundred and fifty pounds. It broke with a loud crack and the squire crashed to the ground. Immediately everyone turned in the direction of the squire's howls, hastening to offer aid.

Everyone but Letty Potts.

She was standing on the embankment, having stalked Catherine Bunting's yellow ball there. She'd been anticipating sending it careening across to the other side, but as soon as she heard the sound of splintering wood Letty, ever quick to recognize an opportunity, decided the time had come to end the game—as the victor. After all, she reasoned, you can't win if you can't find your ball.

With these thoughts chasing one another in less

time than it takes to draw breath, Letty raised her mallet between her shoulder blades and hauled off with a stupendous swing, a swing so marvelous and so powerful that the momentum of it pitched her clean off her feet and over the edge of the embankment—even as it missed the yellow ball.

She somersaulted down the hillside like a wheel of cheese, head over heels in a flurry of ruffles, tumbled hair, and flying limbs before coming to an abrupt stop at the bottom. She lay flat on her back in the thick green sedge, her breath coming in ragged jerks, the clouds overhead spinning madly. She moved her hands gingerly down her torso. She was unbroken but indecent, her skirts rucked up under her bum.

She tried to sit up to adjust them but fell back with a thud. Stars rollicked across the black backs of her eyelids. Far off she heard a woman call, "Where did Lady Agatha go?"

The blood drained from her face. She'd die of mortification if that spoiled, pasty-faced Catherine Bunting caught sight of her like this, smelling of sedge, legs bare, hair mired with grasses and twigs. With a wince, she gingerly turned her head and squinted up the hill.

A masculine figure stood near where she'd gone over, his back to her. There was something familiar about his silhouette, the breadth of those shoulders, the dark clipped hair that brushed the stiff white collar . . . Sir Elliot. Of course.

She held her breath and prayed for him to go away. She'd rather Catherine Bunting saw her than him.

He was looking up and down the field. "I don't

believe she's here," he called back. "Hm. She's apparently left you the field, Catherine." He bent over and picked up the yellow croquet ball. "Here's your ball. Ah, well." He laughed, bouncing it lightly in his palm. "I guess she realized she was outmatched."

Only by supreme effort did Letty choke back a growl. She didn't hear Catherine's words, but she didn't need to. Her tone conveyed her gloating quite clearly.

She heard Elliot again, answering some man's query. "By all means. I'll just wait a bit for my father. He's nipped down to the stables to see Taffy's latest litter and shouldn't be but a few minutes."

The sound of other voices droned on a bit more and then faded altogether. Letty counted to a hundred and then to five hundred. A cricket scurried across her arm and she caught back a gasp. Her legs began to itch.

Finally, Sir Elliot thrust his hands in his trouser pockets and began walking down the ridge toward the house. Letty released a soundless sigh of relief. He stopped.

"I say." He turned his head and looked directly into her eyes. "Would you like some help climbing out of there?"

Chapter 13

If it's got a beard or a battery,
you're going to have trouble with it.

LETTY HAD ONCE PLAYED THE PART OF A girl who fainted whenever confronted with a dicey situation. Right now, she couldn't think of a better response. So she raised the back of her wrist to her brow and closed her eyes. "Oh," she moaned softly. "Oh ... dear me. Can you? Please? I ... I feel a bit ... light-headed. ..."

Sir Elliot's skeptical expression vanished, replaced by one of gratifying concern. He plunged down the steep hill and dropped to his knees beside her. She started to rise, but he pressed her back, his distraught gaze roving over her.

"Just lie still," he said, and his voice held such honest concern that she felt an odd, unpleasant sensation prickling her ... her what? It took her a second to identify the source of her discomfort and when she did, she was amazed.

She was, she realized, *ashamed.*

She had no compunction about using a man's vanities and pettinesses to finesse him into acting the way she wanted. But a gentleman shouldn't be penalized for being . . . well, *decent.*

Besides, she thought defensively, she didn't want the grass staining those perfectly tailored trousers.

"Should I fetch Dr. Beacon?" Elliot asked.

"No."

"But you just fainted."

She acceded to her stupid conscience with poor grace, struggling up to her elbows, and blowing a strand of hair out of her face. "No, I didn't. Not even a little bit."

"But you said you were light-headed." He looked so uncomprehending. But then, she reminded herself dolefully, he was just a simple country gentleman, magistrate duties notwithstanding, and no match for the wiles of a sophisticated, worldly woman such as herself.

"Wishful thinking." She flipped her skirts down over her knees. "If my sensibilities were a bit more accommodating, I would have nipped off into la-la land as soon as I realized my petticoats were showing. Unfortunately, they're not and I'm not."

She smiled lopsidedly at him and, instead of chastising her as she fully expected him to, he started laughing. She liked the way he laughed; she liked the way his eyes crinkled up at the corners and how the thick fringe of his eyelashes then hid his blue-green eyes and how deep dimples scored his lean cheeks. But most of all she liked the sound of his laughter, the surprised pleasure in it.

He held out his hand to help her up, and she took it. His hand was big, his fingers long. It engulfed hers.

"I suspect you think me a terrible romp," she said.

"No. I think you are charming." He pulled her to her feet. She came upright, promptly tripped on a divot, and fell straight into his arms. Her hands flattened against the hard wall of his chest and were caught between their bodies.

She looked up. His smile faded. His heart beat slow and powerfully beneath her palms. The heat of him sank into her flesh and coursed up her arms. She was holding her breath, she realized, and he was going to kiss her.

He bent closer. Her eyes drifted shut. Yes! She wanted to kiss him, only . . . only . . . A needle of panic plunged through her anticipation.

Only how the bloody hell did a lady *kiss?*

If she kissed him in the manner her body and her mouth and her heart—and the rest of her—clamored for her to do, he would find her out for a fraud as soon as their lips touched. No gently bred lady kissed the way she wanted to. Her response was sure to betray her. But how *did* a—

His lips brushed hers with exquisite gentleness. They were warm, firm, and velvety. Her fears stepped back, thrust into a corner by the sweetness of the sensation.

So, she thought vaguely as his lips burnished hers, this is how gentlepeople kiss. He molded his mouth more firmly to hers. She sighed, wanting to open her mouth, just a bit, just enough to experience his kiss with the sensitive inner lining of her lips. The desire seemed so natural. . . .

But a lady *wouldn't* open her mouth, she told herself severely, and clamped her lips tightly together.

He laughed against her mouth. *Laughed!* Gently. Like his kiss. Tantalizingly. Like his kiss.

He swung her lightly around, supporting her with his arm, bending her backward and following. He teased her with his gentleness, while the same gentleness taunted her with wicked promises. He cupped her chin with his free hand and brushed his thumb lightly over her lower lip while nibbling along the edge of her jaw, working his way inexorably toward her lips. Then he touched the very corner of her mouth with the tip of his tongue.

Sensual shocks jolted through her.

Her resolve to be ladylike shimmered like mist, insubstantial and weak and fast-fading. He kissed her again, a full, open-mouthed kiss this time, demanding and hungry. It burned her thoughts to cinders, leaving only wonderful awareness of the strength of his arms, of the desire that rippled and spread between them even as her mouth opened and . . . oh, Lord!

His tongue swept between her lips, stroked her tongue with masculine possessiveness, plundered her mouth with infinite skill. Nothing in all her vast, urbane experience had ever felt so wanton. Pinpricks of light exploded across her eyelids as she sank unresistingly into pleasure.

Mouth and heat, thundering heartbeat and steel-banded arms. And sounds! Sweet sounds of abandonment. Inarticulate, intoxicating, purring sounds rose from deep within her throat. She clutched his tense upper arms, seeking an anchor because any minute she'd be swept away, lost in him.

He lifted his head, his rapid breath sluicing over her heated face. She raised her hands and combed her fingers through that silky, clipped hair, trying to draw his head back down to hers. He resisted.

She opened her eyes, feeling woozy and dull-witted and sensual, but mostly just anxious to return to kissing: innocent, wicked, wondrous kissing.

"Forgive me, Lady Agatha." His voice was rough. His chest rose and fell in deep, harsh cadence. "I am, after all, a simple country gentleman and most unused to the temptations of a worldly woman such as yourself."

She blinked uncertainly up at him, still drugged by passion. *Simple country . . . ?* She frowned. He smiled.

Understanding plunged through her. *He was mocking her!*

She pushed against his chest as hard as she could, but he only smiled more broadly. That was the worst of it—his smile wasn't sardonic or cruel! It was indulgent and . . . and *gentle!*

Ah!

"Let me go! Release me this instant!"

His amusement disappeared. "Agatha, please, I didn't mean—"

"No!" she demanded shrilly. "If you are the gentleman Little Bidewell seems to think you are, you will unhand me at once!"

He looked shocked.

Ah, yes! she thought bitterly, he could mock a poor

girl all he liked, but let anyone cast aspersions on his all-holy gentleman's honor and *that* made him blanch!

At once he lifted her to stand upright. As soon as she was upright, his hands dropped to his sides and he stepped back.

"Agatha—"

It was too much. He hadn't even been kissing *her!*

"Do *not* call me Agatha!"

He inclined his head. Whatever emotions he was feeling by now he'd hidden behind a grave, unreadable mask. "I beg your forgiveness, Lady Agatha. I know you have no reason whatsoever to believe me, but I give you my word I am not in the habit of forcing my," he swallowed, the only sign he felt any real regret, "my attentions on unwilling women."

"Oh?" she asked haughtily. "You generally force your attentions on willing women? How noble of you."

He flushed but continued doggedly on. "I suspect I deserved that."

No, he didn't. She hadn't resisted his "attentions" at all. She resented his mocking her after she'd so apparently enjoyed those blasted attentions. Of course she couldn't tell him that.

"Please, try to understand," he said. "I am—"

Her glare cut off his words as effectively as a muzzle. "If you *dare* tell me you are a simple country gentleman again, I shall ... I shall ... I don't know what I shall do, but it will be very, very *loud!*"

His brows drew together. He scowled. He opened his mouth, clamped it shut, gave her a quick assessing glance, and opened his mouth again. "Excuse me for being dull-witted. May I ask whether I am apologizing for kissing you or for teasing you?"

"Teasing?" she echoed disbelievingly. "*Teasing?* I'd call it jeering, sir."

"I am an unconscionable cad. I should never have teased you except—" He didn't look like an unconscionable cad. He looked delicious, his dark hair tumbled, his mouth relaxed—not a bit of mortification to him. In fact, he looked a touch predatory. Satisfied.

There was more that he wanted to say. She'd have staked a month's pay on it. If she'd had a job.

"You should never have teased me except what?" she prodded.

He leaned in toward her and lifted her chin with two fingers. Drat her treacherous body; she shivered. His smile was lazy but his gaze was piercing. "Except that I couldn't resist."

"Resist what?" she asked, and cursed the high, breathless quality of her voice.

"Resist demonstrating that your worldliness was more fiction than fact," he whispered. "You, Lady Agatha, in the common parlance with which you are so fascinatingly familiar, 'ain't so tough.' "

"Mother of Mercy!" Grace Poole breathed, bending out of the second-story window, Master Bigglesworth's binoculars pressed to her eyes.

"Lemme see!" Merry demanded, tugging at the cook's sleeve. "Your turn is up!"

"Oh, dear," Eglantyne murmured, wringing her

hands. At her feet, dear little Lambikins yawned. "It's not only improper, it's possibly immoral, spying on them like this."

"T'aint really spying, mum," Merry explained. "We're only gaugin' how effective our methods is been to date. How're we to know what to do next if'n we don't know how far things is progressed?"

With a sudden preemptive thrust of her hip, Merry knocked Grace Poole away from the window and at the same time snatched the binoculars from her hand. Grace, eyes ringed with circular dents, didn't even protest. She staggered back from the window, her hand pressed to her chest. "I got me palpitations!" she whispered.

"They're not fighting, are they?" Eglantyne asked.

Merry didn't appear to hear. She stood in the window, staring through the binoculars, murmuring, "My. Oh, my. My," over and over.

Eglantyne vacillated over what to do.

The party had moved inside and were enjoying a lovely buffet. When she'd noticed Agatha's absence, she'd gone in search of her. Instead, she had discovered her wayward staff in this upper bedroom, spying ... or rather gauging the success of their match-making plans. Eglantyne still wasn't quite sure how she'd become part of their schemes.

Doubtless it was the result of all these wedding plans. No one seemed to be able to converse about anything but brides and happily-ever-afters. No one seemed to realize that there weren't happily-ever-afters for those the bride left behind. That the child one had loved and adored, whose hair one had

braided and whose scrapes one had bandaged, that
that child would walk out of the only home she'd ever
known and never return.

Eglantyne sniffed and felt a preemptory paw beat
against her skirts. She looked down. Lambikins was
grinning up at her, his pink ribbon of tongue curling
foolishly. He tapped at her hem again. Why, he wanted
to be picked up! She bent and scooped him up. He
gave her a quick lick on the cheek. She smiled, oddly
comforted by his warm weight in her arms.

She hitched her shoulders, forcing her melancholy
away. Of course, she'd agreed to help Grace and
Merry with Sir Elliot and Lady Agatha. She was most
fond of Elliot and always had been.

He'd been a charming rapscallion in his youth and
had matured into an honorable and conscientious
man. Sometimes she wondered if he wasn't too conscientious. Sometimes he looked so vulnerable in his
gravity, and so alone.

What better woman to chase away somberness than
the vivacious Lady Agatha? Certainly her bohemian
ways had provided a tonic to Elliot. She couldn't remember the last time he'd looked so wholly and
pleasurably immersed in the moment, or laughed so
openly.

Anyone could see that Elliot and Lady Agatha
would suit. And clearly they were interested in one
another. But just how interested? She mustn't be a
coward. Resolutely, she set Lambikins down and held
out her hand. "Merry, I would like the glasses."

At once, Merry stepped back from the window and
handed over the binoculars. Eglantyne raised them to

her eyes and after a second or two of scanning the embankment found . . . oh, my!

She would never have believed him capable of such behavior! Decent, courteous, and chivalrous Elliot was accosting Lady Agatha!

He was kissing her, his dark head obliterating hers from Eglantyne's view, one arm clasped her around her waist, arching her back like a bow, while his free hand held the back of her head. Her auburn hair spilled down, brushing the grass, and her hands were pressed in tight fists against his chest—though, oddly, she didn't appear to be struggling.

Then, quite suddenly, Sir Elliot swept Lady Agatha back to an upright position. At the same time, Lady Agatha seemed to return to her senses, for she beat her fists once against Elliot's chest.

To do him justice, Elliot released her at once. She looked furious. For a second she wobbled unsteadily in place, but then jerked her chin in regal dismissal of Elliot and began stalking off up the hill. Only she didn't stalk so much as stumble, first one way then the other, as if she wasn't exactly sure in which direction the house lay. Which seemed rather odd, but one had to account for her undoubted shock.

Eglantyne glanced at Merry and Grace. Grace was still leaning against the wall fanning herself. Merry was peering through the window through a piece of paper she'd rolled into a tube. Both looked appropriately nonplussed. So much for their matchmaking.

"Oh, Elliot," she murmured. "How could you?"

"Could what?" Merry asked.

"I don't think they like each other very much."

"Huh?" Grace asked disbelievingly, but then perhaps the housekeeper hadn't seen Sir Elliot accost Lady Agatha. Not that Eglantyne was going to inform her of it. It was her duty as a responsible employer to protect her servants from such knowledge.

"They've parted ways and are returning to the house separately," she said.

"Oh?" Merry said, and Eglantyne glanced once more through the binoculars. Lady Agatha was still weaving her way up the embankment, finally heading in the right direction. Elliot still stood at the bottom, his arms folded across his chest.

He must be enduring the most grievous remorse by now, Eglantyne thought with a touch of sympathy, as appalled by his actions as Lady Agatha. He probably considered that his sins toward Lady Agatha were unforgivable—and rightly so. He would be in despair. He would be raking himself over coals of remor—

Eglantyne's eyes grew round. Sir Elliot had turned to watch Lady Agatha disappear from view. Finally Eglantyne was afforded a look at his face.

He was unabashedly grinning.

Chapter 14

Some days you're the cockroach,
some days you're the boot heel.

SHE HAD TO GET OUT OF HERE. NOW. TODAY. Tonight at the latest. Tomorrow at the very, very latest. Things were getting far too complicated.

Letty pushed open the terrace doors and entered the room where the croquet party crowded. Faces swelled and retreated, disembodied voices surrounded. She veered off. She couldn't concentrate on what they were saying or what they asked. She had to get out of here before she gave herself away.

The absurdity of it bubbled up. She'd never flubbed a line in her life, never missed a cue ... until now. She couldn't go on with the show. Where was her understudy?

She desperately needed a moment alone. Her room. Like a drowning rat spying a floating board, she fled toward the door opposite and into the hallway.

Blast! A group of people milled about the bottom of the stairs that led to the upper bedchambers. They turned to her eagerly and she returned their smiles with a frantic gaiety, sheered off, and hastened toward a closed door at the end of the corridor.

She opened the door and stumbled in, slamming it shut behind her. She turned the key in the lock and heard the sweet click as the bolt slid into place. She slumped against the door and took a deep breath, looking around. She was in a small morning room. A settee stood before her, its back to Letty, a pair of chairs flanking it.

She was safe for the moment. She needed to think. Plan. When to go? What to take?

The sound of heartbroken sobs broke through her frantic checklist. Someone else was in here. She nearly sobbed back in despair.

No. It wasn't fair. She wasn't up to this. She spun toward to the door, but the idea of facing those friendly, interested faces—She couldn't. She turned back as a head of soft blond ringlets rose from behind the back of the small settee.

"I'm sorry, Lady Agatha." Angela sniffed and dashed the back of her hands against her red-rimmed eyes. "I didn't think anyone would come in here. There were some people outside with whom I . . . I didn't wish to speak just at the moment."

"Please, don't explain," Letty begged her. She didn't want to be this girl's friend. She was an employee, not a confidante. Damnation, she wasn't even that! She was a fake. A fraud.

"—if you don't mind."

Letty refocused her gaze on the girl. "Excuse me?"

"I'd just as soon wait here until the people outside have gone," Angela apologized.

Try as she might, Letty couldn't ignore Angela's misery.

She took a few steps into the room. At least this way she could focus on something besides *him* . . . and what he must think of her. "It's your home, Miss Angela. Besides, I'm afraid we're both in the same pickle. I'm rather looking to dodge the crush myself."

"You?" Angela asked with dull curiosity. "Why should you seek refuge?"

"You'd be surprised," Letty murmured.

"I daresay," Angela replied politely and then, abruptly, her pale eyes filled with tears, her lower lip trembled, and her head dropped out of sight.

Muffled sobs rose from the other side of the divan.

I should just sit in this chair and leave her to it. Gentlewomen loathe having witnesses to any outbursts. Chin-up and put a brave face on it, was the English gentlewoman's creed. Nope. She wouldn't thank me for asking what's wrong.

Somehow Letty had crossed the room and was standing behind the settee, her hand resting gently on the girl's shuddering back. Angela's sobs only grew louder.

Letty rubbed small comforting circles between her shoulder blades. "Angela. What is the matter?"

Angela lifted her damp, red-nosed, wholly unappealing little face. "I can't tell you. I daren't tell you. You'll think I'm . . . I'm . . . horrible!"

"No, I won't. Never," Letty promised. What sort of

fix had the chit gotten herself into, anyway? What sort of fix *could* a girl get into in a place like Little Bidewell?

"Yes, you will. And you'll ... be ... right ... to think it, too!" Angela's head plunged down between her arms again.

"Whatever you've done, or think you've done," Letty amended, "I'm certain it isn't so horrible it could affect my good opinion of you."

"Oh!" Came the smothered reply. "You don't understand. I ... am ... so ... ashamed!"

Letty cast about for some personal incident on which to draw in order to comfort the girl. It was all too available. And from uncomfortably recent experiences.

"Sometimes," she began uneasily, "one does things without first giving them proper consideration."

"What sorts of things?" Angela asked dolefully. "I'll wager you're not speaking of the sort of thing *I've* done!"

"Well," Letty said, picking her way carefully. She felt as though she were traversing a mine field laid with potentially explosive truths. "One might do these things, these rash, ill-considered things, and never really realize how ... how shabby they might seem, or even *be.*"

She struggled on, a light sweat breaking out on her brow. "And then, one day, one looks back on them from the vantage of time and distance and then one is ... one is ashamed. And one wishes, with all one's might, that one hadn't done what one has done, only there's nothing to be done about it. It's done!"

There. She'd confessed—er, she'd said it. She blew out a deep breath. She felt ever so much better. "Does this make any sense to you, darling?"

The girl eyed her doubtfully. "A bit."

"Of course it does. The fact of the matter is, that what's done is done and there's no good stewing about it. You don't want Marquis What's-'is-face going all gloomy because his little bride's in the dumps over a bit of a gaffe she committed years ago, do you?"

She patted Angela's head and gave her a bracing smile, to which Angela responded by going milk-white, throwing herself back down on the settee, and howling brokenheartedly into the cushion of her arms.

So much for rallying Angela's spirits. Clearly it was time for strong-arm tactics. She grasped Angela's shoulders and dragged her into a sitting position.

Angela was so startled she stopped howling.

"Come now! Out with it, miss!" Letty said in her sternest voice, the voice she'd used to such effect in her role as Marvelle Magwhite, the strict governess in *The Saucy Miss Sally*. A minor role, but juicy.

"I mean it, Angela. Either you tell me what is caus-ing this waterfall or I shall be forced to think," she cast about for something that Angela would consider unendurable, "or I will be forced to think that *you are enjoying yourself!*"

Angela looked stricken, but after a few seconds suddenly clasped Letty's hands in her own and squeezed them tightly. "Swear to me that you will try awfully hard not to think too badly of me," she begged.

"Of course, I won't."

The girl pulled her narrow shoulders back. "All right, then, here it is. I once had a ... more than a sisterly regard for Kip Himplerump."

Kip Himplerump. Kip Himplerump ... "The squire's sullen-looking boy?"

Angela nodded. Finally, things were getting interesting.

"And he had feelings for me. Or, I thought he had."

"I see." And did she! The memory of her own passionate response to Sir Elliot came rushing back with tidal force.

"There. I can see you think the worst of me, don't you?"

"Of course I don't," Letty said. She felt only profound empathy with Angela. The poor little duck, carried away against her better judgment, at the mercy of irresistible forces, caught on a riptide of attraction. Why, if she and Sir Elliot hadn't been in a field in full view of the house, who knows what might have transpired? Thank heavens for that, at least.

At least, she *ought* to thank heaven.

"Well, m'dear," she said, "you've made a clean breast of it. Now, forget it."

"I would. But now—"

Letty pushed Angela gently away, holding her at arms' length. She studied her face gravely. "What, Angela?"

"Kip. He has a letter I wrote. A most revealing, incriminating letter! Oh! I should die if my darling Hugh ever sees it."

"Why should he see it?" Letty asked, but she

already knew the answer. Because Kip was threatening to reveal the letter, was blackmailing this poor girl. Just like Nick had blackmailed all the "rich, worthless, faceless sots" who found themselves in his power. Only now they weren't faceless anymore. Or worthless. They had this girl's face. And this girl's worth.

Even if she hadn't been an actual party to his blackmail, she'd known full well where the money Nick spent on her came from. She'd been as culpable in her silence as he was. She felt an inner recoil, a deep disgust with herself.

"How much does he want?"

"How much?" Angela echoed blankly.

"Money."

Angela looked shocked. "He doesn't want money."

"What does he want then?"

"He wants me to meet him at the witch tree to say good-bye."

The boy wasn't looking for money? Fine, then. There was no problem. "Well, if you don't want to go, don't."

"He says he'll mail my letter to the Sheffields if I don't go and then Hugh will know all." The tears had begun to course down her face again. "Could you . . ." Angela's gaze dropped to her lap. "Would you come with me? I'd feel ever so much braver if you were with me. I'm afraid he wants more than to simply say farewell—"Angela broke off, blushing fiercely.

So it was blackmail after all. "There's only one way to deal with such a creature, Angela. Squeal him out." At Angela's puzzled expression, she clarified her words. "Tell your family."

"I couldn't!" Angela exclaimed. "I can't tell Papa. He'd be as hurt as Hugh. And Aunt Eglantyne would simply curl up and die."

Just how far had things gone between Kip and Angela?

"Angela," Letty said, "it is very important that you answer me directly and without euphemism. Just what have you and Kip Himplerump done? How far had your affair gone?"

"I . . . I let him . . . kiss me!" She covered her eyes with her hands, too mortified to face Letty. "And then I wrote to him about it! About how it made me feel so . . . *womanly!*"

Letty stared blankly at her. "You kissed him?"

"Yes!"

"Once?"

"Several times! Don't speak anymore of it. I should have never kissed any man but my darling Hughie. I," her head dropped, "I go to my Hugh a *sullied woman.*"

Letty nearly laughed with her relief. For a moment there, she'd thought the girl had a pressing reason to cry. But then, she'd learned early in life that the concerns of the privileged were not the same ones as those of her sort. Though judging from Angela's tragic expression, they seemed just as dire to them.

"Oh, come on, ducks," Letty said, chucking her under the chin. "You must admit you've piled it up a mite high, eh? I'm sure that even if your Hughie does read your little note—"

"He mustn't! Really, he'll be so . . . so hurt!"

"Oh, Angela." Letty shook her head. "He won't. Believe me. As a woman of the world—"

"But that's just it. He *isn't* a man of the world. He's sweet and honest and trusting. He isn't like you at all!"

The unintentional slap instantly sobered Letty. Why, even now, the poor girl was so distraught over her marquis's potential disillusionment that she didn't realize what she'd said. But the condemning words chimed loudly in Letty's mind. And it wasn't a faulty judgment, either. She deserved that. Far more than Angela knew.

But Lord, it hurt.

She rose to her feet, still holding Angela's hands. "You may be right, ducks," she said softly. "But even kind, cloistered, unworldly men aren't going to condemn a girl for being human."

"You don't understand!"

Letty released the girl's hands and stepped back. Once more, the girl was spot on. And that was the problem, wasn't it? For Angela and everyone else in Little Bidewell, this was all real. The emotions, the loyalties, the trust, and even the betrayals.

But for Letty, it was play-acting.

And as long as she was pretending to be someone she wasn't, it always would be.

"But I do understand," she replied softly. *"Because* of the sort of woman I am. I've known men like Kip Himplerump. Don't encourage him by running to do his bidding as soon as he snaps his fingers. You're only setting yourself a pattern." She placed her hand on the doorknob, eager to be gone.

"Won't you help me?" Angela asked tragically.

She stopped. "I thought I did." What more could

she say? Why was she even giving advice? Angela wasn't the one who'd had to run away from her home and her life because of her own stupid choices.

Still, she disliked this sense that she was failing the girl. She cast about, trying to buy some time. "I'll consider what you might do. But you must promise to think about what I've said."

Without waiting for Angela's response, she unlocked the door, pulled it open, and hastened out into the corridor, hurrying down the hall, feeling breathless and undone.

The play had gone on too long; the plot was spinning out of control. The secondary juvenile lead was playing a far greater role than Letty had intended for her to play, and the part of Agatha Whyte wasn't as pat as she'd thought it would be. And the more involved with the Bigglesworths she became, the more dangerous it grew. Too many traps yawned before her, too many ways she could reveal herself as an imposter.

She didn't know what the next act would be or what lines she should speak, but one thing she did know: She had damn well better bring down the curtain soon, or she'd be playing out the last act from a jail cell.

Chapter 15

*If you're in doubt about the reception
your performance will receive,
leave the stage before the final curtain.*

"MERRY, DEAR," EGLANTYNE SAID AS THE maid appeared from behind the green baize door, "have you seen Lady Agatha this morning?" Since the croquet party yesterday, Eglantyne hadn't seen their august guest-cum-employee.

"Aye," Merry said, wielding her feather duster like a baton. "She was upstairs packing one of her satchels when I went in to make her room up an hour or so back."

"Packing? That's curious. Did she say why?"

Merry regarded her as if she had made a very poor joke. "Well, I dinna speak to her," she said in exactly the tones one might use if asked if they'd sworn in church. "I popped in, saw she was still occupyin' the premises, if you will, 'n popped out."

"I see." A movement near the top of the stairs

caught her eye and she looked up to see the silhouette of a crouched figure clad in a long duster. "Lady Agatha!" she called.

The figure slowly straightened. Merry, seeing that it was indeed Lady Agatha, promptly bolted back into the kitchen.

"Yes, Miss Bigglesworth?" Lady Agatha called down the stairs. "How can I help you?"

Eglantyne flushed. "I was wondering...that is, Anton is in the library and we were rather hoping ...That is to say, we thought it might be nice if we, well, if we began talking about the wedding preparations."

"Wedding?"

"Yes." Eglantyne nodded encouragingly, but Lady Agatha didn't give any sign of comprehension. "*Angela's* wedding?"

Poor Lady Agatha, thought Eglantyne, her head was probably positively *swimming* with all the weddings she had to keep track of.

And she'd been about to go somewhere, too.

"That is, if I'm not keeping you from important business in town?"

"In town?" She'd come to the top of the stairs and now stopped.

"Yes," Eglantyne said. "Merry said you were packing a bag and you are wearing a coat."

"Oh!" Lady Agatha looked down at her coat and her eyes widened as if she'd forgotten she'd put it on. "Oh, this! Ah, er, no, nothing that won't keep. I was ... I was just going in to Little Bidewell to see if...I... could ..." she smiled and cleared her throat, "find some lace...to match...to match some materials that I'd packed in my bag!" she finished triumphantly.

"But that can wait." She unbuttoned her coat and dropped it over the railing. "I'll just come back here after our conversation and fetch my coat."

She swept down the stairs with her usual élan. "Where are we going?"

Eglantyne gestured down the hall. "The library. Shall we?"

They arrived in the library to find Anton perched in his chair behind his desk, trying to look fiscally responsible, and—how lovely!—Angela had joined him. Everyone necessary to making the wedding go as wonderfully as possible was here. Even Lambikins, Eglantyne noted with pleasure, was curled up on the window seat.

"Lady Agatha," Anton said, rising to his feet. "So good of you to come. Pray, won't you be seated?"

Wordlessly, Lady Agatha sat down and arranged the skirts of her biscuit-and-rose-madder plaid morning dress. No one else with auburn hair would dare wear that color combination, but Lady Agatha made it look chic.

Eglantyne took the window seat, picking up Lambikins and resettling him on her lap, fondling his silky ears thoughtfully. How had someone whose taste was acknowledged to be unassailable ever come to christen her pet—and so unique and intelligent a creature, too—with such a vapid name?

She looked up. Anton looked helplessly at Eglantyne. Eglantyne looked at Angela. Angela looked at her hands.

"Well." Anton smiled. "Well, then." He cleared his

throat. "Perhaps it would be best if we all made a clean breast of things, what?"

At this, Lady Agatha's head popped up. "Sir?"

"Yes," Anton said, nodding rapidly and forging ahead. "So, here it is. We're simply country folk, Lady Agatha. We know nothing about the Society into which Angela will be marrying. Though," he hastened to say as Angela's lower lip began to wobble, "though we know our darling girl will do her new family proud."

At *this*, Eglantyne's lower lip began to wobble. Really. Sometimes men could be so callous. As if she needed further reminders of the loving child she would soon lose!

Anton divided his alarmed glance between the two women. "Just as she has been a source of great pride to us, her natural family."

"And will continue to be," Lady Agatha said. "She's marrying a marquis. Not entering a nunnery."

Anton turned to her gratefully. "Just so! But as she is marrying a marquis, we look to you to guide us, Lady Agatha. Everyone has assured us that the best we can do is to place ourselves wholly in your hands.

"So, here we are. In your hands. Totally in your hands." When this brokered no response, he went doggedly on. "Think nothing of expense. Whatever you advise, we shall be guided by."

He looked at Eglantyne. She nodded approvingly. He'd said it all very well, just as they'd rehearsed. Now it was up to Lady Agatha.

"Fine," Lady Agatha said.

Anton rubbed his hands together, like a yeoman

about to embark on a long, arduous day of plowing. "Angela tells us you've already chosen the fabric and style for her wedding dress, and we have contacted the modiste you recommended. She'll be arriving late next week to begin work. So, what next? Where do we begin?"

Lady Agatha thought a moment. "Food?"

Anton and Eglantyne traded confused looks. "But ... the caterer. I was given to understand that he would do all the food."

A pink flush swept over Lady Agatha's high cheekbones. Whether it was from annoyance or some other emotion it was impossible to tell.

"Well, yes," she said. "He'll prepare the food and I am sure he has arranged for the standard fare, but not the ... the ... pièce de résistance. I always insist on choosing *that* with my clients."

"Oh," said Anton, nodding sagely. "What do you suggest?"

"Ah, but it is not *my* wedding," Lady Agatha said with pretty demureness. "What does our bride like?"

Three sets of eyes turned toward Angela. "I don't care."

"Well," Lady Agatha said. "What of the groom? What does he like?"

Once more everyone looked at Angela. And waited.

"Simple food," she finally said. "Simple ... honest ... decent food!" She turned her head quickly, blinking and staring out the window.

"Fine, then," Lady Agatha said flatly. "We'll have turnips and cabbage."

This brought Angela's head wheeling around,

mouth agape. She met Lady Agatha's direct gaze and flushed.

"Well?" Lady Agatha asked, a challenge in her tone.

"Turbot would be nice, I think," Angela murmured humbly.

Lady Agatha smiled encouragingly. "And?"

"The crabs are very fine at this time of the year."

"Oh. Oh?" Lady Agatha breathed. For the first time since entering the room, a sparkle lit her dark eyes. "A fish motif?" she murmured. "That might be interesting. Or a seaside theme. We could have the stage—I mean, we could have the lawn set with little striped marquees."

She paused and pondered. "No, it won't do. We need something a bit more exotic to impress the aud—the odder guests."

It was wonderful to see Lady Agatha in the throes of the creative process. Her brow furrowed in fierce concentration and her dark eyes flashed as she mused.

"What's fishy yet exotic?" she muttered to herself. "Something like . . . a Brighton Beach wedding?" The question was obviously self-directed, as was the grimace that followed it. "Whatever am I thinking? The Regency is so *done,* don't you agree?"

The others nodded uncertainly. Lady Agatha's fingers tapped against the arm of her chair. Suddenly she straightened bolt upright, her eyes wide as if she were witnessing an inner vision. "I have it! We'll do *The Mikado!*"

"Lovely," said Angela.

"Enchanting!" enthused Eglantyne.

"What's a mick-a-doe?" asked Anton.

Thank heaven for her brother. The word "mick-a-doe" was vaguely familiar, but she couldn't have said where she'd heard it, let alone what it was.

Lady Agatha gave a burble of laughter. "It's a musical farce. A production by Mr. Gilbert and Sir Arthur Sullivan. Surely you've heard the song 'Titwillow'?"

"Yes!" Anton said happily. "Catchy little tune, eh? But what's that got to do with Angela's wedding celebration?"

"It's just a jumping-off point," Lady Agatha said. "Gives us a theme to work with, and cohesiveness. Very important, cohesiveness. Can't have a bunch of subplots jumping in all over the place, eh?"

"Subplots?" Anton asked, clearly confused. Not that Eglantyne was feeling particularly sanguine herself.

"Discordant elements," explained Lady Agatha kindly. "Things that distract the . . . the guests from enjoying the main event."

She edged forward in her chair, her eagerness apparent in her avid expression, her voice earnest.

She loves this, Eglantyne thought. *No wonder she's so good at what she does. Her enthusiasm is absolutely catching and the way she explains things is fascinating!*

Why, Eglantyne quite felt excited herself. Anton looked suitably impressed. And even Angela, who must be experiencing that time of month herself if one was to gauge by her hitherto unhappy demeanor, looked grudgingly intrigued.

"You see," Lady Agatha went on excitedly, "the whole thing must fit together, building toward the final, triumphant moments as the central characters—that would be the bride and groom—are toasted by the happy company of revelers. Everything from setting, to costuming, to timing and lighting, must work together." She flipped her hand in a Gallic gesture of disgusted dismissal. "Otherwise, the thing's a second-rate production."

"I'd no idea," Eglantyne breathed.

Lady Agatha smiled complacently and sank back in her seat. "Few people who attend these things understand the careful orchestration that goes into pulling one off smoothly. That's how one knows one has succeeded. When it looks easy."

"Ah!" said Anton, grinning and rubbing his palms together. "By Jove, I guess we've the real goods in you, Lady Agatha. Pray do whatever you like—" He broke off abruptly, his gaze going first to Angela and then to Eglantyne. "I mean, as long as Angela and Eglantyne here are happy with it—"

"By all means!" approved Eglantyne.

"Oh, yes!" said Angela.

"Oh, dear!" whispered Lady Agatha.

Chapter 16

A conscience is like a pet: If you spoil it
by paying too much attention to it,
it'll start yapping at the most
inopportune moments.

IT WAS EARLY AFTERNOON THE DAY AFTER the croquet party when Elliot received an answer to his inquiry about Lady Agatha. He stepped out of the telegraph office and tucked the telegram he'd received from Whyte's Nuptial Celebrations into his coat pocket. As he did so, Lady Agatha emerged from the train station depot trailing her small dog behind her. An unwieldy satchel banged heavily against her legs as she strove to walk erectly. The wind that had been rising since morning played havoc with the ridiculous and absurdly fetching hat she wore.

She was so intent on her swollen luggage that he reached her side without her noticing him. "Allow me."

He leaned over to take hold of the handle. The satchel dropped to the street with a thud and her head shot up. The brim of her hat caught him under the chin.

"Sir Elliot!" The color leached from her face.

"Lady Agatha." Could she still be thinking of their kisses? She'd not be alone in that. All morning he'd sat in front of piles of briefs and petitions, unable to concentrate on any of them, still feeling her in his arms, her mouth open to his, supple and yielding.

He'd never given in to impulse the way he had when he'd kissed her. It was as unlike him as swearing in the presence of a woman. And it had awoken a storm of hunger in him.

"Oh, dear. My hat has scratched your face." Her hand hovered tantalizingly near his jaw before dropping. He hadn't realized how much he'd anticipated her touch until its promise was taken away. "I am sorry."

"Think nothing of it," he said. Before he realized it, he'd reached out and set her hat back at its rakish angle atop her auburn hair. Once again he'd acted on instinct, heedless of convention or appearances. *She* did that to him, and if she kept looking up at him like that, he'd—

"Here," he said again, reaching for her satchel, a wary eye on her hat. "Allow me."

She hastily grabbed the handle with both hands and hefted it to her waist. "No need," she panted. "I have it."

"Where are you going?" he asked. A surge of alarm flowed through him at the notion of her leaving here. Leaving him.

"Going?" She blinked innocently. "Why, whatever gave you that idea?"

"You came from the train depot. You are carrying luggage."

"Oh, this?" She glanced at her bag. "I thought to take the train to that little town on the coast a few miles north. What's its name? Whitlock?"

"Whitlock is thirty miles from here."

"Is it?" she asked innocently. A fine sheen had sprung up on her brow. She shifted the baggage with a little grunt. "No matter. The train to Whitlock isn't running today."

"The postal runs daily, but the passenger trains only run every other day," he explained. "Little Bidewell is a very small, very remote town."

"So I gathered."

"Why would you want to go to Whitlock, anyway?" It was presumptuous as well as none of his business, and once more he'd seriously breached the rules of etiquette, but the habit of inquiry was a hard one to break. And anything this woman did interested him.

"The Bigglesworths and I have decided on a theme for the wedding reception and I was going to Whitlock to . . . to look for shells. For ornaments." She looked inordinately pleased with herself. "So if I disappear for a day or so, that's where I'll be. Collecting nice, big, seashells in Whitlock. Not that my comings and goings would be of any particular interest to you, Sir Elliot."

He regarded her skeptically. He'd held her, kissed her. She'd responded. In light of that, her comment seemed disingenuous. "You underestimate yourself, Lady Agatha, and I would wager that's rather a rare occurrence with you."

"You would?" She batted her eyelashes. "I'm sure I don't know what you mean, Sir Elliot, but if you are referring to yester—"

"Forgive me for questioning you. As a barrister, I've obviously fallen into disagreeable habits," he broke in. He wasn't ready to brook *that* subject. Not yet. "I only meant to offer you my assistance. Should you desire to go to Whitlock, I'll be happy to drive you."

"No!" The word popped out so quickly Elliot was taken back. Until he recalled that she had every right to be wary of being alone in his company.

She'd pricked his pride yesterday, what with all her veiled comments on his provincialism. Stupid of him to have been provoked. He couldn't imagine any other woman being able to accomplish it. He'd thought to teach her that she was not the only one with experience and sophistication. Instead, he'd discovered in her an inexpert femme fatale who'd clung to him with an ardor that had stunned him, almost as much as his answering hunger that had risen in response.

He didn't know who was more shaken by the encounter, she or he, but he did know he'd done a far better job of masking his reaction. Whatever her past, she wasn't nearly as tough as she pretended. He'd have to go carefully. She was far more fragile than she'd admit and now he knew it.

"I promise you, despite what you have every reason to believe, you are quite safe in my company."

She eyed him dubiously while swinging the satchel to her other side. It hit her leg with some force, drawing a wince from her.

"Please. Won't you let me carry that for you?" he asked. "It looks rather heavy."

She stopped, clearly of two minds before lowering the bag to her feet. "I'd be much obliged. It is rather heavy. On my way to the station I stopped by the local shops and found some things I thought might make nice favors for the tables, but it's made the bag cumbersome."

"It will be my pleasure." He reached down and hoisted the satchel. Good gads! She must be planning to decorate the Bigglesworth bridal tables with quarry stone. "Where can I take this?"

"Well," she said, "that's something of a difficulty. Ham has already driven back to The Hollies. I thought I'd be in Whitlock, you see."

"Allow me to drive you back."

"*You,* Sir Elliot?" She looked him over very slowly and very thoroughly, much in the manner one might inspect a fish at the market that is being sold as fresh but that one suspects is days old. Even her dog, flopped bonelessly at her feet, lifted his head and regarded him balefully. "Hmm."

She was purposely trying to disconcert him. He ought to be offended. Instead, he was amused. At some point in her life she'd gotten the notion that the best way to get on was to put others at a disadvantage.

"I suppose," she finally allowed and promptly tucked her hand in the crook of his arm.

"We'd best hurry," he said, trying to ignore the feel of her pressed lightly against his side. "Unless I miss my guess, there's a bit of weather coming in off the coast." He motioned toward the western sky.

She glanced at the horizon. "Then, by all means, let's hurry, as I suspect weather is a particular area of expertise for you 'simple country gentlemen.' "

Ah, the beauty. She'd best have a care teasing him; he already found her near irresistible. "You are too kind," he returned. "My carriage is by the telegraph office."

She looked down at her dog. "Come on, then," she said. "It's back to laps and lollies for you."

The dog leapt to his feet and dashed down the street as if he knew exactly where Elliot had left the buckboard. Indeed, he was waiting for them when they arrived.

Elliot heaved Lady Agatha's bag up onto the floor, Lambikins leaping in on top of it. He turned to Lady Agatha. "I'm sorry I don't have the brougham. I hope you don't mind sharing a seat?"

"Not at all." She turned around and waited for him to assist her up into the carriage. Her slender back fanned out into unfashionably straight shoulders. But there was nothing unfashionable about her small waist or the extravagant way it curved into rounded hips.

She looked over her shoulder. "Is anything *wrong*, Sir Elliot?"

He liked her self-assurance and the obvious pleasure she took in her womanliness. He even liked the candid way she used her charms to her advantage. It was a wise woman who knew her own worth, and Elliot had always been attracted to intelligence complemented by practicality. In fact, he liked everything about this woman. It was too bad. She'd be gone soon.

"Nothing at all, Lady Agatha." He clasped her small waist and lifted. She was not a featherweight, though hardly heavy. There was substance to her, pliant swells and smooth curves . . .

He released her and went around to unhitch the horse. He climbed up onto the bench, gathered the reins, and clucked. The horse moved forward, tossing its head anxiously as it sensed the coming weather.

They went a mile and then two. The air carried the ionized scent of the sea with it, while overhead, the black-hooded gulls cut through the cloud-heavy sky, buoyed on a high sea-born wind.

The horse fidgeted as the road narrowed, leading them through an apple orchard where the wind whipped up again, pulling the blossoms from the heavy flowering branches and showering them in blushing petals. Lady Agatha laughed, lifting her face and closing her eyes like a child waiting for a kiss.

Elliot watched, as captivated as he was alarmed by the power of her fascination. A swaying apple bough caught the brim of her hat, knocking it off. Her hair tumbled down and was seized by the wind's spectral fingers and sent rippling behind her.

"I love storms!" she called out, catching her hat.

"The feeling looks mutual," he answered, and her brows flew up at his spontaneous bit of nonsense. But she laughed again, and sweeping her hat to her chest in an impromptu bow lost her grip. The wind tore her hat from her hand and blew it from the carriage into the field.

She stood up, heedless of the danger, making an

involuntary sound of dismay. Elliot reached up, clasping her wrist and pulling her down beside him.

"Stay seated!" he shouted, wrestling the recalcitrant horse off the road and into the field. With a touch of his whip, he sent the gelding racing after the tumbling hat.

It was hardly the stuff of a maiden's dream. Within a hundred yards, her hat got caught up on a patch of gorse. It was a simple enough matter to lean out of the carriage and snatch it up.

He straightened, the prize in hand, and pulled the gelding to a halt. He dusted the twigs and grass from the hat, presenting it to her with a rueful smile.

"Thank you," Lady Agatha whispered, her eyes shining. He stared at her, the blood rising in his face. She bemused and confused and confounded him. One minute she was a cheeky vixen, the next she smiled at him as though no one had ever done anything so gallant for her before.

"Not at all," he said, horribly self-conscious. He passed a hand over his hair. "It would be a crime to lose such a fetching hat."

She stared at him a second more and then threw her arms around his neck and kissed him on the cheek. "My hero!"

His arms ached to return her embrace, but he didn't dare. He was afraid he'd scare her off. For the first time since he'd met her she seemed completely relaxed and carefree and happy. She pushed him lightly away, grinning broadly as she fussed with the bedraggled hat, twitching the ribbons back in place and blowing at the crushed silk flowers.

This had gone on long enough.

"Lady Agatha, we need to talk."

"No, we don't," said Letty, looking up sharply.

He knew. He'd found out that she wasn't Lady Agatha. Her throat closed in panic.

The disarming and oddly appealing vulnerability Letty had glimpsed was gone. An austere and determined—though still utterly gorgeous—man sat beside her, his gaze so concentrated she felt he was reading her thoughts.

"We can't talk here properly, anyway," she said in what she hoped was a reasonable voice. "Let's just—"

"I am sorry to insist, but I have waited too long as it is."

Letty stared at the rear quarters of the suddenly placid horse. Why couldn't the drat thing bolt or rear or something? Why couldn't Fagin wake up and jump out of the carriage? She nudged him with her foot. He grumbled sleepily, rolled over to his back, and began snoring.

"I owe you my deepest apologies."

She went still. "What?"

"I wish to apologize."

Of course. He was a gentleman. How could she have forgotten? She closed her eyes, savoring her relief. "Ho," she breathed. "*The kiss!* Think nothing of it. I accept your—"

"No." The wind ruffled his dark hair, coaxing loose the deep waves he kept so severely under control. It made him look younger, almost boyish. Especially when he smiled like that. "I am sorry if you were distressed, but I am *not* sorry I kissed you."

A little thread of pleasure coursed through her.

"No. I apologize for being suspicious of you."

Again, she froze. The wind rose again and fluttered her skirts. The gelding fidgeted and was checked by a slight movement of Sir Elliot's strong, tanned hands. "Oh?"

"When you arrived, you . . . well, you were not what I expected. So I telegraphed your offices in London and asked them to verify your whereabouts as well as send me a brief physical description of you."

"And?"

His look was sardonic. "You know quite well the answer. 'Lady Agatha currently in Northumberland. Stop. Description. Stop. Red-haired, late twenties. Full stop.' "

Late twenties? Letty thought incredulously. *Lady Agatha?* The woman was thirty-five, if a day. But God bless her for her vanity. If she'd admitted to her real age, Letty couldn't possibly have passed for her. . . . In the blink of an eye, Letty's amusement turned to pique. Lady Agatha may well be satisfied to pass as twenty-nine, but *she* was only twenty-five.

Good gads. What was wrong with Sir Elliot that he couldn't recognize her youth? Perhaps he wasn't so perfect after all. Clearly, he wanted spectacles.

"Is something wrong?" Bronze color filled his lean

cheeks. "Of course something is wrong. I checked up on you as I would have some vagrant who'd arrived in town with a line of patter and empty pockets."

Letty swallowed, disagreeably conscious that a satchel stuffed with Lady Agatha's things leaned against her legs. Guilt reared its ugly, and hitherto happily unfamiliar, head. "Don't feel bad. I'm sure you had good reasons." Though what they might be, she couldn't imagine. Her impersonation had been spot on. "Just what *were* your reasons?"

"They hardly bear comment," he answered uncomfortably.

"I imagine I've more flash than you'd expected from a duke's daughter."

"Yes." He leapt on her suggestion. "That's it."

She settled back. "Ah, well, then. In that case your caution was perfectly understandable. You *are* the local magistrate, after all."

"You're kind as well as generous. But my actions are nonetheless inexcusable."

"I beg to differ. I excuse them." She waved away his gravity. "So, see? No harm done."

"But there is," he insisted. "Suspicion and caution have been my talismans, Lady Agatha, and I have obeyed their dictates because I have learned it is better to err on the side of distrust than to put people at risk through blind acceptance."

The rising wind blew the lapels of his jacket against his throat. He didn't even notice. He was speaking of some specific incident, she was certain of it.

Alarm bells jangled along her nerves. She didn't want to know more about him— No, that wasn't true.

She wanted to know *everything* about him and that scared her. She'd never met a man like him. She probably never would again.

"Where did you learn such a thing?"

For a moment, she thought he would evade her query. He was too much of a gentleman to tell her it was none of her affair.

"In the army. In the Sudan. I was under the command of a . . . an officer known for his tactical genius. I was so proud to be his subaltern." His bearing had become stiff.

"He betrayed you."

"I was idealistic. So young." He glanced at her and his smile was apologetic. "My brother Terence had died in the Zulu Wars and upon hearing of his death I enlisted immediately, itching to take up the banner. I was sent to the Middle East.

"You've met my father." His gaze softened with affection. "You might imagine the sort of upbringing we had. We'd been taught since the cradle that England is the greatest nation in the world and that her greatness rests firmly on a foundation of justice for all her citizens."

"Yes. Justice."

"The officer of whom I spoke drank heavily, but never in the field. Except for one time."

She waited.

"It was late and my troop was ten miles inland, on point duty. We didn't expect any action. Things had been quiet for days, but that night one of my scouts returned with some information that the enemy was amassing to the east of our main encampment. I sent a messenger with the information at once."

"To the commanding officer."

"Yes. There was no reply. The next day, as was expected, the enemy attacked his forces. We arrived too late for the fighting. It was...a disaster. So many dead and maimed." His eyes were filled with remembered horror. "I sought out the commanding officer to find out what had gone wrong. He claimed he had never received my message."

This time when he looked at her there was a savage bitterness in his face. "I then found the messenger, a man I'd trusted implicitly. He was in a field hospital. He'd been horribly wounded in the battle and must have been in terrible agony, but it was the slur on his honor that consumed his final thoughts.

"He swore to me he *had* delivered my message, but that the commander had been too sotted to read it so my man had read the message aloud. He also swore that he thought the information had sobered the commander sufficiently for him to act or at least call upon those who would act in his stead. He was wrong. But that's the devil of it. There weren't any witnesses. The commander was alone."

"How terrible," Letty breathed.

"Yes. It was a betrayal, not only of a soldier this officer was responsible for, but of all the principles for which we fought. And the commander got away with it. Do you know, he actually was in the process of bringing a court-martial against the messenger when the poor man died?" A deep mystification and ineffable sense of personal failure suffused his tone.

"What did you do?"

"I confronted him. He was ... most disturbed that I believed my man's word over his and at first kept to his story. But I would not stop. I knew there was no chance he would ever confess publicly to his lie, but I would have the truth." The look in his eye made her shiver.

"And did you get it?"

"Yes. He admitted to me that he had 'perhaps been incapable of adequately performing his duties,' but insisted he had no memory of a message having been delivered. Of course my note had vanished. He also said, and I remember this most of all, that the English army could not afford to lose his tactical genius and that the soldier's sacrifice had, in the long run, been worth it. Wasn't it happy, he asked me, that he'd died before things had gotten ugly? And what more glorious death than to die in the service of one's country?"

"You disagreed."

He flung her a grateful look. "Fervently. The man died fighting for a nation that promised him justice and honor, and in the end he was betrayed by promises we did not keep.

"I have made it my life's work to make certain justice is more than a chimera. In order for justice to be served, we must in turn serve her. She can never be taken for granted."

Silence fell between them. Even the wind died down. Only the slight rustle of the grasses disturbed the stillness.

"What happened to the commander?"

"He was investigated." He didn't need to say under whose insistence. "But no evidence of any wrongdoing was ever established. The case never came to court. A few years later he died of natural causes."

He looked at her gravely. "I did not tell you this story to win your pity. I told it by means of explaining my actions toward you. But explanation does not serve as an excuse. It is I who am sorry."

"Please, there is no need."

"There is, though," he disagreed. He paused, his gaze lingering wonderingly on her face. His voice softened. "It is ridiculous to distrust that a vibrant, uninhibited woman is just exactly what she appears to be simply because I have never met her like before."

No. Oh, no. Letty shifted uncomfortably. "To be wary is no crime, Sir Elliot."

"No, but unwarranted scrutiny can too easily become persecution," he said. "I thank you for reminding me of that before I could do unforgivable harm to an innocent person."

She was struck mute with guilt. He *should* be wary. He should heed the lesson he'd learned at such terrible cost. He shouldn't trust anyone. Especially not her. Worst of all, when he finally *did* discover how she'd duped him—and he would—he'd *never* trust again. Not anyone. But how could she tell him without putting herself in danger? To even consider it was madness—

"I think you were right to send a query about me," she blurted out. There. She'd said it. Good enough.

"Pardon me?"

"You can't trust appearances. Believe me. I know."

Why in God's name was she still talking? "You should always make certain you know what cards you've been dealt. Take a good, hard look at anything fishy."

Good God, she *was* going mad!

"Be careful. The world is filled with tricksters, liars, and thieves. And they don't go around wearing placards announcing themselves. You were right to check up on me. Believe me, I know what I'm talking about."

He regarded her gently. "I wish you didn't."

"Excuse me?"

"Clearly from the ardency of your voice you, or someone close to you, was betrayed. I am sorry."

She remembered just in time to keep her jaw from going slack. Good heavens, he meant it. She couldn't speak, couldn't say a word. She could only stare at him and wish that she was the woman he thought she was, that she deserved his tenderness, his concern.

She was a sham, a compilation of second-rate characters from abbreviated farces. The stage directors had all been right. She'd never be a star. She couldn't tap into the deeper emotions because she didn't have any. She was the consummate understudy. An empty vessel waiting to be filled with other people's emotions.

"I am sorry, Agatha."

"Letty," she murmured miserably.

"Excuse me?"

She started. She couldn't believe her blunder. If she insisted on acting like an idiot, she might as well just turn herself in here and now. But she *wasn't* going to turn herself in. She was overwrought. That was all.

She must snap out of this self-destructive frame of mind. She plastered a smile on her face. "My friends call me Letty."

"Letty," he repeated, testing the syllables and seeming to like them. "It suits you. A pet name?"

"My middle name." It was difficult to cling to hard practicality when he smiled at her like that. His eyes were so beautiful, his smile so tender.

He reached out and swept a tress of hair from her brow. His finger stayed, lingered, following the shallow indent at her temple, the outer curve of her cheek, the line of her jaw. Scintillating, devastating desire began to spill liquid heat through her limbs. She forgot her unpleasant introspection. She forgot her fear. She inclined her head a little, leaning in to his caress.

"I fear I am doomed to spend most of my time with you apologizing," he said. But he didn't look in the least remorseful.

"Why is that?"

"Because I can't seem to keep my hands off you."

Her heart thudded in her chest. "Oh."

His hand circled to the back of her neck. She closed her eyes. Gently, he brushed a kiss across her mouth, a sweet, honeyed kiss, a whetting of passion. Her lips parted a sliver, her head tilted back in anticipation of more.

None came.

She opened her eyes. He'd settled back in his seat, regarding her with a hungry, amused, and heated intensity. One side of his mouth lifted sardonically.

Was he playing her for a fool, or teasing her, or was she—unbelievable as it seemed—simply out of her depth?

"Just what is this game?" she demanded. "What exactly are you doing?"

"Why, Letty," he answered. "I'm courting you."

Chapter 17

Nothing seduces vanity
like the word "help."

"YOU CAN'T LEAVE," CABOT SAID. HE STOOD inside her bedroom door, his jowls even droopier than usual.

"Now, Cabot-me-love, who'd have thought that you'd go sweet on me." Letty bit through the thread and dropped the spool back into Lady Agatha's workbasket.

"Please refrain from levity, Letty. I mean this. You can't leave The Hollies."

Letty held the needle up to the light and squinted as she slipped the threaded end neatly through the eye. "I'm not leaving. I'm sewing. And I won't be able to finish sewing and get this dress done for dinner unless you let me get on with it."

She picked up a fold of the deep green-and-lilac-striped muslin. She wished Cabot would leave. Her head was crowded with unnerving thoughts, ridiculous thoughts.

What had Sir Elliot meant, saying that he was "courting her?" He couldn't mean it. There had to be some explanation. "Courting" probably didn't have the same meaning to his class as it did for her sort. He couldn't really mean what she thought he meant ... because then she ... Well, he just couldn't mean it, is all!

"—In order to protect you, I burned it."

Cabot's last words penetrated Letty's thoughts. "Burned what?"

"Lady Agatha's letter to Miss Bigglesworth."

"What?" The dress slipped from Letty's fingers. "What letter?"

"The letter Miss Bigglesworth received from Lady Agatha while you were in Little Bidewell yesterday afternoon. For heaven's sake, Letty, this is important. You really must make every effort to attend," he said.

Letty ignored his peeved tone. If she intended to bolt, she'd need to know how much time she had to do it in. "What was in the letter, Cabot?"

Cabot sniffed. "It was a private correspondence, Miss Potts. I would never—"

Letty wasn't having it. "If you'd burn it, I don't think you'd have any compunction about reading it. So what did she say? *This* is important, Cabot."

Cabot's superiority fell away with a sigh. "It was short. She apologized for the inconvenience caused by her marriage and sent a money order reimbursing the Bigglesworths for their initial outlay. She then listed some firms in London whose services she could recommend to replace her own, and closed by stating that she would be out of the country for several months. On her honeymoon."

Letty blew out a deep breath. Good. Lady Agatha was still safely away and the Bigglesworths none the wiser. Her immediate danger passed, she found herself smiling. She lifted the seam she'd been working on again. "Good for her," she said.

"Good for her," Cabot intoned, "but not good at all for Miss Angela."

"Well, there is that," Letty conceded, her needle flashing expertly. It left little Angie in the lurch, and Angie already had problems enough, what with the former boyfriend making threatening noises. Not that it was any of her lookout. She smoothed the newly created seam with her fingers. A bit of lace would cover the crease on the outside and dress it up a bit.

"And that," said Cabot, "is precisely why you have to stay and arrange Miss Angela's reception."

"Are you out of your mind?" Letty asked flatly without looking up. "I won't even *be* here tomorrow night. I wouldn't be here today if the dratted train ran on a regular schedule."

She cast a weathered eye on the satchel. It stood where she'd left it. No sense in unpacking. She'd already purchased the train ticket. Not to Whitlock, as she'd told Sir Elliot, but south to York. She had one more night in which to be a lady. One more night in which to—One more night. He probably wouldn't even be there.

"Letty. You can't leave. I mean it."

"Just watch me," she said, feeling suddenly dismal.

She snipped off a length of the lace she'd selected, stabbing pins into it as she fixed it to the seam.

"If you leave," Cabot said, "I shall immediately go to Sir Elliot and tell him who—and what—you are."

Letty stopped what she was doing. "The man I knew wouldn't have blackmailed a friend," she said.

"You leave me no choice," Cabot replied, refusing to drop his gaze.

It was she who broke off their staring contest. She was being unfair. Cabot was only trying to do right by the family who'd earned his loyalty. It wasn't Cabot's fault that what he suggested was exactly what she most wanted to do. But that didn't mean she'd risk her life to do so.

"Don't be ridiculous, Cabot," she said. "I've kept to my part of the bargain. I said right from the beginning that I wouldn't be here more than a few days. You didn't object then. Nothing's changed. The Bigglesworths are in exactly the same boat as they were when I arrived. Why, they wouldn't have even received Lady Agatha's letter until today. At most they'll have lost a few dozen hours in which to find a new wedding planner."

"And what do you expect them to do when they discover they've been abandoned by their miracle worker and duped by the woman they put on a pedestal?" he asked.

That hurt. But she was growing used to her heart being pricked and bruised. It didn't matter if you hurt. It only mattered if others saw the weakness. And Cabot wouldn't see hers.

"They'll just have to find someone else," she said.

"What with all Anton's money, I'm sure someone in London will be willing to light a fire under his staff." She only wished she felt as certain as she sounded.

He gave her a look that spoke volumes, but refrained from comment.

She hated this feeling, this alien, horrible, bewildering sensation of guilt. She didn't have anything to feel guilty about—well, not very much, anyway.

"Besides," she said defensively, "the Bigglesworths should be glad I came. And they will be as soon as they see Angela's dress made up to my design and her looking every bit like a princess in a fairy story."

"I know," Cabot said. "That's exactly why you should stay." He sat down on the settee next to her and took hold of her hand. "You can do this, Letty. I know you can. You've your mother's eye for style and your stepdad's sense of drama."

She gave him a sour look. "Being raised by a first-rate costumer and a second-rate magician beneath the footlights of West End music halls doesn't exactly qualify one to plan a Society wedding, Sammy."

He lifted the skirts of the gown she was working on. "Yes, it does. Why, only look what you did for Miss Angela and what you're doing here. You're as dab a hand as your mother with the needle, Letty. And you needn't worry about the food, or dishes, or the waiters and other attendants. The caterer is already taking care of all that."

When she didn't reply, he went on. "I heard Miss Bigglesworth telling Grace Poole about your idea of tricking the place out in an Oriental manner. She's most enthusiastic about it."

"Dear Lord," Letty said faintly. She felt a bit ill. She'd been carried away by her role, was all. Carried away by the challenge and excitement of being a part of something. Something that didn't have an ulterior motive to it.

"I was just babbling," she said. "Just rambling so as they'd think I knew what I was talking about."

"But you do!" Cabot insisted. "I heard what you said about capturing the audience's fancy, and you're right. A wedding reception is a production just like any of a dozen you've been involved in. I remember how you were always playing about with the stage settings of our acts."

"I just muddled about a bit and besides, those were stages," Letty protested desperately, because—God help her—she was beginning to think that just maybe she could pull this off. If she did, it would be the biggest con of her life. And the prize? A young girl's happiness.

And a few more days with him.

"Letty—" He squeezed her hand.

"Just let me think for a minute!" It was madness to even consider it. She pulled her hand free of his and clasped her head between her hands, squeezing her eyes shut. Immediately, his image sprang to life, his black hair tousled by the wind, the way he'd smiled before raising his eyes to meet hers, his gaze intent yet deferential.

She'd never met anyone like him, a man who could set her pulse to racing, and who made her want to be someone else. The men she'd known were crude, rough, eager for the fight, hungry for the smell of fear and the taste of blood. There was no violence or coarseness in Sir Elliot—the men she knew would eat him alive—but he was still bewilderingly, potently masculine.

She gave a little moan. If she stayed, wouldn't she just be making it harder not only on herself when the time came to leave but also on *him*?

For the last six years, she'd been used to thinking only of herself, of taking care of Letty Potts first and last. She backed suspiciously away from the notion of putting his welfare above her own. A habit like that could make her soft, make her incautious. Besides, she thought defensively, in what way would her staying be unfair to him?

He was Sir Elliot March. He had wealth, property, and friends who both loved and admired him. She closed her eyes even more tightly, struggling through a quagmire of conflicting emotions.

"Letty—"

"Someone would know. Someone would find out," she said frantically, opening her eyes.

"No, they won't. You'll be gone in a week or so, long before any of the Society folk who might know the real Lady Agatha arrive. The wedding is two months out yet.

"You'll just make the plans and send out the instructions to those places Lady Agatha recommended in her letter. Then you'll go away. I'll help. Grace Poole will help, also. You can do this, Letty. *You can.*"

"And what about Lady Agatha? What about when she comes back?" Letty asked harshly. "Angela will be the laughingstock of the town if anyone discovers she let a...a...limelight lark plan her party." There it was again, this odd insistence that she take into consideration others' problems, even ones that didn't affect her.

"Who's going to tell?" Cabot asked, his bulldog features grave. "There aren't any pictures of Lady Agatha. And you heard what she wrote: She'll be on her honeymoon for months. *When* she comes back, *if* anyone even remembers to say anything about the party, she won't dare admit she wasn't here. She'd look not only a fool, but a scoundrel. Her reputation would be in shambles if it was learned that she'd abandoned a sweet, innocent girl to..." he trailed off abruptly, his face turning brick-red.

"—to the clutches of a gold-digging confidence trickster?" Letty supplied sweetly. She gave a little, painful laugh. "That's all right, Cabot. You're right. No reason to suspect I'll change now."

He didn't deny her allegation, and that hurt even more—and that surprised her. Time was she would have laughed at such an estimation of her and hooted "spot on, ducks" to her denouncer.

"There's another reason you have to do this, Letty," Cabot said.

"Yeah? Besides the little matter of you turning me over to Sir Elliot if I don't? What's that?"

"Because, despite what you think, I *know* that if you don't do this, no one else will." He took her hand once more in his. "So, will you do it, Letty?"

She tried to find another reason besides syrupy

sentimentality and a partiality to being "courted," a reason that better fit her idea of who and what Letty Potts was. She found one.

What a flash dodge it would be! The best of her jaded career. Bless Sammy, he'd reminded her just in time who she was: Letty Potts, who dared anything and anyone and laughed while doing it.

"Lighting, set, wardrobe. Plan a few entrances, teach the bride to hit her marks, that about the size of it?" she asked roughly.

"Yes. Will you? Please. I'll even give you the money order Lady Agatha sent."

She knew, right then, that if she decided to light out this very minute, Cabot wouldn't turn her in. He didn't have it in him. He was soft. Not like her.

And she also knew that he didn't think she'd help the Bigglesworths out of simple decency, or sympathy, or pity, or any of the impulses that led people like Sir Elliot and the Bigglesworths and Dr. Beacon to do things. Because Cabot thought she was hard. Not like them. And he was right. So why did she feel like crying?

"Letty." His voice was soft and pleading.

She blinked away the treacherous tears and faced him. "Stay and help these folks with their wedding and in the meantime sleep in a feather bed?"

"Yes."

"Wear rich clothes?"

"Yes."

"Eat fine food and drink fine wine?"

"Yes."

"And then get a nice fat purse for me trouble?"

"Yes."

And be with him.

"Sure," she said. "I 'spect worse things 'ave 'appened to a girl."

Chapter 18

When the plot is thin,
add a fat costume.

NOT TWENTY MINUTES AFTER CABOT LEFT, stammering his thanks and backing out of the room before Letty could change her mind, another knock sounded on her door. She sat up on the bed where she'd flopped down flat on her stomach to read, shut her book, and slipped it under the pillow.

"Come in." Angela entered carrying Fagin. The dog looked decidedly plumper than he had a few days ago. And much better groomed.

"Aunt Eglantyne asked that I bring Lambikins to you," Angela said, depositing the dog on a pillow. Fagin gave Letty a cursory glance before jumping down, trotting to the door, and sitting down in front of it. He looked over his shoulder at her.

"I think he likes Aunt Eglantyne," Angela said.

What's not to like? Letty asked herself. He was well

fed, safe, content for the first time in his life. And for the first time in his life he didn't have to worry about dodging London traffic or getting picked up to be used as a bait animal in London's illegal dog pits.

She didn't blame the little blighter for wanting to suck every bit of sweet from the situation that he could. She was certainly doing the same. She and Fagin were two of a kind. Both living here under assumed names, posing as things they weren't. Wishing it could go on forever.

"And Aunt Eglantyne is ridiculously fond of him," Angela said.

"Then they should be allowed to enjoy each other's company," Letty said. "Please, will you let him out? I'm sure he'll find his way. He's clever that way."

"Thank you," Angela said with her gentle smile. "Aunt Eglantyne is most appreciative of the company. She would never say as much, but I think she will be lonely after I'm gone." She opened the door and Fagin at once stood up and trotted out. He didn't look back.

"Are you busy?"

"Busy?" Letty swung her legs over the edge of the bed and picked up the tablet of paper she'd been scribbling notes on. She'd been trying very hard to keep from thinking of Elliot and distracting herself by poring over Angela's copy of *Our Decorum* that she'd nipped from the library.

"I was just jotting down some ideas for your wedding party."

"I'm sorry to bother you. I was just looking for my book and wondering if you might have seen it."

"Book?" Letty shoved *Our Decorum* farther beneath

the pillow behind her. She couldn't very well own up to having it: What sort of duke's daughter would need to consult a book on etiquette? "What book?"

"Oh, just that silly book about Society manners I was reading," Angela said self-consciously. "I suspect I'll find it later."

"I'm sure you will." *This afternoon. After I've finished reading it. Who would have guessed the social world contained so many rules?*

Still Angela hesitated, and Letty was reminded of her youth and anxiety. "Have you heard anymore from Kip Himplerump?"

Angela colored fiercely. "No."

"No? Well, there you go," Letty said, pleased. "The snake has tried his hand at blackmail, dangled his bait, and having discovered you aren't taking it, slunk back under his rock."

"Do you really think so?" Angela asked eagerly.

"Of course. Do yourself a favor, Angie, and forget the whole thing. You ought to be enjoying yourself. Not fussing after some girlish peccadillo."

"You don't understand."

"Yet another thing I don't understand?" Letty murmured.

"Kip is most possessive. He felt he and I had an understanding."

"Well," Letty returned reasonably, "he was wrong. Blackmailers are basically cowards. Once you stand up to them, they back right down. Don't worry any more about it."

Unless the blackmailer was Nick Sparkle. She shivered.

She hadn't thought about him in days. She hoped—no, she prayed—he'd given up trying to find her.

"What if he doesn't back down?" Angela asked.

"You are going to be a marchioness, Angela," she said, taking hold of the girl's shoulder's and looking her gravely in the eye. "If Kip Himplerump makes demands, *simply deal with him.*"

The girl paled but did not argue. She nodded. "That's a girl, Angie," Letty said kindly. "You'll make a fine marchioness."

Angela gave her a tremulous smile. "I'll try," she promised.

"Good." Letty patted a place on the bed next to her. "Come and sit by me. I was just writing down some suggestions for your party."

"Oh?" Angela said, settling down beside Letty.

Letty flashed her a crooked grin. "Come on, Angie. You'll have to try harder than that. 'The bride-to-be, in transports over her upcoming nuptials, waxes enthusiastic over their preparations,' " she quoted the stage directions from a curtain raiser she'd appeared in last year.

Caught off guard by Letty's supercilious tones, Angela burst into a chuckle. "How'd you do that?"

"Oh, I am a virtual trove of undisclosed talents," Letty said piously. *And I'd better be careful that those talents don't land me in the clinker.*

"What sort of things were you thinking of?" Angela asked.

"I was considering possible entertainments."

"Entertainments?" Angela asked in surprise.

"Yes," Letty said. "An orchestra is all very nice for your run-of-the-mill Society wedding, but the really au courant wedding celebrations feature more interesting divertissements."

"They do?" Angela asked, round-eyed.

"Definitely," she replied, patting Angela's hand.

At least this one would, if Letty had her say. Once Letty Potts gave herself over to an endeavor, she gave herself fully over to it. In for a penny, in for a pound, Veda used to say. Well, she was in for a good sight more than that.

The first thing she'd decided was that three hundred people, many of whom were strangers and most of whom came from wildly different strata of Society, some country gentry, others worldly sophisticates, needed more than a few waltzes to occupy them. Anything less didn't seem wise or, more to the point, fun. While Letty was willing to concede that the wedding ceremony itself ought to be formal and reverent, she felt strongly that the celebration afterward ought to be . . . celebratory. "*Most* definitely."

"What sort of entertainment?"

She knew a troupe of performers who'd starred in the variety acts at the Grandeur Theatre. Since it had closed this past winter—due to liquor license troubles—they'd been out of steady work. They'd come cheap and at short notice, and they were very, very good.

"Well," Letty said, drawing out the word. "How do you feel about midgets?"

Chapter 19

The lower your décolletage,
the less the need for conversation.

"LOOKS A RIGHT PRINCESS, SHE DOES," SIGHED Grace. Merry, standing behind Grace's shoulder, bobbed her head in mute agreement.

"Lovely," breathed Miss Eglantyne. "I hope he appreciates how handsome she is."

As one, the three women peered over the gallery railing to the floor below, where Lady Agatha stood frowning into a mirror in preparation for the Bunting's party this evening. She'd no cause to frown.

She was dressed for the evening's party—well, mostly dressed—in a gown of soft buttery satin that showed her remarkable figure to unfair advantage. Billowing sleeves of delicate transparent muslin fell off her shoulders. Her throat, shoulders, and bosom rose above the deep décolletage. The rich satin flowed over her torso like molten wax, snugging her small waist before falling in sweeping, gored panels to the floor. She twirled lightly, her gaze assessing the effect on her elegant chignon. The thick taffeta petticoat she wore beneath the gown rustled flirtatiously.

"Oh, you need have no worries there, mum," Grace said. "He'd have to be half dead not to be, er, impressed." "Impressed" would have to do, though "hot as a stallion at stud" was more in the way of what she meant.

Lady Agatha lifted her slender arms, encased by pristine white opera gloves, and pinned an errant lock.

"He won't be able to keep 'is hands off her," Merry blurted out.

"Hush!" Eglantyne whispered, scandalized, and then, "Do you really think so?" She *liked* Lady Agatha and the thought of gaining so agreeable a neighbor helped ease the pain of Angela's nearing departure a bit. Still, there was the matter of Elliot's, ahem, ardor to overcome, though apparently he'd made an acceptable apology for his bold behavior on the croquet field, because the two seemed to be very much in accord these last several days.

"Absolutely," Merry said, with the air of a connoisseur. Just how she'd acquired such assurance in these matters Eglantyne didn't even want to know.

"For certain," Grace agreed. "He came over yesterday just to see Lady A. And Dr. Beacon's Sal 'eard him asking Lady Agatha to go drivin' with him after church last Sunday, which Lady Agatha didn't, but I just know she would 'ave if she weren't workin' so 'ard on Miss Angela's wedding."

"But you say Cabot thinks our," Eglantyne coughed delicately, "endeavors toward matchmaking are futile."

"Cabot's an old lady," Merry said in a disgusted tone.

Beneath them Lady Agatha bared her teeth at her reflection and tilted her head to the side, checking her teeth. Merry stifled a giggle. "I didn't think as ladies did that!"

Eglantyne didn't bother hushing her this time. She was too busy thinking about Sir Elliot and Lady Agatha. She wished she felt more optimistic. Not that Lady Agatha didn't give every appearance of being enamored of Sir Elliot. She did. She blushed and glowed and sparkled whenever she was near him, and he . . . Well, the way he looked at her made Eglantyne uncomfortable, as though she was witnessing private and passionate moments.

But there was an undercurrent she couldn't quite name in Lady Agatha's response. Something that tainted the anticipation and pleasure she evinced in his company.

Something like desperation.

Atticus came into the hall to find his son grimacing at his reflection. Amazing. He hadn't seen Elliot disconcerted in years, and in the last week he'd seemed nothing but.

"Nothing left over from dinner in there, I trust?" he asked mildly.

In his present state of mind Elliot didn't note the humor in Atticus's query, but only peered more closely into the mirror and muttered, "Gads, I hope not."

He smoothed his already smooth hair and tugged

on impeccable cuffs. He looked nervy as a racehorse and just as impatient. Atticus liked it. He liked seeing the fire in his son's eyes, the possessiveness with which his gaze tracked the lovely Lady Agatha, the deep timbre in his voice when he spoke of her.

It also helped that Atticus liked Lady Agatha. There was humor in her direct gaze and perceptiveness in her conversation. She didn't seem the sort of woman to take offense easily or become involved lightly. And unless he was mistaken, she wasn't altogether comfortable with her feelings for Elliot.

Which was good, Atticus thought happily. Love shouldn't be comfortable.

That had been the problem between Catherine and Elliot. His affection for her had been "comfortable." At least, that was Atticus's opinion—because his gallant, reticent son would never have disclosed anything that reflected poorly on a lady. But it was Atticus's belief that one of the reasons Elliot was so courtly toward Catherine was because he felt guilty about the relief he'd felt when she'd broken off their engagement.

Atticus couldn't see Lady Agatha as inspiring anything in the least bit "comfortable" in a man. And if Elliot was impatient and ardent, Lady Agatha was equally affected. Witty and saucy she might be, but as soon as Elliot was near her she became breathless and bemused. Again, good.

"Are you ready?" Elliot asked, breaking Atticus's pleasant reverie.

Atticus patted himself down. "I think everything is in order. Pants. Shirt. Waistcoat. Jacket. Tie. Begads, I even remembered my shoes. Yes. I believe I'm ready, Elliot."

"Good."

Atticus shook his head as he followed his son out the door to the waiting carriage. He'd seen it happen before, a man becoming so focused on a woman that he lost all sense of proportion. He'd just never seen it happen to Elliot.

Atticus grinned.

Catherine Bunting had a high, perfectly pitched and abysmally bland soprano voice to which, after ten minutes of polite encouragement, she finally treated her guests. For forty-five minutes.

Letty grew so bored she barely refrained from yawning. There was nothing to do but sit and watch Fagin twine Eglantyne around his dewclaw because no one dared speak while Catherine droned on.

She hadn't even left Letty the undeniable pleasure of sitting next to Elliot. Not content with having monopolized him for every minute since Letty'd arrived, Catherine had now commandeered him into turning her sheet music as she played the piano. Oh, yes. She played the piano, too. Adequately. The woman's accomplishments were legion, if not legend.

Finally Catherine came to the end of her repertoire after lisping out some saccharine song about little bunnies, chirruping crickets, and the other assorted vermin lurking about in a "little country woodpile."

"Oh, no. I couldn't possibly impose upon you anymore," she said coyly. "Surely we have other singers amongst us?" Her gaze touched on Letty and dismissed her.

The woman was *so* annoying, always watching her, especially when she was trying to find a moment alone with Elliot. Because they hadn't had any minutes alone. Not one.

He'd seen her every day since he'd told her he was courting her, and never once had he repeated either his profession *or* his kiss. Because there was always *someone* about. He seemed to have planned it that way. In fact, he'd been a perfect bloody gentleman and it was driving her to distraction!

"Florence?" Catherine was saying, peering over her guests at James Beacon's sister. "But, my dear, you have a *lovely* voice! How about 'Sweet Robyn, Come to Me?' Of course, you know it. It goes like this..." She began to warble the chorus.

This time Letty could not contain her yawn. Catherine stopped singing. Caught, Letty's guilty gaze rose to her hostess's pink face. Well, she *had* covered her mouth with her hand....

"Ah. Lady Agatha! Were you motioning me?" Catherine asked sweetly.

Letty cleared her throat. "No. I—"

"I should have realized you were a songstress," Catherine said. "A woman of your obvious," she emphasized the word ever so slightly, her gaze flickering for just a split second on Letty's bodice, "accomplishments."

Letty's face muscles tightened.

"Oh, *do* favor us with a song!" Catherine implored. The rest of the guests turned in their seats and began applauding lightly, their kind faces wreathed in expectation. Only Elliot looked doubtful. Why? Didn't he think another woman could match his former girl-friend stride for stride?

Not only could she match her, she could outpace her. Bunnies, indeed.

"Well," she said, rising to her feet, "if you insist."

"I do. We do. Don't we, Elliot?" She put a proprietary hand on his sleeve.

"Only if Lady Agatha feels comfortable doing so," Elliot answered tactfully.

"If you kind people promise to forgive me if I make a little blunder here and there?" Letty demurred modestly, and at the crowd's quick assurances, she dimpled and swept up the aisle to the front of the room.

"May I accompany you?" Catherine, ever the gracious hostess, offered.

"No, thanks." Letty slipped by her and scooted to the middle of the piano bench. She wasn't a great musician. Her instrument was her voice, but she knew the chords and had a keen sense of rhythm.

Uncertainly, Catherine moved aside. Elliot took a seat near the edge of the room, his gaze puzzled.

Letty ran her fingers lightly over the keys, producing a perky tune. Then smiling fully at the audience she began singing.

> *On a tree by a river a little tom-tit,*
> *Sang "Willow, titwillow, titwillow!"*
> *And I said to him, "Dicky-bird, why do you sit*
> *Singing 'Willow, titwillow, titwillow'?*
> *"Is it weakness of intellect, birdie?" I cried.*

"Or a rather tough worm in your little inside?"
With a shake of his poor little head, he replied,
   "Oh willow, titwillow, titwillow!"

The crowd loved it. But then, any Brit in the land loved Gilbert and Sullivan.

Amazing.

Elliot leaned back in his chair. Seated near the edge of the audience, he could study her without calling attention to himself. She was magnificent. Her voice was a clear mezzo, bold and rich. But it was the manner in which she sang that most impressed one.

When she reached the lyric about titwillow's "weakness of intellect," her expression transformed into bewildered ingenuousness. The audience laughed, joining in the fun.

That was her gift, Elliot thought. She had the knack of making things fun, of drawing people into her charmed circle and making them feel clever and witty.

As he watched, she tossed her head and swung her arm out, inviting the listeners to join the chorus and, begads, they did. He even saw one of the Bunting's maids busily collecting empty cups at the back of the room, mouthing "titwillow" as she worked. Letty, made bold with their approval, segued seamlessly into an old music hall standard, "Champagne Charlie."

Her expressive, mobile face became bluff and

good-natured, her voice slurred and sly, perfectly capturing the nature and Cockney accent of the song's title character. The audience began clapping, keeping time to the music.

Clapping! His neighbors! As though they were in an alehouse and not Lord Paul Bunting's drawing room. Not that Paul seemed to mind. He was clapping right along with the rest. Florence Beacon was tapping her foot and Rose Jepson was swaying from side to side. Only Catherine remained motionless, a smile fixed on her face.

Letty reached the chorus and sang, "For my name is Champagne Charlie!" and held her hand to her ear, as though listening. The guests didn't hesitate but sang the refrain back to her with gusto, "Champagne Charlie is my name!"

She threw back her head and laughed with pure, unadulterated gaiety. She was still laughing when she looked into the crowd. Abruptly she stopped. Her eyes grew wide. Elliot turned in his seat. There was nothing in the direction in which she'd stared as though seeing a ghost.

She touched her temples and gave an unconvincing smile. "I'm so sorry. I've forgotten the next lines."

A universal sound of disappointment arose from the exuberant crowd.

"No, no. Really, you are too kind, but I must decline." She stood up, bobbed a quick curtsy, and scooted toward the back of the drawing room.

Who was she? Oh, yes, he knew her name: Agatha Letitia Whyte. Letty to her intimates. But even though each day he learned more about Letty, he had the oddest feeling he knew less about Lady Agatha.

Letty scooped Fagin up in her arms. That had been close. She'd been having a right jolly good time of it when she'd suddenly seen the little beggar standing dead in the middle of the aisle that separated the audience's chairs.

Only he was standing on his back legs, his front legs tucked close to his body in preparation for his hop down the aisle to her side. Worse, he would be hopping with Catherine Bunting's reticule clamped in his mouth. She should have realized he'd pull something like this.

An actor's need for attention was nearly insatiable, and Fagin was a true son of the bards. He'd only needed to hear applause to launch into his routine. A routine she'd taught him. As she'd taught him to nip lady's purses in the audience. She'd never imagined he'd combine the two skills. Thank God no one else had seen him.

She dropped the purse and kicked it under a row of chairs. The servants would find it later when they cleaned up. She turned, Fagin wiggling in her arms. A little crowd was gathering behind her.

"What a lovely voice you have, Lady Agatha!"

"I haven't enjoyed myself so much in months."

"You have such talent, Lady Agatha, don't you think so, Sir Elliot?"

"Extraordinary."

She turned her head. He stood beside her.

"Lady Agatha," he greeted her.

"Sir Elliot." Could that breathless whisper be hers? "Sir Elliot."

"May I compliment you on your performance? It was enchanting."

Oh, Lord. He really must stop looking at her that way. It made her feel light-headed and muzzy and ...

He stepped back and another gentleman took his place. When next she looked, he was gone. It was fifteen minutes before she could break free of her well-wishers. She moved through the crush, smiling her thanks as appreciative comments followed her, looking for him.

She finally found him in a crowded anteroom. He was seated by the window, one elbow on the arm of his chair, his knuckles pressed to his lips as he listened gravely to a thin whippet of a man. As Letty watched, another gentleman approached Elliot from behind and touched his shoulder.

Elliot lifted his hand, forestalling any interruption, and the man left. There would soon be another to take his place. Wherever Elliot was, he drew people like steel tailings to a magnet.

As if he felt her studying him, Elliot lifted his eyes and met her gaze. For a second it was as if they were the only two people in the room. She couldn't hear anything except the thudding of her heart. His mouth softened, curved into the promise of a smile.

"Lady Agatha?" Someone touched her elbow. She blinked, coming up from the dense, all-pervading awareness of him, of what he did to her with just the hint of a smile.

"Yes?" She turned to face the gentleman. It was Mr. Jepson and he was brilliantly red in the face.

"Ah, er, you weren't thinking of coming in here, were you, Lady Agatha?" he asked unhappily.

"Of course not," Letty said with a regal sniff. "Why wasn't I?"

"Because, ah, this is the, ah, smoking room."

Of course it was. Any idiot could see that. Smoke hung in a thin blue blanket in the air. Of the twenty or so men, half held cigars while the other half held brandy glasses. The women—There were no women. Oh.

"Do excuse me. I was looking for the ladies' room." Pray God there was such a thing.

"Of course!" Mr. Jepson said. "Down the hall and the first door to the left."

She glanced at Elliot before she left, but he was now thoroughly engaged in conversation with the thin, gray man. She left and retraced her steps toward the drawing room before thinking better of it. A chitchat with some of the local tabbies might prove entertaining. With that thought, she followed Mr. Jepson's direction, finding the door to the ladies' room slightly ajar. She approached half expecting a cloud of perfumed talc to come wafting through the opening. Instead, she heard Catherine Bunting's voice.

"Of course, one would not say 'vulgar.' "

Letty stopped.

"No, but one *could* say 'common,' " came the response. It was Squire Himplerump's wife, Dottie. The woman had never spoken to Letty beyond muttering, "How'd y' do?"

"You know what people are saying?" Dottie asked in dramatic tones.

"You know I don't listen to gossip, dear," Catherine replied, without the slightest reproach.

"Of course not, but this is really more in the order of speculation, not gossip."

"Oh. Well, then. What do people speculate?"

"They say Sir Elliot is, and I put this in the vulgar parlance in which it belongs, bowled over by her."

Letty smiled. *They do?*

Catherine laughed. Letty's smile faded.

"Elliot? 'Bowled over'? Ridiculous!"

"He certainly acts besotted," Dottie replied.

Hear, hear!

"My dear, need I remind you that I was engaged to the man? Not to be unkind, but Elliot isn't the sort who's ruled by his emotions. Supposing he has them."

If that was Catherine trying "not to be unkind," Letty would hate to run into her when she was feeling nasty. She began to turn away, certain that if she stayed much longer she'd do something impulsive.

"You really don't see what's going on, do you?" Catherine asked Dottie.

"Well," Dottie said, "I think he thinks she's got a nice shape? My son certainly does. He says she—"

"No," Catherine clipped out. "That's not what Elliot is thinking." She sighed. "It seems so clear to me. I would have thought that a woman of perception such as yourself, Dottie, would see it, too. Well, if you don't, you don't, and I shan't say a thing. But I think Elliot is making a grave mistake."

"Oh, tell!"

"No. It's too poor of me even to think."

"I'm sure you only have Sir Elliot's best interest at heart."

"Of course I do!"

"What do you suspect?"

"Well," Catherine said comfortably, and Letty could just imagine her scooting her skinny bum closer to where Dottie sat. "Elliot's rather come up in the world over the past years, hasn't he?"

"Yes."

"And he has always been ambitious, and since his return from the east, quite keen on politics. Believe me, he won't be content with a knighthood."

"Oh?"

"Indeed, no. And what better way to assure his rise in status than to marry a duke's daughter?" Catherine paused a second before remembering to gasp. "There. I've said it and now I feel just *terrible!* You must know I wouldn't have said *anything* to *anyone* but you, dear Dot."

"Of course not," Dottie answered solemnly.

"I just hope he knows what he's getting into with a woman like that. And," Catherine continued quickly, "you must believe that my concern is not all for our dear Elliot."

"Of course."

Of course, Letty thought grimly. *And if you believe that, Dottie, you'll believe that son of yours will be the next Prime Minister. Which you probably do.*

"Lady Agatha can't possibly appreciate an intellect like Elliot's. Brilliant men seldom experience deep emotional bonds with others. They give all their resources over to higher faculties. Which would be fine for a like-minded sort of lady, but very difficult for a . . . a . . . a perfervid creature like Lady Agatha."

Perfervid? Letty thought with a little inward cringe. She tested the unfamiliar word. It sounded very like "lecherous."

"She is, isn't she?" Dottie whispered in the delicious tones of the confirmed gossip. "A hot sort of woman. Why, when she's with Sir Elliot they fair singe the air, what with the looks passing back and forth. Fair puts me in the vapors," she finished piously.

"Hmm. I daresay the looks are passing much more in the direction from Lady Agatha toward Sir Elliott than vice versa." Catherine's voice had taken on a notable chill. "I rather pity her, if truth be told."

"You do?"

"Oh, yes. I mean, she's obviously given to female hysteria, being a spinster and all. Poor dear."

"You're a saint, Catherine."

Letty pushed her knuckles into her mouth and bit them hard to keep from erupting into a string of West End profanity. Sounds of movement came from the room. Letty lifted her satin skirts and dashed around the corner and from there headed for the drawing room.

Catherine was lying. Elliot *wasn't* paying her attention because he thought she was a duke's daughter. He was just as passionate as she, not *perfervid*—damn Catherine for putting the word in her head! Nor *hot!* He *did* feel the same irresistible pull as she. He couldn't have feigned that. No one was that good an actor.

But if he found her so damned irresistible, why hadn't he kissed her again?

Chapter 20

No one ever fell in love gracefully.

ELLIOT LOOKED UP AND FOUND HER WATCH-
ing him from the billiard room doorway. Their eyes
locked, and for a moment he had such an acute sense
of her that she seemed much closer. He could have
sworn he saw the dark pools of her pupils dilate, the
soft flush spread up her throat, the light spangled in
her hair.

After she left he had a hard time returning his attention to Will Macalvie. Even now he didn't know
what he'd promised he'd do, but it must have been
enough to satisfy Macalvie for he'd gone away molli-
fied.

Henry Smith immediately filled the vacant chair.
But Elliot wasn't about to make any more rash promises, and arranged to meet Smith at his office Monday
next. From there he went in search of Letty.

He found her in the drawing room, surrounded by people—primarily male people, he noted with grim amusement—being scintillating. Which she did with amazing ease.

He paused, rethinking his course. If he were wise, he would keep a nice, safe distance from her, because dressed in buttery soft satin, her white bosom swelling above the shimmering fabric, her eyes flashing, her laughter teasing... Well, frankly, he didn't know whether he was up to the task of resisting her tonight.

One more hour of wanting her and forcing himself to obey Society's rigid rules of courtship, and he would likely be driven to his knees. She didn't know that, of course. She had no idea how viscerally she affected him.

Not that that was any excuse. He was more than willing to exercise every bit of willpower he owned on her behalf, though it would be a good sight easier if she gave some slight indication that she understood and appreciated his efforts. She didn't, though. She didn't seem the least bit flattered by his restraint. Mostly she seemed confused. Even a bit irritated.

She looked up and caught his eye. Something was wrong. He made his way to her side, where she acknowledged him with a bright, false smile and continued to charm the men standing three deep around her. He studied her profile. Though her playfulness was general and her coquetry without a specific target, he was definitely being excluded. He disliked it.

The dinner bell sounded, signaling that the buffet was ready. The group around Letty melted away as the gentlemen left looking for their dinner partners and the ladies positioned themselves to be found. Letty was left standing beside him in strained silence.

"Are you going in?" he asked.

"Perhaps in a while. I'm a bit overheated." For some reason, as soon as she said this she blushed profusely.

"May I wait with you?"

"That won't be necessary."

He frowned. Surely, he'd heard her wrong. "I assure you, it won't be a matter of necessity on my part. I'd be indulging myself."

She turned a hard gaze on him. "I owe you an apology, Sir Elliot."

"How so?" he asked in surprise.

"When I arrived, I thought the residents here would be quaint, provincial, and uncomplicated. But you, sir, are as adept with words as any cit."

He regarded her closely. "Adept or facile?"

She lowered her eyes. "I would not judge."

"But I think you do and I think you have and I would very much like to know on what grounds I have so tumbled in your estimation."

"Tumbled? You've risen in my estimation, sir. I am most impressed by your eloquence."

"It's not your estimation of my eloquence to which I'm referring, Letty."

Though he'd never yet seen her shy away from candor, she did now. "I don't know what you mean. We barely know one another. In fact, I don't really know you at all."

He stared at her, confounded. He felt he'd known her all of his life, that he'd simply been waiting for her to appear to give a face to the woman he'd been seeking his entire adult life. It had never occurred to him that she might not feel the same.

"I am most eager to rectify that," he assured her.

A challenging light kindled in her eyes. "Are you?"

"Indeed. And if you allow me to escort you in to dinner, I shall spend the duration of the meal striving to make you familiar with me."

"What of your unfamiliarity with me?" she asked with a toss of her head.

He moved a step closer. The scent of jasmine enveloped her like a veil. Her warmth shimmered between them. "But I know you," he said. "I know you."

She shivered and backed away. "No. You don't."

She sounded frightened and that had never been his intent. So he let her retreat. "Then dinner will correct both oversights."

She hesitated. He could sense her vacillation, and for an instant she seemed heartbreakingly defenseless and uncertain. And then the vulnerability disappeared, hidden by a thin, hard veneer. "I have a better idea. I'm not in the least hungry and it's a lovely evening. I've yet to see Mrs. Bunting's famous rose garden. Would you like to accompany me?"

She threw out her proposal like a challenge, which, he realized, it was. He could either let her go alone—ridiculous, as it was dark—or he could accompany her—ridiculous, as it was dark. *And* she was a single woman and he a bachelor. This wasn't London. It was a small, provincial town where Society, and its rules, hadn't changed that much since mid-century.

"Well?"

"Perhaps we might find some others—"

"I don't want to find some others, Sir Elliot. But I don't wish to importune you. Please, don't let me keep you from your dinner."

She was courting scandal. He ought to refuse her for her own good. But the alternative was to allow her to go out there alone, thereby opening herself to all sorts of speculation.

"Don't be ridiculous," he said grimly. "I am delighted to accompany you. Here." He thrust his arm out.

"You sweet-talker, you!" She dimpled, taking it. "How can I resist such an offer?"

He shook his head helplessly. She was headstrong, rash, and incorrigible. And despite the folly of this, he found himself relaxing. He might as well enjoy what he could of this ill-advised walk. He had the notion that any man who spent much time with Lady Agatha should get used to the feeling of walking a tightrope.

She sailed past the few stragglers left and headed toward the French doors at the back of the house. Outside, the leaves and grass were dusted with twilight, their colors indistinct and smudged against the twilight sky. He led her down the crushed-shell path.

"You are fond of roses?"

"They're lovely."

"Do you have a rose garden yourself?" For some reason this elicited a burble of laughter from her.

"The only roses I've ever had were the ones on my wallpaper," she said, and then, sobering, "I haven't really had the time for roses or gardens. I lead a very busy life."

"Ah. A pity. And yet," he paused, eyeing her closely, "I don't see you tending a rose garden."

"No?"

"No. It seems too," he searched for the right word, "too mannered a hobby. Too formal."

"And I am not a formal woman?" Her tone was careful.

"You are perfectly natural," he answered in just as careful a voice.

"I am surprised yet again, Sir Elliot."

"Elliot, please."

She shot him a sharp glance. "Elliot."

"And how is that?"

"Usually—Oh! Forgive me. I shouldn't use that word in reference to you and me."

"What word?" he asked in confusion.

"My *dear* boy," she said in false, sophisticated tones, "we haven't known each other long enough for there to be a 'usual' between us."

She leaned close to him. It was a blatantly defensive affectation. She didn't want intimacy, and perversely—and effectively—used feigned intimacy to achieve distance.

She was maddeningly elusive. Valiantly, he strove to remind himself of the vulnerability that had touched him so deeply only moments before.

"What were you saying about me surprising you?" he asked, trying to distract himself from the feel of her breast pressed against his arm.

"Oh. That. Only that *usually* I would expect a gentleman such as yourself to apologize for making such a personal comment."

He tensed. "I do apologize if you feel I have overstepped myself."

"Good God," she breathed, the unctuous accents dropping from her voice. "Are you always first and last a gentleman? Does 'what's done' and 'what's not done' mean more to you than what you *feel*?"

There. Finally. This was Letty. This was the real woman. Her voice was spiced with disappointment. Her one-sided smile was rueful.

He didn't answer her because he couldn't think how to do so. She was being ridiculous. She couldn't possibly think he valued manners above emotion ... but, didn't he? For the last few years hadn't he subjugated his emotions to his intellect?

She stared at him a long moment before looking away, her expression filled with exasperation. She unlinked her arm from his. He should let her go so that she'd return to the house before anyone remarked their absence.

"Letty—" He clasped her wrist, halting her.

She swung around, coming back to him at once and resting her free hand against his heart. He stared down at her, trying to read her expression, unable to concentrate. Every nerve seemed attuned to the shape and warmth of her hand. He could feel the imprint of each finger, the way her palm rode his breast on each ragged breath.

"Yes?"

He'd told himself he hadn't kissed her again because he did not want her to have any doubts about his intention, any reason to spurn him. It had been only partly true.

He hadn't kissed her again because he was afraid. Afraid that her passion would create a spark, setting ablaze a fire that could consume them.

He'd bent her over his arm five days ago and kissed her, and it had taken all his self-command to stop. Somehow he'd conspired to make a jest of it, but he hadn't been able to keep himself from the knowledge that desire had roused like a sleeping beast within him, ravenous and dangerous.

He sensed it. Now. Here. He stood in the mild night air, her hand barely touching him, and he shivered with want. He, who'd never shivered with wanting anything before.

"Yes?" she repeated softly, her breath caressing his throat.

He covered her hand with his and somehow pulled it away from his chest. "Letty. We should be getting back."

"Should we?" Her voice was teasing; he could just make out her smile. Her hand worked its way free of his clasp and flew like a nesting bird to his chest, slipping beneath his shirtfront, her fingertips against his skin.

Her touch galvanized him. Petrified him.

"Don't." It was all he could say, a hoarse invocation against overwhelming temptation.

She hesitated. For a minute he thought she'd withdraw her hand, leaving them both embarrassed, and him a good deal more. She didn't.

"Mrs. Bunting says you are cool."

"God." He couldn't believe this.

Her fingers pushed deeper under his shirt. His hands clenched into fists at his sides.

"And unemotional."

He hadn't any words, yet he sought desperately to find them. "Please. Letty."

"And she says that you are interested in me because I am a duke's daughter." She stumbled over the words. Not that it made much difference. He barely made sense of them. His entire body, every one of his senses, was focused on the swirling patterns her two fingertips were making on his chest. "That a duke's daughter would be an asset to you."

He heard the rich, swishing sound of her petticoats as she stepped between his legs.

"Is she right?"

"No."

She was standing inches away from him, and this close he could make out the dark seam of her lips, the wide cheekbones and sharply angled jaw. She tilted her head back.

Unwise, he thought. His heart beat like a drum in his chest.

"You aren't only an intellectual?" Her fingernail skimmed over his nipple. He shuddered.

"Or an automaton?" Her lips brushed his chin.

He seized her shoulders, crushing her to him, his mouth covering hers.

One minute she was caressing a chest as hard as rock and just as immobile, the next he'd lifted her in his arms and carried her behind the screen of a rowan tree. He set her down, pushing her against the tree, his mouth already open over hers, kissing her hungrily, passion pouring out of him, drenching her in his heat, his urgency. His tongue swept deep within her mouth, mating with it, insistent, willing her compliance, her own participation.

She wrapped her arms around his neck and he dipped down, lifting her up, holding her pinned between the hard wall of his body and the tree behind. The bark scratched her naked shoulders. She didn't care.

He wanted her. *Her.* Nothing could take that away from her. Ever. He wanted her, not the status he thought her purloined name could bring him. He pulled his mouth away, dropping his head into the lee of her shoulder and throat, tremors migrating along his back and arms.

She clung to him. He was big, bigger than she'd realized. Taller and stronger. Heavy shoulder muscles bunched beneath her hands. The bulge of his biceps, the long taut sinew in his thigh, all of his masculine, hard body had been hidden by his perfectly tailored white shirts and flawlessly pressed trousers. But now she felt the breadth of him, his hardness and urgency.

"I expect you to withdraw your charge as soon as you've slapped my face," he said against her throat. His voice was ragged.

"All right," she said breathlessly. "You aren't cold or unfeeling."

His laughter was frayed with desperation. "Dear God, no. Not where you're concerned."

She raised her hand and cupped his jaw. He turned his mouth and kissed the center of her palm. Electricity swirled from under the contact and speared along her arm, pooling in her belly. It was a good thing that he held her, because her legs felt too weak to stand.

He eased himself away from her, and the cooling night air rushed between them like a vigilant chaperone. He was coming back to himself; she could sense it. His momentary loss of self-control was over. All that masculine power was once more his alone to command.

"But you are controlled," she said accusingly.

"Not as much as I'd like to be," he said ruefully, his palms skating down her bare arms. She wanted him back. Wanted his arms around her and his mouth open over hers, his body straining.

She stood on tiptoe, bracing herself with her hands flat against his chest. His heart belied his calm mien. It thundered, thick and resonant beneath her palms. She nipped the hard angle of his jaw delicately.

"I could make you lose that control."

He closed his eyes. "Don't."

He hadn't denied it, and she took a perverse pleasure in that. He felt something. Something that he hadn't felt for Catherine Bunting. Maybe something he hadn't ever felt for another woman. She would cherish that. Remember that. That an honest, noble, good man had once wanted her so much that he trembled for her.

"Why shouldn't I?" she asked.

His beautiful lash-banked eyes opened, dark glittering gems in the dim light. His smile was touched with sadness. "No challenge," he said. "Too easy."

The light wind died. A lark bunting fluttered from

the branches of a rowan tree. The sound of distant voices, the clink of glassware, seeped from open windows and carried across the garden. She stared up at his shadowed face, trying to read his expression.

"Why is that?" she asked quietly.

"Because," he said, "I love you."

Chapter 21

The audience never boos the chorus.

SHE COULD HAVE PROBABLY HANDLED THAT better.

Somehow Letty doubted the real Lady Agatha would have hiked up her skirts and run away from a declaration of love. Come to that, glib, dry-witted Letty Potts wouldn't have either. The trouble was, thought Letty as she pressed her poor scratched back against the billiard room door, she didn't feel much like Letty Potts these days.

She had to get hold of herself. Put things in perspective. She'd seen this before, actors and actresses who became so immersed in their roles that the lines between who they were and who they portrayed were blurred.

She'd become carried away, was all. And was it any wonder? She'd fooled them all. Especially Elliot. Was it so surprising she'd fooled herself as well?

Because for a moment there, for the space of two heartbeats, she'd almost replied, "I love you." Almost.

Thank God, she hadn't. Because he didn't really love her—no matter what drivel she'd been dosing herself with about him wanting her and not this duke's daughter that didn't exist. It was all of a piece.

Stage-door Johnnies were always falling in love with a heroine created by a playwright's prose, a director's dab hand, and a lighting crew's artistry. So what if she'd authored her own lines, and blocked her own moves? It was still just an act.

She should really be getting a good laugh out of it. She'd almost bought into her own illusion. And why not? It was a nice illusion. A borrowed personality, some remade clothes, and a man who loved the resultant woman. How long could she keep the illusion going? If she tried very, very hard, how long could she be the woman Elliot thought she was, the woman he loved? Her heart raced.

Ultimately, he'd have to know she wasn't Lady Agatha. And there was no way his feeling for her would last beyond that revelation.

But what if it did?

Couldn't she make it work somehow? She'd almost convinced herself she was the woman Elliot believed her to be. How hard would it be to complete the transformation and become that woman? Maybe she was already. Just a little.

And they didn't have to stay in Little Bidewell. No one had to know. They could go away for a few years. She could dye her hair, lose or gain some weight, work on a different accent, and they could come back here again.

Her breath came rapidly. Her hands clenched in unconscious supplication.

Maybe there was a future out there somewhere for them.

"I've never seen him so utterly nonplussed."

Letty whipped around at the sound of the male voice. It was Atticus March, standing quietly beside the window, half turned so she'd not seen him immediately upon entering, his evening dress so dark his figure was lost in the shadows.

"Sir?"

He nodded toward the window. "My son. He's pacing about the back of the garden."

"Oh."

He smiled at her. He was fragile-looking, his tall frame stoop-shouldered but his face was still handsome. And so like Elliot's. "You've quite over-set him, m'dear. I do hope you intend to put him out of his misery soon."

She regarded him cautiously.

"I hope I haven't shocked you. I don't think I have. I have been watching you, you see, and you don't seem the sort of young woman who takes exception to straight talk."

Was that a good thing or a bad thing? She wasn't sure so she remained mute.

"Look for yourself." He motioned her over to the window. She went, drawn in spite of herself, and peered down into the garden.

Elliot stood beneath the window. The rising wind whipped his coattails and ruffled his dark hair. Behind him the sky had darkened to a velvety black.

Lightning flickered far off on the horizon. A storm was coming. It would find a kindred spirit in Elliot.

His expression was set, his skin pale in the weak light cast by the sconces outside the French doors. He was grimly regarding the door through which she'd run, obviously considering his course. If he came for her, what would she do?

"Look at the poor devil. Angry. Confused. Disheveled. Uncertain." Atticus leaned forward, squinting. "Begads, I do believe he's forgotten to do up his top shirt button." He shook his head. "Let's hope his current sartorial obliviousness passes. I doubt the Queen would appreciate her new baron making his bow with his shirt unbuttoned."

Queen? Baron? Atticus was speaking as if she knew what he was talking about, and she hadn't a clue.

He regarded her quizzically. "You don't know, do you? He hasn't told you. Forgive me, my dear. I should have guessed he wouldn't say anything, but I assumed . . ." He held out his hand. "What say you give an old man the pleasure of your company for a few minutes? Over here. Where we can sit."

He led her to a leather-covered sofa, and after seeing her seated, lowered himself next to her. "Now, then," he said, "it isn't my place to tell you this, but really it is the poorest kept secret in Little Bidewell. Anyone could and would tell you."

"Tell me what?" Letty asked

"That at New Year's Honors this year, the Prime Minister shall recommend to Her Majesty that Elliot be created a baron."

But that meant . . . No. No.

"What if the Queen refuses?" she said. "What if she decides not to act on the Prime Minister's suggestion?"

Atticus smiled. "Why ever should she refuse?" he asked. "While not nobility, March is a venerable and august name. My son's past is stellar, his character is unblemished, his associations above reproach, and his career marked by brilliance. I don't think she'll have a problem with his proposed elevation." There was no mistaking the pride in his voice.

But all Letty could hear were the words, "his associations above reproach."

That had been before he'd become "associated" with a music hall performer. If the powers that be ever found out about her . . . She swallowed the thickness in her throat.

The future that had beckoned so irresistibly dissolved and vanished, snuffed out like a candle flame, leaving her in darkness. There had been a slight chance that Sir Elliot could make a future with a music hall performer. But Lord March couldn't. Even if Elliot could forgive her her past, the Queen never would.

She turned to Atticus, her voice tinged with desperation. "He doesn't *have* to accept it, does he?"

His brow furrowed. "Well, no. He could refuse the honor," he said mildly. "But . . . he's worked for years for this opportunity. I don't see him letting go of it."

"But he's already a knight," she countered. "That's prestigious enough. Being a baron won't make him any better or worse than he is now!"

"Of course not," Atticus said, his gaze troubled but his voice kind. "But surely . . . as you know Elliot, you must realize it isn't the title Elliot seeks but the opportunity that comes with it."

She stared at him, dawning understanding making her mute. Of course.

"As a member of the House of Lords he can rise in the judicial branch . . . but you know these things. You must know how important this is to him and, I am vain enough to believe, to our country." He patted her hand and smiled.

"From what I've seen of my son lately, he hasn't exactly distinguished himself for his eloquence. But one makes allowances for extenuating circumstances." He twinkled at her. "You'll have to take my word for it, Elliot is a most gifted and persuasive speaker. He is particularly eloquent on the subject of judicial reform. Before he came back here because of my illness, he'd made quite a name for himself at the Old Bailey."

"The Old Bailey?" She'd thought that, except for Elliot's years in the Sudan, he'd been in Little Bidewell all his life. "He spent time in London?"

"A decade," Anton corrected her.

What a fool she'd been, teasing him about being a country cousin when all the while—

He regarded her with an unreadable expression. "Elliot once said that the price England paid in soldiers' lives could be sanctioned only if it purchased justice and freedom." His gaze was piercing. "You *do* understand? Ambition does not drive Elliot; commitment does. He will achieve a great deal of good with his title. A great deal of good." He sank back, smiling proudly. "Do you doubt it for a minute?"

"No." She didn't. Elliot's innate decency, his

integrity, his determination, his *passion* for justice would be formidable proponents for good. A wave of pride swept through her. Lord Elliot March, the man she loved.

Loved. She loved Elliot. Because he was generous and honorable and decent, qualities she'd doubted existed and so had jeered at as the products of the weak and sentimental. Because he was gentle toward Elizabeth Vance and compassionate toward her father. Because he discounted his efforts on others' behalves and made it seem that he was receiving when in fact he was bestowing. Because he never belittled in his conversation or was dismissive in his replies. Because he was scrupulous in his efforts toward fairness and patient with those who were not.

But she also loved him because his kisses made her feel hot and yearning and powerful. Because her body thrummed like a tuning fork whenever he touched her. She loved him because he was Elliot, unlike any man she'd ever met or ever would meet again.

Atticus was watching her closely. Then, as if he'd read her thoughts and knew how much she loved his son, he broke into a puckish, unexpectedly charming smile. "So, knowing what you now do, exactly what are your intentions toward my son, Lady Agatha?"

She could have handled that better, too, thought Letty, hurrying along the hall. She shouldn't have blurted out, "I don't have any intentions!" and bolted like a scared rabbit.

But the intentions she had were not the sort one revealed to one's intended lover's father. *Lover.* Letty had had ample opportunities to take a lover, but she never had. Because she'd never *loved* before, never understood what led a perfectly reasonable, intelligent woman to go all sappy and soft-headed over some man.

Until now.

She knew there was no future for Elliot and her. It didn't matter. She wanted to make love with the man she loved. She deserved that much, didn't she? There would never be another man like Elliot. She could spend a lifetime looking for him and she'd never come close to finding his like. Because no one got that lucky twice in a lifetime. Few women got that lucky once.

But she *had,* she thought fiercely. And she wasn't going to throw away one minute of happiness. And minutes were all they'd have.

Seducing Elliot would be difficult but not impossible. She knew him. He needed to be led to believe—as, being Elliot, he would—that their lovemaking was just a prelude to their marriage.

Her pace slowed. She stopped, amazed at her own audacity. She couldn't. He wouldn't. She daren't. What had become of her that she was making such wild plans?

She felt anguished by how far she'd allowed things to go. Her head throbbed with too many thoughts and her heart ached. She hated that she might have caused him pain. She needed to go to him, to steal what moments of happiness she could. Maybe, in the end, that's all she really was: a thief.

She looked around as if awakening from a troubled sleep. She'd made a circle of the lower level and was back where she'd entered the house from the gardens. People were starting to emerge from the dining room.

She had to find Elliot. That's all she knew.

A hand clasped her wrist. Letty turned, startled. Angela stood beside her. "He wants me to meet him at the witch tree tonight!"

"Kip? He isn't even here," Letty said, her gaze scanning the crowd for a dark, elegant head. "His parents offered his regrets to the Buntings. I heard them."

Elliot had to be somewhere. He wouldn't leave his father to make his way home alone. Was he angry? Disgusted?

"He sent me a message, just before we left," the girl said. "He says if I don't meet him he'll send the letter to Hugh by tomorrow's post! I should deal with him firmly, just as you said I should, shouldn't I?"

Letty stared unseeingly at Angela's taut face. She had to know what Elliot was thinking. He mustn't believe she didn't want his love. He couldn't.

"Lady Agatha?"

He mustn't leave without her seeing him. "Yes," she murmured.

"Really?" Angela insisted.

"What? If it comes to it, yes. But it won't come to anything tonight," she said distractedly. "A storm's coming."

"You don't know him," Angela whispered, but Letty didn't hear her. She'd seen Elliot's figure and was already hurrying through the crowd.

Chapter 22

Storms always make for
good theater.

LETTY MADE HER WAY TO THE FRONT DOOR just as Elliot's carriage drove away.

For the first time in her memory she didn't know what to do. The play didn't have a "next act."

She wandered through the rooms, smiling, murmuring inconsequentials and moving on, her thoughts wrestling hopelessly with what she wanted and what she must do. Finally, she grew light-headed with the strain of the irresolvable situation. She went to find Eglantyne to ask if she might have Ham drive her back to The Hollies. She found her speaking with the Buntings.

"I'm sorry, Letty," Eglantyne apologized upon hearing her request. "Angela had a headache, so Ham drove her home a short while ago. He hasn't returned yet and, well, I told him there was no need to hurry back as I expected we'd be here awhile."

Angela had left. An itch of anxiety penetrated Letty's preoccupation. Her gaze strayed to the window. Rain sparkled on the glass, and far beyond, in the darkness, she could see a stand of cypress trees snapping about, lashed by a strengthening wind.

Angela wouldn't have actually gone out to meet Kip in this? The memory of the girl's determined gaze and hard voice came back to haunt Letty.

"If you're not feeling well, you must stay the night with us," Paul Bunting offered. "Mustn't she, Catherine?"

"She must," Catherine agreed woodenly.

"No," Letty said. "I mean, I couldn't impose. I have these little spells, you see, and when I feel one coming on there's nothing that will do but that I take my tincture."

"Tincture." Catherine nodded eagerly. "I am all in sympathy, m'dear. I've heard that many Society ladies have problems with . . . excitability." The look she shot Dottie Himplerump was smugly satisfied. "You must return to The Hollies at once. Call for our carriage, Paul."

Letty thanked her profusely. Let Catherine gloat, she thought; there were more important matters at hand. She considered telling Eglantyne about her worry regarding Angela, but thought better of it. If she was wrong in her suspicions, she would only have succeeded in betraying Angela's secret.

Best to just go back to The Hollies alone. Angela was probably tucked into bed already, poor kid.

Ten minutes later, having left Fagin to a doting Eglantyne, Letty was in the Buntings' carriage heading down the drive. Driven by a heightening wind, the rain lashed the carriage roof, the racket deafening. Letty pulled her cloak tighter, peering out into the churning darkness. They made slow progress passing over the little bridge that led to the main road.

Off in the distance, illumined by lightning like something in a fairy-book illustration, she saw the skeletal oak they called the witch tree. Back of it a quarter mile sat the Himplerump house, while a bit farther up the road she spotted the formal outline of the Marches' manor house, the lower windows glowing through the rain.

He was still up, then. Was he hurt? Or had her running away from him snapped him back to his senses, and was he even now toasting himself on his good fortune?

A short time later she stood alone, dripping water in the great hall at The Hollies. At least Merry had had the courage to let her in before bolting. But as Letty shed her coat, Merry reappeared, leading a puffing Cabot and Grace Poole. Both looked awful, their expressions frightened.

"What is it?" Letty asked at once.

"Miss Angela. She's taken a horse and gone off riding and she wouldn't take any of the lads with her."

"Oh, no," Letty said, her worst fears realized.

"I don't know where she's gone!" Grace Poole said, her mouth forming an *O* of despair. "I couldn't stop her. I tried, Lady Agatha, but she was set. More determined than I'd ever seen her. Went right out to the stables and had the boy saddle her horse."

"When did she leave?"

"A quarter hour. No more. I'm sending one of the lads to the Buntings' to tell—"

"No!" Angela would die of humiliation if anyone discovered the reason she'd gone. Much more important was her safety. The storm was intensifying. What she needed was to come home, and it was up to Letty to see that she did.

"Who knows she's gone?"

"Just Grace Poole, Merry, and myself," Cabot said, gnawing his lip anxiously. "Why?"

"Listen to me," Letty said. "I know where Angela is. I know where she's gone but I can't tell you why. I can say this, however, it is imperative this goes no further. No one but us must know. Got that?" As little as she cared for Society, Letty was not so naive as to believe an affianced girl could ride out in a storm to meet a man other than her betrothed and not cause a terrific scandal.

Cabot and Grace Poole nodded and Merry said "aye," thrusting her little chin out determinedly.

"Her happiness depends on it."

A week ago she wouldn't have believed she could make such a melodramatic pronouncement and mean it. But she did. Personally, she didn't give a rap for Kip and his blackmail and Angela's marquis's tender feelings. But she'd learned a few things in the past week, and one of those was that just because something wasn't important to her didn't mean it wasn't important.

"I'll go. I'll bring her back. If we're lucky, we'll arrive back here well ahead of the Bigglesworths." Each minute the storm grew louder. The rain wasn't just pouring from the skies now; sharp spears of water hurled down from the heavens.

"But there's no carriage," Cabot exclaimed. "Ham went back for the Bigglesworths."

"I'll ride." She grimaced at Cabot's skeptical expression. "Who do you think exercised the Sultan of Arabis's Penultimate Palominos when Old Bill was seven sheets to the wind?" She ignored Grace's quizzical look and Merry's downright baffled one. Cabot nodded.

"Send someone down to the stables and have a horse brought round. I'll—"

"Hobbs already has a saddled horse waiting out the kitchen door," Cabot said. "I was going to send him off to the Buntings' as soon as I wrote a note."

"Good." She started down the hall toward the kitchen, Grace and Merry trotting along in her wake. "There's no time to lose."

"I should go," Cabot suddenly said. "I'm a man."

Oh, God. She didn't have time for this. "Good call. But completely irrelevant. If Angela sees you, she may well ride off. I'm the only one who knows where she is and why. Besides," her voice grew gruff, "she trusts me."

Cabot hesitated and stepped aside.

"I'll be fine, Cabot," Letty promised. "We'll be fine. Now, I'd appreciate something better than this cloak to wear."

"Here." Cabot opened a narrow door and withdrew a heavy oiled slicker. "This'll keep the weather off best as can be."

She thanked him, shrugging into the oversized

coat, and then, without looking back, opened the kitchen door and dashed to where the boy waited with the horse.

The horse was already nervous. What with whirling leaves and clashing rents of lightning, he needed no encouragement from Letty to run. She leaned over his neck, clinging like a burr as she set his head toward the witch tree road, thanking God she'd once helped exercise the trained horses in a variety act. Within minutes her heavy satin skirts were soaked and the wind had ripped the hood from her head, raking her elegant coiffure loose and sending long sodden streamers of hair whipping across her face.

She ignored it. Ignored the cold and ignored the wet and concentrated on holding on. By the time she raced into view of the witch tree she was soaked through and shivering with each strike of lightning.

She made the top of the rise and pulled her winded mount to a stop by the long-dead tree. She peered through the driving rain. She couldn't see a horse anywhere. She stood up in her stirrups. Nothing.

Fear grew like a canker inside her, spreading tendrils of panic. She wasn't surprised not to find Kip there; only a fool would be out on a night like this, a fool or a desperate girl.

Angela had to be here. Letty hadn't seen a rider on the road and there was only the one between The Hollies and here. She kneed her horse forward, moving out in a wide arc. She'd gone about fifty yards when she saw a darkish mound on the ground.

In a trice, Letty slid from the saddle and stumbled through the mire toward the figure lying so still. She fell to her knees. It was Angela. She must have fallen from her mount. Brief flickers of lightning illuminated a face as pale as alabaster, a smear of something dark seeping across her forehead.

Please God, please let her be all right.

Her hand trembled as she shoved it beneath the cloak, seeking a pulse. She caught back a sob when she found it. "Angela!" she shouted. "Angela, wake up!"

The girl shifted uncomfortably. "Agatha?"

Once more a sob escaped Letty. "Yes. Yes, dear. It's me."

The girl muttered something. Letty bent nearer to hear her. "What, Angela?"

"You were right," the girl mumbled. "He didn't come."

Letty's sob turned to laughter. "No, he wouldn't risk his neck. I told you he was a coward."

"You are a woman of the world," Angela murmured weakly. "I endeavor . . . to remember."

"Quiet, Angela. Be still."

"We'll drown if I'm . . . still . . . too long," the girl muttered.

"I'm afraid you're right," Letty said. "Can you walk?"

"I think so."

Letty eased the girl to a sitting position and felt her flinch. She shifted behind Angela and wrapped her arms around her waist, bracing her feet and pulling. Angela gasped in pain but scrabbled weakly to find her footing. It was no good. With a moan, she sank silently to the ground.

I'll kill her at this rate, Letty thought desperately. She cast about trying to think of what to do. She didn't dare leave her here and ride for help. Angela was already insensate, her body cold and wet. But they could not stay, either. Angela couldn't long endure being soaked in frigid rain.

She'd told Cabot that she would find Angela and bring her safely back. She'd fail. She should have let Hobbs ride to the Buntings.

She sank to her knees, wrapping her arms around Angela's unconscious body and pulling her into her lap. Her cold fingers fumbled at her slicker. As soon as it was open, she spread it as best she could over the motionless girl, and huddled over her, shielding her from the rain.

Tears welled from Letty's eyes, slowly at first, a mere coda to the rain, then faster until they streamed down her cheeks and her throat. A floodgate opened and a lifetime of tears coursed down her face, unexpected because they'd never been acknowledged, never been allowed. Veda had told her not to cry. Not ever.

She'd told her not to cry when Lady Fallontrue had forbidden the tutor to read Letty's poems. And the one time Veda had taken her to see her father, the viscount, he'd stood behind his desk, his auburn hair burnished in the sunlight, and looked at Letty's hair with startled and pleased recognition. Until he'd caught Veda's eye. "You can't prove she's mine," he'd said, and Veda had told her not to cry.

And Veda had even told Letty not to cry as she lay dying, her once robust frame reduced to a delicate frame covered with gossamer skin.

Because tears meant weakness; tears meant *they'd* won.

But while Letty could spit in anyone's eye on her own account, she was scared to death for this girl.

She threw her head back and shouted, "Help! Help us, please! Help!"

And Elliot March rode out of the blackness.

Chapter 23

*You can figure out what the villian fears
by his choice of weapons.*

LIGHTNING SCORED THE SKY, LIGHTING
Elliot's face.

It might have been better for Letty if it hadn't.

Because gentle Sir Elliot March didn't look so gentle at
that moment. He looked like something a watery hell had
spewed up to deal with unworthy petitioners. His head
was bare, the black locks curling wildly, water streaming
down his face. His brows were lowered in a dark vee, his
scowl thunderous, his mouth a hard, tight line.

His horse danced beneath him, a huge black gelding snorting fumes of mist from its flaring nostrils and
tossing its big, bowed neck. He held the big horse effortlessly, heeling it closer. His gloved hands gripped
the reins as if he were choking them ... or her.

"I didn't believe them when they said you'd gone
out in this!" he bellowed, his voice carrying above the

wind. "Good God, woman! Have you lost your bloody mind? And where is Angela?"

Letty shielded her face from the rain, peering up at him as she gently peeled her coat from Angela. "She must have been thrown from her horse. I tried to get her up, but I think she's fainted."

"Dear God," Elliot muttered, leaping from his horse and kneeling down. His hands moved with practiced gentleness behind Angela's head and down her neck and shoulders.

"She might have a concussion," he said. "My house is the closest. We'll go there. Can you hold my horse still while I mount with Angela?"

Letty nodded, ridiculously happy to have him take charge of the situation. They were safe now. No one was going to die. He wouldn't allow it. Elliot would take care of the situation, *any* situation.

She gathered the reins and stood by the horse's head as Elliot lifted his foot into the stirrup. He balanced Angela against his hip, shifting his weight forward onto the stirrup. The movement caused Angela's arm to swing free and slap against the gelding's leg. The startled horse reared, pulling Elliot's leg out and sideways, his foot still caught in the stirrup.

His teeth flashed briefly in pain. Letty fought to bring the gelding's head down. By the time she looked up, Elliot had swung into the saddle and was holding Angela across his lap. He looked down at her, his unwillingness to leave her written on his face.

"Go on," she shouted, shielding her eyes with her hand. "I have to catch my horse. I'll follow as soon as I can. Don't worry. I'm a very good rider!"

"I can't leave you!" he shouted back.

"You have to! You have to get Angela out of this weather! Go!"

He could not argue with her. With an unintelligible sound, he touched his heels to the gelding's sides, riding off into the storm as Letty watched.

The girl would be well. Elliot would do his part, and now, by God, she would do hers.

"Wake up, Kip," Letty said.

"Huh?" The boy in the curtained bed flopped onto his back, dragging the sheets with him. He hadn't even bothered to undress, Letty noted in disgust. Her nose wrinkled as the smell of stale beer erupted in a yeasty burp that penetrated the curtains surrounding the four-poster.

"Wake up, you young idiot."

That opened his eyes. Bleary eyes. Red-rimmed, unfocused eyes. Good. This would play out even better if he was drunk.

"Huh? Who're you? What're you doin' in here?" He started to roll out of the bed, but she snagged the sheet twined around his legs and pulled him back.

"Uh-uh. You just stay right where you are, m' lad."

"Lady Agatha!"

"Bright boy."

"What're you doing in here?" Confusion now, extreme confusion. A tiny kernel of an idea sprang to light in his clouded eyes. "Hey. How'd you get in here? Bribe the doorman?"

"No," Letty said impatiently. "No one knows I'm here. I climbed up the ivy outside."

His disbelief was obvious. Not that she gave a fig. "It doesn't matter how I got here, does it? Only that you may rest assured that *no one knows.*"

His brow furrowed, then smoothed as a smug expression of self-satisfaction dawned on his face. He nodded, grinning and raising a finger to his lips. "I won't tell."

"Oh, I know that." She shifted and her wet shoes made a squishy sound. "As to why I'm here, I've come for the letter Angela wrote you, you nasty, despicable, blackmailing little toad."

"Hey!" His complacent smile dissolved, replaced by stunned aggrievement. "You got no right to talk to me like that!"

"Of course I do. I'm speaking the truth. You're a vile extortionist of the very worst type, that being the type that holds an innocent young girl's dreams ransom for his own sordid ends."

Kip struggled to a sitting position. "Her dreams? What about *my* dreams? We were going to get married."

"Not that she ever knew of."

The boy's lower lip thrust out sullenly. "Well, I hadn't got 'round to asking her yet, but that doesn't mean I wasn't going to."

He truly did sound hurt, and for a second she softened. "She doesn't want to marry you, Kip."

He flopped back, his hands behind his head, and smirked. "Oh, yeah? Well, she wanted to 'something' with me, I can promise you that."

So much for Kip's tender heart. She placed her hands on her hips. "You arrogant boy. Let me explain a few things to you. Like any healthy, inquisitive young girl, Angela was curious about kissing. But unlike most healthy, inquisitive young girls, because she's a dear, naïve, and proper young lady, she decided she must be in love if she wanted to kiss you."

He laughed. Not very nicely.

"Yes," Letty said. "We both know that that is a bunch of bunk, don't we? Angela realized it pretty quickly herself. Unfortunately not quickly enough. She wrote you a letter first. And she wants it back. She *wants* to marry Hugh. So give me back her letter and we'll just chalk this attempt to victimize Angela up to a youthful lapse in judgment, eh?"

His eyes had narrowed angrily. He crossed his arms over his chest. "I told her she could have the letter. All she had to do was come and get it. Nothing was going to happen that hadn't happened before. Maybe a bit more." He leered.

"She sent me."

"Her mistake."

She had had about enough of Kip Himplerump. She was standing in a pool of rainwater, sopping wet, her satin ball gown growing heavier with each moment, cold of foot, wrinkled of hand, and with a three-mile ride in a storm still to come.

She ripped back the bed curtain. "Your mistake. You will now fetch me that letter and this is why. If you do not, I shall ruin your reputation."

At his look of amazement, she smiled grimly. "Yes, you simple young male, *your* reputation. And when I am done, no woman in London, let alone Little Bidewell, will have you. Your friends will snicker behind your back and your parents will duck their heads in shame." She leaned forward and jabbed him in the center of his chest. "I shall say you tried to seduce me."

"Really?" Kip asked eagerly. Then, masking his delight, he sank back on his elbows and examined his fingernails with studied nonchalance. "Go ahead. Tell everyone you want." He leered up at her. "You see, I don't care if all Little Bidewell, York, Manchester, or London thinks I'm the Marquis de Sade himself. I don't care for my reputation at all."

"Oh, I think you do." Not only was he simple, he was profoundly simple. "You aren't listening, Kip. I said I shall tell everyone you *tried* to seduce me."

He frowned, the shadow of understanding just beginning to penetrate his thick skull.

"I shall say you were," she leaned forward, her lips inches from his ear, "incapable."

He tensed.

"Fallow."

She straightened just in time to avoid being hit by him as he bolted to a sitting position.

"Limp."

He stared her in the eyes, his gaze disbelieving.

"Dormant."

He gasped, hurled the covers back, scrambled from the bed, and dashed across the room.

"Quiescent."

He fell to his knees before a bureau and wrenched open the bottom drawer.

"In a word: Impotent."

He dug his hand deep in the drawer and with a cry of triumph, withdrew an envelope. He leapt to his feet and ran back to her side and thrust it into her hand, panting heavily.

She almost pitied him. Almost.

She accepted the letter, pocketed it, and grinned. "Thanks, chum." She turned around.

"You're a bitch," she heard him mutter.

She looked back over her shoulder. "Flaccid."

He blanched. She chuckled.

"I was just pulling your leg, Kip. Now, off to bed with you," she advised pleasantly. "And if I hear of you saying anything at all about Angela, if you so much as breathe her name in a disrespectful manner, well . . . I shouldn't."

He didn't answer, just slunk back to his bed and slipped under the covers, glowering at her over the edge of the blanket like the naughty little boy he was.

"Good boy."

She opened the casement window, squinting out through the rain. It had let up some, but she still couldn't see twenty feet in the downpour. The trees were nothing but a vague impression. She looked down. Below her the wall disappeared into darkness.

She took a deep breath, steadying her nerves. She'd worked a rope act once, hadn't she? What was the difference between twenty feet of living ladder and crossing an inch-thick rope thirty feet above the ground?

A net, that was what.

Well, she didn't have a net and she didn't dare be

seen by the Himplerump servants. Without giving herself a chance to back out, she hoisted herself over the sill and, after noting Kip had had the good sense to stay abed, lowered herself cautiously. She felt for a toehold and found one, but the water had made the leather soles of her shoes slick and her foot slipped. For a half a minute she hung from her hands twenty feet above the ground, her sodden skirts dragging at her, the rain pummeling her face.

She considered calling out to Kip for help, and discounted the idea. He'd probably pry her fingers from the sill.

She wasn't going to fall. She wouldn't let herself fall. She had to see Elliot. She scrambled amidst the ivy leaves, found purchase, and carefully relinquished her weight to the vine. It held.

The rain made it difficult, but slowly she worked her way down the ivy-covered brick façade, the cold rain pelting her face. Finally, she looked down and saw the ground directly beneath her. She dropped from the wall, hit the earth, and stumbled to her knees.

It didn't hurt. Nothing could hurt. She was alive. Angela was alive. And she had the letter. Now, she only needed to get the horse and off she'd be.

She lifted her face to the pouring heavens, grinning with relief and the sheer, giddy feeling of having won. And looked straight up into Elliot March's furious face.

Chapter 24

Love has no place in a love scene.

"I TRUST YOU'RE HAVING A BLOODY GOOD time," Elliot ground out between his teeth. If he was angry before, he was livid now. The storm swallowed up the color from his eyes, leaving them pale and terrible looking.

Letty swallowed. Before she realized what he was about, he'd bent and lifted her by her arms, pulling her roughly to him, his fingers digging into her forearms. "God. When I saw you hanging from that ledge—" He choked off whatever more he might have said.

"Angela?" she asked. "Is she all right?"

"She'll be fine." His teeth clamped shut as he turned, dragging her roughly in his wake. He limped heavily, leading her to where she'd tethered her gelding. Elliot's black stood beside it.

Without a word, he scooped her up and deposited her in the saddle, then swung up onto his horse's back. He glared at her. "Will you follow me back to the house?"

She nodded. Through the driving rain he led the way down the road and to his home. Once there he dismounted, cursing as he dropped from the saddle and his leg buckled. She slipped at once to the ground and went to him, but the glare he threw her warned her against offering her assistance.

He took the horses' reins and moved with painful deliberation toward the stables. He did not look back. "The door is open. Go in."

She did as he bid her, entering the house with a little wistful sense of anticipation. Elliot's home.

The redbrick manor house was built around a central hall and a graceful staircase that switchbacked up three stories. Behind this, a hallway led to the back. A set of doors faced each other across the foyer in which she stood. The one on her left was partly open.

She peeked inside. It was evidently a woman's room. White-and-poppy-red floral chintz covered a pair of sofas and a hassock. On delicate piecrust tables stood bell jars filled with brilliantly hued butterflies and porcelain figurines. Above the mantel hung an oil painting of a dark woman flanked by two curly-headed boys. The older one looked composed and thoughtful, the black-haired younger one gay and inquisitive.

The front door opened behind Letty, causing her to jump back from the door. Elliot came in, shedding water like a great spaniel, flapping his arms and shaking his head. He peeled off his jacket and tossed it over the stair rail.

"The Buntings sent a boy on horseback here an hour ago," he said. "Thank God someone showed some sense."

He was soaked through to the skin, his white dress shirt and vest plastered to his arms and chest. Through the fabric she could see the play of his muscles. She looked away, her cheeks warm. "I'm sorry. What were you saying?"

"The Buntings' bridge is flooded and too dangerous to take carriages over. The Buntings' guests will be staying until the morrow." He met her gaze grimly. "Angela came to as soon as we arrived. No, don't look like that. I meant it. I've seen my share of head wounds. She'll be fine. I promise."

She nodded. If Elliot promised Angela would be fine, she accepted that she would. Elliot would never disguise the truth. Unlike some.

"How did you know where I'd gone?" she asked. It didn't occur to her then to ask how he'd known she and Angela were at the witch tree to begin with. She'd needed him and he'd come.

"As soon as I got Angela inside and into my housekeeper's care, I realized that you weren't 'right behind me.' " His look was condemning. "I went back to the witch tree, but you were gone, so I rode for The Hollies. You weren't there, but I heard a great deal from Cabot, little of it to my liking."

"I hardly dared believe my suspicions were correct, but I had no other leads to follow so I headed for

Himplerump's house. Imagine my amazement when I saw you creeping down the wall.

"Although in retrospect, I don't suppose I should have been surprised. You had already, after all, evinced a certain interest in ivy and the climbing of it." He finished his sentence between stiff clenched jaws.

She swallowed. He looked very, very angry.

"I . . . I had to fetch something that . . . that's—" she began to stutter.

"Angela told me about the letter," he broke in.

Of course. Everyone relied on Sir Elliot March. Everyone told him their secrets and their past transgressions, their fears and their little crimes. Everyone but her. But then, no one's crimes were quite as damning as hers, either.

"She told me about Kip's demand and why she'd gone there. This storm might be our salvation yet. We're lucky."

Not *she* was lucky, not *Angela* was lucky, but *they* were lucky. He'd already assumed responsibility, made their problems his own.

"As I said, I've spoken to Grace Poole and Cabot. They're eager to help and most willing to put about the story that, being unhappy with the notion of Angela and you alone at The Hollies on such a night, I fetched you both here.

"Do you understand? Do you agree?" He was short to the point of curtness.

She nodded and caught her movement in the mirror. She glanced sideways. She looked awful. It wasn't fair. While he looked like Poseidon taking on mortal form, she looked like a sea hag. Beneath the streaming slicker, her skirts hung from her waist in sodden, mud-smeared folds. Her tangled hair dangled in wet ropes, slithering along her neck, and her skin was so white it looked bluish.

"Would you tell me what you were doing climbing the Himplerumps' wall?" he asked as though the query was forced from him.

Her gaze met his in the mirror. For the first time in her adult life she couldn't think of a glib story to account for her actions. She didn't try. She was tired of speaking lines, of dodging verbal traps.

"I went to get Angela's letter from Kip Himplerump. I got it."

"Did Kip Himplerump see you?"

She nodded.

"Will he tell anyone?"

"No. I guarantee it." He was so aloof. So coldly efficient. She *had* hurt him. She hadn't wanted to. "Elliot, I have to tell you something. My reaction to what you said to me earlier this—"

"Good," he broke in. Clearly, he didn't want to hear anything of an intimate nature from her. "Though just to be on the safe side, perhaps I should make a morning call on my young neighbor."

Good God, she thought, her breath leaving her, perhaps he regretted saying he loved her. She felt hollow inside, as though a vacuum had suddenly developed around her heart. "Things will all turn out all right," she managed to say.

"What I would like to know," he said in a careful

voice. "What I would very *much* like to know, is why you risked life and limb to play cat burglar with that . . . that . . . boy. You might have been killed!"

The last words exploded from him causing Letty to flinch. He saw it and cursed vividly under his breath, raking his hand through his hair. "Where did you learn to climb like that?"

He *cared*. The realization made her giddy. "A youthful peccadillo?"

"I won't even honor that with a response," he grated out. "Might I suggest you take that wet coat off?"

She tried to comply but she was shaking so badly her teeth were clicking. She fumbled at her slicker's fastenings with fingers too numbed to work properly. Before she realized what he was about, Elliot had brushed her hands aside and, with cool competence, unbuttoned the slicker. He turned her with a hand to her shoulder and stripped the coat from her. All very economical and all most impersonal.

"Thank you."

He stiffened. "I don't want your gratitude." He looked as if he wanted to say more but decided against it, instead tossing her coat over his. "You'll need to get out of those clothes. We only have a housekeeper, Mrs. Nichols. She's sitting with Angela right now, but I'm sure she'll help you with your dress."

"No need," she said. "I'll be fine. Really. Angela will want her."

"Fine." He motioned for her to precede him up the stairs and she went, her wet skirts slapping against the risers. Behind, she heard Elliot's slow progress. At the top she turned around. Elliot's face was ashen, and tension marked the corners of his eyes and mouth. He was hurting.

"Elliot, please. Is there something I can do for you?"

At once, his expression became remote and imperial; the quintessential British gentleman, stiff-upper-lipping it straight into perdition. "Nothing. Thank you for your concern." He pointed down the short hall. "Angela is at the far end left. Your room is two doors up from hers."

She hesitated. "Elliot, please—"

"I'm sure you'll find everything in order," he said, and walked stiffly down the opposite hall. He did not look back.

Elliot limped across his bedroom floor, heading for a small cabinet. From it he withdrew a squat brown glass bottle and measured out a good ounce of liquid into a shot glass. With a grimace, he tipped his head back and swallowed the draught. Morphine.

He disliked its effects. It clouded his thinking and tricked his senses, but as a painkiller it was undeniably effective. And tonight, tonight by God, he was in pain.

It occurred to him to try to use the deep throbbing ache in his thigh as a distraction. But he doubted it could distract him from thoughts of her. Instead, he'd opted for the narcotizing effect of the drug. If he were very lucky, it would help him forget that she was in his house, sleeping in his bed, so close to being where he wanted her, but under such completely different circumstances.

For the first time since finding Angela and Letty at the witch tree, he allowed himself to think back on the events that had driven him from the Buntings' party.

He'd told her he loved her. He'd never told another woman that, and when he did, she turned as white as Dover sand. Clearly, she'd been shocked. He'd been shocked himself. But as soon as he'd said the words, he'd known they were true: deeply, incontestably true.

For a fleeting instant something that sent elation coursing through him flickered across her expressive features, only to disintegrate into horror. Then she'd run. She couldn't have gotten far enough, fast enough. His hands balled into fists at his side.

He'd tried to stay on at the party, but the thought of Letty avoiding him, laughing nervously in his company, of his vibrant, audacious, unguarded Letty becoming stiff and clumsy with him—he hadn't been able to stand the idea.

It had been no more palatable here at home where, after an hour of relentless pacing, he'd come to understand a vital truth: He would rather have some small part of Letty's friendship than nothing of her at all.

He'd written her a letter, explaining that he would not ever again infringe upon the friendship he most sincerely desired and felt them already to enjoy. She must not worry he would ever again distress her with talk of his feelings. That was his intent, anyway. He'd prayed to God that he was strong enough to carry it out.

Then, loath to have a single day pass without doing everything in his power to put things right between them, he'd ridden to The Hollies intending to give the letter to Cabot, to be delivered as soon as she arrived home. From there things had gone to hell.

Elliot poured a half tumbler of brandy and swallowed it in a gulp, washing the bitter flavor of morphine from his mouth. Experience had taught him how easily liquor compounded the drug's effects. It couldn't act fast enough for his purposes.

He unbuttoned his vest and stripped it off, tossing it to a chair. From there, he pulled off his collar and tie and began unbuttoning his shirt as he limped to the window and stared out at the darkness.

Angela had told him about Kip and the letter as soon as they'd discovered Letty wasn't 'just a few minutes' behind them. He couldn't believe she'd broken into the Himplerumps' house to get the damned thing. He smiled unwillingly. Had he called her audacious? Reckless.

His smile faded as he recalled his eviscerating fear as he'd watched Letty dangling from the ledge and knew there was nothing he could do to help her. Nothing had ever scared him so profoundly. Nothing in war or peace, no threat of injury, nor foreboding of defeat, nothing. Once she was on the ground, it had taken all his self-restraint not to haul her into his arms.

But he didn't have the right. She didn't want that

from him. She'd made that clear enough. The letter promising he'd never importune her again lay folded in his pocket, a bitter reminder of his pledge.

Being Letty's friend was quite possibly going to kill him. But what in God's name was he to do? He couldn't think clearly anymore. His thoughts were distant, as was the pain in his leg, both dulled by the encroaching effects of the morphine. He braced his hands on the sill.

She would be asleep by now, hair the color of mahogany spilling across crisp white linen, warm skin delicately flushed. He pressed his forehead against the cool window.

He'd spent a lifetime subjugating his emotions to his intellect, trying so damned hard to keep control, to maintain balance, to act judiciously, prudently. He smiled bitterly. Thirty-three years had brought him to this place, to the point of awakening, to this sharp, bittersweet shattering of his heart. How many more would it be before it no longer hurt?

"Elliot."

Her voice.

"Elliot, please. Turn around."

"Why? You're not real," he said practically, sensible even in his drugged state. "You're a combination of morphine and brandy. And want," he added as an afterthought. "Unbearable want."

"I'm real. Please. This is difficult. Turn around."

What difference would it make? He turned and inhaled sharply. She stood inside his door, wrapped in his father's old dressing gown. Her hair, glorious and unbound, rippled down her back and spread like a veil over her shoulders. Beneath the robe's frayed hem, her feet were bare. Slender, narrow, delicate as gulls' wings, white and unspeakably vulnerable.

She shouldn't be here. But then, she didn't know about the morphine and the brandy. She didn't know that the restraint he'd always found his most formidable challenge no longer seemed an issue. "Go back to your room."

She didn't move. A cherry-colored stain swept up her throat and flamed in her cheeks. "I can't," she whispered.

His hands clenched on the sill behind him. He didn't dare move. "You're an adventuress now?" He tried to make his voice light. It sounded ragged.

"I guess so." She didn't sound like an adventuress. She sounded lost, and as hungry for love as he was starved for her.

"God, Letty. You haven't a cautious impulse in you, do you?"

"I guess not."

She doesn't want love from you, he reminded himself savagely, hoping that the knowledge would somehow give him the strength to resist this. Resist her. Because she was set on seduction. The rawest boy could see that. There was nothing subtle about her. Apprehensive, anxious, skittish, yes, but also expectant, breathless, and irresistible.

She moved toward him, her unbound breasts moving beneath the ruby silk. By God, she was naked under the robe.

"I'm cold."

He would not do this. He *would not* do this. It went against everything upon which he'd based his life. He was stronger than this. "I'll get you an extra blanket."

"I like *that* blanket." She pointed to the blue duvet on his bed.

"Here," he clipped out, striding across the room and snagging the corner of the blanket. He flung it at her. She made no effort to catch it. It landed on the floor.

She swiveled slowly, deliberately bending at the waist. The silk robe stretched across her derriere. She looked back at him, her hair falling forward provocatively.

"Don't."

She flicked her hair behind her ear and smiled, wise and knowing and merciless.

"You don't understand, Letty." He fought to hold to the ragged edge of his control. He was a civilized man. No matter what the provocation, he had always maintained self-control. It was a standard he not only lived by but believed in. But he'd never been tested in such a manner or to such a degree. He wanted her. He ached for her.

"I wouldn't want to leave you wanting." She piled the blanket in her arms. He saw, too late, that he'd handed her the excuse she needed to draw nearer. She moved toward the bed, coming within a few feet of him, still smiling enigmatically, her perfume filling his nostrils...

He didn't even know what happened. One minute she was moving past him, the next she was in his arms and he was lifting her up, walking her backwards, his mouth open over hers, hunger pouring out of him, engulfing her, overpowering her.

And she was clinging to him. And her mouth was open. And her hands were on him, touching him, his shoulders, his arms, his chest, delving beneath the open edges of his shirt and setting him on fire.

He yanked her belt from her waist and pulled the silk lapels open, peeling the robe from her shoulders. She pulled back, looking up at him, her gaze no longer knowing and worldly, but uncertain, a bit frightened.

"Perhaps . . . I . . . I shouldn't . . . we shouldn't—"

"Too late." Far too late. There were no codes here. No rules. Just imperatives: Want. Desire. Love. "You know it as well as I."

He released her in increments, letting her slide down his body and feel the hard evidence of his desire. Her breasts dragged across his shirt, her robe caught on his waistband and twisted up, rucking up around her thighs.

Letty shivered. Her toes touched the ground but her ankles felt liquid and her knees weak. His hands dropped to his side. He didn't step back. Each breath he drew brought their bodies back into brief, tantalizing contact.

She looked up into his face, her gaze dazed. She needed something to hold on to. She wrapped her fingers in the edges of his open shirt, twisting the cloth, her knuckles pressing into the hard muscle of his chest.

"If you want to leave, go. Last chance, Letty. Last chance for either of us." He bent and traced a kiss across her mouth. "But I think you should stay here."

She stepped back a little. He followed, dipping his head so that his lips teased her ear. "Stay." His breath warmed her ear, sent gooseflesh rippling down her throat and arms.

He didn't touch her, *hadn't* touched her since releasing his grip, and yet he surrounded her, enveloped her in longing, kept her anchored here, wanting...

His fingers touched the side of her breast and with gossamer lightness he traced its curve, following the nether swell. His fingertips moved up to her nipple, outlining the silken areola, round and round. His gaze never left her face, lupine with intensity, unwavering and mesmerizing.

She didn't recognize him. Reserved, genteel Sir Elliot had vanished, leaving behind a stranger in his stead, a stranger who played with her body with deliberate nonchalance while the hunger in his eyes dragged her soul from her.

"Please," she whispered. His white shirt was two thirds of the way open, affording tantalizing glimpses of hard muscles and the dark hair that covered his chest.

"Why did you come here, Letty?" he whispered, dropping a soft, warm kiss on the corner of her mouth.

She couldn't tell him the truth: that she had come to make love with him. Because if she told him she loved him, he would expect, would have every right to expect, that nothing barred an honest relationship or stood in the way of their marrying. Because in Elliot's world, people who loved one another married.

She should leave, wrench herself away from here, but she couldn't. Because if she left here, she left behind the one chance she might ever have to *make love*.

And she wanted that. So much. Her skin danced with awareness. Her limbs trembled with anticipation. Liquid desire pooled in her loins and the tips of her breasts. What if he told her to go away? How could she live with that? Without ever knowing what it would be like?

"I've come for a tumble." She sounded desperate.

He went utterly still. A heartbeat passed. Another. Again. She found herself holding her breath, trying to read his unreadable expression, fighting the panic that threatened.

Why wouldn't he touch her? Say something? *Do* something?

When his response finally came there was nothing vague about it. "You want lust? Lust is easy."

Without lifting his gaze from hers, he unfastened his trousers in one short, efficient, sexually charged motion. Before she understood what he intended, he flicked the edges of her robe open and bent, one large hand closing on her thigh, his other forearm looping beneath her derriere. He lifted her, hitching her leg over his hip, spreading her most vulnerable, sensitive part against the opening of his trousers.

She gasped at the sudden intimacy and flung her arms around his neck to keep from falling. The position was flagrant, the hard length of him ground against her, his objective blunt, crude, and rousing.

His skin was hot, his body hard.

"Elliot—"

He ignored her, the look in his eyes killing her voice. This was raw, focused desire. He walked with her dangling thus until her shoulders hit the wall. His head dropped to the side of her face, his mouth fell open on her throat. His hips pinned hers to the wall.

He moved, a slow, heavy tilting of his loins that sent thought-destroying floods of pleasure careening through her body. Her fingers sank into the white broadcloth covering his shoulders, trying to hold on, caught in a primal wave of need she couldn't escape, terrified, elated, wanting to do to him what he so effortlessly did to her.

Even beneath the shirt she could feel his muscles shift and bunch, sleek and hard. He rocked his erection against her. She gasped. He trembled.

He moved again and again, little pulsing thrusts that exploded bursts of ever-mounting pleasure within her. And now he added a new torture to the game, lifting and settling her in counterpoint to his thrusts. It was excruciating and tantalizing.

"Elliot. Elliot," she panted.

He did not answer. His expression was set, strained, his throat corded and veined with his exertions. He was one-minded, intent only on sexual gratification.

She couldn't think, could only feel. She'd never realized how big he was, the breadth of him, the heaviness of him. He enveloped her completely, surrounding her with sensation, hot and satiny-smooth skin, crisp starched shirt and cool, damp hair.

She wanted more. She wanted him inside her. Filling her. She wanted to complete this ancient dance.

She closed her eyes. Her hips found the rhythm he urged and moved with it. Against her throat he drew a sharp breath. Abruptly he reached down, clasping her other thigh and lifting her higher, settling her at his waist. She was naked there, and he ... With a start of trepidation she recognized the blunt width pressed against her. Her legs tightened involuntarily.

He groaned, lifting his head and, slanting his mouth over hers, kissing her fiercely, possessively, a thin edge of anger in his aggression. She returned his kisses, her hunger rising.

He pushed and slid into the sleek, swollen entrance. He tore his mouth from hers. She heard him draw a ragged breath, felt him bracket her face in between his hands, pinning her motionless to the wall.

His breath sloughed over her lips. She opened dazed eyes, needy and agitated.

His glittering eyes locked with hers.

"I want to see you. I want to see you take me."

He pushed slowly. Her eyes flew wide, startled by the sensation. He was thick, stretching her as he pushed slowly into her. She inhaled with discomfort as her body tried to accommodate him.

Something flickered in his gaze. He stopped moving, his chest working like a bellows, his skin dusky, a sheen of perspiration covering him.

But the stopping was far worse than the slight pain.

"No." She shifted. His jaw worked reflexively. His eyelids squeezed shut. But he didn't move.

She pushed herself down, just a bit. His lips parted in a grimace. She moved, taking him deeper inside, past the pain, leaving only the thick feel of him buried within her. Want returned, redoubled. She moved again.

"Please," she said. "Please do that again. Move again."

"God!" The oath burst from him, releasing the tight rein of self-control. He drove deep into her, thrusting urgently. Again and again, he thrust into her, building her need all over again, taking her past the point of no return, riding the wave now, cresting with it, making it her own.

"Give in to it," he urged hoarsely, straining above her.

She did. She threw her head back and felt him around her, in her, above her, working her, giving to her. Pleasure engulfed her, speared through her, and blossomed, rippling through her until she sobbed with the pure beauty of it, collapsing in its wake, a house of cards undone by a tempest.

And when it was over, and her arms hung limp about his shoulders, he eased himself from her body, still potent and hard and unsatisfied. Effortlessly, he lifted her and carried her to his bed and laid her down on it.

Dazed and uncertain, she watched him stand up and finish unbuttoning the brilliant white shirt. He stripped it from his body in one fluid movement and tossed it behind him. He was just as beautiful as she'd imagined, athletic and lean and clean-limbed. The black hair covering his chest narrowed and thickened into a dark band that rode a flat belly corrugated with muscles.

He pushed his trousers from his hips, and her appreciation of his body turned to awe.

"What are you doing?"

"You've had sex," he said grimly. "Now, for the rest of the night, we make love."

Chapter 25

Passion is tragedy-in-waiting.

ELLIOT HAD NEVER BEEN ANGRIER IN HIS life. She'd stood there, shaking like a leaf, and told him she wanted a "tumble." As if he were some cicisbeo she could use to garner experience on instead of a man who loved her heart and soul, body and spirit.

He hadn't meant it to go so far, but the longing, the desperation and hunger had all conspired against him, driving him to one thought, one intent: She wanted lust. Fine. He could teach her about lust.

But by the darkest hour of the night, by the time the storm had finally broken, they'd both learned about love.

He looked down at where she lay deep in slumber beside him. The glow from the sconce above wrapped her in a soft cocoon of diffused light. Damson-colored highlights gleamed in her hair. A golden lacquer washed the satiny hill of her naked shoulder. The pristine bedsheets were tangled about her hips. One slender arm stretched out, her throat arched as though arrested in her culmination, leaving her in her satiation both defenseless and exposed.

Once again, he felt the stir of desire. They'd been in his bed for hours. He could not press her again. There had been a tincture of desperation in her hunger for him that she hadn't been able to hide. Whatever its source, he would vanquish it.

He loved her and, by God, he knew she loved him. She had not said so, but her arms and lips and touch had spoken far more eloquently then simple syllables could have done.

In Letty he had rediscovered his own heart, his own capacity for pleasure, for pain, for passion. He could not go back again. And, by God, he wouldn't. Not now. Not when he knew she loved him.

He gathered her to him, intending only to revel in the feel of her, and closed his eyes. But soon exhaustion and passion and morphine wrested consciousness from him and he, too, finally slept.

Morning steeped the room in light the color of weak tea. Letty woke instantly, panic already closing her throat, anguish humming through her like an electrical current. She was in Elliot's arms, a leg draped across him.

For one all-too-short minute, she forced all thought from her mind, absorbing the sensations, the flat hardness of his male body, the denseness of the lean muscular arm thrown over her waist, the velvety ladder of his ribs. But her thoughts gnawed at her pleasure, driving her to raise her gaze to his face.

He was beautiful. His nascent beard darkened his jaw; his lashes lay like thick smudges on his cheek. A small line knit a crease between his brows, and the corners of his mouth curved downward as if his slumber was troubled.

Dear God, he would hate her when he discovered who she was, what she was. She had to leave.

A tear slipped from the corner of her eye. She mustn't sob; she mustn't wake him. She would simply take what she could, a thief gathering stolen moments from a borrowed life, and slink away. She couldn't stay; she had nothing left to give him. No more lies left. Just the truth: She loved him.

And she would *not* stay to watch his love turn to hatred.

She was a coward. She had always been a coward, afraid to love. Too many lessons had conspired to teach her the dangers of it. Too many lessons had convinced her it was better to live life as a merry pretender, acting whatever part made it easiest to slide by uninvolved where you might be uninvited. Indeed, she was so afraid of love that she couldn't even sing a love song convincingly.

A damn music hall singer and a coward, that's what she was. That was the sum total of Letty Potts.

She had to get out of here. Before he woke up.

Carefully, she eased his arm off of her and shifted her weight from the bed. Quietly, she donned the silk robe and pulled it closed before slipping from the room and hastening down the empty corridor to her room.

Within twenty minutes she'd dressed in her damp, mud-stained ball gown, found her slicker, and entered Angela's room. A comfortable-looking, white-haired woman was snoring in a corner chair, her stockinged feet propped up on a little stool. The motherly Mrs. Nichols.

Letty tiptoed over to Angela's side. The girl was resting comfortably, her breathing relaxed, her color even. Letty smiled. At least Angela's problems had been easily enough fixed.

The girl stirred and her eyes opened. "Lady Agatha?"

"Quietly. We don't want to wake the worthy Mrs. Nichols, do we? And, please, my friends call me Letty."

A blush of pleasure tinted Angela's round cheeks. "Letty. Where did you go last night? I was so worried, and Sir Elliot was beside himself."

A few days ago she would have been tickled that she'd caused Elliot distress. Now she only felt a stab of guilt. She plastered on a cocky smile. "I went to fetch your letter, little goose," she whispered. "Can't have incriminating missives floating about, can we?"

"You did?" Angela's eyes widened. "Did you . . . did you get it?"

"Yes." Letty pulled the letter from the pocket of the slicker and handed it to Angela.

"And Kip?" Angela said, eyes wide on the incriminating paper. "He isn't angry? He's accepted that I love another?"

It took an effort not to make a sharp retort about

what Kip Himplerump could do with any ire he felt, but she refrained. It was not her place to question what value Angela set on her past friendship with the boy. It was but another of the lessons she would take with her from Little Bidewell.

"He's seen the light," she said.

A smile lit Angela's young face, and seeing the beauty of that suddenly unburdened smile, Letty found herself glad she'd gotten the dratted letter. With a vigor that boded well for a quick recovery, Angela tore the soggy letter into little scraps.

"How can I thank you enough, Lad—Letty?"

"Dictate any future correspondence," Letty suggested dryly.

"Henceforth I shall only write letters to my Hughie."

"And don't call your poor marquis 'Hughie,' " Letty said. "At least not in public."

Angela nodded solemnly.

"Have you seen Sir Elliot?" Angela asked.

The question caught Letty off guard. Her cheeks warmed, and from the interested expression on Angela's face, she knew they'd colored up as well. Luckily, Angela was too well raised to make a remark about her blush.

"Yes. I have. And I have thanked him for his aid." She knew her words sounded stilted but she couldn't help it. "But now, I have to go back to The Hollies. At once."

"Why?"

"Ah. Because. Because . . . Sir Elliot didn't realize I would be in such a pitiable state when he manufactured his story about fetching us from The Hollies during the storm. It would be rather hard to explain why I hadn't bothered to change before going off with him.

"So, you see, I must return to The Hollies before your father and aunt arrive home." Thank heavens her wits hadn't entirely deserted her. The excuse even made a sort of sense.

"But what shall you say then? Why would I be here? Alone!" Her eyes widened. "I mean, well, Sir Elliot is very old and very honorable and quite above anything *untoward, but . . .*"

If she only knew, thought Letty. "Angela, don't worry. I shall tell everyone that we both came with Sir Elliot last night but that you slipped upon exiting his carriage and hit your head. I shall explain that I came back at first light so I could be there when your aunt and father arrived to inform them of matters."

Angela scooted up against the pillows. "But that still means I have been here alone. And I am, after all, an unwed woman, and he's—"

"Mrs. Nichols has been in here with you all night. She's still here. Asleep—if you haven't woken her up, that is. Your reputation is safe."

The girl sighed gustily. "Of course." She looked a little sheepishly at the recumbent figure across the room. Mrs. Nichols snored blissfully on. "Silly of me. I should have realized Sir Elliot would take every precaution against compromising a lady."

"Every precaution," Letty agreed tonelessly.

"In fact," Angela went on, chuckling, "if he thought he'd been the least degree lax in guarding a lady's reputation, he'd be at the church this very Sunday demanding the banns be read. He is *such* a stickler for propriety."

The girl couldn't know that her words stabbed Letty's heart like a knife. "Indeed? I had best be going. I should like to creep down the back stairs before the rest of the staff is about."

And find a corner and curl up and die in it.

"All right." Impulsively Angela held out her arms, and after a second's amazement and another's awkwardness, Letty bent down and embraced the girl.

"Now I can forget all about Kip and that letter and concentrate on your wonderful plans for our wedding. Oh, Letty, heaven must have sent you," Angela whispered, a little catch in her voice, "because you have set everything right."

The devil must have sent her.

It was the only conceivable explanation. Because after leaving him breathless with wanting her, after sharing every intimacy with him, after flinging wide the doors to his cautious heart and making it her own, she'd left. Without a word, without a scribbled note of explanation. With only the memory of her lovemaking to cloud his thoughts, fire his blood, and inflame his anger.

Somehow Elliot contrived a calm expression for Angela, who sat being spoon-fed broth by Mrs. Nichols.

"And did Lady Agatha say whether she expected to return?"

"I don't think so," Angela said. "She said she would have to hurry to get everything ready for the wedding by the time she leaves."

"Leaves?" A more attentive listener might have noted the careful timbre of Elliot's voice.

Angela's mouth pulled down in the corners. "Yes. She has another wedding celebration to plan. She can only stay to finish the arrangements here, and then she plans to return to London forthwith."

"Does she now?" Elliot smiled around his clenched teeth. "Well, I had best leave you to your recovery, Miss Angela. I'm sure your father and aunt will be visiting soon. I'll show them up as soon as they arrive."

"Thank you.

Elliot bowed before exiting the room and shutting the door behind him. There, in a calm and moderately pitched voice, he let lose a string of every profane word in his vocabulary.

As a former army officer, he had an impressive command of the vernacular.

Chapter 26

The toughest role is real life.

"PROFESSOR MARCH SHOULD BE PLEASED with the results of his party, no doubt about it. Everyone's having a grand time, and Miss Angela looks beautiful." Merry whispered to Grace Poole from her position beside the white-draped sideboard at the far end of a long drawing room.

She, Cabot, and Merry were at the manor on loan from The Hollies, since the March household was inadequately staffed for this large a party. Mrs. Nichols, bless her soul, was a fine daily but hardly a chef—a term Grace had taken to applying to herself since Lady Agatha had delegated her to make the bridal cakes for Miss Angela's wedding. And since all the guests were clustered around Miss Angela, at the other end of the room, it was safe to chat quietly.

"Wouldn't know she'd hit her head and been laid

up in bed less than a week gone by now, would you?" Grace commented softly, watching as a small disembodied hand emerge from beneath the tablecloth and began an exploratory journey toward the candied grapes. Tommy Jepson, if she guessed right.

"Looks happier than I've seen her in a good while, too," Merry agreed. She'd spied the creeping hand, too, and rapped its knuckles sharply, but only after it had nabbed a cluster of grapes. "Knocked the jimjams clean out of her, I expect."

"Too bad things between Lady Agatha and Sir Elliot aren't going so well," Grace murmured, sliding more hot turnovers onto a silver chafing dish beside the punch bowl.

Merry pursed her lips. "I'm sure you're wrong. Why, you can see clear as day that he's head over heels for her. It gives me the flutters the way he watches her when he thinks no one's looking." She blushed at the memory of Sir Elliot's face as he'd watched Lady Agatha at church last Sunday. It had definitely not been a proper "church" sort of look.

"Well, that much is true," Grace agreed. "Not that there's been much chance for him to look at her. She's kept to her room all week long, busy at her work. And when she does come out of her room, her eyes is all red-rimmed and her face is pale. She'll work herself ill at this rate."

She selected a petit four from a tray, lifted the tablecloth, and waved it enticingly beneath the table. A little hand emerged, snagged it, and disappeared. Stifled giggles emerged from beneath the table. Tommy Jepson and his sister Sarah, too.

"Well," Merry said tartly, her voice low, "I think Lady Agatha is a trace, well, *scared* of Sir Elliot."

"Scared?" Grace chuckled. "Merry, you innocent goose. He fascinates her. And she's miserable about it. Though why a handsome woman being courted by a man like Sir Elliot should be miserable is beyond me."

"Perhaps she doesn't feel she can marry so far beneath her station?" Merry suggested.

"What station?" Grace hissed in exasperation. "When all is said and done, Merry, Lady Agatha is a woman who hires out her services to whoever can afford them."

"When all is said and done," Merry whispered back heatedly, "she is a duke's daughter."

"Yes, yes," Grace said impatiently. "But she don't seem full of herself, in spite of it. Besides, clear as clear, she's in love with him."

"How can you tell?" whispered Eglantyne, who'd come up unnoticed beside them. Lambikins lounged in her arms, eyeing the turnovers hopefully.

"She's miserable," Merry said.

Eglantyne turned her head and studied Lady Agatha standing across the room. There was no arguing there. The strain of the last days was clearly written on her remarkable face. Dark shadows bruised the flesh beneath her eyes and her complexion looked waxen. A tendril of hair had escaped her heavy chignon and she looked thinner, as though she'd lost a bit of weight.

"She's been working too hard," Eglantyne murmured.

"Fingers to the bone," agreed Grace Poole.

"Burning the midnight oil," Merry nodded.

"Maybe that is why she's been unable to find a single moment to give my son," Atticus said quietly from behind them. All three women jumped. "I hadn't realized you were such a slave-driver, Eglantyne."

Merry and Grace didn't bother refuting such nonsense. Everyone in Little Bidewell knew Eglantyne Bigglesworth was the kindest soul alive.

"Oh!" said Eglantyne in mortification. "How awful you must think us, Professor March, gossiping like this. You must believe that we are interested in Elliot and Lady Agatha only because of the affection we bear them."

Atticus waved aside her agitation. "No need for you to apologize *or* abandon your current fascinating topic of conversation," he reassured her. "You might say I have a vested interest. And I hope you will not think me too terrible if I admit that we share a mutual ambition."

The three women regarded him in surprise.

He nodded. "It's true. I've spent the last few days singing Lady Agatha's praises to Elliot until I've half convinced myself to marry her."

Eglantyne giggled, but Merry shook her head. "She won't have you. She wants Sir Elliot."

"Then why doesn't she *have* him?" Atticus asked in an exasperated stage whisper. "Elliot became so tired of hearing my paeans of praise that he finally told me—and please forgive the use of hard language, but I quote my son in order to illustrate the extent to which he has been pressed—'If I knew what the hell to do, don't you imagine I would have done it by now? The lady will not see me!' "

"He's right," Eglantyne agreed forlornly. "She won't see him. If he arrives by the front door, she scurries out the back. If we have him for lunch, she's too busy to come down. She only came here today because I told her Elliot had been called away on his magisterial duties."

"But he hasn't. He isn't," Atticus said. "He's in the front hall talking to Anton."

"I know," Eglantyne replied placidly.

It took a full minute for the import of her statement to sink in.

"Why, Miss Eglantyne, I never!" breathed Grace Poole. Atticus chuckled and Merry beamed approvingly.

"Here he comes," Merry suddenly whispered.

Elliot had entered the room, his head bent as he listened attentively to Anton, his dark brows drawn together. As Eglantyne watched, he raised his head and saw Lady Agatha. His eyes narrowed, became focused, more intense.

Eglantyne's gaze swung to Lady Agatha. She, too, had seen Elliot enter. For a heartbeat, she froze where she stood. Her dark eyes grew darker and more lustrous, her lips parted, and then her gaze abruptly snapped around, as if gauging her distance from the various doors. She moved back. As if on cue, he paced her, moving forward, his gaze never wavering from her.

There was nowhere for her to escape. She moved quickly toward the open door leading to the garden, but Colonel Vance, who'd dropped his cane at her feet, barred her path. She had no choice but to retrieve it, and by the time she'd returned it to his gnarled hand, Elliot was beside her.

The guests had quieted, as if aware of a drama unfolding in their midst. Even at this distance, Eglantyne could see what little color remained ebb from Lady Agatha's cheeks, the defensive adjustment of her posture, and the anxious tension at the corners of her eyes. By contrast, Elliot was a study in composure. He took possession of the hand she reflexively offered. He bent his dark head over her hand and raised it to his lips and slowly, deliberately, pressed upon her trembling fingers the most ardent kiss Little Bidewell Society had ever witnessed.

The watching ladies reacted variously and tellingly. Most looked a trifle wistful, some were amused, some shocked, but only one looked like she was on the verge of fainting: Lady Agatha.

"Dinner!" Grace loudly prompted Atticus.

"What?" Atticus asked.

"Announce that it's time for dinner!" Grace said urgently. "He'll offer her his arm. She'll have no choice but to accept, and then ..."

"Ah!" Atticus nodded. He stepped forward, clearing his throat. "My dear friends," he announced, "may I invite you in to dinner?"

Elliot was smiling wolfishly down at Lady Agatha. Her chin tilted upright, acknowledging the challenge. Though Eglantyne could not hear him, clearly he was asking Lady Agatha to dine. She saw Lady Agatha hesitate. Then she touched her fingertips to her temples, shaking her head. Elliot stiffened.

Lady Agatha fled. Elliot took one betraying, uncontrollable step after her, and stopped. His face smoothed of expression, only his stiffness betrayed his heightened emotions. Eglantyne's heart twisted with pity.

"Something has upset you, Miss Eglantyne?" Catherine Bunting, moving with a group entering the dining room, paused beside Eglantyne.

Before she considered her words, Eglantyne replied. "I fear Elliot is much affected by Lady Agatha's avoidance of him."

"Affected? Elliot? I doubt it." Catherine smiled sanguinely. "Perhaps his pride has been pricked. Elliot is a most proud man. With every reason to be, of course," she added.

"Catherine, my dear, you'd best have a care lest people think you unfeeling," Atticus said in a low, cool voice. He had overheard her dismiss his son's pain and it made him impatient with her.

She swung on him, color like flags in her pretty cheeks. "I assure you, *I* am not the unfeeling one."

Her eyes were bright. Gads, she was on the point of tears. Hurriedly, Atticus offered her his arm. "Catherine," he said loudly, "before dinner, might I ask you to take a peek at my heliotrope? It looks a bit leggy."

She hesitated a second, but then allowed him to draw her out the door to the garden where they could be alone. "I am sorry, my dear," he said. "I did not realize until just now."

She did not pretend to misunderstand. It was past that. "Please, don't be sorry," she said. "It's really not necessary. I am quite content with my life and Paul."

She took a deep breath, hoping that in voicing these things she could finally purge them from her mind. "For years, Elliot has nurtured the idea that he stood bravely by while I married his best friend. I suppose I should be grateful. I would rather people think I broke his heart than have them pity me." She gave a brief laugh when she saw Atticus's expression. "Apparently he did not even allow you into his confidence. How like him."

Atticus regarded her soberly.

"I broke things off between us, yes. And have since comforted myself with the conviction that war changed him into a man I could not love. The truth is somewhat less palatable. You see, *I* am a woman *he* could not love."

"My dear," Atticus said sympathetically, "I know without question that Elliot loved you once."

"Yes," she said, "he did. But even then, even when he was young—you remember how passionate he seemed when he spoke of certain things, the delight he seemed to draw from the simplest acts? It was just his manner. There was no basis for it."

"My dear," Atticus said, reaching out to pat her hand. She snatched it away.

"I know. Because he never . . . He was never carried away by his love for me."

Before he had left for the Sudan she'd gone to him, knowing she would find in his arms the thing that had always eluded her, the passion that he hoarded, that she'd never tasted and wanted so much. He'd told her he respected her too much, that there were consequences he could not allow her to risk.

"When he returned so changed, I was glad. Do you understand, Atticus?" She'd never called him Atticus before; they'd never been close despite their proximity and having shared such important places in Elliot's life.

"I think so."

"The man I had loved never existed except in my imagination. I will not accept that I was unable to make him . . ." She broke off. "And that *she* can succeed where I failed." How she hated Lady Agatha, with her laughter and her brilliant eyes and her casual manner.

"But of course, I never really tried." She lifted her chin. "By the time Elliot had returned, Paul and I had grown close. He loved me with all the ardency I had wanted from Elliot."

She gazed at him proudly. "There were tears in Paul's eyes when he confessed he loved me. Tears." Her expression was challenging. "Can you imagine Elliot crying? For anything? For anyone?"

Atticus stared at her mutely and she had her answer. She'd made a mistake; she should not have confessed these things after all.

"He has been so very alone, Catherine. He has spent his lifetime searching for a woman he can love as ardently and wholly as Paul loves you," Atticus said gently.

Paul. She had never doubted his love. He was there for her. Always. Supportive and admiring and adoring.

"Perhaps, it is time to let old admirers go," Atticus said and she saw in his careful wording the same respectful consideration his son had always shown her when she had wanted his fire.

Let Elliot go? She'd never had him. But she did have her pride. And she had Paul.

What the devil was Lady Agatha thinking? And what was she doing? Before she realized her own intent, Eglantyne found herself at Elliot's side. For a moment she thought he might excuse himself, but his manners were far too deeply ingrained.

She did not bother with subtlety. She had watched him take his first fence and had rapped his knuckles for stealing apples from her larder. She loved him.

"Lady Agatha has been working so very hard to complete the preparations for the wedding party," she explained. "Every day she receives dozens of telegrams, orders and arrangements. She personally has overseen the sewing of a hundred little silk fans as wedding favors."

"She has reason to be exhausted," Elliot concurred politely.

"Oh, yes!" Eglantyne exclaimed hurriedly. "And there are the floral designs she's made, and she's drawn up plans for the seating arrangements. Very modern, I admit, but most practical, when she explains how the best seats in the house, the ones with a full frontal view of the wedding ceremony, ought to be reserved for the marquis's family. And ours, of course."

"I can see she's been very busy."

"I am sure she would not leave your father's party unless she felt an overwhelming need to do so."

"I am sure you are correct."

There now, Eglantyne thought with satisfaction. He didn't look quite so tense anymore. His usual impeccable manners were standing him in good stead. He even smiled at her, once more the polite gentleman she'd known since his return from the Sudan, fully in command of the situation and himself.

"Will you excuse me, Miss Eglantyne?" he asked and she nodded.

He strolled casually but directly from the nearly empty drawing room. He did not turn into the dining room as Eglantyne expected, but instead walked into the hall and turned to close the door carefully behind him.

A sudden loud crash made her jump. She hurried to the hall door and opened it, looking outside. No one was there. But the large porcelain vase that generally stood on the hall table lay on the floor, shattered into a thousand pieces.

As if someone had hurled it against the wall.

An hour later, Letty sat in the library at The Hollies. She heard one of the maids speaking to someone who sounded very like Elliot. She rose swiftly, and the silk fan she'd been listlessly embroidering fell to her feet. For a moment, panic and pleasure vied for precedence until logic took hold. Elliot would never leave his guests. She stooped to retrieve the fan.

"Letty."

She bolted upright, clutching the fan like a talisman to her chest. He looked so handsome and severe. He searched her face, and she wished she knew what he read there, wished she could adequately hide the ache in her heart.

She wanted to run to him, she wanted to feel him enfold her in his arms. All she had ever desired reposed there. It made standing motionless the hardest thing she'd ever done.

But the knowledge that whatever joy she might know in his arms could only be temporary stayed her. The world would not vanish, the past would reach out and rip her from his embrace. And the longer she stayed in Little Bidewell, the more likely the wound caused by that rending would be mortal . . . to both of them.

He was a knight, soon to be a baron. He had a family name to honor and a position of trust and responsibility to uphold.

"This can't go on any longer." His voice brooked no argument. "This is absurd."

He was right; this couldn't go on. Every day she'd tried vainly to find a happy ending for them. There should be a way. In all the popular plays, the poor girl managed against all odds to gain the handsome aristocrat's heart. But this was not musical farce, and the happy ending she so desperately sought refused to materialize.

He moved cautiously closer. "Letty. You can't tell me you have no feelings for me. I won't believe that."

She wouldn't deny it. Or him. He held one hand out. She shook her head, fearful that if he came closer all her resolve to spare them both would vanish.

"Don't back away from me, Letty. I couldn't stand that. I won't press myself on you," he said. "I have done this poorly. I understand. And I know that a woman like you expects a certain standard—" He broke off abruptly and raked his hand through his hair, looking away.

"Damn it, Letty, there is *no* woman like you," he said, suddenly savage. "How am I to follow some template of behavior when everything in me urges me to act from the heart? Do you know," his gaze speared her where she stood, "that since I have loved you, I have not regretted one word, one glance, one touch? And I am so certain in loving you, so sure of it, of us, that I cannot conceive that you regret any of these things, either."

He gave a humorless laugh. "Loving you has made me a monster of egotism, my dear. But there it is. I am fearless of misstep, unable to conceive that I could err so gravely that you would turn from me." His voice strained with his need to convince her. But she needed no convincing. She knew he loved her.

"I could never turn from you," she breathed. He did not hear her. He'd paced a few steps away from her, once more raking his hand through his hair before turning back. When he next spoke his agitation had vanished; his voice was deep and ardent and clear.

"A heart filled with such conviction cannot exist independently. I could not be so certain without your love, Letty. All I ask is that you give me a chance to woo you. Tell me what you want and I will do it. But do not run from this. Do not deny it. Do not deny us."

Dear God, when he spoke like this she could almost believe that he did not care for convention or dignity or Society, and that loving her was the most important thing in his life. She trembled on the cusp of hope.

"I don't dare. Things are much more complicated than they appear and I am . . . I am ashamed."

Darkness flooded his face. His gaze sharpened. "I never expected things to be easy, Letty. Only confide in me and I swear I will make things right. As for shame, I am convinced there is nothing you have done that is unforgivable."

She believed him, God help her. She only needed to tell him. She held out her hand and instantly he was by her side, wrapping her hand in his and raising it to his mouth, kissing the back of her hand before turning her fist over and uncurling her stiff fingers and pressing his lips to the center of her palm.

Without quite meaning to, she raised her free hand to his bowed head. Her fingers shivered a fraction of an inch above the dark, silky locks she longed to caress.

"Letty," he murmured against her open palm, "Please, trust me."

"I do. I want to. I—"

"Lady Agatha!" Cabot's voice boomed anxiously from the doorway. Letty looked about in confusion. She hadn't even heard him knock and he stood in the open doorway, his face filled with horror.

Elliot straightened slowly, his expression taut with anger as foreign to his face as humility was to a lord's. "What is it, Cabot?"

"A gentleman to see you, Lady Agatha."

"A gentleman? What gentleman?"

A figure appeared behind Cabot. Of medium

height, the man was barrel-chested and heavy through the shoulders. He doffed a smart bowler as he entered, and his thick blond hair shone like guineas in the late afternoon light. He spied her, and his square, bluntly handsome face bloomed with an expression of undeniable pleasure.

"Why, Letty, my dear," he said in an accent that had never quite lost its Cockney tang. "None other than your fiancé, Nick Sparkle."

Chapter 27

If a man brings a cabbage to
the theater, he is going to throw it.

"QUITE A PLUM SETUP YOU 'AVE 'ERE, LETTY-me-love," Nick said. He strolled restlessly about the library with his hands clasped lightly behind his back, gauging and evaluating the contents.

Letty could not take her eyes from him. It was as if she'd wakened to a nightmare. She could barely breathe. Her pulse hammered thickly in her temples.

Elliot had left within minutes of Nick's entrance. There had been one instant when his gaze had swung on her and she had seen his betrayal and shock, and then Nick had been in front of him, pumping his hand and introducing himself. Elliot had responded in kind, every vestige of the emotion he'd revealed erased from his face as though they'd only been figments of Letty's imagination. He'd not looked at her again, not even when he'd bid them good-bye.

Something died within her. Something precious and fragile and essential was irretrievably lost.

"Done well this time, Letty. Small wonder you come over all high-minded and moral. You had other plans. Better plans than mine."

"How did you find me?" she asked tonelessly.

"Old Sammy here tipped your hand, love," he said motioning toward where Cabot stood miserably.

"I'm sorry, Letty," Cabot said. "I didn't realize when I wrote Ben that he'd say anything to *him*."

"Well, now, Sammy, you mustn't blame the old bugger. He weren't exactly forthcoming with the information. Needed a spot of encouraging, he did."

Cabot's face flamed with anger and he took a step forward. The pleasant façade dropped from Nick's handsome face like a cheap mask, revealing the pitilessness that was the true reflection of his nature. "I wouldn't, if I was you, Sammy. You'd be heaving your guts up inside a minute."

"Listen to him, Cabot," Letty cried, putting herself between the two men. "He's right. You'll only get hurt."

Nick watched Cabot hopefully. When it was clear the older man would not fight, he sneered and turned to Letty.

"Ah, relax," he sneered. "I didn't touch the fool. I only told him he was gettin' a bit long in the tooth to be blown across a stage, and a word in the manager's ear would have him out in the streets by nightfall."

His expression turned offended. "Whatcha think, Letty? That I'd hurt the old codger? You oughta know I'm not that sort. Or do you think a bloke has to have a silk cravat like your gentleman friend there in order to have fine feelings?" he sneered.

She wouldn't discuss Elliot with him and turned her head. He grabbed her arm and she winced. Once again, Cabot tensed. "It's all right, Cabot," Letty said quickly. "If you would go into the hall and keep an eye out for the Bigglesworths, I'd appreciate it. I need to talk to Nick."

Cabot didn't look happy about it, but he did as she asked. As soon as he was gone, Nick flopped down on the chintz-covered settee, his checked suit and gaiters as out of place in these surroundings as a . . . as a music hall singer, Letty thought morosely.

Something of her thoughts must have shown on her face, for Nick's grin widened. "There's my girl. A little bitter to counter all that sweet."

"You have to leave, Nick. This isn't what you think. I didn't plan on this at all. I just found a ticket and arrived here and the folks thought I was—"

"This here Lady Agatha," Nick interupted, nodding. "Yes. I know all about it. Ben showed me Sammy's letter."

"Cabot," Letty corrected in a low voice. "His name is Samuel Cabot."

"You can call him whatever you like. To me and the rest of the world, he's Sam-Sam, The Spaniel-Faced Boy. Just like you're Letty Potts, sometime musical artiste, but much more often an artiste of a different persuasion, eh?"

She felt ill. Hearing it said out loud, she knew exactly what she was and always had been. She'd thought of con games as nothing more than a laugh and a wink at people who could afford it. It had never seemed wrong. It did now.

It wasn't the money. The Bigglesworths and their sort could afford to have a few pieces of silver nabbed from them. It was that other theft that mattered, the theft she'd never recognized before: stealing their trust and abusing it. The victims of that sort of theft always got hurt.

Nick shook his head. "I got to hand it to you, Letty. You always did have a knack for falling into the slops and coming up smelling like roses. And you've done so this time, too."

He wagged a finger at her. "But don't try and tell me you weren't thinking to take advantage of your good fortune, 'cause I know you, Letty. Never let an opportunity pass without milking it for all it's worth, and never will. So out with it. What's the dodge?"

She regarded him with repugnance. He was wrong this time. She couldn't hurt these people. She wouldn't.

"There is no scam, Nick. I'm just helping these folks out in exchange for a soft bed and some nice meals. As soon as I'm done, I'm leaving, and that's the gospel truth, take it or leave it."

The cockiness faded in his expression along with his smile. "I'll leave it."

He pushed himself to his feet and came to her side. He tilted her chin up with a blunt, stubby finger. "Don't think I don't understand, me girl. You come 'ere, get treated like royalty, everyone all sweetness and light, and pretty soon you're thinking what decent sorts they are and what a shame it'd be to hurt their feelings. And you like it that you're feeling all expansive and treacly. Makes you feel good about yerself."

She stared at him in fascinated horror. His words came too close to the truth. What if it was all self-delusion? What if she'd only convinced herself she'd changed because it didn't cost her anything, or anyone else, either?

He read the confusion in her eyes and smiled. He'd always been a baffling combination of perceptiveness and brutality. It was what made him so good at his job.

"It's easy to be pious when you got a feather bed to sleep in. But this ain't real, love. It's time to wake up, Letty." He moved closer. "How's it go in all those fairy tales? You wake the princess with a kiss."

He clasped her shoulders and leaned toward her. She stood very, very still, willing herself not to cringe when his lips met hers. He'd kissed her dozens of times, but this time it felt awful, not only a violation but a betrayal. And not only of Elliot, but of herself.

He drew back. His face was ugly, his voice rough. "So that's the way it is, eh? You and that black-haired sap. I shoulda known it would take more than a feather pillow and a butter cake to make you forget what's what. How much more? *How far has it gone between you and him, Letty?*"

"You're talking nonsense," she said stiffly. He'd always been jealous. Once he'd even beaten a particularly persistent admirer. She didn't dare think what he could do to Elliot if he wanted.

His eyes narrowed. "Lookit you. Pissed as poison that I should even sully 'is name by speaking it."

"You're being silly. He's a knight."

"And he thinks you're a duke's get. And a good thing, too. 'Cause if I thought 'e had enough red blood in him to do anything with you, I'd kill him. God! Don't look at me like that on some other man's account!" Real hurt flared in his bright green eyes. His skin grew mottled with blood. "Damn you, Letty. Damn you! Think you're too good for the likes of me, do you?"

"No, Nick," she answered, reaching out to clasp his forearm. "No, it isn't—"

"Shudup!" He flung her hand away with such violence she staggered back. He reached for her as though he regretted his act, but then the ugliness flowed back into his face and his hand dropped to his side. "I loved you, Letty. No man loved a woman as much as I loved you."

"Nick—"

"Treated you like a queen, I did. Like a bloomin' lady. I never pushed to get you into bed, never asked more than you were willin' to give, because I always figured someday we'd get wed and you'd be mine and you'd appreciate the time I took with you. Because I cared what you thought, Letty. I cared about what *you* wanted."

The rims of his eyes had grown red. "I never hurt one person you cared about. Not even when I was trying to get you to seeing things my way with that little job I'd planned. I could 'ave. I could 'ave brought you to heel, by just breaking someone's leg or arm. But I didn't. Because I didn't want to hurt *you*, Letty."

He had loved her. At least, as much as Nick could love, and he really believed that stopping at burning down her house and only threatening theater managers were acts of charity on his part. And because Letty loved just as hopelessly as Nick did, she understood his pain.

"Nick," she said. "I am so—"

"*Don't you say it!*" he broke in violently. "No one's sorry for Nick Sparkle. *No one.* 'Specially not some daft cow wearing airs. Think *'e'll* want you when 'e finds out you're just a skirt-wearing dodge?" He laughed nastily.

"I know," Letty said. "I know. But it doesn't make any difference, Nick. I still won't help you."

"Listen," he said, ignoring her. "I got my own plans and you're part of them. You just keep these Bigglesworths happy for a few days and leave the rest to me."

"And if I don't?"

"And if you don't, well, I guess I'll just have to leave."

She looked up, suddenly hopeful. "Oh, Nick!"

He stroked the side of her cheek with his thumb. "Course, I'll have to write a little note to this Sir Elliot and these Bigglesworths. A little note that says just what 'Lady Agatha' is been up to these past five years. You know. A few details about a mind-reading scam down Kensington way, and a bean-and-cups game—"

"I get the idea, Nick. No need to continue."

His caress turned into a pinch. "Good. Then, like I

said, you just keep on doing what you been doing and I'll take care of the rest. That sound good to you, Letty?"

She stared at him with disdain.

He chucked her lightly under the chin. "I thought so."

Atticus's guests had left. Outside the French doors, the garden was blanketed in warm, perfumed night. A perfect evening for courting a woman, which is exactly what Atticus had assumed Elliot was doing when he disappeared from the party. He'd thought Elliot had gone after the fleeing Lady Agatha. But perhaps he'd been wrong, because certainly Elliot hadn't been absent long.

When Merry had whispered in his ear that Elliot had returned, he'd fully expected his son to rejoin them. He hadn't. So after bidding his guests good evening, he'd sought his son. He'd found him prowling the length of the library, his back and shoulders tensed as a caged tiger's.

"It's a shame Lady Agatha was taken ill," Atticus said carefully.

Elliot stopped his stalking. "Yes."

"She doesn't seem a woman in fragile health."

"No."

Atticus knew his son. Elliot was proudly self-sufficient. He'd never willingly burden another with his problems, and the watch he'd kept on his emotions was ever vigilant. *She'd* been changing it. But now . . .

"Still, Eglantyne says Lady Agatha has been most

assiduous in her work, quite determined to have it completed before she leaves. Undoubtedly that accounts for her indisposition."

"I am sure you are correct," Elliot murmured. He stared unseeingly out into the night.

"Did you go to see how she was faring?" Atticus asked mildly. "I hope you found her comfortable?"

Elliot looked up, frowning thoughtfully. "Excuse me, sir? You were saying?"

"How did you find Lady Agatha?"

"With her fiancé." Elliot's frowned deepened, his expression absorbed and his voice distracted. "And, no, she does not look well."

Atticus's jaw dropped. A sense of betrayal swept through him, stunning him with its force. In no manner, by either direct word or inference, had Lady Agatha suggested she was betrothed. How dare she play so fast and loose with Elliot's affections? How *dare* she pretend to a freedom she did not own?

"Dear God, Elliot," Atticus said, aghast. "I had no idea . . . I . . . I don't know what to say. That she was affianced never occurred to me."

Elliot looked up. "It didn't occur to anyone else, either," he said slowly. *"Anyone."*

"Elliot," Atticus began, but his son had picked up his coat from the chair on which he'd flung it.

"I'm going into the village," he said. "Don't bother waiting up for me."

"We can't let him rob the Bigglesworths. Especially since he's already announced he's Lady Agatha's fiancé."

Cabot paced back and forth in Letty's room, his hands clasped in a white-knuckled grip behind his back. "Can you imagine the scandal? The Bigglesworths will be the laughingstock of Society, first to be duped by a feather merchant pretending to be a duke's daughter, and then to be robbed by her associate. I wouldn't be surprised if the Sheffields called the wedding off."

Guilt and remorse combined to set Letty's hands shaking like an old woman's. She clenched them and unclenched them, focusing on making them still so that she wouldn't have to think. There was nothing she could do except that which she already was doing.

Cabot stopped his incessant pacing. "Why, do you know he's downstairs with the Bigglesworths right now? Introduced himself as smoothly as oil on flat water, registering offended surprise that you hadn't told them about him."

He blew out an unhappy sigh. "He can do the gentleman act when he wants to, you know. A young flash modern, but still just enough manners to make him look authentic. You taught him that."

Letty twisted her hands together. "I know."

"He told them he 'couldn't stand to be separated from you for one more day' and that he was sure they'd understand and, by the way, was there some small inn somewhere that might accommodate him while he was here?'

"It made me cringe to hear. Miss Eglantyne did exactly what you would expect: She begged him to stay here."

"Oh, no," Letty murmured, sitting heavily on the edge of the bed. "Poor Eglantyne."

"Yes," Cabot avowed. "And looking guilty as sin."

"Guilty?" Letty asked in confusion. "What has she to be guilty about?"

"Oh, Letty," Cabot said despairingly. "Didn't you notice . . . of course not, you were too occupied with him and that's exactly how they wanted it to be."

"What are you talking about?"

"Miss Eglantyne and the rest of the staff have been doing everything within their powers to make a match of you and Sir Elliot."

Dear God. The fools. The darlings. "And you allowed them to do so?"

"I didn't have any alternative," Cabot defended himself. "How was I to explain that the two of you were unsuited for one another? And how was I to know that their machinations would actually bear fruit."

She glanced up.

"Don't deny it, Letty. I've seen how you react to one another." The paternalistic disapproval abruptly vanished, leaving only fatherly exasperation. He sat down beside her. "What the devil were you thinking, girl?"

"I wasn't thinking." *I was feeling. I still am feeling, God help me.* "And Miss Eglantyne was also involved?"

"Yes. And from the look of her when she was presented with your 'future husband,' she is overcome with remorse at having interfered in your life. She doesn't do that sort of thing, you know. She must have felt very strongly to act as she did."

"If you are trying to make me feel guilty, you're too late," Letty said. "I am already full up with guilt."

He sighed heavily. "Forgive me, Letty. I'm as much

to blame as you are. But we mustn't let Nick hurt them more than . . . well, we mustn't!"

Letty stood up. "He isn't going to rob the Bigglesworths. I promise."

She lifted the satchel she'd packed Lady Agatha's belongings in and dumped the contents onto her bed. She began stowing different clothes inside, warm clothing that she could wear on a packet ship across the North Sea.

"What are you going to do?" he asked.

"I shall write Sir Elliot a letter and tell him who Nick Sparkle is," *and who I am,* "and what he plans to do." *And what I planned.*

"But, Letty—"

"I'll go into Little Bidewell at first light. The passenger train departs the station at ten. I'll be on it." She folded a shirtwaist. "If you could just hold off sending the letter to Sir Elliot until noon, I'd be much obliged."

Cabot frowned. "What about Nick? What if he comes looking for you?"

"He won't. Nick Sparkle never met a morning he didn't despise. If he asks after me, tell him I'm sick in bed. He ought to believe that readily enough."

Cabot nodded. "All right. You'll stop Nick from stealing from the Bigglesworths, but what about the scandal? What about Miss Angela?"

Was there no end to the skein she must unravel? Letty closed her eyes briefly. Her head throbbed. She had to concentrate on Angela. She mustn't think about Elliot. About what his expression would be when he read her letter, about the repugnance he would feel, about how disgusted he would be at having told her he loved her.

"Tell the Bigglesworths that I once worked for Lady Agatha. They'll believe you." She held up her hand forestalling him. "As you once pointed out, it's in Lady Agatha's best interest to support me if she returns to England.

"And if she doesn't return, who's to refute my claim that I was once her assistant? Nick? We only met five years ago. You've known me longer. You can support me.

"Tell the Bigglesworths that I only fell into bad company after my mother died. Tell them I know what I'm doing, and that everything will be fine as long as they don't mention me to the Sheffields."

"You don't think anyone in Little Bidewell will tell the Sheffields?" Cabot asked, unconvinced.

"With whom in Little Bidewell is the Marquis of Cotton's mama going to be exchanging tattle?" Letty asked flatly. She snapped the satchel shut. "No. You need only get the wedding over and done with. Later, if something should leak out, well, it will only make the Sheffield's dinner parties more interesting. Scandal is always more palatable if it's anecdotal."

It didn't matter that it was her life, her heart, that would be discussed, then abandoned along with the fish course.

Cabot's gaze met hers and slid away. "Is there any reason the Bigglesworths shouldn't follow the plans you made for the wedding party?"

She flushed. "Everything is nearly done," she said

quietly. "Grace Poole and the caterer are taking care of the food and the service. I've ordered in all the decorations. The favors and garlands are complete.

"Angela, Eglantyne, and you, for that matter, know how things are to be arranged, and I have no doubt the servants can set things up. I've left sketches. Merry does my room; I've no doubt she knows where all the bills, receipts and correspondence are kept.

"Don't worry. Everyone I've contracted with in London is trustworthy and utterly dependable."

She realized how amusing that must sound coming from someone who was running away, and smiled. "I mean it, Cabot. It will not be a walk in the park, but it's doable."

Chapter 28

A professional knows
when the performance is over.

THE DAWN CREPT IN MOIST AND GRAVID, the air condensing on the backs of the dray horses standing before the greengrocers. The peony at the front of the teashop bowed under the weight of dew and the lace café curtains drooped.

Letty stood on the platform outside the train station with her ticket in her hand. Ham had dropped her off in town a half-hour ago. It would be another hour before her train left.

Only a few people were on the streets, the dampness being uncomfortable. Letty didn't mind. The air smelled freshly washed and fertile, green with spring's promise and dark with earth's wealth.

The scent awoke memories of walking hand in hand with her mother down a country lane. She'd thought she belonged there, until Vernice Fallontrue had told her she didn't. Just like she'd thought her father would love her if only he had the chance. And that the music hall was her home and the performers her family . . . until her mother died and Alf had been too grief-stricken to work. Then she'd discovered that her "home" held no place for a girl who wouldn't wear tights and who spoke with a high-class accent. So she'd found work in the musical productions and been told she didn't have the emotional range necessary to make it big.

All her life she'd made the best of bad situations. Then one night, soon after her mother had died, the same night Nick Sparkle had introduced her to champagne, one cold, sleepless night when a girl from the chorus had thrown herself into the Thames because she was pregnant, Letty decided to make things happen *for* her and not *to* her.

She'd stood by that creed. No softness, because the world wasn't soft; lots of laughter, because if you were in on the joke, the joke couldn't be on you; no wanting what you couldn't take, because the world never gave.

Or so she thought.

But here she was again, standing with a packed bag, waiting for the next act. She was just a journeyman after all.

But life still hadn't brought her to bay. She smiled. She was still on her feet, still running strong. She looked down. Fagin, on the other hand, didn't appear to have any desire to run, walk or, for that matter, stand. He huddled in a miserable little pile at her feet, staring up at her disconsolately.

He hadn't wanted to come with her. She'd had to lure him with a bit of sausage and lead him after her with a braided length of satin. Something tightened in her throat.

Fagin had never worn a collar in his life. He'd never needed any encouragement to get him to follow her. He'd always been her shadow, because if she disappeared he'd be on his own. Poor little blighter. In the whole world she was the only thing he could depend on, and that had been more through his vigilance than hers. She'd taken him for granted.

"Come on, Fay," she coaxed. "We've had an adventure is all. And we'll have others, you'll see. We'll go to Norway. You think kippers are tasty? Wait until you taste salmon."

He looked off in the direction of The Hollies and Eglantyne. Eglantyne who'd never taken his affection for granted.

"It's a chance to start all over again and, by God, if that isn't a lark, what is?"

Fagin stood up to walk to the end of his tether. She felt her smile freeze.

"G'day, Lady Agatha." Mrs. Jepson's nursemaid bobbed her head, hurrying by pushing the perambulator in which the youngest Jepson wailed enthusiastically. The gulls wheeled overhead, crying plaintively. A cat slunk from under the platform and darted across the street. Fagin watched it listlessly.

"All right," Letty whispered, untying the satin ribbon from around Fagin's neck. "You just take care of Eglantyne, you hear?"

Fagin cocked his foolish, furry face, his gaze as somber and impenetrable as ever. He didn't lick her face. He wasn't a licking sort of dog. But he wagged his tail once, tentatively, and then trotted off down the street, dodging the farrier's cart as he headed back to Eglantyne, back home.

She watched him go with tears in her eyes, wanting to follow him so much that it felt as if her spirit were pulling free of her flesh to do so. But she couldn't. She didn't belong. She wasn't Lady Agatha Whyte. She was Letty Potts, whoever that was. She sniffed, trying to find a caustic smile for the thought and failing.

There was only one possible way she could ever discover how much of Lady Agatha was Letty Potts and how much of Letty Potts was Lady Agatha. And that was ridiculous. She looked overhead. The spiraling flock of gulls was fading back to the horizon, returning to the sea. In the distance, Fagin was a small dark blotch, running now. "Get," she whispered hoarsely. "Run faster, Fay."

She clutched the train ticket tighter and waited for the sense of escape to come over her as it had a dozen times before, that heady sensation of having just scooted through the clanging gate, of eluding the thrown net. It didn't come. She was running again, but she wasn't escaping. She'd been chased to ground a long, long time ago.

And there was only one way out, she realized with sudden and absolute certainty. She tore the ticket in half, adjusted her hat, and stepped off the train platform.

Whoever she was, Letty Potts was no coward.

* * *

The flustered-looking clerk showed her into Elliot's office. He was seated behind a desk covered in papers and ledgers and such. A brawny young man she recognized as the local constable stood on the other side of it. On seeing her, Elliot rose immediately to his feet. The young constable stammered a good morning before suggesting that he should be going.

Elliot came around to her side of the desk, his expression careful and his manner, as always, impeccable. She searched his face for some signs of the pain and betrayal she knew he had felt when Nick had introduced himself as her fiancé. His mouth was tense, his eyes looked weary.

"Lady Agatha, won't you be seated?"

"I prefer to stand."

"Then would you be so kind as to wait while I show the constable out? I shan't be but a few minutes."

"Of course."

He shut the door behind him, leaving her in the office. She moved farther into the room, looking about. It was a serviceable, impersonal room, the furnishings undistinguished and not particularly comfortable, the cabinets mismatched and overflowing. On his desk lay a broad fan of letters.

She glanced down and was surprised to recognize some of the names she saw. They were from politicians and labor organizers. She stepped back, frowning slightly. She'd no idea Elliot was so well known amongst London's political elite. But hadn't his father alluded to such?

The door opened and Elliot reentered. "Please, won't you be seated?"

She shook her head. She couldn't pretend this was a social call. And of course, he could not be seated in her presence. "As you will. Brown, would you please go down to Shrimpton's and bring us tea?" he called to his clerk before returning his attention to her.

He looked exactly as he had the first day she'd seen him. His boiled white shirt could not have been crisper or whiter. Beneath the starched collar, his gray silk tie was perfectly knotted. The dark blue coat stretched across his broad shoulders would be a tailor's pride. Even his hair was immaculately neat.

Only his expression had changed. He looked cool, politely interested, and wary. He made no effort to close the distance between them. She might have been a client he'd only just first met, and not a woman with whom he'd shared his bed and body.

"You have something you wished to see me about, Lady Agatha?" he asked. She could hear the effort his placid manner caused him in his tone.

"Yes." She took a deep, steadying breath. "I am not Lady Agatha Whyte."

His brows drew together. She'd expected an outburst, some expression of outrage. None came.

"My name is Letty Potts," she said, hurrying now, fearful that if she stopped she would not have the courage to continue. "I am a musical comedienne." With difficulty she met his gaze. It was impossible to tell what thoughts he held behind those guarded eyes. "At least," she said, "that is what I do most of the time."

He studied her for long moments. "And what do you do those times you are not onstage?" he finally asked.

She swallowed. "I work with Nick Sparkle."

He betrayed himself for an instant in the involuntary tightening of his jaw. "Your fiancé?"

"No!" The word burst from her. "I never . . . you *know* I have never . . . I *would* never—" This was one offense she *could* not let him think her capable of. "I would never have made love with you if I had promised to marry another."

A muscle jumped at the angle of his jaw. "Letty—"

"Please. Let me continue." She would not let him think she would use their relationship to win free of her past.

"Nick and I duped people out of their money. It's as simple as that. I'd act the lady, luring the toffs into feeling comfortable with whatever scam Nick had running. And then Nick would put the sting on them."

She could not put it more clearly, nor could it sound any uglier. That had been her intent.

"I see," he said. "And what was the 'scam' in Little Bidewell to be?"

"There wasn't one," she said. "This was all an accident."

He drew back as though she'd struck him. Too late she realized what she'd implied. A cry of distress broke from her. "My coming here was an accident," she said. "Nick had this plan, this con he wanted to run. I didn't want to do it, and when I refused to be part of it, he made it so I couldn't get any legit work in town. When I still wouldn't do it, he burned down my boarding house, thinking I wouldn't have any choice then."

The words tumbled out, her heartbeat racing to keep up. Her hands were so tightly clenched together that her fingers were growing numb. But she didn't dare stop now. She stared fixedly at the floor because if she looked at him she feared her courage would flag.

"So I ran away. To the train station. Only I didn't have any money on account of the fire, and I couldn't afford a ticket, and then this lady came by and she was with this French chap and he talked her into going off with him and she dropped her ticket on her way out and I . . ." She glanced up. "I just took the opportunity as it presented itself."

He watched her steadily, his expression unreadable.

"I didn't mean to impersonate her," she said earnestly. "It never even occurred to me until I stepped off that train and all those people were there staring at me as if I were the answer to their prayers.

"And I wouldn't have done anything even then, except that someone said her things were all waiting for me. I didn't have anything, you see. It was all burnt in the fire. So that decided it, because I'm not a good person."

Why wouldn't he say something?

"I tried to tell you that day in the carriage not to trust me. But I swear, I didn't think it would hurt anyone, except maybe this Lady Agatha. But she wasn't going to need her luggage. I did."

There. The recitation she'd practiced all the long

way down the street to his offices was nearly over. "So I came to The Hollies. Only it wasn't as easy as I'd thought it would be. Because there was Angela with her problem with that rotten boy, and Eglantyne who was breaking her heart over missing her chick before she'd even left the henhouse, and Anton with his worries about being good enough for the Sheffields, and . . ." *And you.*

"I knew Cabot from when from my folks were in the variety shows. Before I knew it, he'd convinced me I could pull this wedding thingie off and no one would get hurt. Only Nick found me." She finished, squeezing her eyes shut, a coward after all.

" 'No one would get hurt,' " she heard him say in a tone she could not interpret.

She opened her eyes. His face was stark, his eyes bright with unmasked pain. She could not stand it. She went to him, reaching out to touch him, only he grabbed her upper arms first, trembling with the effort it cost him not to shake her.

"Did you think I told you I loved you to get you into my bed?" he demanded.

"No," she denied vehemently. "No!"

"How could you think no one would be hurt when you let me love you, let me . . . How could you think *this wouldn't hurt?*"

Her face became ashen, her eyes stricken. But he'd withstood as much as he could; he was not as strong as he needed to be. From the moment she'd walked in and it had become clear she had come to confess he'd been lost, unable to think clearly. At first he'd been dubious, then cautious. Finally he'd seen that her anguish was sincere, her resignation real. And by the obvious omissions that would have guaranteed her his sympathy, if not leniency, she'd made him fall in love with her all over again.

She wasn't Lady Agatha Whyte. He didn't care. She was brave and valiant and trying so damned hard to make it right. Honesty was easy when it was rewarded, not so easy when it brought only the promise of punishment. And yet, she was here, unflinchingly proclaiming her own culpability. She was not looking for forgiveness, he realized. She wanted atonement.

But when she'd said she hadn't thought it would hurt anyone, his temper had flared, aggravated by sleeplessness and the jealousy that had cut mortally deep when that man claimed her as his.

"Forgive me," he said stiffly. "I had no right—"

"You have every right," she said heatedly. "*I didn't think.* I was selfish. I wanted the first time I . . . made love to be with someone I loved. And who loved me." Her mouth twisted wryly. "Or at least loved the woman he thought me to be."

Her answer drained the last bits of anger from him. She loved him. Nothing else mattered. His hands slipped down her arms to her hands.

"Letty . . ." He turned her palms up. "Letty, I—"

He forgot whatever he'd been about to say, stunned by the sight of the dark purple smudges that stood out like brands on her wrists. "Did he do this?"

"It doesn't matter." She tried to pull away. He could see the fear in her. This had not been the first time she'd known violence, he'd swear it.

"Please," she whispered. Fear for Elliot climbed in

her throat. She could see his desire for retribution in the fire of his gaze, the tension in his neck and shoulders. He would only get hurt. Nick was strong and merciless. He didn't fight like a gentleman; he fought to hurt his enemy by any means possible. "Please. It was an accident. He didn't mean to hurt me—"

A sharp, perfunctory rap interrupted her. Elliot released her hands and stepped away from her. "Come in."

Nick Sparkle entered. His broad grin thinned when he saw her, but he strode through the office with all appearances of confidence.

"Agatha, my dear," he said. "So, here you are. The Bigglesworths' driver said he'd taken you into Little Bidewell for the day. I couldn't imagine why. Not much here to keep a body busy all of a day." His bright, malicious gaze flickered toward where Elliot stood coolly appraising him. "Or is there?"

His words stank of innuendo. Color rose in Elliot's face. Letty moved quickly between the two men just as the clerk returned bearing a wooden tray. With a shy smile, he placed it on Elliot's desk.

"Tea," Nick said. "How cozy. And how like you, Agatha, to make such warm friends in so short a time."

"I dislike your tone, Mr. Sparkle," Elliot said.

"Really? I dislike your familiarity with my bride-to-be." Abruptly, Letty realized that Nick had no idea why she was here. She almost laughed. Of course not. It would never occur to him that she might give him—and, in the course of doing so, herself—up to the law. Instead, he thought she was here on a tryst!

"If you will excuse me a minute, Mr. Sparkle," Elliot said. He motioned for his clerk. "Be a lad and run down to the farrier's. Tell Kevin I'll likely need his help with that gelding I told him about earlier."

The young clerk's eyes grew round. With a bob of his head, he hurried out of the room.

"Didn't want the boy to hear what you been up to, aye?" Nick sneered. His gentlemanly mien had fallen off. He looked ugly.

"Nick, please," Letty begged.

Elliot had moved forward, but her voice checked him. With a sound of frustration, he turned his back on Nick and went round to the other side of his desk, as though needing to put some obstacle between them.

"Mr. Sparkle," Elliot said, "whatever the young lady and I have been 'up to' is no concern of yours."

"Well, that's a right cosmopolitan view of things," Nick said with a bitter laugh. "Mayhaps I'm a bit old-fashioned, but I don't like my future wife playing fast and loose with another man."

"I wouldn't, either. If the lady in question was, in-deed, promised to me," Elliot said coldly. "But this lady says that you are not now, nor ever have been, engaged to be married."

At this Nick shot her an uncertain look. "What does she say we are, then?"

The sound of hurrying footsteps clattered heavily in the outer hallway. The door swung open and the young constable, Brown, came through it followed by a huge, powerfully built man.

"Garth, too? Very well," Elliot said, regarding Nick

with unmistakable loathing. "And to answer you, Mr. Sparkle, she says you are partners in confidence games. A charge I have the verification for here, in this telegram." He lifted a sheet of paper from his desktop.

Nick's surprise lasted only a few seconds. He hadn't survived in his profession by being slow-witted. He swung around but found his path barred by the two large and formidable-looking men, one of whom held a baton.

"You are under arrest, Mr. Sparkle, for conspiracy to commit fraud," Elliot said. His cool, unreadable gaze swung to Letty. "As are you, Letty Potts."

She knew it was coming. It was why she'd come here, after all. To get it done and over, to mark the bill paid, once and for all. But the breath still left her lungs in a whoosh, and her head spun dizzily.

She was so intent on Elliot that Nick nearly got to her. He lunged at her, reaching out to take her hostage, or simply to punish her.

Elliot, caught behind the desk, shouted. Kevin, standing closest, grabbed Nick's arm, wrenching it savagely up behind his back and thrusting the baton under his chin, jerking it back. At the same time, Garth seized his other arm.

Nick didn't fight long. He was no fool; he knew when he was outnumbered. But the look he cast at Letty made a thousand vile promises.

"You stupid bitch!" Nick ground out. "You stupid, useless slut. I hope it was worth it, whatever pleasure you got on him."

"You will shut up, Mr. Sparkle," Elliot's voice was

quiet and low, but lethal. Even Nick must have sensed that Elliot held his fury in check only by the slimmest thread, for though he glared at her and spat at her feet, he remained mute.

Only as the two men dragged him from the office did he dare speak one last time. "I hope it was worth your life, Letty."

"I'm sure of it," she answered.

Chapter 29

The villain gets to cheat, lie, steal,
and kick the dog, because in the end
you shoot him.

ELLIOT ASKED THE CLERK TO ESCORT LETTY back to The Hollies and ask the Bigglesworths to allow her to remain until he'd sent word. It would take a few days for him to call together a hearing. He disliked it, but he could see no alternative. She'd confessed to criminal intent and he was the magistrate. And while he could have quite easily released her to her own devices, she quite clearly expected him to act impartially.

Odd that it should be this, her implicit belief in his honor, that kept him honorable.

"What are we to do with him?" Kevin asked, jerking his head toward the spare back room in which they'd locked Nick Sparkle.

"Ever been to London, Kevin?" Elliot asked.

"Nah. Been here all my life and well you know it, Sir Elliot."

"Then it's time you went," Elliot said. "I want you to go down to the train station and buy two tickets in a private compartment to London on the dinner train tonight. On the way, stop at the telegraph station and send a wire to the Chapel Street Police Station, to Lieutenant Runcorn, stating that you will be arriving with your prisoner, Nick Sparkle, at Paddington Station on the eight o'clock tomorrow morning."

The young man's face reddened with pride. "Coo, sir. You mean it?"

"I do. And you'd best also stop and get some locks for the windows and door."

"Right." With a smart click of his heels, Constable Brown marched out of the office, making Elliot smile. It faded abruptly as his gaze moved toward the room in which Nick Sparkle sat. The memory of the bruises on Letty's wrists rose in his mind, bringing with it cold, unappeasable rage.

A sudden, loud crash shook the storage room door, a string of muffled curses following.

"I suggest you quiet down, Mr. Sparkle," he said gently.

"Do you?" came the sneered response. "And what are you going to do if I don't? Arrest me again?" His laugh was sour. As if to press home his contempt, the door shuddered again, the sound of splintering wood accompanying it.

The man was going to kick down the door at this rate, Elliot thought with a tincture of pleasure. He really couldn't allow that. As magistrate, he owed it to his constituency to protect public property.

He flipped back the bolt and pulled open the door.

Nick stood in front of it, his head lowered. His gaze dwelled in open hatred on Elliot's face before traveling to the empty corridor behind him.

"Where's the bully-boy with the knuckle-duster?" he asked innocently.

"Down the road a ways," Elliot answered.

Nick nodded, his expression lax but his gaze sharply assessing. He was weighing his advantage, measuring the breadth of Elliot's shoulders against his slender build, the big hands against the immaculate attire. Clearly, Nick liked the odds. Clearly, he'd have liked to make them even better. And that was where he made his mistake.

"I been sitting in here wondering something," he said, pursing his lips.

"Oh?"

He nodded, eyeing the ceiling reflectively as he wandered casually toward Elliot. "I was rather 'oping you'd 'elp me out. Bloke to bloke, you understand."

Elliot stood very still. The man was incredibly obvious. "And how can I do that, Mr. Sparkle?"

"Well, I was wondering." Nick's lips spread back over his teeth in a feral grin. He leaned closer. Just within arm's reach, he asked, "Was she any good?"

He lunged forward, but Elliot anticipated him. He stepped sideways, clamping his hand down on Nick's shoulder and spinning him around, pitching him back into the room. Nick staggered against the far wall, his face slack with incredulity.

"Men like you, Mr. Sparkle," Elliot began, and then he stopped, the blood rising fast and fiery in his veins. He *hated* that this animal had spoken about Letty like that. *Hated* that he'd left marks on her, hated him in an intense, personal, and profound way.

"Men like you," he repeated again, "who live according to whatever impulse strikes them, always make the mistake of thinking other men are just as easy to manipulate as they themselves."

Nick surged forward at the insult and stopped. "You're lucky you have your boys within calling distance, *Sir* Elliot, or I'd show you a thing or two about impulse. Like I intend to show Letty as soon as I beat this rap and run the bitch to ground."

Elliot stared at him, suddenly calm and absolutely clearheaded. "*That* was a mistake," he whispered.

"What?" Nick demanded.

Elliot didn't answer him. Instead, he smiled. It was not a pleasant smile. "Constable Burns is at the train station where he will be occupied for at least another half an hour. Garth is back at the stables.

"Now, Nick my lad, there's a back door to this building. A quarter mile behind here is the north road. It's a well-used road. Plenty of travelers. Some going to the coast, some north, some south. You'd only have to flag one of them down and you'd be far away inside an hour and no hope anyone would find you."

Nick regarded him narrowly. "What are you saying?"

"I am saying that the only thing that stands between you and freedom is me."

"And just why are you telling me this?" Nick asked. At his sides, his hands had curled reflexively into fists.

He would try rushing him low, Elliot judged, catching him in the belly and pounding him in his kidneys. Elliot shifted his weight forward, preparing to side-step him once more.

"Because I want you to try and escape," Elliot answered truthfully. "I have seldom wanted anything more in my life."

Nick grinned just as his fist shot out and caught Elliot full on the jaw, dropping him to his knees.

"Happy to oblige," he said.

Chapter 30

The audience is the only critic
that matters.

THEY HELD LETTY'S HEARING IN THE BIG-
glesworths' Great Hall, it being the largest room in
the county and therefore the only one that could adequately seat those who'd come to see the questioning
of the imposter. Little Bidewell Society was out in
force, jockeying for the best seats, their voices humming.

Everyone was deeply sympathetic toward the victims, the Bigglesworths. It seemed inevitable that
Miss Angela's wedding would be touched by scandal,
and everyone bitterly regretted that. Those who'd
looked fondly on the romance between Sir Elliot and
"that woman" were further aggrieved.

Plainly put, their sympathies were not with the de-
fendant. Not only had this Letty Potts played fast and
loose with Angela's future, but she'd also deceived

them, what with her charming ways and ready laughter. And it confused them that she could be so bad, when she'd seemed so dear. Everyone, that is, except Catherine Bunting, who'd been suspicious of Miss Potts from day one.

Cabot had cordoned off the far end of the hall with a satin rope. Behind this a trestle table had been set up, a straight-backed chair behind it while its mate sat at an oblique angle in front. This is where Letty would be seated to answer whatever questions the magistrate deemed appropriate in judging whether or not she should be held over for trial. The rest of the room had been divided into two sections filled with chairs and separated by an aisle.

The hum of voices grew as Sir Elliot entered from a side door carrying a pair of books under his arm. His bearing was as precise as ever, his hair combed to a polish, his attire faultless. His face was not quite so unremarkable. A yellowing bruise spread across his chin. Another darker mark raised the flesh beneath his right eye.

The murmuring in the room grew hushed. They had been ill-used by this woman, but Sir Elliot had been in love with her. How could any man help but want to punish the woman who'd so deceived him? Yet, knowing Sir Elliot, they trusted him not to let his personal feelings interfere with the outcome of the inquest. In Little Bidewell's opinion, Letty Potts was immeasurably lucky.

Elliot set the books down and nodded. He took his seat while Constable Burns hurried toward the back of the room and poked his head behind the door. A moment later, the door swung open and out stepped Eglantyne Bigglesworth, her face set in unaccustomedly grim lines. Behind her came Letty Potts.

She was dressed in the same lilac lace dress in which she'd arrived. The huge picture hat balanced atop her glossy deep red hair somehow looked gallant above her pale face. She looked neither right nor left, but kept her gaze fixed on her destination.

Dazzling rectangles of light coming from the upper-story windows lay on the parquet floor, and as she passed through each, the strain of the last few days was clearly and remorselessly revealed. Her skin looked waxen, the blue veins beneath her eyes prominent. Quiet unrolled behind her like a carpet as she passed.

At the end of the room, Eglantyne took a chair behind the satin rope. Letty took her seat. Only then did she raise her eyes to Elliot and see the bruises on his face.

She half rose from her chair, her lips parting in an inarticulate sound of distress. Her head swung around, her eyes sought Eglantyne. Eglantyne leaned forward.

"It is said that he and Mr. Sparkle had an accident," she whispered. "If it is any comfort, Dr. Beacon says Mr. Sparkle took the brunt of it. He had to be carried to the train station."

The first shock of seeing him over, Letty relaxed slightly. She smiled bitterly. "How am I to be comforted by the knowledge that Elliot was hurt by a man he never would have met if I hadn't come here?"

"We seldom anticipate the consequences of our actions, my dear," Eglantyne said gently.

Elliot nodded and the constable paced to the center of the room and called out in a loud voice for everyone to be seated. Elliot rose to his feet.

"This hearing is to determine whether or not a crime has been committed by Miss Letty Potts," he announced. A buzz of excitement filled the room. "Over the course of the last four days I have been in constant communication with the law enforcement officials in London regarding the criminal activities of Mr. Nicholas Sparkle, who is awaiting trial on a variety of charges."

Again, voices rose in speculation.

"Please," Elliot called out. The murmurs died away. "Now, while Mr. Sparkle has been unremitting in his accusations that Miss Potts aided him in his criminal activities, the London police cannot find anyone desiring to bring charges against her, nor can they find anyone to attest to her complicity in Mr. Sparkle's crimes."

At this, Letty pushed herself to her feet. "That doesn't matter," she said. "I freely confess my involvement."

Elliot regarded her dispassionately. "This is not London, Miss Potts," he said. "Please be seated. It is not my province to hear cases outside my jurisdiction. I could extradite you, and *would* extradite you, if you were wanted in London. You are not."

"But—" She began to protest but he raised his hand, silencing her. He was a stranger, utterly imperious and decidedly not to be gainsaid. She sank down in her chair.

"That is not to say you cannot be tried for any crimes committed, or in the process of being committed, in Little Bidewell. And will be, should it be warranted."

Squire Himplerump shouted, "Hear, hear!"

"Now," Elliot said, turning back to Letty. "Let us begin . . ."

At the end of half an hour, Elliot had finished questioning Letty. She was exhausted. If she'd feared that he would gloss over her initial motive in coming to Little Bidewell, if she thought he would hide the fact that she'd intended to steal Lady Agatha's belongings, she needn't have worried. Cool and detached, he led her through the last three weeks, beginning with the fire at her boarding house and ending with Nick Sparkle's arrival.

The spectators listened in fascination. Many eyes had widened on hearing that Letty was a musical actress. Some had nodded knowingly. A few had pursed their lips when she described how she'd intended to flee.

Letty couldn't have guessed what they thought of her. She'd spoken only to Eglantyne since Constable Burns had escorted her to The Hollies four days ago, and Eglantyne simply refused to think badly of her. But then, Eglantyne would.

Letty gazed along the lines of avid faces listening to Elliot's summary. Angela appeared more puzzled than anything else, while Anton looked openly bewildered. Behind him sat Atticus, his brow furrowed thoughtfully. Dr. Beacon and his sister wore identical expressions of troubled uncertainty. The Jepsons simply seemed sad. Colonel Vance had fallen asleep and was snoring peacefully, while beside him Elizabeth worried her hands anxiously. Near the back of the room stood Merry and Grace Poole, Merry looking disgusted and Grace Poole angry.

Even the Himplerumps seemed subdued, but for this Letty had an explanation. Angela's letter was the one point that had not come to light during the hearing. Letty assumed the Himplerumps would just as soon keep it that way.

"Has anyone anything to say or ask Miss Potts before I make a decision about whether she is to be bound over for trial?"

Conversation bubbled forth again. Letty waited uncertainly. Things had not gone as she'd imagined. She'd thought she'd be arrested by now. Instead, it appeared she was only "rather" arrested and even that was unclear.

"Yes, Mrs. Poole?" Elliot said.

Grace Poole marched down the aisle and turned around. Her face was flushed, but she carried herself with dignity. "Seems to me," she said, "that if we're to stick strictly to the law, no crime 'as been committed against anyone in Little Bidewell."

"That is not strictly true, Mrs. Poole," Elliot said calmly. "By her own admission, Miss Potts has used and altered Lady Agatha Whyte's clothing and, again by her own admission, doubts whether Lady Agatha shall ever be able to use those garments again. Unless," he scowled at the notes he'd taken, "Lady Agatha 'suddenly develops a bosom and shrinks three inches.' " Snickers of laughter erupted in the room.

But Grace was not to be so easily quieted. "I said,

Sir Elliot, no crime had been committed against anyone what was *in* Little Bidewell.

" 'Strictly speaking,' sir, Lady Agatha ain't here to
make no complaint against Miss Potts, and since she
ain't a citizen of this town, I don't see as how it's our
duty to do it for her. Besides which," she sniffed audibly, "if Lady Agatha had been doin' *'er* job, what the
Bigglesworths hired her to do, we wouldn't be having
this hearing in the first place now, would we?"

At this the snickers turned into outright laughter.
Someone from the back shouted, "You tell 'em,
Gracie!", which caused the housekeeper to go beet-
red to the roots of her improbably black hair and
beam with delight.

"I should hate to stand across from you in a court
of law, Mrs. Poole," Elliot said.

"No chance of that as long as we women can't vote,
now is there?" Grace shot back.

"Oh, no!" Constable Burns shouted. "None of that
suffrage claptrap here. Not now, Grace, or I'll arrest
you for disturbin' the peace."

"Wouldn't be the first time," Grace muttered flatly,
inciting another peal of laughter.

Letty looked around in stunned confusion. Where
was their animosity, their sense of betrayal? The
whole proceeding was taking on the aspects of light
entertainment. They *must* want her to pay for her
crimes.

She frowned, baffled and uneasy. A slow warmth
was unfurling deep within her. She distrusted it,
feared it. People were never so ready to forgive. She'd

spent four days trying to get used to the idea of prison: cold, drafty rooms; gray uniforms; no music; no laughter. No Elliot.

"Quiet down," Elliot called. "Mrs. Grace Poole has a point. Does anyone here wish to bring a complaint against Letty Potts and act on Lady Agatha's behalf?"

Eglantyne Bigglesworth cleared her throat and slowly rose to her feet. It was a monumental act of bravery for a woman so naturally reticent, and the laughter died away as everyone strained to hear her.

"I rather think the point is that Miss Potts has *already* acted on Lady Agatha's behalf."

Several people nodded thoughtfully.

"Lady Agatha had left us, as Mrs. Poole pointed out and as Miss Potts would so colorfully phrase it, in the lurch. Miss Potts, as Colonel Vance would so picturesquely put it, leapt into the breach."

Letty felt the corners of her mouth lift. The darling would never make a playwright, not with mixing metaphors like that.

"She has done all the work we asked of Lady Agatha and she hasn't been paid a red farthing for her efforts. Regardless of whether you make Miss Potts stand trial or not, I believe we owe her our thanks. *And* Lady Agatha's fee."

Letty gasped. Behind her Dorothy Himplerump gasped, too. Grace and Merry cheered. Anton puffed out his cheeks and said, "Good show, Eggie."

Angela stood up and linked her arm through her aunt's. "I owe Miss Potts far more than my thanks," Angela continued. Behind her Letty heard Mrs. Dorothy Himplerump gulp anxiously. "She has become my friend. She has offered me invaluable advice and aid. And if you do charge her with some ridiculous crime, Sir Elliot, I shall personally see that she has the finest counsel in England represent her."

Elliot arched a brow, considering the girl a moment before releasing her from his gaze. "Anyone else care to comment?"

Colonel Vance chose that moment to awaken. His cane clattered from his lap to the floor and his head snapped upright. He blinked, looking around and scowling. Spying his daughter beside him, he shouted, "What's happened? What's going on with the girl who used to be Lady Agatha?"

"Nothing, Father," Elizabeth replied loudly. "They're still deciding."

"Deciding what, for God's sake?"

"If she's a criminal!" Elizabeth shouted back.

"Well, of course, she ain't. She gave me a strawberry trifle, didn't she? What criminal gives a fellow a cake?" he said with such profound disgust that no one could help but smile. Including Letty.

They were the kindest, most generous people in the world. But she couldn't allow them to forgive her so easily. She deserved punishment. Perhaps she needed it. She cleared her throat, but before she could speak, Atticus March did.

"Well said, Colonel." He struggled painfully to his feet. "If I might speak, Elliot?"

Elliot nodded, watching his father closely.

"It seems to me we have a twofold problem here," Atticus said. "The first, whether Miss Potts has committed a crime for which it is Elliot's duty to charge her, seems to be resolved. No one wants to press charges, and in light of Miss Potts's efforts toward Miss Angela in Lady Agatha's stead, there is some question as to whether it is even ethical to do so. I believe we all agree it is not."

The crowd rumbled with sounds of concurrence. Except for Catherine Bunting, who remained silent. Letty stared ahead, dazed by their magnanimity.

"The second problem is a bit trickier. It involves scandal." The voices abruptly died away. "In little over a month, a large number of Londoners will arrive in Little Bidewell. They will be here only a short time, a week or so, and then they will be gone. They will take our Angela with them when they go, our daughter, niece, and friend."

Angela lowered her eyes modestly.

"I am sure we all want Angela's happiness."

Everyone nodded; every smile was tender with affection for the pretty, sweet-natured girl. Even Kip Himplerump looked sentimental in a sulky sort of way.

"We all know that if these strangers ever hear about the background of the woman who planned Angela's bridal party, if they ever hear anything about her profession or where she came from, Angela's wedding ceremony will be forever stained by scandal."

Grumbles and dark looks shot back and forth between the spectators, as though everyone was already searching for the lout who'd ratted out the story of Angela's actress-*cum*-wedding planner.

"We can't allow that, can we?" Atticus waited a minute for the shouts of "no" to die away. "Now, if we arrest this poor girl," he gestured toward Letty, "and she is held over for trial, and possibly from there remanded for the Session Courts, the story *will* leak out."

The spectators traded worried glances.

"However, if she is *not* charged with any crime, I am reasonably certain that we can keep the whole affair quiet.

"Of course," Atticus said soberly, his gaze touching on every person in the room, "there is one small matter. If anyone should ask, which it is very doubtful they will, we must all of us to a man—and woman— agree that Miss Potts was here under Lady Agatha's auspices."

Letty waited. She understood why it would be best if she wasn't charged with a crime; she conceded that if there was a chance to save Angela humiliation, it would be worth releasing a two-bit con artist.

But there wasn't a chance. They couldn't carry it off.

Letty knew far more about lies than they did. You needed to keep them simple and you needed to let as few people in on them as possible. There were upwards of fifty people in the room.

She stood up and said so in a clear, carrying voice.

Atticus regarded her politely as she explained the madness of their plan, and then he waited just as politely for her to sit down again.

"While Miss Potts's concern certainly does her credit—" Letty moaned. They mustn't insist on attributing her with characteristics she didn't own. "—she does not understand Society."

Now *that* was doing it a bit rough! Letty started to stand up again but a sharp glance from Elliot put her grumbling softly back in her chair.

"There'll be scant chance of any one of us spending time in lengthy conversations with the Marquis of Cotton's friends and relatives. Except for Paul and Catherine, of course." He nodded toward the Buntings. "Most of us won't speak to them at all. We need only keep mum for a few days, for a few minutes at a time. I daresay we can pull that much off."

"Of course, we can!" Paul Bunting cried. But Atticus knew very well who in the room could be counted Letty's friend and who her foe.

"What do you think, Catherine?" he asked, his gaze holding hers. "Can we remain mute for Angela's sake?"

She was caught as neatly as a rabbit in a snare. Struggle though she might, there was no way out. The smile on her face was stiff. "Why, of course we can," she said clearly and, just as clearly, "For Angela's sake we can do anything."

The others had added their voices of assent until the whole room rang with their intention. Atticus turned back to where Elliot sat in broody thoughtfulness.

"Well, Elliot," he said quietly. "What's it to be? Is Miss Potts under arrest?"

Elliot stood up. Letty trembled as he regarded her, afraid he would release her, equally afraid he would not. She stood up and waited for his judgment.

"Miss Potts, you are free to go."

Chapter 31

Don't try to turn a tragedy
into a musical.

MERRY BURST INTO THE MARCHES' MORN-
ing room, her white maid's cap askew and her eyes
bulging. "She be leavin' on the noon train ter
London!"

Elliot rose from his seat at the breakfast table.

"I got Ham ter drive me over, but you best hurry if
you're thinkin' to stop 'er, Sir Elliot, sir."

"Ring for Mrs. Nichols, if you please, Father, and
have her bring Merry a glass of water."

Atticus reached for the bell but Merry shook her
head. "Thank you kindly, sir, but I'll be fine as soon as
I catch me wind. I have to get back and slow her
down." She glared meaningfully at Elliot. "And *you* had
best hurry. She has The Hat on!" And with that perti-
nent bit of information, she wheeled about and disappeared.

Atticus regarded his son worriedly. He'd no doubt that Elliot loved Letty, and from what he'd seen, she felt the same about Elliot. But whether they could be brought to act upon their emotion was another thing entirely.

"Miss Potts is an uncommon sort of female," he said.

"I am glad to have your opinion," Elliot replied.

"Ah." Atticus nodded. "Then you have given thought to Miss Potts and her future."

"Quite a bit, actually." Elliot watched him closely. "She probably ought to be in prison."

"I imagine there are those who would take that view," Atticus admitted.

"*I* am not one of them," Elliot said quite forcefully.

"Oh? Neither am I."

"Good," Elliot replied flatly, and then gave his sire a half-smile. "I'm sorry."

His dark face set into naturally imperial lines. "Father, I love Letty. I have never loved a woman in the same way, and before you advise me of the dangers of being intrigued by a woman because she has such a diverse background from my own, let me assure you I have told myself the same thing time and again."

Atticus hoped the poor, honest fool hadn't said as much to Miss Potts. Being a woman of sensitivity she would—

"It's not true," Elliot said. "I do not love her for what she is, but for who she is."

"And that is?"

A smile of such extraordinary pleasure appeared on

Elliot's lean countenance that Atticus drew a breath. "Why, a woman who would give a fellow a cake."

Letty placed the sheaf of papers on Eglantyne's desk, satisfied that the directions for the wedding festivities were as complete as possible. She glanced at the wall clock. The London train left at noon. Until then she could only pace and wait, memories of him standing at her shoulder and whispering in her ear.

Where had he gone after yesterday's hearing? What was he thinking? Did he regret making love to her? Would she ever see him again? If she occasionally walked down past the House of Lords, would she ever see him come out and catch a carriage, bound for a late-night dinner? With a lady? A real lady?

"Miss Potts?"

Startled, Letty turned. She'd been so immersed in her thoughts she hadn't heard Eglantyne enter. She was carrying Fagin.

"Yes, Miss Eglantyne?"

Eglantyne held Fagin out. "I've brought you Lambikins. I gather, what with all the distractions and so forth, you forgot him." Her grave expression clearly told what she thought of such an oversight.

"His name is Fagin. At least that's what I've always called him. I suspect you might call him anything you like and eventually he'd answer to it. He's a smart little beggar." She took a breath. "And I didn't forget him, Miss Eglantyne. He chose to stay."

The older woman's eyes grew round.

"He was never my pet, just a mate that shared the road for a ways, is all. Never thought we'd see the end of the line together, and looks like I was right." She smiled at Eglantyne's disbelief. "Why should he go searching about for what he's already found? Someone who loves him as much as he loves her."

"Oh, Miss Potts—"

"Letty. Please."

"You're pulling my leg. Dogs can't love."

Letty shook her head. "If there's one thing I've learned in the last few days, it's that none of us can say who ought to love who, and if it's right or possible or proper. It just *is*, Miss Eglantyne. Love just is."

"Are you sure?" Eglantyne asked, slowly withdrawing her arms. Fagin relaxed, cradled against her thin chest.

"Doesn't matter if I am," Letty said, a hint of roughness in her throat. "He is."

"Thank you," Eglantyne whispered. Her eyes were overly bright, and the thin hands stroking Fagin's head trembled. "Thank you so much."

A discreet knock sounded on the door and Eglantyne turned, overcome with emotion, leaving Letty to answer. "Come in."

Cabot opened the door and stood back. "Sir Elliot."

She hadn't expected to see him again, and his appearance caused her heart to flutter uncontrollably. He looked so beautiful: Clean and masculine and fine. Yet there were subtle signs that he had come in haste. His shirt cuffs weren't straight, and his tie was slightly askew. She longed to fix it.

He saw her and his body tensed. His gaze traveled

past her to Eglantyne. "Miss Eglantyne, if you would be so kind as to allow me a few minutes of Miss Potts's time?" His voice was cultured and resonant and velvety, sending shivers through Letty.

Eglantyne didn't answer. Still holding Fagin, she simply brushed past Elliot, closing the door behind her.

The morning light filtering through the windows picked out glossy blue highlights in his hair. The crinkles at the corners of his extraordinary eyes looked deeper, as did the lines bracketing his nose and mouth. The bruises on his face had faded a little, the darkest areas blooming yellow.

"I am so sorry he hit you."

"I assure you it was a mutual exchange." His smile was self-conscious and utterly disarming. "I ought to regret it, I suppose. It's a childish sort of way of expressing oneself." His smile grew wry. "But it was vastly satisfying."

She couldn't help laughing. His gaze warmed with shared amusement.

"He didn't hurt you too badly?" she asked.

"No. The worst thing about it is not being able to boast of the manly way I dispatched the ba—the bounder."

"And why can't you do that?" she asked, her tone still flavored with amusement.

He shrugged. "It isn't done. You'd think me coarse."

Her smile faded. *"Never."*

The single word seemed to bring him abruptly back to the reality of their situation. He clasped his hands behind his back, and it looked to her as if he wasn't sure how to begin or what to say. Such indecision was foreign for him, she was sure. He frowned, glanced up at her, frowned again, and paced a few steps. He stopped abruptly.

"That," he said, his gaze rising above her face, "is the most confoundedly attractive hat I have ever seen."

Whatever she'd expected, it hadn't been that. Her bewilderment relaxed him and he moved closer, his gaze traveling with flattering attention over her hat. "Audacious, bold, yet vastly feminine." His gaze fell to her eyes. "Exactly the sort of hat one would expect you to own."

She couldn't think of how to reply. She had no idea where he was leading. She could only stand helplessly, wanting to fix his tie, wanting to be in his embrace.

"Merry said you were leaving this morning. Going back to London."

She nodded.

"Isn't that rather precipitant? I mean, it was assumed that you would finish making the arrangements for Angela's wedding."

"I've finished," she said. "Or as good as. I've made sketches of the set designs and instructions. The caterer and wine merchant are already engaged and the extra servers hired. The staff has all been apprised of their duties." She lifted her shoulders. "Everything is done."

He did not look convinced. "But won't this need someone to oversee the lot?"

For the first time since he'd entered, she smiled. "Grace Poole and Merry are more than up to the task."

"I see." He didn't appear pleased and she understood his displeasure. He didn't know these women as well as she did.

"It will all be well," she promised. "Besides, I received a telegram this morning. I'm to testify at Nick Sparkle's hearing."

His brows drew together. "And you will do so?"

"Yes, of course."

"If he is set free, are you concerned he'll seek retribution?" he asked. His scowl had become fierce, his expression dangerous.

Could he still care?

"No," she answered breathlessly. "That is, I don't see any possible way he can be set free."

Elliot moved within a few feet of her. His gaze was somber, his concern clear. Despite what she'd done, planned to do, despite having stolen his love for one night, he cared for her.

"But if he *is* set free?" he insisted.

She could no longer resist. She reached up and jiggled the knot until it aligned with the fall of his tie. "Well, that's why I'm going to testify. To make certain he isn't."

"If you married me, I would make certain you were safe."

Her hands froze. He covered them with his own, enveloping them in warmth. She could see the slight abrasions that covered his knuckles. The dusting of dark hairs on the back of his hands.

Careful, she cautioned herself, though her heart was racing and her knees felt weak. *This was to be expected; it was simply all of a piece.*

They'd made love; she'd been a virgin. It wouldn't matter to him that she was a bastard and a criminal. He would see marrying her as an obligation, a matter of honor. And he would even do it without ever, by inference or action, showing regret, because that was not his nature. He was a gentleman.

"Letty, please. Do me the honor of being my wife."

The paralysis gripping her broke and she pulled her hands free. "No, no," she said struggling to keep her voice light. "That isn't necessary. I swear it. Nick would never hurt me. Really. He's a bully, but not a killer. And I suspect that after the trial, even if he is freed, which I cannot believe for an instant he will be, his influence in London will be greatly reduced."

He followed her retreat, his face grave and intent. "I said that badly. I don't want to marry you to protect you. Or yes, I do, but that isn't the—" He broke off abruptly and reached up, caressing her cheek with the back of his scraped knuckles. Involuntarily she closed her eyes.

"I love you, Letty."

"Elliot." His name came out on a sigh of hopeless longing.

"It's the truth. I love you. I've loved you from the moment I saw you smile. Please, Letty, look at me."

She opened her eyes and saw his sincerity. He cupped the side of her face.

"I love you, Letty. I don't want to live without you."

"How can you love me?" she asked, forcing herself to say the words that would kill the tenderness in his eyes. "You don't even know me. You know 'Lady Agatha,' a composite, a character, a role I played."

He shook his head, his negation gentle but certain. "I didn't fall in love with a character, a title, or an occupation. I didn't fall in love with you because of your past or despite it.

"I love you because of your intensity and passion, because you make me want to be better than I am, because seeing my reflection in your eyes *makes* me better than I am. I love you because you laugh easily and honestly. I love you because you carried an ugly mutt into a drawing room as though it were a prince and because you gave an old soldier a strawberry trifle. I love *you*, Letty."

"No." The more she wanted to believe him, the more strongly she denied him. He should choose someone of his class, someone who was as much a lady as he was a gentleman. And he would. "You'll go to London and become a baron and meet some fine, beautiful lady whom you will be proud to introduce, who will be your equal in birth and in nobility."

"No," he said gravely. "I won't."

She laughed, a horrible fake sound. "Yes, you will. You'll see. It just feels like you won't now. But you reconciled yourself to Catherine's marriage. Why, you live in the same town. And it's not as if we'll be forced into each other's company to remind us. London is so big."

His eyes were like fire pits, burning with intensity. "You are not Catherine. This is not the same. I can promise you that no city in the world is large enough to hold the both of us if you refuse me. The entire damn island will be too small."

"Elliot—"

"Please, stop." His tone was harsh. "If you don't feel you can marry me, you needn't come up with excuses."

A mask of imperturbability was falling over his features, but not before she saw the bone-deep wound she'd caused. She couldn't let him think that he loved and was not loved in return, not to save her soul she couldn't.

"Elliot, I love you."

The mask fell from his face. His eyes were fierce. "Then marry me. Or tell me you don't love me."

"I can't."

"Listen to me, Letty. I don't want a courteous, lukewarm relationship. I don't want to greet a paragon every morning and say good evening at her bedroom door each night. I don't want a polite, civilized union."

Abruptly, he seized her and pulled her close. Silver pins fell from her hair and scattered across the dark red carpet, pinpricks catching the light like stars on a wine-red sky. His eyes grew dark and lambent, as sensual and caressing as his touch. "I want you, Letty, in every way imaginable. Fresh from your bath with your hair still wet, coiling about my wrist and dripping on my chest.

"I want you cool and regal, earthy and impertinent, spoiling for a fight and abashed by your own temper. I want you flushed with exertion and rosy with sleep. I want you teasing and provocative, somber and thoughtful. I want every emotion, every mood, every year in a lifetime to come. I want you beside me, Letty, to encourage and argue with me, to help me and to let me help you. I want to be your companion and lover, your mentor and student."

"And when you are made a baron, will you want me to wear a coronet?" she asked breathlessly.

"Of course," he said. But she'd seen it, the flicker of hesitance, the little mote of darkness in his eyes. She understood. She knew him so well. It was not that he wouldn't be proud to give her a coronet. It was that there would be no coronet to give.

The Queen would never grant a barony to a man who'd wed a music hall actress.

She'd known. Atticus had told her. From that moment on, none of her wildest dreams had found a way past that irresolvable point.

She forced herself to confront head-on everything that stood between them, not only their pasts but also their futures. It wasn't just that she was a near felon and he a magistrate, it was also what he *would* be: a baron, a member of the House of Lords, "a powerful proponent for good."

If she married him she wouldn't only be robbing him of his barony; she would be hurting all the people for whom he could someday speak. She gazed long and sadly into his eyes and gently touched his cheek.

"I love you, Elliot. I swear I did not know the meaning of the word before I came here. Nothing in the world would give me greater joy than being your wife. But I can't."

"For God's sake, Letty, why not?" he ground out.

"The Queen will never make you a baron if you wed me."

He did not deny it. Instead, he caught her hand and pressed an ardent kiss against her knuckles. "I have lived thirty-three years without being a baron; I assure you I can survive without the honor," he said, his voice a warm caress against her skin. "I don't know that I cannot survive without you, but I do know that I don't want to."

She brushed his cool, silky hair with a feather's touch. "It's not just you, my most . . . It's not just for your sake."

"For whose, then?" His turned his head, his brilliant gaze locking with hers, demanding an answer.

"For those who need you to speak for them. For the soldiers and the children and the women in the factories and the men in the mines. Justice needs you, Elliot. The poor dear is already blind; she mustn't be mute as well."

He dropped her hand and backed away with a muttered curse. "You can't do this. You can't rob us of our future for the sake of nameless people." But she saw the torment, the agony of conscience it cost him to say the words.

"Elliot, you said I made you better. That you saw yourself through my eyes and was a better man for it. It's the same for me, Elliot. Don't rob me of my nobility. Don't see me as less than what you want me to be, what I can be.

"How could I realize a moment's honest joy knowing I'd purchased my happiness with the silence of a thousand people, or bought my joy with their loss? How could I be happy knowing that because you married *me*, I diminished *you*?"

His expression was desperate; his face ravaged by an inner torment she'd unleashed.

"What of me, Letty?" he demanded. "What of what I am willing to purchase for joy? What have I ever had of it, except your love? Is that all the heavens have allotted me? A taste, to carry me through for the rest of my life? A taste to let me know what I am missing each and every hour of my existence?" he ended in a rasp of pain and outrage so intense the tears sprang to Letty's eyes.

"I don't believe that!" He grasped her arms, shaking her slightly. "There is some way. There must be. I won't accept this!"

"What do you want me to say, Elliot?" she asked.

"Give me something, Letty. Anything. Some reason to hope."

She could give him hope. It would hurt her more, because she knew it would be an illusion. But by the time he realized it, his pain would have faded. She couldn't refuse him. She couldn't let him hurt one bit more than she had to.

"Come to me after you're a baron. After you've taken your seat in the House of Lords, find me. If you still want to marry me then, I'll be your wife."

His gaze scoured her face intently. His hands tightened around her upper arms. "You swear it? You promise that once I have sat in the House of Lords you will marry me?"

"Yes."

Abruptly he released her. He stepped back, with that precise military grace she so admired. Formally, as though accepting a commission or a sentence, he bowed, his manner grave, his face wiped of emotion.

"I shall hold you to your word."

Chapter 32

Happily-ever-afters
happen only at matinées.

APPEARING IN THE *LONDON HERALD'S* SO-
ciety pages:

The wedding of Miss Angela Frances Bigglesworth to
Lord Hugh Denton Sheffield, Marquis of Cotton, took
place Saturday at The Hollies, country home of Miss
Bigglesworth's father, Mr. Anton Bartholomew Bigglesworth
of Little Bidewell, Northumberland. The extensive guest list
included Society's most notable lights as well as many
of the bride's friends and acquaintances from neighboring
estates.

(Omitted here: three paragraphs citing the names
of those participating in the ceremony and two
columns devoted to an intricate analysis of the wedding party's apparel.)

The postnuptial celebration was not only wonderfully festive but highly original, as could only be expected having been orchestrated by Whyte's Nuptial Celebrations, although in this instance it surpassed all expectations for novelty and élan.

After the wedding the bride and her groom were driven from the church in a victoria of striking beauty, the vehicle painted in ebony lacquer and having real orange blossoms pressed into the paint, achieving the artful effect of japanned papier-mâché inlaid with mother-of-pearl. This pretty and frolicsome Oriental flavor established the tone and tempo of the subsequent festivities.

Arriving at The Hollies, the guests were greeted by servants dressed in Oriental garb, the women clad in kimonos and the men in loose trousers and blouses of silk, bowing silently. Their delightfully feigned obsequiousness continued through the evening.

From the front of the manor, the guests were escorted to a gently uncoiling path strewn with fragrant jasmine blossoms that led beneath arches twined in flowers and topped with fluttering silk kites in the various and wonderful shapes of goldfish, swallows, and butterflies.

At the back of the venerable Bigglesworth estate, the guests were greeted by the sight of a little colony of pagodas atop a grassy knoll. Brilliantly colored striped silk pavilions had been set beneath the lofty branches of beech and flowering rowan. Below, on the mirrorlike expanse of a picturesque lake, male servants poled miniature sampans, while from within the exotic boats a sextet of singers, so diminutive in stature one suspected they were children, sang popular ballads in consummately beautiful three-part harmony.

Under the pavilions sat long tables resplendent with exquisite blue-willow china and silver place settings. At each setting were small favors, the gentlemen receiving red silk smoking caps with black tassels and the women exquisitely painted silk fans depicting scenes taken from the surrounding countryside.

(Omitted here, a lengthy discourse on the various food items served, including a full column devoted to the wedding cake prepared by one of England's hitherto undiscovered treasures of the culinary arts, Mrs. Grace Poole.)

Incense in cunning little ceramic bowls placed discreetly amidst the pavilions scented the air nearly as sweetly as the singers' voices, while a flock of swans foraged along the lake's bank. As dusk fell, little paper lanterns bobbed in the light breeze, casting playful shadows upon the Oriental wonderland. Yet, the festivities were not finished, for once darkness had fully enveloped the landscape, fairy lights appeared amongst the rhododendrons and deep within the pine copses bordering the knoll. These heralded the arrival of a troupe of Oriental acrobats, dancing and somersaulting and brilliantly displaying the athleticism of their kind in a variety of amazing maneuvers. After which the festivities were brought to a spectacular close by a display of fireworks set off across the lake that spangled the night sky with glitter.

The unanimous opinion of those fortunate enough to be counted amongst the guests at this exclusive, enchanting, and startlingly original fete was that, much to Society's regret, the Season will not see its like again this year.

The following excerpt from the *London Sentinel*'s review of *The Bohemian Girl* appeared approximately six months after the preceding article:

> . . . *Miss Letty Potts in the role of Arline is a revelation. Miss Potts may be remembered for her roles last year in a series of curtain raisers, when she was lauded as a contralto soprano of fine voice and delightful comedic timing, but thought to be generally lacking the depth of emotion necessary to inspire an audience. Clearly such criticisms have been premature, for in the character of the Gypsy-girl-cum-aristocrat, Miss Potts sings with an ardor and sincerity that is astounding.*
>
> *One song in particular, "I Dreamt I Dwelt In Marble Halls," continued to bring audiences to their feet. Though the song is a standard sentimental favorite, Miss Potts has imbued the ethereal aria with such delicacy of feeling and poignancy of phrasing that not one eye in the house remained dry. Brava, Miss Potts, brava!*

One month later, the *London Sentinel* carried this notice on the bottom of a page devoted to politics:

> *Lord Elliot March, lately created Baron March of Bidewell, having received his writ of summons, will take his seat in the House of Lords in the opening session of Parliament this afternoon.*

Letty folded the newspaper and handed it to the boot boy. "Thank you for going out in the rain for this, Vinny. Put it in my room, there's a duck, and don't set it on the makeup. I want to keep it nice and clean, right?"

"Right, Miss Potts," the boy said, and nipped off to do her bidding. Letty's gaze followed him, her determined cheerfulness dimming.

This afternoon had been the day, then. Elliot had taken his seat in the House of Lords and the world would be a better place. She pulled back the curtains and looked out across the audience. Good house tonight in spite of the storm outside.

Good for both of them, then. Elliot had his barony and she had the career she'd always wanted. She ought to be glad. And she was.

After all, it wasn't as though she'd expected to hear from him again. She'd always known he'd come to his senses. And he *had* come to his senses. Not once, in any manner or form, had he attempted to contact her. Not once had he come to see her perform.

She knew; she'd asked the manager to keep an eye out for him. And no one, least of all the manager of a theater looking to draw the swell crowd, would have overlooked the presence of one of London's rising politicians. No, he hadn't come to her, but he'd gone other places. The newspapers loved him.

He'd been seen shopping in Mayfair with a wealthy philanthropist's daughter. He'd dined with the widow of a socially prominent politician. He had been to the opera and the legitimate theater, but he'd never gone slumming down in the West End. It was as if he didn't want to risk the embarrassment of accidentally running into her.

Aye, the newspapers loved the new Lord March. And what's not to love, Letty asked herself with a little laugh. The illustrations didn't do him justice, but even those were handsome in a severe sort of way.

When he smiled, he probably bowled them over in droves. Not that he seemed to smile much. Words like sober, serious-minded, and stern appended themselves to his name in newspaper articles. He took his duty seriously. He took life seriously.

And *that* she regretted. For his sake. Because he'd laughed easily once. With her. It seemed a pity that he should lose that.

"Two minutes, Miss Potts," the stage manager whispered as the end of the first act drew near. She watched the scene rise to a climactic conclusion, with the little girl who played Arline as a child swept into the Gypsy's arms to be carried away from her father's court.

At the audience's gasp, the stage crew hauled down on the ropes, snapping the curtains shut. Silently the workers swarmed the stage, positioning the new set. Letty twitched the ragged paisley shawl into place over her breasts and shook out her Gypsy mane of hair so that it tumbled loose about her shoulders.

She hurried onstage and dropped to the floor, lying curled on her side. The second act opened twelve years later. She closed her eyes, willing herself into the role. She was Arline, stolen daughter of an aristocrat, beloved fosterling of a Gypsy tribe, well versed in guile and connivance yet still dimly remembering another life, another time.

She felt the rush of air as the curtains swept open,

and heard the murmurs from the audience. She waited for her cue and then opened her eyes. The footlights blinded her, and a blaze of color surrounded her as the Gypsy dancers gathered around.

She'd played this role three dozen times, knew in her heart that it was hokey and trite and overwrought and the essence of the gooey, sappy, sentimental drivel she'd once so bitterly denounced. But tonight . . . tonight . . .

Perhaps it was hearing the door shut on the last of her hopes. Perhaps it was seeing the evidence of his success and knowing she'd loved him enough to give him up. Perhaps it was the words to her opening aria, words that seemed a mirror reflection of her own experience in Little Bidewell, that for a short dreamlike time, she'd been a lady and had known the love of a gentleman. And perhaps it was because she, too, had wakened from the dream—but not from being in love.

Whatever the reason, she sang as if her heart were breaking, sang as if every word was an entreaty, every phrase redolent with dying hope. Yet still her dream was so beautiful, so perfect, that even the memory of him filled her heart with unutterable joy . . . and love.

When she was finished, not a rustle disturbed the silence in the packed house. Every breath was held, every face riveted on the piquant figure kneeling center stage.

Suddenly the doors at the back of the house burst open. Surprised by the unexpected interruption, Letty peered into the darkness. She couldn't see anything, but she heard the murmurs of the curious audience and the sound of boot heels striding down the long aisle toward the stage.

And then there was a tall figure standing below her, just past the lights. A hand appeared on the edge of the stage, flat on the flooring, and a man vaulted lightly from the audience up onto the stage.

It was Elliot. His white tie was askew and his black hair was dripping wet. Rain had soaked through his coat and darkened his trousers. But his eyes glimmered behind their twin banks of black lashes, and there was a stubborn set to his chin. She stared up at him in amazement. He took one step toward her. The audience held its collective breath.

"I took my seat in the House of Lords this afternoon at five o'clock and stayed through the evening session," he said. "When I came out I could not find a cab and I would not wait, and so I must ask you to forgive my appearance."

She gulped.

"Forgive my appearance," he continued harshly, "*and* keep your promise."

"My promise?" This could not be happening. The other actors onstage had slowly drifted back, leaving them alone in the center of the stage.

"You said I was to come to you after I took my seat in the House of Lords and that then you would marry me."

"But . . ." She had to be dreaming. She was delirious. He wasn't here. He hadn't even written her a note. "You didn't even write a note," she mumbled through her delirium.

He grasped her arms, gentle but firm and—by God! he didn't feel like a mirage! He felt like flesh and blood and masculine strength and Elliot, dear Lord! He felt like *Elliot*.

"I didn't dare. I didn't dare because I knew that if I ever saw you I would not have the strength or resolve to stay away, and I knew that you would accept nothing less from me than the best I could give, not only for you, but for myself. So I didn't write and I didn't come, but God knows the torture it has been, and now you must end it!" he ground out, his eyes blazing with passion and promise and everything she had ever wanted. "You must!"

Abruptly, as though he could not stand his torment a second longer, in front of eight hundred audience members, Baron March swept the rising musical star Letty Potts up into his arms.

"You must marry me. You must, my darling, beautiful, audacious Letty," he said his voice softening to a low rumble that only she could hear. "Now, quickly, before I kiss you and embarrass you in front of all these people, say you will."

She grinned, delighted and triumphant and dizzy with happiness, raining kisses on his chin and cheeks and throat and mouth.

"Oh, yes," she said. "Yes and yes and yes."

Letty Potts was no fool.

*Watch for Connie Brockway's next "bridal"
romance in the Fall of 2002.*

Read on for a preview. . . .

London, England
1895

"IF YOU DO NOT WANT BLOOD ALL OVER THIS carpet, I suggest you call a physician," Evelyn said as she pushed her spectacles back into place.

The tall man who'd walked into the library with his head bent over the pages of an open book abruptly stopped, caught in a pool of bright mid-morning sunlight. He wore shirtsleeves, the white cuffs rolled halfway up sinewy, tanned forearms, the collar undone and open at the throat.

"Which carpet?" he asked, looking about for her.

Ten years had passed, but it might have been yesterday that she'd last seen him. The light, easy, imperturbable voice was the same, as was his slender, loose-limbed build and disheveled good looks.

"Here," Evelyn called. "On the floor by the window."

Justin Powell closed his book and came round the side of the desk. Looking up past the high polish of expensive and expensively maintained shoes, she could now see the subtle changes a decade had wrought. Thin lines radiated from the corners of his eyes, and little comma shapes bracketed his wide mouth. A dusting of gray threaded through dark, rumpled hair in dire need of a good clip.

Mutely, he gazed down at her. Just as mute, she returned his regard.

What was wrong with a man when even the sight of a woman bleeding to death on his floor couldn't excite him to action? Evelyn frowned. Well, perhaps she wasn't precisely bleeding to death.

"I understand how the sight of a woman lying in a pool of her own blood might be offputting, Mr. Powell. But can I do anything to dispel the paralysis that seems to have gripped you and encourage you to act?"

"Woman, eh?" he murmured, calmly setting the book on the desk. He hunkered down, his elbows on his knees and his hands hanging between his legs, and cocked his head. Gingerly, he lifted the torn flap in the knickers she'd "borrowed" from her nephew, Stanley.

She dared a glance at her leg, saw the blood, and averted her face. She looked at him, intending to read the severity of her injury in his expression, but instead found herself staring in fascination at his eyes. They were just as she remembered, too, a fascinating, glinty-soft greenish. Forest pond in dappled light. Gold leaf swirling through liquid jade—

"You aren't bleeding to death," Justin said matter-of-factly. He released the flap of twill. "And that spot isn't a pool. Blast." He frowned at his blood-tipped fingers, looked around, and ended up wiping them on her pant. "Now, as I was saying, though the cut is long, it's not very deep."

"Thank heavens!" She released the breath she'd been holding. She was, admittedly, a bit of a sissy where blood was concerned.

"Not much more than a scratch," he said calmly. "A tad messy but nothing any English schoolboy hasn't suffered a dozen times over."

His lack of sympathy made her bristle. "I am *not* an English schoolboy."

He gave her a superior look. "Since Mrs. Boyle's Finishing School opened in the neighborhood, I have learned that the difference between the average English schoolgirl and the average English schoolboy isn't very much."

She frowned. "Whatever are you talking about?"

"I'm wondering just what the enticement was to get you to dress up like a boy," he said, his gaze drifting in a purely impersonal manner over poor Stanley's blouse, knotted kerchief, and ruined knickers.

Evelyn scowled at the idea that he thought she was from the local girls' school! "I dressed this way only because I expected I would need to crawl up the trellis outside your library window in order to get in here."

"Ah. I see. Now that you explain it all, it makes perfect sense."

She was wounded and he was being sarcastic. She lifted herself to her elbows, preparing to deliver him a stinging setdown, but as soon as her head rose above her chest and she saw the red, sticky flap of cloth, her head swam and she dropped back with a moan.

"Are you hurt elsewhere?" Justin asked quickly, the slight coldness vanishing from his manner.

"No. It's just that . . . Blood! Ugh!" she burst out. "I'll be fine as long as I don't look at it."

"Then by all means, don't look. You're as white as Devon sand." He uncoiled. "Just lay there quietly while I nip off and raid the old medicine cupboard. I'll be back in a trice."

Only after he'd left did it occur to her that he hadn't asked how she'd come to be lying in such a condition on his library floor. Simple deduction would have told him she'd entered through the broken window overlooking the walled garden at the rear of his town house, but most men would have demanded to know why she'd made such an entry. At the very least, they would have been unnerved by her sudden, unheralded appearance. But then, she recalled, Justin Powell had no nerves.

She twisted her head, looking about the library. A small, untidy working library, just the sort she'd have loved to explore—and put in order. A pair of deep leather club chairs faced a two-story bookshelf outfitted with a rolling brass ladder. Across the room, a library desk basked in the light pouring in through a now permanently open east-facing window.

She was squinting through her glasses, trying to read some of the titles on the bookshelves, when she heard footsteps. A second later Justin came in with a tray filled with medical paraphernalia: a ceramic bowl, a pair of scissors, a stoppered brown bottle, a roll of linen bandages, and a terry cloth.

He didn't waste time fussing about proprieties, he simply knelt down beside her and proceeded to cut off the right leg of her nephew's knickers five inches above the knee. He then wadded the ruined pant leg up and tossed it into the wastebasket beside the desk before dipping the end of the towel in the bowl. "I'm going to clean you up a bit, all right?"

Before she could answer, he gently dabbed at the wound. She took a deep breath and stared bravely at the coffered ceiling overhead.

"Nice wood, that," she said in a high, thin voice.

"Cherry," he replied casually.

She winced as the warm water seeped into the cut. "You're sure it's not deep?"

"Very sure."

She sucked in her breath as his dabbing became more pronounced—very like scrubbing, in fact. "It *feels* as though it's been cut to the bone. Tell me. I can take it."

"True, you're slender, but really, it's nowhere near the bone," he replied, sitting back on his heels and tossing the washcloth after the pant leg. "There. All nice and clean. Have a look for yourself."

"Thank you, no. If you'd be so kind as to put a bandage over it, I'm sure I can finish tying it up." She began struggling to a seated position, but he stopped her, his big hand enveloping her shoulder.

Gently, he pushed her back down. "Not a bit of it, m'dear," he said cheerfully. "Besides, always finish what you begin. Or so me old granny used to say."

She breathed a heartfelt thank-you. She hated being brave about blood. She'd never even seen any real value in it, except that it made everyone else feel better just when you were feeling your worst, which was generally the time a girl needed a bit of sympathy.

"You just rest easy and think of something else. I know," he said, as if a novel idea had only just occurred to him. "Why don't you tell me why you broke into my house?"

"Broke . . . Oh. That. The insufferable person who answers your door kept insisting that you were not at home. As I had to see you, I had no choice but to find an alternate means of gaining access."

"Beverly told you I wasn't in? How reprehensible!" Justin said, and then, "I suppose there was some good reason you didn't believe him?"

"Of course, " she answered. "I saw you."

"Saw me?" Justin repeated mildly. He opened the little amber bottle and withdrew a small glass wand from it. Carefully, he guided it along the cut.

"Ow!" Evelyn squealed, pulling away and glowering at him with the air of one grossly betrayed. "You *hurt* me!"

He grimaced apologetically. "Sorry. Carbolic acid. Should have warned you it would sting a bit."

"I should say," Evelyn muttered bad-temperedly.

"Almost done. Just a bit of bandaging and you'll be right as rain. Now then . . ." His hand slipped behind her knee. His fingers wrapped impersonally around her leg. "You were saying how you spied me in the house and thus deduced Beverly to be the lying knave he undoubtedly is. Where did you see me?"

"Through the back window here."

"Ah." Justin nodded. "So having been told I was not at home, you at once became suspicious of Beverly's villainous mien and decided to walk around the house, climb over the alley wall, and look through the windows. Most enterprising."

Evelyn frowned. "Put that way, it sounds rather . . . intrusive."

"No, no," Justin said affably. "I'd say the actual

intrusive spot came when you broke into the house. Up to that point I'd call you merely . . ." He looked at her hopefully, as though she would supply the word that eluded him.

"Prying."

"Ah, *prying*," he said happily. "Yes. That might do."

She couldn't detect the least bit of sarcasm in his tone, but it was there right enough, as was his amusement. She thought over all the reports she'd heard of him through the years, which were plenty.

Eccentric. Reclusive or was it *exclusive*? *Clever. Unflappable.* Some people had deemed him inattentive, others preferred oblivious. Obviously none of them had ever spent any time with him, for clearly a razor-sharp intellect lurked beneath his pleasant, obliging manner.

"And exactly why were you prying?" he asked.

"Because," she replied, "it was absolutely essential that I speak to you."

"Me? How flattering! Young girls are so seldom resourceful. Or persistent," he exclaimed, unrolling the linen bandage and clipping off a length. Deftly, he wound it around her thigh and secured it with a piece of sticking plaster. He admired his work. "The medical field will ever feel my loss, I'm afraid."

She grinned at his nonsense. He definitely had a way of getting around a girl.

He uncoiled with feline grace and she was reminded of another adjective that had on occasion been associated with him. *Dishy*. He seemed so gentlemanly, without being the least bit stiff, that for a moment she'd forgotten the circumstances under which they'd originally met. But being the recipient of his indisputable charm and seeing him move with such fluid ease, it all came rushing back. A dark hall long past midnight, another man's wife, another man's room.

He was a Lothario.

Not that for one second she feared *she* was in danger of exciting any romantic efforts on his part. Heavens, no! But that didn't mean she couldn't see why other women found him hard to resist.

Though now that she thought of it, it was odd that since that night she hadn't heard any sordid stories about him. Perhaps it was because one heard stories only about incompetent Lotharios, the ones who got caught. She glanced up at Justin. He didn't look in the least incompetent—

She gasped as he suddenly stooped down and scooped her up in his arms. She blushed, warmed by the notion that he'd read her thoughts.

"You can put me down. I can easily walk."

"Of course you can, if you want," he replied in the tone one would use on a recalcitrant child. He didn't stop, however. He strode into the narrow, carpeted hall, heading for the back of the town house. "But why do so? A lift is the least I can offer you by way of making reparation for owning such shoddy, easily broken windows, as well as for employing such a scoundrel for a butler."

Her eyes narrowed on his face. "You're mocking me."

"Never!" he denied. "I'm perfectly serious. I'm just thankful you aren't this very minute sending for your parents' lawyer in order to press suit, and wish to express my gratitude by offering you a nice cool glass of lemonade. Which is in the kitchen. Which is where I am taking you."

Gads! Listening to him, she could almost believe she *was* in the moral right and he *ought* to be making amends, when she knew very well that she should be offering him every apology she could think to keep him from ringing up the local constable and having her carted away to the jail for breaking into his home.

"Besides," he was saying, "I should dearly love to hear why it was 'essential' that you spoke to me."

She hesitated, knowing she should protest further. But he didn't seem to mind carrying her and she didn't seem to mind being carried, not in the least, so she relaxed in his arms and sank comfortably against his chest.

It was a nice, broad, hard chest. And warm under the starched white shirt. He smelled fascinating, too. Sharp astringent soap, earthy warmth, and something else, something unique.

She closed her eyes, trying to pinpoint the

aroma, and finding instead a whole new vista of sensations opening before her. The easy, rhythmical motion of his stride carrying her, the gentle swing of her legs in counterpoint, the soft feathering of his breath on her face, and the steady rise and fall of his chest. She held herself still, soaking up impressions. Lovely.

She smiled and opened her eyes, looking up just as he looked down and knocked her glasses askew with his chin. She shoved them back into place, the movement causing her to shift in his embrace. Easily, he jounced her up, settling her more comfortably, and in doing so his hand slipped up her rib cage, his fingers brushing the nether curve of her breast. His hand jerked back. His brows suddenly dipped in a scowl.

"You're not from Mrs. Boyle's school, are you?" he asked in a voice tinged with accusation. He looked down into her upturned face, peering past the faintly smoked lenses, touching on her mouth and moving to the dark tumble of hair that had come undone during her escapade and now swirled like a Gorgon's tresses around her shoulders. "Why, you're not a *girl* at all!"

"I beg your pardon." Evelyn stiffened.

"*You* are a woman."

By God! He'd thought she was . . . a *child*! That's why he hadn't castigated her, or sent for the authorities, or treated her as a real person at all. He thought she was from this girls' school he'd

been babbling about and that this was a . . . a girlish prank!

Evelyn, who had spent the last decade fighting
the prejudices roused by her youthful appearance,
who was always, in spite of her best efforts, a *little*
too aware of her lack of female curves and thus a
tad defensive about her womanliness, spoke before
she thought. "I'd heard you were sharp. Do tell,
whatever gave me away?"